TOUCHING SIN

J. SAMAN

Photography by WANDER AGUIAR

Cover Design by Shanoff Designs

Edited by Gina Johnson

Playlist:

After The Storm - Mumford and Sons
Cold Desert - Kings of Leon
Liar (it takes one to know one) - Taking Back Sunday
I Wanna Be Yours - Arctic Monkeys
High Hopes - Kodaline
Angela - Lumineers
We Don't Know - Strumbellas
How to Disappear Completely - Radiohead
Panic Switch - Silversun Pickups

Prologue

You wanna know an ugly truth? People hurt people. It's a part of human nature we rarely like to discuss or acknowledge. Mostly because we've grown to accept it as if it were the changing of the seasons.

An inevitability.

Sometimes the hurt is inflicted intentionally. Sometimes it isn't. Regardless of the process behind it, our natural inclination is to make excuses for it. We rationalize what should never be rationalized because the truth hits harder than your loved one ever could. And so it goes…

Until finally, something unforeseen occurs. We stop making excuses for the inexcusable. And when that happens, we gain power over that person. Over that hurt. It can start out as a slow burn. An aching sigh. A flicker of some long-forgotten hope you had previously thrown out like the useless, cluttered trash it was. Eventually that slow burn smolders, growing, absorbing oxygen and energy and blood and sweat and tears and pain, until it becomes a brush fire. Wild and uncontrollable. A real motherfucker to contain and put out.

That's the moment of freedom.

When you declare that enough is enough and make it stop.

That might be your defining moment. It was for me. At least, for a while. Because I ran. I got away. But it was all for naught, because in the end, he managed to find me anyway.

"TRUTH IS, everybody is going to hurt you: you just gotta find the ones worth suffering for." ~ Bob Marley

Chapter One

Mia

The acrid smell of burning oil is suffocating. Even with all the windows down and the vents blowing in outside air, it's unbearable. The smoke billowing from the hood of the car is even more alarming. I need to stop. Probably now. I know what this means. It means I'm stuck in the middle of…where the hell am I?

Cold realization slaps across my face. I have no idea where I am.

I can't remember the last time I've seen a town or anything other than flatland, desert, and mountains.

All around me is dark. Not just dark, pitch black. So black I can't see anything other than the narrow, meager glow the ancient headlights struggle to let off. It's like two flashlights shining out of the front of the car, only illuminating what they touch. Useless.

I can't even run away right. Can one person be this pathetic?

The smoke is most definitely getting thicker now, blowing directly into my face through the vents and the open windows. I can't breathe or see through it, and whenever I do, it burns my throat and eyes. It would be ironic to asphyxiate on the fumes from a stolen car when I could have taken my mother's Mercedes. It's just been sitting in the garage since she died. Niklas wouldn't have noticed if it went missing. At least not for a while. But it has GPS tracking, as do all our cars, which is why I left it in favor of the gardener's old clunker.

The car makes a sputtering noise before it jerks and then jerks again, the steering wheel shimmying to the point where I can barely maintain my grip on it. Now I'm out of options. The internal lights flash on and off, on and off again, and suddenly, the engine dies and I'm forced to roll to a stop at the side of the road.

The completely vacant road.

Shit.

Well, I certainly didn't plan on this happening. I'd laugh if it weren't so tragic. At least it's summer and warm out.

I have no idea how far I am from the nearest town. I left Dallas yesterday and went west. I definitely went west because, for a while, I was following signs for Flagstaff and then Las Vegas. But somehow, I allowed myself to become distracted, and now I'm here.

On the road to nowhere.

The car is dead. It makes the worst grating noise when I try to turn the key. Like metal against metal. The smell is even worse than the noise, and I wonder if I can even stay in the car.

What if it catches on fire?

Do cars actually do that, or does that only happen in movies? I have no idea. But nothing about this situation is reassuring. I need to think.

I fumble for my purse on the soft fabric cushion of the passenger seat, and my hand closes around the strap. I can't even see my hand in front of my face, that's how dark it is in here. Digging through my purse, I locate my new cell phone and press the button. It illuminates, showing me the home screen. I groan when I realize I have no service.

I tap on the search engine, but the screen tells me I have no internet connection either.

What the hell am I going to do now?

Tears prick the backs of my eyes, and it has nothing to do with the toxic smoke. How could I have let this happen? I should have paid closer attention to street signs instead of obsessing over all the ways my life has gone wrong. I refresh the internet page again with the same results.

No cell or internet service. No working car. No idea where I am. No food or water, either. Not even a goddamn blanket. Not that I could stay in this car anyway. I'll probably suffocate if I try.

This. Sucks.

I slam my hands into the plastic steering column as I belt out the shrillest shriek I can manage past my smoke-clogged lungs. It does nothing to ebb the rising panic and frustration. Peering around, searching everywhere I can out the open windows, I come up empty. No moon. Just useless stars that offer no warmth or light to see by.

Right as I'm about to get out and walk, bright lights flood the glass of my rearview mirror, temporarily blinding me. I squint reflexively and jerk away before I realize it's headlights. *Oh, thank God.* It's too dark to visualize the car approaching, but at this point, I don't care. Unless it's the police. That wouldn't be so good. Anyone else is fine.

Until I notice it's a big truck, high off the ground and so loud the world vibrates with its power.

All I can see of it are those headlights as they hone in on me like a spotlight.

On the one hand, I'm relieved they stopped. On the other, I'm a young woman alone in the middle of nowhere, suddenly at this person's mercy. *They could rape and kill me and then dump my body in the brush.* Right. There's that scenario. Not a whole lot I can do about that now.

Why didn't I bring a gun? I'm from freaking Texas. We had guns all over the goddamn house. Why didn't I think to bring one? Then again, knowing me and my luck, I'd probably shoot myself instead of any potential assailant. Especially since I have zero idea how to actually shoot one.

Perhaps they'd accept cash bribes in lieu of rape and murder?

One can hope.

The driver's side door slams shut with a dull click, and I watch through my side mirror as a tall, dark, hooded figure slowly strides up to my car. My heart is exploding out of my chest, my breathing erratic, my knuckles white from my grip on the steering wheel. I can't move, nor can I tear my eyes away as the figure draws closer.

He reaches my window, staring down at me through eyes I cannot see. His hood obscures his entire face in shadows. All I can discern is that he's tall and broad and can easily snap me like a twig in seconds.

At first, he just watches me as I cautiously peer up at him, completely immobilized by his presence. I'm the goddamn pathetic equivalent of a deer in headlights.

"Are you okay in there?" he asks, and the way his smooth whiskey baritone rolls over me like it's being poured from crystal onto ice has me releasing the breath I've been holding. "Do you need help?"

The last thing I want to do is open the door to this guy, but I don't think I have a choice. Especially since my voice still doesn't seem to be working. He steps back when the lock on my door clicks, giving me a wide berth like he's expecting me to get out.

My hands tremble violently, and I doubt my legs will support my weight if I attempt to stand. Instead, I sit, shifting on the thin, lumpy fabric of the seat, turning slightly in his direction with the door partially ajar.

What the hell have I gotten myself into?

"Are you hurt?" he continues at my silence.

"No," I reply as I stare down at his feet—dark stains on black hiking boots, and old, worn jeans covering his strong thighs—my voice soft, but loud enough to be heard over the vociferous engine of his truck that seems to be mocking my useless car.

"From the smell of it, your car is burning a lot of oil. Can it turn on?"

"No," I repeat, wrapping my arms protectively around my stomach as the meager contents inside swish and sway. I feel way too vulnerable and exposed right now. I'm ill at ease around men on the best of days and in the best of situations, and this is certainly neither of those.

He mutters something indiscernible under his breath and then says, "Come on then." His gruff directive gives me chills and I can't decipher if they're the bad kind or not. But if he was going to hurt me, wouldn't he have done it already? I don't know. I have no frame of reference on the methodology rapists and killers employ with their victims.

"Where are we going?" I manage, my voice holding more strength than I would have believed myself capable of.

I lean back in my seat, my gaze finally traveling up. His hands are clean and well kept, unlike his jeans or boots. His face is shrouded in darkness, for which he takes no action to fix even though my intent must be obvious. His reluctance for me to see his face raises my fear factor to an eight. He could be mangled and getting ready to do the same to me. He could be the psycho from the Texas Chainsaw Massacre.

"I'm going to drive you into town," he explains like it should be obvious to any sane, rational person. But I am neither sane nor rational right now. I've been driving for two days, practically non-stop. The only sleep I've had was when I pulled into a twenty-four-hour Walmart and parked in the back to close my eyes for a few hours.

Town. He's going to take me into town. Which town is he referring to? Is Las Vegas considered a town or a city? But if he takes me into town, that probably means he won't rape and kill me, right? *Or he could be lying,* the girl in the back of my head reminds me. God, this situation sucks. I have no choice but to trust him.

I certainly can't stay here.

I'm in the middle of the fucking desert.

"Okay. Thank you. I'd appreciate that."

He steps back further, like he's just as wary of me as I am of him. I stand, the gravel and dried earth crunching beneath my riding boots. At least I'm wearing appropriate clothing. I look up at him, only able to catch a glimpse of his mouth and stubble-lined jaw. Angled lines and smooth, full lips to be precise, but the rest?

"Can you, um…," I swallow hard, shifting my stance. "Would you mind removing your hood?"

He rumbles out a chuckle. "Want to make sure I'm not Leather-face or something?"

I laugh, too, but it's awkward and comes out shaky, because he just echoed my exact thoughts. Right down to the creepy horror film.

He draws back his hood, and my breath catches for an entirely different reason. He's beautiful, which seems comical given how manly and rugged this guy appears, but it's the first word that pops into my head.

"Satisfied?"

I just stare at him. Beautiful doesn't mean safe.

A crooked smile quirks up the corners of his lips. His head shakes ever so slightly as his hands fly up in surrender.

"I'm not gonna hurt you. I promise. But I can't leave you here twenty miles from the nearest town." *Twenty?* "You're lucky, actually. I just so happened to be passing this way after going to the dam. I decided to drive around for a bit and took the very long way home. Good thing, too," he emphasizes that last bit, running a hand across his jaw and eyeing me from head to toe. "You could have been out here all night without a car passing."

What dam? Like, the Hoover Dam? Where the hell am I?

"Lucky," I parrot, tasting the sourness of the word on my tongue, because I don't think I've ever uttered it in relation to myself before. It almost makes me want to laugh at the absurdity of it. "What's your name?" I ask, staring up into his eyes. I think they might be brown. I can't quite tell, but that's what I'm betting on. His hair is slightly tousled, longer on the top and shorter on the sides. The color, barely decipherable in this light, appears as dark as his eyes. That strong, chiseled jaw is lined with a decent layer of lazy-man's stubble.

He's a lumberjack, I muse. A sexy one at that.

He smiles, and his teeth are perfect. White and straight. An interesting and welcome contradiction to his otherwise roughness. And that smile. Holy wow. It makes me relax for some odd reason. Like the quality of his dental hygiene and the fact that he has a gorgeous smile is an indication of character. When did I become this stupid girl?

"Jake," he introduces, looking me over slowly, languidly, his eyes sweeping along every inch of me, before they find my face again. His expression alters, growing skeptical and cautious as they bounce around each feature on my face. I wonder if he recognizes me. I hope not. I doubt it somehow. I can't imagine I'm known in this part of the world. "What's yours?"

My name. And this is where I hesitate. Which name do I give him? Certainly not my real one.

"Mia," I blurt out, my eyes skirting his.

"Okay, Mia. Why don't you grab anything you have in there that you want to keep and follow me? I have a buddy who can tow your car into town."

I nod, but I don't get a chance to respond before he stalks off, back to his truck, his impressive silhouette framed in a halo of light. I don't waste a moment in grabbing my purse from the passenger seat of the stolen car.

I bite my lip. Is there anything else in here I need? Anything that could link me to this car?

Other than where you got it from and your fingerprints?

I growl out a slew of curses under my breath. The moment this car is made, I will be, too. But this guy says he knows someone who can tow it, and maybe I can offer them cash to dispose of it. No one will be the wiser.

Walking around to the trunk, I open it and lift my suitcases out one by one, setting them onto dusty ground. Jake is already there, waiting on me, his headlights glowing across the back of my car, paving a path for me to see by. My license plate is also visible, and I inwardly cringe. The word TEXAS in bold caps along with the picture of the state. Too late now, I sigh. I can only hope he's not the most observant of men.

Jake wordlessly lifts one of my suitcases for me. I follow after him, dragging the other behind me, the wheels catching on the cracked earth. We weave in between his truck and my car and then he opens the passenger side for me. Grabbing my suitcase from my hands, he effortlessly picks it up and tosses it onto the small backseat behind the passenger side with my other suitcase.

His impressively large hand reaches out to touch my arm, and instinctively, I jerk back like his fingers are made out of fire. "Don't touch me," I snap.

His hands fly up, dark eyes wide. "I was just going to help you up."

"Oh. I'm sorry, but I believe I can manage it, thank you," I murmur, feeling a small pang of guilt for my outburst.

I hoist myself up into the clean, cool cab and breathe in the enticing scent of woodsy cologne and new car. This truck is nice. Expensive, if I had to guess—given the soft leather of the seats, wood paneling and massive dashboard filled with buttons and dials and all sorts of technology.

Then it hits me. The guy who tows my car could look it up before I can even strike a deal with him. I need to get as far away as possible. Maybe it's better if he doesn't call anyone. If we just leave it here in the middle of nowhere.

"You don't have to call your friend," I say when he gets in the car, buckling his seat belt. "We can leave the car here. I think it's dead and it's really old. Is there a place nearby where I can buy a new one?" It'll be a risk, but what choice do I have? Then again, I have no idea what kind of car I can afford with my meager budget. Probably not anything better than what I was just in.

Jake stares at me, long and hard. Like he's trying to figure me out. It makes me anxious and impatient to get out of here. It feels as though he can see straight through me with those eyes of his and it takes all of my concerted effort not to shift my position or my gaze. I was right about the brown eyes, but they aren't just any brown. They're warm, milk chocolate.

"If we leave your car here, the police will eventually pick it up." He watches me intently for a reaction, and though my heart is pounding wildly in my chest, I'm doing everything I can to maintain my stoic mask. "And nothing will be open until the morning."

My eyes close as my breath falters. I could take a bus or a train, but that's a last resort, and I doubt I can get one tonight.

"I'm stuck here," I whisper to myself. "Where am I?" I ask, more out of curiosity at this point than anything else.

"Just outside of Henderson or Boulder City, depending on

which way you're headed," he answers and my eyebrows furrow. "Nevada," he adds.

Henderson, Nevada? I have no idea where that is in reference to Las Vegas, but those were the last signs I remember. Lord, I'm in trouble.

What the hell am I going to do now?

Chapter Two

Mia

The ride into town is long and quiet. We pass through Henderson, and as we're driving, I realize he never asked me where I want to go. He just assumes it's Las Vegas because those are the signs we're following as we glide along the highway. I don't bother to suggest anything else. Las Vegas gives me the most options, and it's where I was headed tonight anyway.

The radio is on, but it's turned down so low it's more of a background hum than actual music. I can't even tell what song is playing.

"What do you think is wrong with the car?" I ask, unable to handle the silence a moment longer.

"I don't know, but if I had to guess, I'd say your engine is shot due to a pretty extensive oil leak."

"Is that expensive to fix?"

He chuckles lightly, rubbing his hand along his stubbled jaw. His reaction irritates me. There is nothing amusing about my situation. Nothing at all. But I guess he doesn't know just how desperate I am.

"That car is probably older than you are, and considering it hasn't been in production for at least a decade, I'd say it's not really worth it. But that's your call, not mine."

I sigh, swallowing down everything that is trying to rise up and suffocate me. Or have me vomit all over his car. "Can you take me to a bus or train station? I can pay you," I add.

Jake glances in my direction, before turning back to the black expanse of the road, his headlights illuminating the yellow dashes of the highway.

He's silent, and that silence draws my attention over to him as I try to patiently wait him out. He's still rubbing his jawline, thinking, I assume. Finally, he pivots his head back to me. Even in the dimly lit cab, I can tell he's trying to read me. His eyes give me a slow sweep before they're forced to return to the road.

"It's late," he says in a measured tone. "Las Vegas is an all-night town, but that doesn't make it a good idea to go to the bus station."

"I don't follow."

"You're a young woman. A beautiful young woman at that. And you're alone. The bus station in Vegas is not a safe place to be at this time of night."

I nod my head, but I can't manage to speak past the lump in my throat. I do take some small measure of comfort in the fact that I'll be in Las Vegas, which is a big place with a lot of tourists.

"Okay," I finally manage. "How about a hotel?"

He nods with an expression that says I'm finally being reasonable. "That I can do. What sort of place are you looking for?"

Anyplace that won't ask questions or require a credit card. Or photo ID.

Which is no place on the planet anymore.

I don't know how to answer him, so I don't. I can't stand this feeling of trapped helplessness. It's smothering. Absolutely terrifying. It's everything I'm running from, and yet, here I am again, in over my head in a situation that has me paralyzed.

No car. No place to stay. No way out.

"Is there anyone you can call?"

"No," I snap, my voice thick with the tears I refuse to let fall. The only people in my life are the ones I'm running from. He was right when he said I was alone. I am. I have no one.

"Where are you coming from?"

I don't respond.

"Where are you trying to go?"

Again, I stay silent.

He blows out a heavy breath, clearly as exasperated with me as I am with myself. And him. I'm exasperated with him, too, though I know I have no right to be. He's been nothing but kind, and I can't stand it. I can't stand his questions or his helpful ways. I can't stand any of this. I knew that car was old. I knew Roderigo hadn't driven it in ages. But it started when I turned the key, and it had gas in it. I couldn't take any other car and I certainly wasn't about to buy one.

I have no way of leaving wherever he's taking me tonight. I've never been to a hotel that doesn't require a credit card. Every single one of my cards has my real name on it. Leaving like I did was impulsive and epically stupid. So fucking stupid.

Now I'm trapped.

It's only a matter of time before he finds me and drags me back home.

And then I lose it. My face drops into my hands as tears pour out of me like a broken faucet. I tremble and shake as sobs rip their way out of me, one after the other. I don't even care that I'm a blubbering mess in front of a stranger. *What am I going to do now?*

"Hey," he says softly. "It's okay. It's going to be okay."

I shake my head, my hands still covering my eyes, because this guy has no idea.

"Listen, I'm not going to leave you at the shop with no place to go. I wouldn't do that. We'll talk to my friend, and then we'll find you a hotel."

I shake my head again, my hands falling to my lap as I peek over at him. "I can't go to a hotel."

He's quiet for a beat, and then he asks, "Can you tell me why?" Another head shake. "I can't leave you at the bus station. It's really not safe. I'm not kidding about that. You might not be familiar with Vegas, but I am."

He has no clue what the definition of unsafe really is. What true nightmares are made of.

"That's not your call to make." I'll take a cab there if he won't take me. I have cash. It can't be that far from whatever garage he's driving me to.

He scrubs a hand over his face before slapping the butt of his palm on the steering wheel. "Okay, how's this? You'll come with me to work, and I'll make some calls," he urges, his right hand drawing away from the steering wheel and over to me like he's about to touch me, but then thinks better of it and puts it back on the wheel. "We'll figure something out. I won't leave you with no place to go tonight."

We, he says. He uses the word 'we' like he's invested. But why? "Why are you helping me?"

He chuckles sardonically, and something in the way it sounds has me wiping the last of my tears so I can see him clearly. It's a laugh that says he has no idea.

"You're alone and stuck in Vegas. I mean, it's not exactly original."

I glare at him. What a rude comment to make.

I think he realizes he just crossed the line into asshole because he follows it up with, "You need help and I'm not the sort of guy who just lets a young woman fend for herself with no place to go." He pauses here, a small, lopsided grin pulling up the corner of his mouth. His eyes, so very dark, sparkle against the blue glow of the dash. "Or maybe it's because I can't stand your tears. Whatever the reason, I said I'd help you and I meant it."

He turns back to the road and focuses on driving, essentially ending the conversation.

I stare at his profile, wondering if he's for real. I've never met a selfless person before. I realize that sounds awful, but it's no less true. Everyone I've ever known has always had an ulterior motive for the things they've done. Even when giving to charity, it was for tax breaks and appearances. How sad is that? But this guy is offering to help me, and I find myself waiting for the punchline.

"What do you want in return?"

His head snaps over and for a fleeting second, he looks wounded that I even asked. Or perhaps that expression was disgust, because there are a lot of ways a question like that can be construed.

But it's a question and not an offer.

He doesn't respond, and I don't know whether it's a positive or negative thing with him. He angrily twists the dial up on his radio and instead of country music or metal, as I expected, it's Arctic Monkeys.

I smile despite myself and my miserable situation. Anthony, my maid's son, liked this band, which is why I know them. He used to play this album for me, but after my father found out we were spending time together, he forbade him from returning to the house.

"You know them?" Jake asks, surprised. My eyebrows knit together as I tilt my head at him. How could he tell that? "You're humming along," he supplies, answering my unspoken question.

Oh. Oops. "Yes. I know them. But not all that well. Just a few of their songs."

He shifts in his seat, and catches my eye before quickly going back to the road. "You have an accent," he starts and then takes a deep breath before he continues. "And your license plate said Texas. Is that where you're from?"

I don't answer; instead, I stare out my window, taking in the Las Vegas Strip that we're slowly approaching as we meander our way through the city.

"Are you in some kind of trouble?" I want to laugh at that question, but he's being serious. I have no way of responding with an honest answer. "Are the police looking for you?"

I don't know the answer to that, either.

I realize I need to give him something. He's helping me out and probably just needs to ensure he won't get arrested for helping a criminal or something.

"I haven't broken the law, if that's what you're asking."

"Are you a runaway?"

I scoff, running my fingers through the ends of my long hair, "I'm twenty-two," I tell him, hoping he understands I'm not some underage kid who ran away from home. The fact that I'm an adult who ran away from home is an entirely different issue. "And you don't have to help me."

He doesn't come back with anything else. He presses some

buttons on his steering wheel and the volume on his sound system increases, drowning out any further ability to speak.

I bet he's regretting picking me up. I would be if I were him. A few minutes later, he pulls into a gas station that says Healey & Sons. The main building and the garage bays are partially dark, but the gas pumps are still brightly lit. When I focus, I notice someone inside the main building with their feet kicked up on a counter.

"That's Brennan." Jake points to the man. "He runs a towing service in town and he can get your car situated." My eyes stay trained on Brennan. I don't know what to do about that car yet. In the half an hour it took us to arrive here, answers to my situation have elude me. "Wait here, okay?" He takes me in, watching me closely. "I'll go speak to him, and then once we get that set up, I can take you to a hotel."

I huff out some air, but suck it back in quickly. I can't go to a hotel. I just told him that.

"I know a place. It's nice and not too far from here."

Nice places want nothing to do with me tonight.

"Sure," I puff with a forced smile. "Sounds perfect." And because I won't get another chance to say it, I pivot my body to face him better and say, "Thank you, Jake. For picking me up on the side of the road and bringing me here. For trying so hard to help me."

He gives me a crooked grin, squeezing the back of his neck. His eyes roam my face, and then he hops out of the truck. I watch him walk toward the main building. I even take a minute to appreciate him as he does.

The moment he steps inside, I get out of the truck, grab my suitcases, and run.

I drag them down the street and away from the gas station. There are cabs everywhere, and part of me is tempted to flag one down and hop in, but where would I go?

He's probably right about the bus station not being safe at this hour. It's well after one in the morning, and even though there are a good amount of people on the streets, they're mostly drunk and loud and leering at me as I pass them. Or maybe that last part is in my head, but it feels like they are. My stomach sinks as I somehow find my way down to the Las Vegas Strip.

It's bright here. Blindingly so, almost disorienting, and even more congested with people walking every which way. Men are handing out fliers for hookers and women are wearing jeweled bikinis with pleasing smiles.

I could go to the airport, but using my ID is a huge risk and a major tip-off to anyone who is searching for me.

I stop, standing in front of one of the massive hotels that line the Strip as I think this through. He said a woman being lost in this city is a cliché, and right now, I believe him. Because that's exactly what I feel like. A cliché.

"Hey there," someone calls out, dragging me out of my reverie and away from the massive gold structure to a group of guys headed my way. They're eyeing me up and down, taking in my suitcases and lost expression. Then, the one who I assume spoke to me, grins in a way that turns my blood cold. "You look a little lost, baby doll. Why don't you come with us? We'd love to help you find your way."

I shake my head at him, my stomach rolling over as I think about what these guys could do to me.

"Thanks, but I'm all set. My husband is waiting for me." And then I book ass up the ramp that leads to the massive gold hotel. I don't look back, and they don't follow me.

I guess this place, The Turner Grand, will have to do until I can figure out a plan. And I have no idea how long that will take given the dire straits I now find myself in.

Chapter Three

Mia

"Checking in, miss?" the valet asks as he holds the large glass door to the hotel open for me.

"Uh," I pause, caught off guard by the question, but I am hauling two suitcases and entering a hotel, so I go with, "Yes."

"Would you like me to help you with your luggage while you do that?"

I shake my head and force a smile. "No, I can manage. But thank you."

He gives me a warm smile and doesn't offer anything else. The small heels of my riding boots click against the marble floors of the lobby. There's a stone fountain of Greek Gods in the center of the atrium, the ceiling dripping with ornate, multicolored glass that appears lit from within. Off to my left is a large reception area, teeming with people checking in. Along the counter closest to me, is the concierge area. One of the smart-looking, suit-clad men glances up the moment I step over and spots me. He gives me a full once-over. I know I'm a mess. Two days in the car and a lot of tears. I quickly scurry off, heading I have no idea where.

I wander around for much longer than I should, fatigue building as the rush of adrenaline ebbs. Jake. I feel bad about running out on him. He was…nice. Helpful. So gorgeous my insides liquefied with just one look from those brown eyes of his. I nearly laugh out loud at that, mentally shaking myself. How ridiculous to focus on that given the situation I find myself in now.

The longer I meander around, the more exhausted I become. I'm also drawing more attention to myself by employees and drunk men, and I'm running out of routes to take and places to peruse.

I spot a sign for the pool and head that way, lost as to where else to go. It's quieter over here, the shops lining this part of the building are all closed now, and most of the action is back over where the casino and bars are.

One of the doors off to the side of the pool entrance catches my attention simply because it's slightly ajar with a sign in front of it that indicates it's under construction. And no one is around.

I look left.

I look right.

Then I book it, keeping my head down and my face averted from the numerous overhead cameras. I slide through the open door, hauling my suitcases along. After I make it through, the door shuts with a loud clatter behind me.

I freeze, standing bone still as I wait for the inevitable security to arrive. But after two minutes and no cavalry to come and haul me off, I ramble out into the warm summer night.

The breeze runs across me, catching my hair and bathing me in the faint scent of chlorine. My boots click loudly against the hardscape, the sound echoing through the night, forcing me to move faster.

To where? I have no idea.

I just need to find a place to hide out. A place to sit and gather my thoughts without curious, prying eyes on me.

Along the back wall, close to a sign that reads, Spa Exit, is a lounge chair partially obstructed by shrubbery. I make a beeline for it, sliding my suitcases next to me and tucking myself down onto the lounger, curling in and making myself as small as possible.

Then I listen.

I have no idea how long I take in the sounds of the pool at

night, to the waterfall and the rustling of trees, but my eyes end up closing, and my mind wanders, only to be jostled awake by visions of everything I ran from.

My head whips around instinctively, my heart rate through the roof as my chest heaves with barely contained panicked breaths. Darkness closes in on me, and I swallow down a sob as I try to remember where I am.

Pool. Hotel. Las Vegas.

Oh God. How did I get myself here? How did this hopeless situation become my life?

I should feel some relief.

I got away. I made it out. But not one ounce of fear has abated. If anything, this feels worse. For a flicker of a moment, I regret my hasty flight.

Homeless. No car. No usable ID. No job. Little money.

I could go to a shelter. That might be safer than sleeping outside. Or I could try to find a place to live like a motel or an apartment that doesn't require anything but cash.

Breathe.

Compartmentalize.

Breathe.

Push everything down.

Breathe.

Formulate a plan.

Sitting up in my lounger, I wipe the residual sweat from my nightmare off my brow. My heartbeat finally normalizes as I take stock of my life and my options. No. I can't focus on my life. I have to focus on getting through this. Right. Focus.

I bite on the inside of my cheek as I regard my suitcases. I can't carry them around. My mother would roll over in her grave if she knew I was about to trash them and most of their contents. Or sell them. Maybe I can sell them? They have to be worth something. The suitcases and everything inside them are designer.

Unzipping the first suitcase, I flip the lid back, followed by the second. Then I take out the large rucksack I threw in at the last minute and begin to fill it with the clothes I'll need. Shoes. Shirts.

Shorts. Blouses. Nice pants. Underwear. I keep going until the rucksack is filled. When I'm done, I close my suitcases and lean back against the wall on the other side of the recliner, mentally making a list.

I need a fake ID. Probably a fake social security card. I need a job or two or three. I need to accrue as much money as I can short of robbing a bank. A fake passport that would clear customs seems impossible.

I'll have to start small and work my way up.

But hell. This is Las Vegas. If ever there were a town to hide out, get a fake life, and earn quick cash, this is the place. Like touching sin, only easier.

I laugh. Loud. It's humorless and maybe a bit psychotic, and when a hiccupped sob finally escapes, I break down. Tears fall from my eyes and roll down my cheeks like a Texas rainstorm.

This is my life now. Mia…Jones? Sure. That works.

"This is your life now, Mia Jones," I say aloud to myself. It's a pep talk. A way to bolster myself up. A way to keep the wrecked devastation at bay.

One thing is for sure, I cannot go home.

Not yet. Maybe not ever.

Another thing is for sure, I'm leaving my old self there.

I need to start over. Reinvent myself. Become the woman I always dreamed of being. The self-assured, smart, in control one. The one with all the answers and none of the fear.

The one who could hit back.

"You don't belong here." A deep male voice comes out of nowhere, and I jump so high off the lounger, I fall to the ground, a startled scream escaping my lips.

"Sorry. Shit. You okay?" A large man bathed in dark shadows reaches out for me, trying to help me up.

I shoot back, slamming into the metal of the lounger, holding my arm to my chest like he just tried to rub my skin with the plague.

"Okay." He draws his hand back, standing up straight and tall. "No touching. What the hell is a girl like you doing out here?"

I glance up, brushing my hair back and off my face, but I still can't see much. The lighting is limited in this part of the pool area. But I can tell from his silhouette that this man is huge. I can't determine exactly what he's wearing, but it doesn't appear to be a uniform. Mostly because I catch the skin of his massive arms and what appear to be jeans on his legs.

"I, um..."

And then I break down again. I just can't do this. I feel like a crybaby and a girl who is losing instead of winning, and it's all just catching up to me. Lack of sleep and my life generally sucking in all the ways that matter and too many men tonight who may or may not be trying to help me out.

"I'm sorry," I say, wiping at my face and grasping my handbag and rucksack. "I'll go."

"Oh, honey," he drawls, and that southern accent makes me smile. Why? Fuck if I know. But when you're at the bottom, you cling to the smallest shred of what feels good, and a southern accent is evidently just the thing I need. "I'm not kicking you out. I'm just wondering why a pretty thing like yourself is hiding out back here."

"Are you going to hurt me?"

I have no idea why I just asked that question so bluntly. Maybe I've officially lost my mind, or I'm at the end of my tolerance. Picking myself up, I slide back onto the lounger, because if he is going to hurt me, I'd rather not be on the hard ground when he does it.

"Hurt you?" he challenges, his voice rising an octave, his tone a mixture of shock and incredulity. "I love women." And then he chuckles lightly. "Maybe a bit too much, according to some. But hurting them, the way you're asking, has never happened and never will. Is that why you're here? Some guy rough you up?"

I laugh. Again, my laughter sounds slightly crazed. Some guy? Rough me up? Yeah, that's hilarious. If only because it's the story of my life. If only because the way he says it makes it sound so painfully inadequate. Like he's unintentionally trivializing something that doesn't feel trivial.

"Do I need to leave?" I go with instead, because evading direct questions seems to be what I'm all about tonight.

"No," he says slowly, carefully taking a seat next to me on the lounger, even though I didn't invite him into my crisis bubble. Into my world that's melting faster than ice cream in the Las Vegas sun. "You can stay here. And if you need help, well, I can be your guy for that."

I shake my head, staring down at the large hands in his lap with his fingers casually intertwined. No balled-up fists. No rigid posture. The sincerity in his tone is weakening me. Is jumbling up my already overworked brain.

"Why would you do that?"

"Because you're alone. Because you're sitting on a goddamn lounge chair, hiding in the darkness of a pool in Las Vegas, surrounded by suitcases. Because you're crying and scared and asked if I was going to hurt you, and I'm a man who does not tolerate any of those things for women."

"You're the second man I've met tonight who tried to help me. Is this a Las Vegas thing, or have I just been hanging out with the wrong crowd?"

He laughs, running a hand through his hair before propping his elbows on his knees and staring off at nothing in the distance.

"Couldn't say. But maybe the latter from the sound of it."

"I'm running away," I announce, wondering why I'm telling him anything when I wouldn't tell Jake. Maybe it's the darkness that's making me brave. Maybe it's because I was attracted to Jake and didn't want him to know just how pathetic I truly am. Or maybe it's because Jake started this fire in me, and now I want to talk, before my truth burns me alive from the inside out. And actually, I sort of wish it were Jake here next to me instead of this guy.

"I'm Maddox Sinclair, Running Away. Nice to meet you." *Oh Lord.* I laugh. I laugh so freaking hard and it's the first genuine laugh I think I've ever had. Like, ever. "What can I do to help you out?"

I shrug. Might as well give up and go for broke. I literally have nothing left to lose. And whatever this guy does with me, well, I'm not sure I care anymore. I can't tell if this rock-bottom stuff is demoralizing or empowering.

"I need a fake ID. I need a fake social security number. I need a job and a new life. And I need to learn how to kick some serious butt."

"Hmmm...," he hums, his tone contemplative, his gaze bouncing over to mine. "Are you a cop?"

Another laugh bursts out. "Seriously?"

He shrugs, shifting to face me fully, trying to read me in the dark. "I have to ask."

"No. I am most certainly not a cop."

"Then I can help you. With all of that, actually."

I stare at him. His dark eyes sparkle against the paltry light of the pool area. He stares back, unwavering and lacking any sympathy or pity. He's serious.

"What do you expect in exchange?" It's almost the same question I asked Jake. With the exact same meaning.

"I like that question about as much as I like you sleeping out here. Can we find you a real place to stay?"

I shrug. "Maybe. But for now, this is my new home. I like it here. I feel safe here. There are no outside people wandering around. Well, except you."

"I work here."

"See," I point at him. "Exactly my point. It's private. There are no sketchy neighborhoods or dangerous people. It's quiet, and it's dark. I like both of those things."

"I'm going to think on that one, because you sleeping outside is really not cool with me."

"What if I promise to find other accommodations?"

"Then I'll help you, Running Away. I'll teach you how to fight, and I'll get you hooked up with some fake-ass shit, and I'll land you some good jobs that pay well if you don't mind wearing something sexy."

"Sexy doesn't mean selling sex, right?"

He sighs, like I just offended him again. "No. Sexy means Las Vegas club or restaurant uniforms."

"I'm in," I promise, because like I said, what do I have to lose? "But if you're playing me, if this is a ploy to hurt me, then you should know I'm a girl with zero fucks left to give. And I never cuss.

At least not outwardly, so this should demonstrate my sincerity on this."

"Since we're bonding here, you should know, I cuss a lot outwardly and I'm a guy with a lot of fucks to give."

I smile. I think I like Maddox Sinclair.

"Another cool fact about me? I was raised by a single mother. Never had a father. I have so much respect for women it's not even funny. I love women. Especially ones who need my help. And you, Running Away, you need my help."

"So, you're going to help me?"

"I am. I'm going to get you exactly where you need to be."

Only, Maddox Sinclair has no idea just how impossible that is. It's only a matter of time before my nightmare catches up with me.

Chapter Four

Mia

"You're new here," a girl says as I stash my large backpack under a shelf and behind a stack of crates. I stand up quickly, hoping she didn't catch exactly what I was up to, and spin around, morphing my expression from nervous to bright and cheery.

"Yes," I beam with a big smile. It's fake. Everything about me pretty much is, but this girl with the bright red lips that match mine and the long, stick-straight, black hair that matches her skin doesn't know that.

Two weeks. I've been in this town two for weeks, and the jobs that Maddox helped me obtain feel like all I have. No, scratch that. They *are* all I have. "First night."

"Great. Welcome, I'm Millie." She steps forward and extends her hand to me. No one has bothered to shake my hand in such a long time that for a moment, the gesture makes me freeze up. But I recover quickly, extending my hand back. "You'll love it here. The rest of the staff is all really super friendly and the bosses are great."

"Mia," I say, though I almost cringe doing it. "Do you work in the bar, too?" I take stock of her outfit. She might have the same red lips, but she most certainly does not have the same outfit on, and that makes me want to frown. She's wearing a mid-thigh white button-up shirt-dress with a thick red belt, whereas I'm wearing a skintight black dress that is so short if I bend over—just a little, not even a lot—my ass shows. As if that weren't bad enough, the dip in the front is low to the point of showing off cleavage without even having to try.

"No," she says like it should be obvious, which probably should be given the outfit difference. "I'm a hostess." Her eyes bounce over to the exit of the back room before coming back to me. "I gotta get out there, and I bet you do, too. Hope you have a good shift. Maybe we'll catch up later."

And with that, she's gone. I don't even get a chance to say, *yeah, you too* or *I'd like that*, which I really wouldn't, but again, she doesn't need to know that. Glancing quickly over my shoulder to make sure my bag is well hidden, I leave the back room, coasting through the crowded restaurant. It's one of those Las Vegas trendy hotspots, complete with lounge areas as well as indoor and outdoor dining. It also has a huge bar that takes up an entire wall set against red glass subway tiles.

Red. This place is all about the red. At least with the décor because the walls are dark, and the floors are distressed oak.

When I was first hired, Cal promised that someone would train me. He never mentioned who, though, so as I approach the entrance to the back of the bar where the staff comes and goes, I hesitate, searching around like someone is just going to materialize and tell me what the hell I'm supposed to do.

Waiters and waitresses are hustling and bustling, filling their trays with drinks and adding garnishes as required. They ignore me as I scoot past them and maneuver around a small corner that leads to the long strip where I'll be working. The floor is rubber over here, to prevent slipping, and it's narrower than I would have expected given the overall size of the place.

"You must be Mia," a girl with short, unnaturally platinum blonde hair, dark eyes, and a septum ring says to me.

"That's me," I reply, hoping my voice sounds more confident than I feel at the moment. Really, I'm shitting my pants. I've never had a job before. I've never done anything of value. Never earned a dollar of my own money. It's a night of firsts. While I should be brimming with excitement, I can't seem to locate any sensation other than nausea.

But money equals freedom, and right now, that's no joke.

"Perfect," she puffs out like I just made her night. "I'm Diamond. I hope you know what you're doing, because Cal said you've tended bar before, and I can't train you."

"Oh." I blink at her. "Well, yes, I have tended bar before, but no one has trained me on the drinks you have here or the register."

Diamond practically growls out her frustration at that. "Kippa no-showed and she was supposed to train you. It's just you and me tonight because the bitch bailed, *again*," she emphasizes like it's my fault this Kippa girl left us in the lurch, "so I can't help you. You're gonna have to learn how to swim on your own."

And with that, she spins on her five-inch platform boots and gets back to work, effectively dismissing me. Swim on my own? I guess I don't have a choice, even though I have absolutely no clue what I'm doing.

"Excuse me, miss?" a man barks, snapping his fingers at me with an air of annoyance as he tries to get my attention. "Are you going to help me or what?"

"Of course," I say with that manufactured smile on my face. My heart ping-pongs around my chest with deafening force, reminding me I'm about to screw this up to epic proportions. "What can I get you?"

"Grey Goose dirty martini on the rocks with three blue-cheese-stuffed olives."

"Coming right up." I offer a closed-mouth grin to his pissed off scowl. I have no idea where anything is. When I was hired, it was very early in the morning, and Cal did not feel the need to give me a tour. I haven't studied the bar menu. I don't know how much the drinks cost. I have no idea how to work their fancy tablet register system, and even if I did, I'm not sure I have a code to access it. Diamond hasn't so much as glanced in my direction, and as I find a glass and fill it with ice, I'm starting to panic.

Rocks means ice. Dirty means olives…I think. At least he helped me out with the type of vodka he wants.

I lied when I said I have tended bar before. Maddox told me I needed to or no one would hire me. But I have made drinks for people. That was part of my hostess duties because my father always felt it was a more personal touch if I did it instead of having the staff do it.

Cal never checked anything out about me. Not my fake ID or the social security card I bought or my bogus work experience.

Nothing.

This is a very legitimate restaurant in a very high-end hotel on the Las Vegas Strip, so the fact that Cal called me and hired me, despite the level of bullshit I tried to pass off as truth, astounds me. I practically passed out from dread as I handed my fakes over to him to scrutinize. The only thing I can come up with is Maddox. He sorta kinda knows my situation, and he must have told him some of it. I honestly don't know.

But it's got nothing on the fears that plague me on a daily basis.

So this panic? This panic feels more manageable to me. Even if it still sucks.

I fill up a shaker, mix this asshole of a man his cocktail, and hope to God he pays me in cash and tells me to keep the change. I figure I can always ring the order up later if anyone ever comes to my rescue or decides to help me out. I finish off his drink, drop a napkin onto the polished wood bar and then slide it to the man.

He's still scowling at me. Did I get it wrong?

"I'd like to open a tab," he bites out.

Now I'm good and screwed.

"I can help you with that," a male voice says beside me, and the relief I feel nearly has me sagging in place.

I glance up, catching my savior's profile.

He's tall, which is saying something coming from me because I'm five-nine plus an extra few inches in my stupid heels. He's well over six feet. His hair is a medium-chestnut brown, and a light layer of stubble in the same warm color lines his angled jaw. I can't make out much else, but when he smiles at the asshole customer, I suck in a rush of air.

Holy Jesus. It's him. Jake.

The guy who picked me up on the side of the road after my car died, and then I ran out on him first chance I got, like a one-night stand. A bubble of nervous energy fills me from head to toe, stealing my breath and coloring my cheeks with a rush of warm heat.

He's wearing a white button-down shirt and black slacks, the same as all the waiters and waitresses, so I can't figure out what he's doing back here. The light over his head casts a shadow, burnishing his dark hair and white shirt with a fiery red glow. *A dark devil,* I think. Only instead of damning lost souls, he's saving them. The asshole customer nods at him, but doesn't say anything else, like thank you, as he accepts his drink and hands Jake his credit card.

Jake pivots to me, catching my eye and giving me a once-over. His expression darkens, hardening to steel. I don't think I've ever felt so embarrassed and small in my life.

"Thank you," I whisper meekly, my voice suddenly caught in my throat as I follow him over to the tablet at the back of the bar like the lost puppy I am. He peeks in my direction, and I feel my cheeks growing warmer, my eyes desperate to lower to the ground—my natural inclination when being observed like this. I force them to stay up, force myself to stay strong.

I forgot how gorgeous he is. Sexy. Large. Muscular. And terrifying because he is all of those things.

"You're welcome. Helping you out is apparently what I do." The bitter note in his sarcastic tone brings me back to the situation at hand.

"I, um…" I have nothing to say to that. He's right. It was a bitch move, but in my defense, I had limited options.

"Watch and learn, okay? I'm hoping you're a quick study, and I'm not stuck here training you all night." Okay. Wow. I'm starting to think that Millie girl was either lying or the only friendly one here. Then again, what do I really expect from him? "I saw you made his drink the correct way, so I guess that's a good start."

I don't say anything back to that. His hostility is causing my stomach to twist and my palms to sweat.

He taps on the tablet at lightning speed, and I do my best to track his every movement.

"I take it you don't have a pin yet?" I shake my head no, and he blows out a breath of frustration. "You'll have to use mine tonight. Just don't screw up the drawer on my name. My pin is three-six-four-five. Should be easy enough to remember."

Maybe I was wrong about the saving lost souls thing. Maybe he's just the devil, and I got lucky that night. I nod.

"You suddenly don't talk a lot, or am I too much of a dick right now for you to handle? Because if it's the latter, you're gonna have to get over it. This is Vegas, and everyone here is a dick."

"I don't talk a lot, and I have no problems handling a dick." The moment the words pass my lips, I realize how they sounded. My face burns hot, and I want to shrivel up into a ball.

Jake pauses, his finger poised over a number on the tablet's screen. His lips twitch with an obvious smirk that makes a dimple sink into his cheek. He chuckles lightly, shakes his head, and then goes back to the screen.

"This here is a price list for our drinks." He points to a laminated sheet behind the tablet, his voice softening some. "It's like a cheat sheet. It will help." He taps a few more things into the tablet, and when he's done, he sets the credit card down in a small box next to the tablet and turns to me. He looks me over once again, until he reaches my eyes, and then he runs his hand through his hair. "I thought for sure you'd be gone by now," he says softly, his tone and expression unreadable. *Me too.* "You ran out on me. I paid to have that piece-of-shit car of yours towed, and by the time I came back out to the truck, you were gone." He blows out a breath. "Two weeks later and here you are."

"I'm sorry," I whisper, shifting my weight, my gaze finally descending to the black rubber floor. He paid to have my car towed. I can't believe he did that for me—a complete stranger he picked up on the side of the road. "I'll pay you back."

He lets out a harsh, humorless laugh. "If I cared about the money, I wouldn't have done it."

He leaves me with that, going back to the waiting patrons of the bar. I follow once again, but if I'm going to swim on my own, as

Diamond said, I can't be his shadow. Plus, I'm a little too uncomfortable at the moment to be near him. As I recall, I had a complete breakdown in his car and told him things I really wish I hadn't, considering I now work with him.

Yet, oddly, I hate that he's angry with me—if that's even what this is.

"What can I get y'all?" I ask a couple of girls who are decked out to the nines, and then mentally chastise myself for the southern twang and slang.

They give me their crazy martini orders, and I do my best to make them without having to ask Jake or—God forbid—Diamond for help.

Jake's watching me.

I feel him.

Out of the corner of his eye, while he's doing other things. He's letting me swim, but making sure I don't get into the deep end just yet.

It's a relief. It sets me at ease, and as I chat with the girls all dressed up for a bachelorette party, I allow myself to pretend like I'm a normal girl, living in a normal world. I allow myself to have fun.

The girls already seem like they're a bit drunk, so I'm hoping they don't notice any mistakes I make. I manage my way through the tablet, even though it takes me much longer than it took Jake, and then I move on to the next person, smiling as I go. It feels like I've got this. Maybe not fully, but it's not as terrifying as I initially thought it would be.

That's how the next twenty minutes go.

Jake doesn't speak to me, but he's absolutely watching me. And when I glance in his direction, he offers an encouraging nod, but no smile. At the moment, I don't care. His positive affirmation is all I need. He might be rough and short-tempered with me tonight, but I can accept that. It actually makes it easier on me. Allows me to keep my distance and not feel as obligated to him as I already do.

Whenever I have a free second, I find myself observing him. Or Diamond. They laugh with each other, and I can't help the pang of jealousy I feel. Not of them specifically, but of their level of comfort with each other. Of their easy friendship. I've never had that with anyone.

"Hey," he says, catching me in the act, and I realize I've been standing here staring far longer than I should have been. "You okay? You need help with something?" The sleeves of his shirt are rolled up to his elbows, and I spot a hint of colorful ink peeking out on his muscular forearms.

I shake my head and take a step back as he approaches me. He tilts his head, studying my face, and I can only imagine what my expression says. I open my mouth to speak when someone interrupts me.

"I'll have a Blanton's single barrel, on the rocks, please," a man in his late twenties requests. Jake glances in his direction, narrows his eyes, before turning back to me and stepping away.

The man has been watching me since he sat down a few minutes ago. I know because I caught him twice already. He didn't even try to hide his interest. I tell myself that he's leering because of the way I'm dressed. Because I'm the bartender for the section of the bar he's in and he's looking for a drink.

I tell myself he's not here for me.

"You got it," I say with a forced smile. There's something about him and that look he refuses to bestow on anyone else.

Spinning away, I find a glass to fill with ice. This particular Blanton's is not all that accessible. I have to stand on a step stool and then reach up. And when I do reach up, I can feel a hint of a breeze on the bottom of my ass cheek. I don't waste time on trying to tug down the fabric, I just grab that bottle as quickly as I can and, in the process, nearly fall off the stool.

"Careful," Jake warns as he grasps my arm, trying to catch me. But before I can even think about it, I tug my arm away, jolting back until I knock into the row of bottles behind me. Mercifully, they don't fall, but they do clank and sway. He throws his hands up in surrender, much the way he did that first night, startled by my reaction. "I wasn't going to hurt you, Sunshine. I was just trying to help."

My cheeks warm for what is easily the tenth time tonight. He makes me feel like the teenager I never was.

"I've got it," I promise with more conviction than I feel. Pushing past him, I grab the glass I had already filled with ice.

Jake is just standing there, behind me. So close, I feel his warmth, breathe in his scent. He hasn't moved on to help anyone else, even though we're fairly busy, and there are customers waiting to place their orders. I don't glance over my shoulder to find him. I just pour the amber liquid into the glass, ignore the stench of it, and the way it makes me feel, and slide it toward the smiling patron with the hungry eyes.

"Thank you," he says, leaning across the bar with a fifty-dollar bill extended for me to take.

I snatch the money from his hand, avoiding eye contact with him, and ring up his order. As I return with his change, he shakes his head at me, his dark brown hair reflecting the dim overhead lights.

"It's all for you, beautiful." His charming smile probably gets him whatever he wants in life.

That's one hell of a tip. "Thank you. That's very nice of you." I pocket the change and then move on to the person sitting next to him. But as he sips his expensive bourbon, that discerning gaze never leaves me.

When I hand the lady next to him her wine, he asks, "What's your name?" And now my heart is really starting to hammer.

This night is going from bad to worse. Right after my reaction to Jake's hand on my skin, this guy asking my name might just throw me over the edge.

"My name?" I echo, trying to buy time.

"Yes," the customer says, giving me that smile again. "I'm Brent."

I open my mouth to respond, when I feel a hand on the small of my back, making me jump forward.

"Excuse me," Jake says to the man in a tone that is not to be questioned. "I need to speak to you for a moment," he whispers in my ear. Spinning on his heel, he marches off.

I offer Brent what I hope is a placating grin and scurry off after Jake. He stops in the corner of the bar where the waiters line up to collect their drinks for their tables. Jake's dark eyes follow me as I cautiously approach him, the thin, white fabric of his shirt straining against the muscles of his arms as he crosses them over his broad chest.

"He's a shark," is all Jake says like I should have some sort of idea as to what he's referring to. "You need to be careful of men like that. I've observed the way he's been watching you, so if you're not into that, don't give him your real name and don't tell him anything personal about yourself."

Don't give him my real name? That almost has me laughing out loud. Jake doesn't even know my real name. It's most definitely not Mia.

I blink up at him, a little stunned by his warning. And that scowl? For some reason, it has me holding back my grin.

"Do I look that naïve to you?"

"Excuse me?"

"I asked if I look naïve to you?"

"No," he growls as he runs a hand through his thick hair. He lets out a loud sigh and then shakes his head in agitation. "You don't. But you look sweet and innocent, and men in this town will jump all over that."

"And you believe that's something I require your assistance with? Keeping men from jumping all over me?"

He bends down, bringing his eyes to the same level as mine. It takes every ounce of power not to flinch, or duck my head, or lower my gaze.

"I'm saying you appear to require my assistance with a great many things. I'm saying he's a shark for the same reason I didn't want to leave you at the bus station in the middle of the night. All he's after is a quick Vegas fuck. They all are, and I don't want to see that happen with you."

I swallow. Hard. My heart racing in my chest. I can barely breathe, that's how close I am to the panic taking over. He's so close. His whiskey eyes are right here in front of mine. *Breathe, just breathe*. I do, but in addition to the oxygen I so desperately need, I take in the addictive fragrance of his cologne and taste the mint of his toothpaste.

"I appreciate the concern, Jake...," I trail off because my voice is barely audible. Just a whispered breath. That's how quiet and weak it is. Clearing my throat of the lump that has formed, I try again. "I appreciate the concern, Jake, but I'll be okay." I force a smile. "And last I checked, it's really none of your business."

He leans in closer as I say his name, his beautiful eyes confiscating my senses. I lose the battle of wills and step back, my hands jutting out protectively. His eyes widen, and his breath catches at my reaction, vacillating between my outstretched hands and my face like he doesn't know which to focus on. Finally, he rights his body, giving me the space I need.

"I want you to switch sections with me. I don't like him talking to you."

I narrow my eyes, trying to hold firm. "You really are a dangerous devil, aren't you?"

A bark of a laugh passes his lips. "Last I checked, this dangerous devil saved you from the hell of a burning car. But you're right, Sunshine. I'm no angel. I'm the guy who gets hit when he's not looking. Switch sections with me. That's not a request."

And with that, he walks off—no, storms off—back in the direction of the bar.

I have no idea what to make of Jake. He unsettles me in so many ways I can hardly begin to categorize them in order of importance.

I decide to ignore him. Keep my distance. From him and that guy, Brent. I don't want men talking to me. I don't want them asking for my name or telling me what to do. And if I didn't need this job, and if it weren't for Maddox who got it for me, I'd walk.

If my bravery existed in the form of action instead of silent words, I'd be done.

I suck in a deep breath, take another to clear my head, and then I go back to work. I smile at Brent, who readily smiles back, but I do not speak to him again. And not because Jake told me not to. No, my days of letting men tell me what to do are over.

Chapter Five

Mia

Reaching into my bag, I slide out my cell phone. In the two-plus weeks I've had it, I haven't used it for anything other than Google searches and getting hired by Cal. I pull up my internet browser and type in my name. Articles about my family and publicity images instantly fill the page, but nothing new in the last two weeks. That has me breathing out a sigh of relief.

It's like the world has no idea I disappeared.

I wonder how long Niklas will keep that up. Maybe he's not looking for me. But I know he is, so I don't understand why I continue to indulge that fantasy.

"Is that real?" a voice on my left asks with a mixture of curiosity and barely contained snark. I didn't even hear anyone else enter the break room.

Jesus. I jerk upright and look over only to realize it's Diamond. She brushes past me, opening up her locker and tugging out her purse. She fishes through it until she retrieves a pack of cigarettes and a lighter, before turning her I'm-going-to-chew-you-into-small-pieces-and-enjoy-a-smoke-after glare on me.

"I'm sorry?" I ask, unsure as to what she's referring to. It can't be my phone. This is a pay-as-you-go, disposable one. I mean, it's a smartphone, yes, but surely, she's seen those before.

"Your bag," another voice says, and I turn to find one of the waitresses standing with her hip propped against the entrance of the door, her dark eyes flashing down to the designer purse dangling from my wrist. "Is it real?"

"Oh." I eye my purse, taking it in for a moment. It is real. And in truth, it never occurred to me to swap it out for something less conspicuous. Not that I have any of those anyway. I have no idea how to answer that question. Do I lie? They're not looking at me with contempt, more general curiosity, so I go with the truth. "Yes. It is."

"Wow." The waitress clucks her tongue. "It's nice. How much that set you back?"

I shrug, glancing around surreptitiously before returning my attention to them. The waitress is smiling, but Diamond is most definitely not. I don't think she likes me very much. All night long, whenever I caught her eye, she was glowering at me like I killed her cat and made a bonfire with its remains.

"It was a gift."

The waitress's eyes widen, but Diamond steps in front of me, crossing her tattooed arms over her chest. Yeah. She hates my guts.

"Jake get you that?"

"Pardon?"

"Shut up, Diamond," the waitress tells her friend. "Just because he was keeping a close eye on her doesn't mean they're together, *right*?" she accentuates, turning her attention back on me. "I mean, he's training you, not fucking you."

Before I can respond, Jake—of all freaking people—passes the waitress with an, "Excuse me." I can feel my cheeks redden and all eyes on me. Silent, evil, expletives slay my skin as he inadvertently shields me from high-school-quality girlish hatred.

"Here, Mia," he says, handing me a laminated book. "It has everything you'll need to learn about working here. What food we have on the menu, what wines and cocktails we serve, even how to navigate our computer system."

I hear the waitress snicker behind him, but I don't dare acknowledge her, and now Diamond is sneering at me. I ignore her as well, because I can play ugly every now and then, too.

"God, Jake," I whisper, shaking my head ever so slightly. A bubble of laughter chokes its way out of me, a bewildered smile spreading across my face. Our eyes lock and the warmth in his has my breath stuttering in my chest and that laugh dying on my lips. "Who are you?" I don't think mercurial hero quite covers him.

He laughs, opening his mouth to speak when Diamond cuts him off as she stalks in closer. "Jake," she purrs, running a blood-red nail along his arm. "Are you gonna hang out for a drink after our shift tonight?"

Jake blinks, his head swiveling over in her direction. Mine does the same, but more out of curiosity than anything else.

"Oh, hey, Diamond. I didn't see you there."

She lets out an indignant huff, but her anger dissipates quickly. She leans forward, revealing more of her cleavage as she does. "I was hoping we could catch up tonight. It's been a while since we have."

"Uh," he peers around the small room as if searching for an escape only to come up empty. "Can't tonight. I have to be up early tomorrow." Jake turns back to me, a wry smile bouncing on his lips. "I'll catch you later, Mia."

"Right. Thanks for the book." I hold it up and he nods, exiting the break room as quickly as he came. The waitress follows after him, a knowing smile on her lips.

What was that? I've been doing pretty well all night. I mean, yeah, I screwed up a couple of the signature cocktails, got the proportions wrong on some others. So maybe he's trying to help me? But it didn't exactly feel like that was all there was to it. It felt like a dare wrapped in an olive branch. Is Jake flirting with me or have I reached the point where I can no longer determine what's genuine?

Niklas used to flirt. Relentlessly, in fact. It was one of the things that initially drew me to him. I was so emotionally starved.

Desperate for anything positive, anything remotely resembling affection or, God forbid, love.

Niklas gave me that.

But this sort of flirting? It's above my pedigree, that's for sure.

"Don't waste your time," Diamond scoffs, snapping me out of my reverie. Diamond has a look about her that suggests she views me as competition. It makes me want to roll my eyes and tell her just how far off she is. "Jake hardly ever dates, and when he does, he loses interest quickly." She offers up a fake sympathetic expression, like I'm the next to fall victim to his winsome ways.

Well, that explains her antagonism toward me.

"Thank you for the warning, but I'm not dating him."

"Of course, you're not," she laughs, like it's all just so funny. Like I'm just this outmatched, dim-witted girl hung up on the unachievable. "But I felt the need to warn you all the same. I saw the way you were looking at him." Diamond plasters a satisfied grin across her face, obviously believing she's put me in my place. She tosses her hair back and stalks off, her cigarettes held firmly in her hand.

Christ almighty. All this drama and it's only my first day. I hate drama. Want absolutely nothing to do with it. It's all I've ever known. Now I just want easy and quiet. Which is ironic given the town and situation I currently find myself in. Yet, I'm oddly inflated by her antagonism. It has me smiling before I catch the traitor on my lips.

Look at my life. The joke is on me. Living in Las Vegas because the car I was driving to get away from my life broke down. It seemed like the best sort of place to hide once I actually gave it some thought. The sort of town where everyone has secrets and anonymity is not judged. I had four thousand dollars in cash and my suitcases filled with clothes.

That was it.

I've been here for two weeks, and I wish I could say the days are getting easier. That the nights aren't as frightening.

That would be a lie. I don't feel safe. If anything, I feel more exposed now that I'm working, but I didn't have a choice, and so far, my fake ID is holding up okay.

But how long will that last?

Especially when money, clout, and resources have no limit.

If Niklas wants to find me, which I assume he does, then it won't be that difficult. It has me jumpy. It keeps me on edge. It makes for restless nights and sick days. But sometimes all the good choices are stripped away from us and we're left with the bad in order to survive —like wearing a uniform that shows more skin than it covers and tending bar with a guy who consumes me with smoldering glances and panty-melting heat.

He already knows too much.

But there are worse gigs to be had in this town, that's for damn sure, and I am in no place to try and find something else. Something that does not include Jake.

The restaurant closes at two in the morning. For Vegas, from what I'm learning, that's early. The hotel, on the other hand, never closes. The hotel, casino, and even some of the bars and places to eat are open twenty-four hours, seven days a week. That makes my sneaking simultaneously easier and more difficult.

After two weeks, I know all the cameras. I think I've figured out where the rare dark spots are. How to play duck and cover with the unavoidable ones.

I think.

Security is something Vegas hotels are notorious for. And not just basic security and cameras. They have all kinds of tricks up their sleeves according to my internet research.

Maddox was not forthcoming. Casinos use high-resolution images, facial recognition, and have more personnel than some small countries probably have.

On the one hand, that makes me feel safe. On the other, sometimes I'd rather not have the security in on what I'm up to.

They'd either have me arrested or kicked out on the streets.

Worse than that, they'd have me fired, and I need the money.

With my backpack hiked up high on my shoulder, I walk briskly down the long hallway that leads back into the main area of the hotel. The casino is bustling for this hour. It's a Thursday night, and this town is known for its weekend gaming. When it's busy like this, and the slots and tables are overrun with action, and money is speaking louder than the drunks placing the bets, no one pays any attention to me.

Gliding along the perimeter of the casino, I walk past the Sports Book, down a hall, and over toward the employee door that leads to the pool and spa areas. This part of the hotel is down a small alcove, and I know there are cameras here, because they make no attempt at hiding them. But I have yet to be stopped, so I wonder how closely—if at all—they monitor this area after-hours.

In the summer, the pool closes at eight p.m. and does not open again until nine a.m. But the staff arrive as early as seven to get things set up for the day. Taking out my universal keycard that I have no business having, I swipe it through the slot, hit the pin that I should not know, and the door gives me a green light and a beep that tells me I'm in.

The warm breeze of the Las Vegas summer night kisses across my face and down my exposed skin. It's welcome and sweet. Like soft kisses and stolen moments. The sounds of wind rustling through palm fronds and water splashing against rocks from the man-made waterfall feeding into the main pool permeate the night. Even though it's dark outside and it's the middle of the night, the lights of the pool are on and the waterfall is still flowing. They never turn them off from what I gather.

The pool serves as the only illumination, casting a dancing blue glow into the air, barely enough to see by. It's certainly not enough to be readily visible if someone, like security, happens to be out here. Removing my shoes, I pad barefoot along the path, snaking my way around the pool and various seating areas over to the back door that leads to the spa and their own private pools.

When I come upon the lounge chair abutting the wall and hidden behind some shrubbery, complete with a blanket and small pillow, I can't help but smile weakly. Maddox. That man has been true to his word every step of the way.

He helped get me my fake ID and jobs and told me that when I have enough money saved up, he'll help me get a safe place in a decent neighborhood that won't question my ID. He hates the fact I still sleep here, but for now, it's where I feel the most comfortable. I don't want to stay with him, nor do I want him to pay for me the way he offered. I don't want to sleep in a shelter, and apartments are costly. Anything I can afford is not in a safe neighborhood. Out here, I'm alone. Out here, I'm safe. Relatively speaking anyway. Even if it is outside.

Lowering my body onto the lounge chair, I cover myself with the thin blanket, rest my head on the somewhat soft pillow, and close my eyes. I'm exhausted. It was a long night of ups and downs and I have to be awake again by six-thirty. I'm going to make these almost four hours count. I set my alarm, close my eyes, and I'm out.

The morning comes quickly. The sun is already starting to rise, and with it, bringing on the incredible desert heat that will resonate on the streets all day long. Getting up quickly, I move the lounger back into the main pool area, fold up my blanket and pillow, and tuck them in the alcove that is hidden behind a small prickly plant that has a name I do not know.

The spa opens at eight a.m., and since Maddox gave me that universal card, I try to slip in early and use their shower facilities before anyone can notice. I have to be at my second job at eight, working the breakfast shift for another restaurant in this hotel. I rarely step foot outside the walls of this resort. Here I know. Here I'm safe.

Out there... Nothing about out there feels safe to me.

Out there is a setup. The punchline at the end of a bad joke.

After I shower and blow out my long, now dark-brown hair into soft waves, I slip into my second uniform, which consists of short-short jean cutoffs, a short-sleeved white button-down that is supposed to be open at the top in the center of my bra, and black and white checked suspenders. The bars, restaurants, and casinos in this town want slutty, and as far as I know, no one complains about it. You want the job, you dress the part.

I tuck down my shame, hoist my backpack onto my back, and then leave the spa like I own the place and belong here just like everyone else. No one questions me. No one stops me. Only a few people are around. And that's exactly how I like it.

But the moment I hit the floor where I know there are cameras everywhere, I tuck my head down so that it comes off like I'm watching where I'm going and let my long, dark hair do the rest to cover me.

That was one thing Maddox encouraged. My hair was blonde before, and he suggested I lighten it or go much darker. I went dark, because I feel like it's less conspicuous. I also cut off about four inches from the length, but it's still to my mid-back.

A man and a woman are laughing, speaking in German to each other. Their conversation is about winning five hundred dollars on a one-dollar slot machine bet, but the accent and the language send me into alarm. My feet pick up their pace without conscious thought. My hand grips the strap of my backpack to steady it against me.

I move around another couple, but the Germans aren't far behind and I can still hear them. Sweat slicks the back of my neck as my heart thunders. I whip past more people and around a corner only to slam into someone. Hard. The weight of my backpack coupled with the force of the blow knocks me back onto my ass with a shockingly painful slap.

A whimper passes my lips as I search wildly around, but the German couple are nowhere to be seen. They weren't working for him. *He's not here. He doesn't know where I am.* God, I don't know how much longer I can take this.

"Mia?" I glance up, brushing my hair out of my face and trying to clear my bleary eyes. When I focus, I find Jake's dark eyes. He seems equally as stunned to see me as I am to see him.

He's wearing a suit. Well, he's wearing a suit jacket and slacks that match, but his light-blue button-down is open at the collar, and his dark gray tie is loose, hanging in a way that suggests he just threw it around his neck before walking out the door. His chestnut hair is still damp from a recent shower and brushed off his cleanly shaven face. Other than the haphazard tie, he looks sinisterly handsome and professional. It throws me for a beat.

Long seconds pass as we stare at each other, and then he reaches out to me, offering to help me up. I don't take his proffered hand, instead I awkwardly maneuver myself with my heavy backpack and pry myself up and off the floor.

He shakes his head slightly at my refusal as he does a sweep of my outfit, and I want to die. He looks like a god amongst mortals, dressed in Armani, and I resemble some trashy, nineteen-fifties, Buddy Holly pinup throwback. If I thought I didn't know what to make of Jake before, this morning, with him dressed like this, it's worse.

And if I thought my embarrassment had met its limit, I was wrong.

"Are you okay?" he finally asks. "I wasn't paying attention."

"I'm fine." I am. At least, I think I am. "I wasn't looking, either. Sorry I smashed into you."

He grins at me. I really hate how gorgeous he is. He would be easier to discount if he didn't make my stomach flutter, my heart spring to life, and my skin tingle every time I saw him. And his eyes. God, I have no idea what to do with those. They're intense and dark, and they give off the impression that he sees everything and reveals nothing.

"You can smash into me anytime. I'm just glad I didn't hurt you." I blink at him, a little disconcerted at his almost-flirtatious comment, and that grin grows into a full-blown smile. "I take it you also work in The Bistro."

It's not a question, but I nod all the same.

"Are you going on a job interview?" I gesture toward his suit.

He laughs and the sound…well, it gives me chills. The good kind. The kind you feel all the way down to your toes. "No. No job interview. Just…work." He reaches for my face and I flinch back, but he doesn't stop or pull away from his chosen path. His hand caresses my cheek, brushing a few strands of hair from my face, and tucking them behind my ear.

A small whimper passes my lips, and I realize my eyes are clenched shut.

"I'm not going to hurt you."

I nod, but I can't speak. Hell, I can barely breathe. It's been so long since a man has touched me for anything other than inflicting pain and punishment. Even when Niklas touched me like this, soft with gentle strokes, I knew it was only the calm before the storm.

"Open your eyes."

I do, but slowly, and when I find him again, he's closer than he was before. Sort of like he was last night when he brought his face down to mine so he could look me in the eyes. He searches my face for an eternity, his body drawing in so close he's all I can see. His body heat wraps around me, the scent of his cologne and masculine shampoo calms me down and speeds me up at the same time.

"You have flecks of gold in your green eyes."

I do. No one has ever noticed before. Everyone assumes they're green, because that's the most dominant color, but sometimes I think they're more hazel.

"And your hair is darker."

I don't respond.

"What's your last name, Mia?"

I shake my head, unable to gather my scattered thoughts. It's his proximity. His touch. His…everything. It's beyond distracting.

"It's none of my business. I know that. And I'll keep my mouth shut because I get the strong impression you need your secrets the way most people need honesty, but I want to know all the same."

I hate myself as I open my mouth and say, "Jones."

He instantly knows it's a lie. His eyes darken and lose some of their luster. He blows out a loud breath, leans back and crosses his arms over his chest as he studies me. He nods his head, not daring to challenge me. He knows I'm a lost girl. He knows I'm a bit of a mess. I mean, what sort of person can't go to a hotel? What sort of person finds herself stranded on the side of the road in an ancient fossil of a vehicle without a proper place to go? Oddly enough, I think he gets me and doesn't feel the need to push further. As he said, it's none of his business.

"Did you get a chance to read over that booklet I gave you?"

"Not yet. But I appreciate you helping me, and I will get to it later. I don't work again until tomorrow night."

"I'll help you with whatever you need," he rushes out before slowing it down. "That's the sort of guy I am."

I half-smile, laughing lightly at his impish tone. "So I'm learning. Thank you for being so accommodating, Jake."

He grins like a little boy when I say his name and leans closer to me again. "Accommodating?" He points to his chest and I smile wide. Why? I don't even know at this point. It just feels too good not to. "Me?"

I nod, my teeth gnawing on my bottom lip.

"I can be accommodating. If you like accommodating, that's exactly what I am."

I shake my head, trying to laugh off his comment as anything but serious. I take a step back. He's too close. He's everywhere. His eyes seeking. His smile infiltrating. His playfulness enticing.

"I need to get to work."

"I'll see you tomorrow then, Mia Jones."

I offer up a closed-mouth grin and a small wave. It's the best I've got. And with that, I turn on my heels and walk off. I don't run the way my body is screaming at me to. I walk. Because I know beyond a shadow of a doubt that he's watching me, and I'll be damned if I show him just how much he affects me.

Chapter Six

Jake

"She's pretty," Maddox says as he walks up, joining me on my right and standing beside me as he appraises Mia the same way I am. "*Very* pretty. Who is she?"

For some reason, I don't want to tell him I found her broken down on the side of the road. That feels like something between me and her and no one else. When I had Brennan get her car towed, I didn't give him any information other than I was helping out a friend. But by the time I made it back out to the truck, she was gone.

It was like a sucker punch to the gut. I even ran down to the sidewalk, searching everywhere I could for her. But she was long gone. That didn't stop me from driving around trying to find her. I did. For longer than I care to admit. And now, two weeks later, here she is.

The woman I never thought I'd see again but haven't stopped thinking about once.

"She works at Valaria's with me. New hire as of last night."

"And you're already talking to her like that? Did you fuck her and that was your walk of shame?" Maddox is incredulous. So am I if I'm being honest, because he's right. I was way more physical with her than I had any right to be.

"No. I did not fuck her. She's just...," I trail off. I have no words for what she is, and I certainly don't feel the need to entertain my best friend any more than I already have. "I'm just helping her out, is all. What's the big deal?"

"No big deal," Maddox says, not even bothering to hide his smug grin. "She looks like a nice girl," he adds.

"Don't start."

He laughs, nudging me in the shoulder. "I came by to tell you I can't make this morning's meeting. I gotta go down the street. Two dealers called out last minute."

I turn to face him, finally dragging my eyes away from the front entrance of The Bistro Mia fake-ass-last-name Jones went through almost five minutes ago. Maddox is already wearing his black dealer's uniform. His light blue eyes give the impression they haven't seen a full night's sleep in weeks, but I doubt mine are much better, so I don't comment on that.

"You felt the need to stop here first?"

He shrugs. "Your phone went straight to voicemail when I called, and I wasn't sure if you'd get my text. I know this is a big meeting, so if you want me to figure something else out for the tables, I can."

"Nah. Go on. Thanks for covering that, I know it's not really your job."

"It's cool. I like dealing, remember?" I nod, because I do remember. "I'll catch you later, then you can bring me up to speed on everything I missed at the meeting."

I slap his large, muscular back. "Sounds good. Later."

"Have fun with your nice girl," Maddox calls back over his shoulder, chuckling to himself as he goes.

She is a nice girl. Maddox isn't wrong about that. She's also very pretty, just as he said. Truthfully, she's downright gorgeous with her long, flowy dark-brown—I can't decide which I like better on her, brown or blonde—hair and green eyes. Tall and slender with unbelievable curves in all the right places. Her beauty is something else entirely. I can't even explain what. It goes beyond her face, her eyes, her lips, her hair and her body. It goes deeper.

Hits you on a different level.

But she's trouble. And I don't have time for a lost girl.

There's a lot more to the story than that, though. A lot more. I haven't lived in this town all that long, only existed in this very exclusive world with infrequency. I grew up on the smaller side of life thanks to my mother, but there was nothing small about my father's world, and as a result, I know what a girl with money looks like.

Mia has money.

Her suitcases were designer. Her purse is, too, and the shoes she wore last night have those signature red soles. And yet, she was driving that piece of shit Chevy that was older than Cal. She wouldn't answer my questions and practically broke down into hysterics when I explained why buses weren't an option. And why couldn't she go to a hotel? I can't imagine money was the reason.

No, it's because she didn't want to produce an ID or credit card.

She said she had no one to call.

Girls like her always have someone to call—a boyfriend or a daddy—and the fact that she said she didn't and was stranded in the middle of nowhere in that car, before running off alone into the Las Vegas night, only to turn up now, is raising all kinds of red flags. It also pisses me off. Like she's been right here, under my nose this entire time.

That didn't stop you from helping her.

It didn't. Her crying in my truck that night dropped me to my knees. And really, what was I supposed to do? Leave the woman stranded somewhere? Or worse, in a Vegas bus station? No way. Never in a million years. I hadn't expected her to run out on me. I'd thought she'd stay and let me help her.

She's scared. Of me personally? Of men in general? I'm not entirely sure yet.

But I do know she doesn't like to be touched, which only seems to make me want to do it more.

I sigh. Out loud and right in the middle of the hall.

Mia Jones. Who are you? And why do I want to know so badly?

I pull out my phone and find that it is, in fact, off. I turn it on, wait for it to power up and text Cal, informing him that I'll train Mia again tomorrow night. Not that she really needs much training. She's a decent bartender, despite being noticeably inexperienced. That will work to my advantage since I hate tending bar. That was not a lie. It's why I became a waiter instead of taking on any other position.

I have plenty of experience waiting tables, which, considering what my life has become in the last six months, makes me nostalgic for that simpler way of living. Last night, when I came in and Cal told me that Kippa had called out and that I was needed to train the new girl, I was not pleased. And when I challenged him on Kippa, he just threw his hands up in the air and said, "Why do you think I hired the new girl? This is your show and you're the only one who can do it."

He is right. It is my show. All of it. So, I sucked it up and made my way over to the bar.

And then I saw her.

My tragic mystery girl.

Even though she looked a little different than the last time I had seen her, I knew her instantly. There's no forgetting a woman like her. I saw her smile at the asshole with the pinched face who was being nothing but rude as he ordered his drink. I watched as she fumbled about making his drink, even though I knew she didn't know how to work the register. I even caught the flash of panic in her eyes when he asked if he could start a tab.

I watched her because I couldn't take my eyes off her.

I had no idea how to process encountering her again. And after two solid weeks.

I resented her for running off on me. I was bitter because I was worried about where she went and whether she was okay. I was furious that after two fucking weeks, I still thought about her.

I wanted to ask her if she knew everything she'd put me through? But more importantly, I just wanted to make sure she was okay, and that frustrated me most of all.

But she's raising more red flags than I care to think about.

I brush off that encounter because I'll have another opportunity to try and figure her out tomorrow night. Walking through the hotel, I pass the main casino and make my way down the hall to the staff and corporate area. The resort chain is comprised of three hotels in Las Vegas and another dozen satellite ones throughout the country. Turner Hotels are quickly becoming exactly what my father envisioned.

As for me? I don't know if he ever anticipated me.

If he ever really figured me into the equation. But the fool thought he was immortal. That a life of alcohol, cigars, and cocaine wouldn't catch up to him, and now here I am. Maybe that's why he paid for MIT and then Wharton after the Army. Not that business was ever my endgame. It wasn't. I just went along with his suggestions because I was at a loss. I had no idea what I wanted my future to be after I left the Army. It was like that bullet to the shoulder flipped my world on its head, and the life I had once envisioned for myself was no longer relevant or desired. So, I went to his fancy schools and when that was done, after he spent hundreds of thousands of dollars on my education, I became a waiter.

I liked waiting tables. I liked going to clubs. I liked meeting women and fucking them. I liked living that life.

Then six months ago, my world flipped upside down once again.

My father died.

He left his girlfriend of ten years some cash, but nothing more. Everything else went to me. The hotels. The restaurants. The clubs. The casinos. The empire. All mine now.

And since he had never publicly claimed me as his son, I was unknown. I did not exist in the media. The tabloids had no knowledge of me. I was the son of the woman he spent a summer loving, and he never had any other children. His will was explicit, and thus far, uncontested.

So, it all fell on me.

I spent four months traveling across the country from one hotel to another, checking them out individually.

And now I'm in Vegas. The end of the line. The biggest cluster of hotels we have, and by far, the most lucrative. The casinos are the main reason behind that. The money they haul in is astronomical. The hotels and restaurants rake it in as well. But you don't get to know, understand, a business until you work in it.

I'm a waiter in the most popular restaurant we have. I'm a pit boss in our most popular casino. And I'm a bouncer in our most popular club.

Each of these are spread throughout the three hotels here in town.

Corporate types have no idea what makes these places run, but if you get on the inside, become one with the culture, you learn more than you ever could while sitting in a boardroom.

It's why we're refurbishing three of our restaurants, expanding our casinos and bolstering our nightclubs. The money is exorbitant, but in the end, we'll make it back and then a shit ton more. I've already seen the changes I've made pay off. Not that there's anyone to challenge me. There is no board. My father was the sole proprietor.

He was also a colossal prick.

But I'm not.

Even though I am technically the one in charge, the name behind the show, I am not the face. Nor do I want to be. I like the fact that the press still have no idea I exist. They think my father's second in command is in charge, and for some of it, he is. Enough to keep him happy at least. One thing my father did right was to hire a dynamic executive team. Despite my age and inexperience, thus far, they've been receptive to my ideas.

I punch in the code, swipe my card, wait for the beeps, and then I'm in, walking down the long white corridor until I reach the elevator at the end. It takes me right up to the corporate suite. I button the top button of my shirt, straighten my tie, and become my most ruthless self.

"Mr. Turner," my assistant says with a warm smile. She's been working here since she was twenty-two and is Vegas born and raised. She's become an invaluable resource. "They're waiting for you in the gold room, sir."

Sir. I almost scoff. I'm twenty years her junior, but suddenly I've become sir to her.

"Thank you, Malerie."

I open the double doors without a moment's hesitation, and when I enter, everyone sits up straight. And if I'm Malerie's junior by twenty years, these men have got thirty on me. I'll give them their dues, because they do not regard me as a kid. The changes I've already enacted in the other hotels are making money on the investments we've put in, and in the end, it's making them richer.

Vegas is our headquarters. It's our start. Everything else is a branching out of the original. Which means it has to be the best. It's why I'm here. It's why I've spent the last two months of my life playing house and learning everything there is to learn about the hotel and casino business.

"Jake, my boy," Morgan Fair says, the smile on his wrinkled face oozing from his voice.

Maybe they do see me as a kid, after all.

He stands up, slaps me on the back like we're close chums and gives a shit, then he sits back down on my right. No coincidence. He's the figurehead.

"Morgan," I say before I greet everyone else at the table. I take my seat at the head of the polished mahogany table, steeple my fingers and sit up straight. I may be young in this game. I may not have a lot of experience. I may be so far out of my depth I'm drowning in the swell.

But fuck it and fuck them.

Twenty-nine is not a boy.

We settle into business, and for the next hour and a half, I talk shop. I discuss the new DJs and music acts who will be headlining our clubs and concert venues. I disclose the new celebrity chef I hired and the theme of the new restaurant we're adding. I describe the new sports betting that's going live later this quarter, which is similar to fantasy sports leagues you see online, all done through a secure app that can be accessed anywhere, anytime. It's a plan to keep them gambling with us, even when they're not physically here. Maddox's dream baby.

All of this goes well. They're in. They're excited.

And I feel fan-fucking-tastic when I walk out of that boardroom.

I don't think about Mia. Not once. Not until the door of my father's condo clicks shut behind me and I'm blasted with the chill of the air conditioning and the quiet of an empty space. Now she's back. Full force. How? Hell, if I know.

This thing with her… This thing that is not even close to being a thing… Well, shit, it's turning me back into a bartender. It's filling my mind with questions I wonder if I'll ever get the answers to. I have so much on my plate. Expectations. Deliverables. Working three different jobs at all different hours in addition to playing CEO.

I don't have time to be the guy on his knees for the girl who doesn't want him there.

I don't have time for the effort she'll no doubt require.

My expensive shoes tap against the marble floor as I make my way to what is now my bedroom. I grew up here in a way. It was the only place I ever visited my father. He may have owned two dozen hotels nationwide, but Vegas is where he liked to be. When I visited, he never took me out. We stayed inside. He'd order room service, which I thought was unbelievably cool, I'd swim in the private pool he has on the large wraparound terrace, and it would be just him and me.

It took a very long time to realize what he was actually doing. Hiding me.

After he died, after his girlfriend took all the furniture when she left, I redid things a bit. Made it more me and less him. But now it's just a giant lonely place that still doesn't feel like home. The balcony is off the master and the family room, but I enter it through the bedroom because that's where I was headed when I decided blistering heat was more favorable than a soft bed.

The heat is so overpowering it steals my breath, instantly covering me in a sheen of sweat. It's well over a hundred today, and that's street level. I'm fifty stories up. None of the other rooms have balconies. Few hotels in Vegas do. My father had this added on and had the railing made out of thick glass that goes up to my waist. I don't dare touch it. It will most likely burn me if I do.

I just stand here, staring out at the Strip and the mountains and the bright blue desert sky. The heat is blistering. The air is heavy, sweltering, and absolutely perfect. I close my eyes and let the sun sear into me. Let it brand me. Let the sweat wash away…well, everything.

That thought makes me smile for some reason.

Like this is the fresh start I've been looking for. Because this is my chance. I'm no longer the middle-class kid from Baltimore. I'm no longer the rich son of the hotel tycoon. I'm no longer the party guy.

I'm Jake Harris Turner.

And that new distinction has made me accountable. Has made me an adult. And has made me want to figure out absolutely everything about the woman dominating my thoughts.

Chapter Seven

Mia

Placing my earphones in my ears, I adjust them until they're the way I like them. I hit play on my running mix, tuck the iPod into the plastic, waterproof protector on my arm and set off. It's raining today. It's the first time I've seen rain since I got here, and I welcome it. Wet and cool. At least, cooler than normal. The scent of fresh rain against hot pavement—petrichor, I once heard someone call it—fills my nostrils as I crack my neck and stretch out my muscles until the tightness releases.

I'm new at this. Not the running part—I used to do that every chance I got. Exercise was one of the few freedoms I had—but the leaving the hotel part, that's new. And the training part. But Maddox offered to help and since he's a huge bear of a man, former Army per him, he knows how to throw a solid punch.

Taking Back Sunday unapologetically blares in my ears as I run down the Strip, heading for less conspicuous territory. This is normally an excessively busy area, but right now, at this very early hour, it's quiet. I find my rhythm quickly, enjoying the solitude of the wet, gray morning.

The cold rain comes down in angry torrents, slapping against my skin with a sting and soaking me through. My mind clears, allowing me to only focus on my breathing and footing on the slippery concrete. It's the only time of day I don't actively think of him. That I'm able to let go.

I jog up the street another two blocks until I spot the black sign with white block lettering that says, *David Torres, Gym and Mixed Martial Arts Studio.* I have no idea who David Torres actually is, but Maddox says he's a good friend and is cool with us using one of his training rooms for free as long as it's before eight.

Slowing down before I reach the door, I walk the last hundred or so yards, hands on my hips, as I pull the cool morning air in through my nose and out my mouth.

Two extremely built guys head straight for the door to the gym, shooting the shit with each other. The people who train here are hardcore. Professionals. Or trying to be. I'm not, nor am I trying to be, but this is the first thing I've done that's made me feel strong, empowered even, since I left.

I scoot in behind them before the door has a chance to shut and head straight for the stairs that will take me to the third-floor private training space. The first floor of the building is the main gym. Every kind of machine and free weights a person could desire is there, as well as a few treadmills, stationary bikes, and elliptical machines. It's also where the locker rooms and saunas are located.

The second floor is set up into four separate spaces. Two are training or class studios and the other two are set up as mock octagons for sparring. The sparring rings are intense and only for the professional fighters that train here. I've never been here during those scheduled hours, but I did overhear one of the other women discussing it in the locker room. Apparently, a man got his jaw broken, and his eye swelled up so badly he couldn't see out of it because he refused to spar with protective gear.

The last thing I want to watch is people getting the shit beat out of them for sport.

The third floor, however, is set up as open space for private lessons. Half of the floor is the regular pale hardwood that comprises the rest of the gym; the other half is hard mats. I have private lessons three mornings a week with Maddox.

When I asked him, again, why he is helping me, he informed me that he has four older sisters. Four.

And so, his rationale was this: "If any one of my sisters were in the position you're in, I'd like to think there would be someone to help them the way I'm helping you." I took that, and I kept it. Maddox is a good man, and I do not know how I'll repay him yet, but I will. Fake IDs, new jobs, personal training and just generally being there when I need him.

He's like the big brother I never had. A gorgeous one, but our relationship is purely platonic. And I know that one works both ways. He doesn't look at me the way Jake does. Jake looks at me like he doesn't know how not to. Like he doesn't want to look anywhere else. Maddox didn't notice I'd dyed my hair until I asked him what he thought of the change.

I make my way up the last step and walk through the large glass double doors that lead to the studio. The door closes behind me with a swoosh, and I'm instantly assaulted with the scent of bleach disinfectant, chemical air freshener, and sweat. It's as unpleasant as it sounds, and yet, it's oddly comforting.

I grab a white towel off the small table where several towels are folded into small squares. I wipe my face and arms of the excess rain water and sweat before tossing it in the bin next to the table.

"You ready to work, girl?" the familiar male voice questions from behind me. I spin around to see all six-foot-six of Maddox Sinclair, standing there with his hands on his narrow hips, watching me expectantly. His standard no-bullshit expression firmly affixed.

I like that about him.

He doesn't waste time with pleasantries.

He calls me girl. It's not even in a derogatory way. He actually believes calling me woman is more derogatory, and since he refuses to call me Mia, knowing it's not my real name, he settles on girl.

To say he's an imposing figure is a mild understatement. His sandy-blond hair is buzzed close to his head, military-style. Deep-set, powder-blue eyes say, 'don't fuck with me or you may not live to regret it.' The smattering of sweat on his brow suggests he's already had a busy morning on the mats. He's wearing a light gray sports tee that hugs his enormous chest and arm muscles, and light blue track shorts.

He doesn't smile.

He rarely does during these sessions, though he's pretty much a wiseass otherwise.

He sees my pain with some of his own. And even though I don't know his wounds, I do know they're deep and so embedded in him that they've become part of his skin. Exactly like mine.

"Most definitely," I grin, tilting my head at him. "Aren't I always?" I raise an eyebrow in challenge. My hands fist on my hips, mocking his pose in feigned annoyance.

"Good." He points over to the other side of the room, "Now get your ass over to those mats, and we'll get started."

I do as I'm told, because, well, he's huge and a special forces guy, if I had to guess, though he doesn't talk about it. You don't mess with these dudes. You'd think knowing he can beat me into oblivion with his pinky finger would scare me after everything I've been through with Niklas, but it doesn't.

I know Maddox would never ever hurt me. Sure, we spar, and he throws me down to the mat, but it's never hard, and it always has a purpose behind it. Something I need to learn or work on. He's never raised a hand to me in anger.

And it makes me respect him all the more for not treating me with kid gloves.

That trust didn't come overnight.

I freaked out within the first five minutes of our first session.

It was my fault, I hadn't been fully upfront with him about my past. That led to an hour-long conversation about what I was looking to get out of our time. Why I was doing it. It meant opening up to him about some things I'd just assumed I'd never speak of again. But I never once saw judgment in his eyes, or pity for that matter.

And it worked. I now trust Maddox and let him direct me in whatever way he sees fit. Simply put, I need him. I need to be fit. I need to be ready. I need to expect the unexpected.

Because Niklas does not come with a warning bell. He does not typically give me a heads-up before he strikes, and he never ever relented because I asked him to.

"I started working the other day," I tell him, a little embarrassed for some reason. "The two jobs at the hotel," I add, like he doesn't know. He got me the freaking jobs. I'm positioned straight in front of him, about six feet away, on one side of the circle that's constructed out of thick masking tape stuck on the blue mat. It gives me boundaries to work within. A way to keep myself focused.

Fighting is an intimate playground. At least, that's what Maddox says. I admit, I sort of treat him like my therapist as well as my trainer and friend. And maybe that's wrong of me. That's not his role after all. But he lets me talk and hears me out so I'm not about to stop while I'm ahead.

"How'd that go?" he asks in a tone that's much softer than before, but the hard glint in his eyes remains unchanged. He knows my history, well, as much of it as he needs to know anyway. He knows I was abused and that I fled. Everything else is above his pay grade.

"Um." I blush and look down, feeling ridiculous and adolescent that my thoughts automatically return to Jake. He's not someone I should be thinking about. I hate the way his eyes make me feel. Or the way my body reacts to him. "It's good. Scary. I'm pretty sure I suck at bartending."

He doesn't laugh like I expect him to, which makes me desperate to read his expression better. There's no pity or sympathy there; he doesn't do much of that. Instead, he looks like he's thinking hard about what I just said, relaxing his hands and his knees a little to a less strained position while he does.

"It's a learning curve, right? Like with any new job, you need to learn the ropes. Give it a chance and try to stay positive. The Bistro you'll pick up, because Julien runs that place like a military drill sergeant. Valeria's is different. Diamond, am I right?"

I laugh and shrug. "She was rough. I guess some Kippa girl didn't show and she couldn't train me so…"

I turn and look away, unsure why I'm hesitant to tell him about Jake. Maybe because I'm afraid I'll blush if I talk about him. I certainly haven't told Maddox how Jake found me broken down on the side of the road in the middle of nowhere.

"So, someone else did? Who?"

I shrug. "Jake," I say, my eyes still fixed on the rain beyond the south-facing window. "I don't know his last name."

He's silent at this, which of course prompts me to look back over at him. He's rubbing his smooth jaw absently like he's thinking seriously about this, a small smirk on his face.

"Jake's a good guy," is all he says. "Just stick it out. Especially at Valeria's. Learning curve, right? Like any new job," he repeats, widening his eyes at me like I should acknowledge this as a truth.

But his words resonate in my soul, filling me with gut-twisting humiliation. I've never had a job before. All I can do is nod, my heart in my throat. Maddox moves his hands out in front of him, waist-high. He's getting into position again.

One foot crosses over the other as he starts to stalk me within the perimeter of the circle, crystalline eyes never leaving mine.

I mimic his position, keeping my eyes trained on his, as I've been taught. Never look at the attacker's feet or hands. They can fool you. Always go with the eyes or upper chest and you'll anticipate their movements and intentions better.

My body poised for attack, leaning forward only slightly as I maintain my center of gravity over my hips. My feet always spaced shoulder-width apart and my hands in front of me in both an offensive and defensive position.

"Try meeting some new people. Make some friends."

I pause, caught off guard by his words before he snaps his fingers at me, drawing me back to the task at hand.

"I'm not ready for that. And besides," I snort out derisively. "What would I tell them about myself?"

"Trust has to be earned," his thick voice says calmly, but full of concentration as we continue our slow dance around the circle. "It's never a gimme. Look at us. You start slow and build from there."

Except trust is a fallacy, a word people throw around when its convenience and purpose suit them.

I shake off the conversation. It's counterproductive. I'm doing my best to focus on his movements now, so I shut up, and so does he. Friends are not part of my objective.

We continue to circle in silence after that, and then, without warning, he launches at me. One punch thrown, which I block by ducking down to the right. I sidestep him, throwing a punch of my own, which he doesn't block, hitting him squarely in the flank. It's not a hard punch and I'm sure it doesn't hurt him, but it still feels good. We're not using pads or gloves at the moment, so our hits are meant to show contact and movement rather than force.

That comes later in the session.

Much of what we do is building my confidence. You can never *really* be prepared if someone attacks you. Especially if they're much larger than you are, which Niklas is. He's a bruiser of a guy. The man lives in our personal gym. None of that matters, though, the confidence in being able to defend yourself is a powerful weapon. I may not be able to *win* the fight, but I may be able to do enough to distract him or partially disable him, which would allow me to get away.

And in the deepest, darkest, recesses of my mind, the thought of hitting Niklas back, of actually inflicting pain, gets me going. If he comes after me again, I will destroy his world the way he destroyed mine.

Maddox doesn't wait, he comes at me again. A one-two punch combo that does hit me, pushing me back down onto the mat, right on my ass with a loud slap.

"Crap," I mutter, slamming my hand onto the hard material before jumping back up to go again.

"Don't get frustrated, girl. This is only your fourth lesson. You're doing remarkably well," he encourages as we circle again, this time only a few feet apart.

"I can't help it." My eyes narrow, disappointment, and maybe some anger, lurking beneath the surface. "I want to be able to kick your ass."

I'm not even joking. I really do. Never in my wildest dreams do I ever expect to, though. It's like a kitten going after a pit bull.

Pathetic and unrealistic. But still, the dream is there, and kittens are notoriously feisty and relentless.

He gives a half-grin, which is the most I've ever seen cross his lips while we train. Probably because I said ass and I don't cuss. Except in my head. "A lady never cusses," my mother always said. It's a difficult lesson to unlearn.

"Believe me, soon enough, you'll be able to. Now, bring it before I knock your ass down again."

And I do. I go after him with everything I have. I throw punches and kicks and elbow shots. I spin and twist and block and duck. I land a few, he lands more.

We spar like this, on and off, for more than twenty minutes. By the time we stop, I'm dripping sweat all over and panting for my life. The adrenaline coursing through my veins is a heady rush. A fucking high I'm quickly becoming addicted to. So gloriously different than the adrenaline that comes from fear.

I guzzle down water from the reusable bottle I leave here. I'm so thirsty I finish half of it before he's even had a few sips of his. Water runs down my chin, dripping onto my sweat-soaked sports tank.

"I'm loving the contact you're making with your strikes," he says, standing in front of me, once again making me feel like that kitten. Mostly because I don't agree with him. He went easy on me. I know this. He knows this. "They're strong and have good power behind them. Your kicks are another story." I peer over at him in dismay, wiping the excess water from my mouth with the back of my hand. "Those are much harder to become comfortable with. Much more so than punching. Kicks can set you off balance and make you feel vulnerable if done incorrectly, so I get it." He holds up a hand to stop me before I can argue. "We'll work on it and make you into a fucking machine. Don't you worry about that."

A reluctant smile tries to break out, before it falls just as fast. I turn to face him head-on, staring him directly in the eyes.

"I need to be formidable as soon as possible, Maddox. I need you to work me hard. I'm not messing around with this."

He takes three large steps in my direction. Each of his steps probably equaling two of mine, at least. His index finger reaches out, pressing into the underside of my chin, and instinctively, I jolt back from him. He doesn't shy away, tilting my face up to his, before it pulls away just as fast. He knows I don't like being touched. Yet he pushes my boundaries with it. Like riding a horse without any reins, I have no way to steer. No direction I can maneuver. I'm at his mercy and he knows it.

"Do you really believe he's coming to find you?" His voice is cautious, but his eyes are telling me he needs a real answer here. Not for himself. I don't get the impression that Maddox Sinclair is afraid of much. Even Niklas isn't stupid enough to take on this man.

I draw in a deep breath and release it slowly, before nodding. "If he figures out where I am, I know for a *fact* he'll come after me." I don't shrink away from him, I stand here and let him make of that what he will. He needs to know this, but more importantly, I need to face it. Two weeks of nothing in the desert oasis that serves as the perfect playpen for escapism will not make me complacent.

Niklas won't send someone. It will be him, and it will be me, and it will be blunt force trauma.

His eyebrows knit together, making his forehead crinkle. Blue eyes dance around my face, then over toward the glass door for a beat before returning to mine.

"I will do *everything* in my power to get you comfortable and ready to attack. I can promise you that…," he trails off like he's not sure if he should continue. I can feel the *but* lingering on his lips, so I nod my head and widen my eyes, encouraging him to continue. When he finally does speak, his voice is bothered, like he doesn't relish the words he's about to utter. "Has he ever come after you with a gun before?"

I shake my head immediately. "No. Never. He's more of a fists and kicks guy. Plus," I pause here, glancing back down at my feet, feeling the color rise up my cheeks. My fingers knot, and I don't know how to say this to someone I hardly know. Sucking in a deep breath, I release it and say, "He doesn't want me dead. He wants me very much alive." *Because I'm worth more alive than dead*, I don't add.

"Despite that, you need more than this if you believe him coming after you is a real possibility."

I raise my eyebrows surprised by his candor. "What does that mean?"

Another step to me. All six-six of him staring down at me, but it's not fear or intimidation he's imposing on me, it's a possessive protection instead. Like a brother protecting a sister. "It means if I were you, I'd buy a gun and join the gun club. I'd learn how to shoot that thing like a motherfucker. I'd also carry pepper spray on me at all times." I open my mouth to speak, but he holds up his hand stopping me. "Physical fighting is one thing, and you may be tall, but you don't weigh much. You're what…" His eyes trail down my body, but not in a creepy way. He's sizing me up. "A hundred and twenty pounds?"

"About that, yes." I've lost weight since moving to Las Vegas. Not intentionally, but irregular meals are what they are.

"You can punch and kick him, and it will help. Believe me, it will help. I'll teach you how to incapacitate an assailant, but, *Mia...*" He pauses, stressing my fake name, directing my attention entirely to him, ensuring I'm absorbing his words. "Sometimes you need more in order to save your life. He might not be out to kill you, and I would never tell you to kill another human being, but you might have to, if you get what I'm saying."

My head snaps away from his penetrating gaze. Unable to hold it, I seek refuge in the large windows. My arms wrap around my chest protectively. The dark, gloomy sky mirrors my insides. I think about this for a moment, and Maddox remains quiet as I mull over his words.

"I've never even held a gun before," I admit quietly, unable to draw my eyes away from the window.

"If you're not comfortable with that, I get it." He pauses again. I know he won't offer to teach me to shoot, though I wonder if that's what was lingering there before he stopped speaking. "But I think the pepper spray is a must."

"Okay," I whisper. Any confidence I had feels like it's now in the bottom of my feet.

"I didn't tell you this so you'd get discouraged. I will make you into a fighter, I promise." I finally turn back to him and the intensity in his expression makes my breath catch. "I will make it so you'll know how to hurt him or any asshole who tries to fuck with you. But hurt is not dead, and sometimes the latter is the only way you come out alive. I just want you to be fully protected."

I swallow hard, before clearing my throat of the lump that's sitting in it. "Thanks, Maddox. I can't express what that means to me."

"Good," he smirks. "Then don't. I fucking hate praise." I smile so big I'm sure all my teeth are showing. "Now, let's get some pads on and see what we can do. You hit me like a fart in the wind."

Nice. Very nice. Men, right?

He marches off, no doubt in the direction of the equipment he has lined up against the far wall, but I take an extra second to collect myself. I was just given way too much information that requires some processing and a lot more thought.

Maddox is right.

And even though I was not raised as a gun-toting girl, it might be time for that to change.

Chapter Eight

Jake

The restaurant, lounge, and bar areas are all packed to the brim, stocked full of weekend travelers, business people extending their stay, and even some locals. It's midnight, but all that means is things are just getting started. The club downstairs has a new DJ tonight, and I've already heard from four people here that they're planning on checking it out after dinner.

I gave them each a one-free-admission card. That means that they have to pay the entrance fee for anyone else, but it also ensures they're more likely to go than they might have been before. In addition to getting more bodies in the door, it builds goodwill with customers. Freebies make people happy. People are more inclined to buy other things if they get something for free.

Economics 101.

I'm not waiting tables tonight, so I have no idea how people are enjoying the food. I could ask the waitstaff what people are saying, but in truth, very few people know my deal. The upper managers, sure, they know. The general staff? No. Because that leads to a whole other world I'd rather not explore. Especially with the catfishers.

Mia came in tonight looking as beautiful as ever. Red lips.

Skintight black mini dress. Long, dark hair flowing. She gave me a cursory glance, and that was it. She went right to work, and she's a fast learner. The customers love her. The men want to fuck her.

She's quick on the register, and if I had to guess, I'd say she knows about seventy percent of our signature cocktails already.

She studied up, and that makes me smile like I won something.

"Do you need a break?" I ask her, making a point to touch her bare shoulder as I do just so I can watch her reaction. She draws back. Again. Like she's expecting me to land a blow. Jesus motherfucking Christ. How do I make sense of that?

She smiles up at me. Big, brilliant, and beaming. That's how. That smile, man. I've never seen anything like it.

"No," she says softly. "I'm good. You go if you need to."

I don't. I'm not going on a break while she's working. And that thought is solidified when I see that cocksucker Brent walk in. He smiles that asshole smile of his at her, throws her a wink and quirks a finger, asking her to approach him. I'm instantly jealous. But I force myself to stay quiet as this vulture swoops in and takes what's mine.

Mine?

Mia is not mine, but I'm having a hell of a time convincing myself of that. I don't possess her. I feel like that's been attempted a time or two by men who should not be allowed near women. So yeah, that's not my objective. But mine feels right. Keeping her close feels right. Watching out for her feels right.

I might be a special level of fucked with this.

She steps back from me, only to approach him. I stand and watch. I don't even hide the fact. Let him think what he wants about me. I don't give a fuck. I don't want him touching her. And hell. None of this is good. It's only going to end badly. I need to get my head on straight, and I need to do it now.

Scrubbing my hands up and down my face, I pull myself together but don't go far. I smile at the women sitting next to the asshole and take their order.

"I was hoping I'd see you tonight," he says to Mia. "I missed you last night, but I see your boyfriend is here keeping tabs on you again." He glances in my direction, and that draws her eyes over her shoulder to me as I mix up a batch of martinis.

I wink at her. Then smirk at him, because he can go screw himself sideways.

She rolls her eyes. Shakes her head. And then turns back to him. "He's not my boyfriend. Just my boss. What can I get you tonight? Same as the other night?"

"Will you stand on the stool to reach for it again?"

She blushes a bright red, and I hate he just humiliated her like that. "I might not have a choice," she grins. She's being playful. Just. Perfect.

I do my best to ignore them, to focus on these drinks and these girls who are flirting with me the way Brent is flirting with her. But I can't concentrate on them. My attention is one hundred percent on Mia.

"Then, my answer is yes. I'm all for anything that gets you to reach for something high up in that outfit. But if it makes you uncomfortable, I'll let it be ladies' choice." She smiles softly now. She likes that answer. "I'm hoping you'll go out to dinner with me some night while I'm here, and something tells me that objectifying you won't earn me that luxury."

She shakes her head. "You're right about that." And then she pauses, straightening herself up a bit. "But I don't date."

"Are you married?" Brent presses.

She shifts her position. "I'm not on the market."

Well, hell.

"Do you have a boyfriend, a fiancé?"

The guy is persistent. I'll give him that.

Her posture stiffens, but she recovers quickly. "No, but I'm not dating right now."

He gives her his million-dollar grin. "I'd love to change that. Here." He slides a card across the smooth wood bar top. "That's my number. Just promise me you'll think about dinner."

"I will," she says and then goes and gets him a nice bourbon from the second shelf instead of reaching up high and showing off her ass. She slides him three fingers with some ice, and he accepts it with a big smile. He doesn't touch her, and part of me wishes he would. Just so I could watch her flinch the way she does with me.

"Are you okay?" she asks softly when she catches me staring at her, but when she realizes I'm not, she takes a step back.

Shit. I'm scaring her.

"I'm fine. Sorry." I shake my head, clearing away everything. "Just tired, you know? It's late, and I was up early again. You must be tired, too, doing swing shifts between here and The Bistro like this." I shut my mouth before I continue my inane babbling.

She shrugs, but she still looks wary. I don't blame her, so I tack on an easy-going smile at the end of my little speech. She seems to buy that because she relaxes her rigid spine and manages a grin of her own. I blow out a breath and pull my shit together, pushing all those thoughts to the back of my mind.

Brent sits there, sipping his expensive drink and eating her up with his eyes while she continues to work. I do, too. I can't even seem to help myself. She's the most alluring drug. I can't help but stay closer to her than I know I should.

A girl walks up to the bar, leaning so far across it her tits practically spill out of her tiny top. "Hey," she coos, offering me a seductive grin.

"What can I get you?"

"Are you on the menu?"

Jesus. I can't stop my small laugh. People flirt with bartenders. They do it everywhere. They think we're all easy game and out for a lay. And sometimes that is most definitely the case. But of all the places I've worked, people are far more brazen in Las Vegas.

"I'm not. But we have a lot of drinks that I'm sure would make you feel just as good."

Her finger glides along the line of her cleavage, but I do not take the bait. My eyes stay focused on hers. And when she realizes this isn't going the way she anticipated it would, she points over to her friends and says, "A pitcher of margaritas."

"You got it."

"But if you change your mind, I'm staying in this hotel. Room 10-050. Come find me. I'm a lot of fun."

"I have no doubt that you are. Thanks for the offer, but I'm afraid I can't." She gives me a pouty frown but leaves it at that.

I start making the margaritas when Mia approaches me, standing close as she mixes a drink she could have easily made on the other side of the bar where she's stationed.

"She was pretty." It takes everything in my power not to smile at that.

I shrug indifferently.

"Why didn't you take her up on her offer?" Her eyes are on the bottle of gin and glass in her hand, but her voice tells me that my answer means something to her.

"Not interested in her."

She nods. That's all. She told Brent she doesn't date, that she's not on the market, but hell, this small nothing of a conversation makes me wonder if she's just not interested in *him*.

"Are you working tomorrow morning?" I ask her, making sure my body slides in nearer to hers. I can feel her warmth, catch a hint of something floral on her skin, and it only makes me want to move in closer so I can absorb more of it. She doesn't back away, but she stiffens.

She shakes her head no.

"Have breakfast with me."

Another head shake. "I don't date."

I anticipated she was going to say that and I have my answer ready. "Perfect," I reply quickly. "Neither do I," I lie. "Have breakfast with me as a friend."

She swallows hard, glances all around her and then goes back to her drink.

"You can come up to my place. We don't have to go out if you'd rather not. I'll cook for you."

"No," she says firmly, pivoting to meet my eyes. "I will not go to your apartment." And then she sighs, but this one is more in defeat than fear, her face dropping to the rubber floor. "You saved me that night and brought me into town. You've helped me learn my way around this job and not once have you mentioned the money I owe you for the tow you paid for." Finally, she finds me again, killing me with the pain I see swimming in those grass-colored depths. "I think you might be a good man, and those are very hard to come by for me, but I don't want breakfast. I don't want dinners or lunches. I don't want whatever you're trying to offer me. I don't want anything that has anything to do with anyone. We can be friendly here, but that's it, Jake. Not friends. Not lovers. Not even casual sex buddies. And that will never change."

It takes me a moment to absorb her words, analyze them, roll them around my brain, and when I do, I realize I have no comeback for that. She left me with no loophole. I know that was her intention because she just walks off like her point was made. And I guess it was. She most definitely won this round.

I should give up. Right here and now.

But she asked me about the girl who gave me her room number. There is only one reason I can think of to ask a non-friend, member of the opposite sex, a question like that, and it's not because she doesn't want anything to do with me.

But she meant what she said. That much was clear.

What happened to you, Mia?

I know the answer to that question before my brain can even finish the question. She's running from something. Or someone. Most likely someone if good men are hard to come by for her.

That gives me pause. Actually stops me in tracks and has me frozen on the spot, clutching a pitcher of margaritas, incapable of movement.

She was scared of me when I approached her car that night. Maybe that was a typical female reaction to a strange man approaching your car, but more than likely, it wasn't. I don't know to be honest. She's formal and inadvertently sweet, a mass of contradictions. Overemotional one minute and completely detached the next. And she lied about her last name. Maybe even her first name as well.

I think someone hurt her. I think someone did something so bad to her that she fled from them in an old piece of shit car. I think someone did something so bad to her that she's terrified they'll find her again so she's giving me a fake name and wouldn't stay at a hotel that would ask her for ID.

I find her, across the bar as she works furiously, trying to read everything she's hiding behind. Blood pounds in my ears, my fists clench, nearly cracking the plastic of the pitcher I'm still holding. I want to kill the man who put her in this position. But more than that, I want to protect her from him. I don't even know her, but that's the feeling I have. And it's strong.

I should give up. Right here and now.

That's what the smart, rational part of my brain is telling me. But a woman has not intrigued me the way she does in…hell, forever. I tell her I'll be right back, and she gives me what I determine to be a genuine, possibly relieved, smile. Diamond is here, so it's not like she's alone. I shouldn't leave the bar. It's busy and crowded and overrun with drunks looking to bump up their buzz. But I'm a man on a mission, and there is no deterring me.

I stalk across the lounge and through the restaurant, past the busy tables until I reach the back room. Cal is there, staring at God knows what on his computer.

"What do you know about her?"

He glances up at me, not bothering with the pretense of asking me who and just shrugs. "She came recommended."

"By whom?"

"Can't say."

I raise an eyebrow at that, and he laughs, shaking his head at me. He does the stare down thing with me; the one guys do when they're trying to not-so-subtly tell the other guy to fuck off without causing a fight. But he knows me well enough to realize I won't back down. Not on this.

Finally, after a very long minute, he goes with, "Someone we trust vouched for her. Said Mia was a good worker, a capable bartender, and in need of a job. Did I miss something? Were they fucking with me?"

I shake my head. "No. She's good. She's a quick learner, a hard worker and the customers love her."

Cal doesn't smile. He doesn't even smirk. He just stares at me for a long hard minute. "Then tell me what the fuck you're doing back here asking about her?"

"I want to see her file."

"For what purpose, man? You just said she's good. Why are you turning over rocks?"

It's a good question. One I have no answer for. I need more information, and that's all there is to it.

"If you didn't own the goddamn place, I'd tell you to fuck off. But I guess I don't have that luxury."

"Not anymore."

He chuckles at that. I've known Cal a very long time. Practically my whole life. He and my father were as close as anyone in their respective roles could be.

"But for the record, I'm not letting you get rid of her."

Dick.

I roll my eyes. "I'm not getting rid of her. I just want more info. That's all." I hold my hands up in surrender, the way I did after I touched Mia and she freaked out.

God, the things that bastard must have done to her.

"Fine. But none of it is legit. I already checked it out."

"I'm going to forget you just said that. Because if you just admitted to hiring someone with fake info, then not only will she get fired, but you will as well."

He doesn't flinch. He knows I won't fire him. Or her.

I sigh, resigned. I can't win this one.

"Just show me."

He clicks a few keys, and by the time I get around his desk to his computer, her face is there. And that address. Holy shit. It's a joke. To anyone who lives locally, we know that no one has that address. It's not even creative. I have no idea who advised her to put that down on her application, but hell, it stands out considering there is a big, bright casino in that location.

Her name says Mia Jones, no middle name. Her ID is Connecticut, not Texas, though that's where the plates on the car she was stranded in were from. Plus, she most definitely has that sexy southern twang. She has a social security card on file with the same name.

Are these IDs fake? Most definitely. A full background check was not done because she's not full-time here, and each restaurant is individual, which means whatever she has on file with The Bistro is not available here.

"She's a sweet girl, Jake."

I inwardly groan. "I'm not out to hurt her."

"But you want her. Anyone can see that." I glare at him, and he visibly backs off. "Hey, I'm not criticizing. I get it. If I weren't married—" Another look and his hands are above his head. "I didn't mean it like that. I'm just saying she's a beautiful girl. But she wants privacy. She's a sweet, innocent kid and a good worker. Just let her be. If you're not invested, let her be."

Right. Let her be.

Am I invested? How can one be invested after such a short time with a woman who lies to them? I don't know this woman, and clearly, she's involved in something heavy if she's using fake IDs and addresses. Something potentially dangerous? Maybe. Could even be illegal for all I know.

"I'm just checking," is all I say, knowing it's not nearly enough but it's what I've got. She turned me down for a date. She doesn't want to be anything more than friendly. Not even friends. I guess that means I walk away.

Why does that thought make my gut wrench?

I leave Cal's office, my mind a blur. I have no idea who is involved. Who recommended her for the job or who got her the IDs. I didn't press it. But why are they putting themselves on the line for Mia?

I reach the bar again and find her leaning over the flat wood top, talking to Brent far closer than I'd like her to be, the curve of her ass just visible beneath the hem of her dress. I hate her in that dress. It wouldn't be so short if she didn't have legs for miles. Smooth, tanned, gorgeous legs that I'd die to have wrapped around me as I sink into her. And that ass. Jesus, my cock is twitching, which only serves to make me feel like more of a creep.

She laughs, and I want to kick Brent's ass. It's juvenile as hell, but I can't muster enough strength or pride to care. I hate the way he looks at her. I hate the way he speaks to her. I just plain hate him.

"It's dinner. Maybe some dancing," he says, and she shakes her head, but she's smiling. "Oh, come on, beautiful. I know you want to. I'm charming, right?"

She laughs now. "That's why it's a no. Besides, I already told you, I'm not available."

"I'm persistent," he warns.

She gives an unconcerned shrug. "Do you live here?"

"No," he replies, and there is actual regret in his voice.

"Then I'm not worried. You'll go home to your wife or girlfriend—or both—and forget all about the bartender you met in Vegas."

"No," he states firmly. "There is no forgetting you. And there is no wife or girlfriend. There is just you."

"Wow," she laughs, tossing a napkin at him. I hate that she just did that. It was flirtatious as hell. "You're good at this. But I'm not falling for your act, so you should just back off now."

"Not gonna happen."

Another shrug. "Do you need another refill or are you done for the night?"

"You really won't go out with me?"

She shakes her head. "I really won't."

"I guess I'm done, then. Don't want to push the lady too hard, too fast." Brent stands up, reaches into his back pocket for his wallet and slaps a hundred on the bar with a resonating smack. That's a seventy-dollar tip. "Until tomorrow, beautiful." He bows like the douchetard he is and then leaves.

She throws me a sidelong glance, like she knows I was watching her, and then goes back to work. That's it. Goddamn, this woman is driving me insane. I want to pepper questions across her lips. Both sets. Have her answer me with screams of pleasure. I want her to beg to be mine and no one else's.

Who are you, Mia Jones?

Why give a fake local address? And that license was not a great fake. The whole name thing keeps throwing me. I knew that last name was bogus. She's not a skilled liar.

Mia Jones. Two weeks and I can't get you out of my head.

By the time we finished up it was past two, but now it's rounding on three. I should not still be here. I should not be planning what I'm planning. Or doing what I'm about to do. It's wrong. I know it's wrong. But I can't stop myself.

I have to know.

I tried rationalizing it by saying that I was doing my job as the owner of the hotel, but that's bullshit.

She's driven me to a whole new level of obsessed.

Some of the staff stick around for a few drinks after hours. Diamond once again tried to get me to join her, but I never do that. Not with any of them. Truth be told, I have no interest in what she's trying to offer me.

Mia is in the back, grabbing her shit, I assume. I need to go home. I need to shower and get some sleep. I try to talk myself out of this move a million different ways. But when she exits out of that back room, skirting quietly along the far wall with a huge backpack on the shoulder facing away from the residual staff, I know I'm not going home.

At least not yet.

She walks out the door and no one so much as throws her a cursory glance. She's invisible to them, which appears to be exactly the way she designed it. I throw a wave, say a quick goodnight, and I'm out the door.

The hotel is still decently crowded. As I said, this is Vegas, and two-forty in the morning is not late here. Especially not on a Saturday night.

She moves briskly down the long corridor that leads further into the hotel instead of out of it. The employee lot is not this way either, so this raises my curiosity another degree. I follow her, knowing it makes me a fucking stalker, but unable to muster the decency to care or stop what I'm doing. She moves through the casino floor, past the Sports Book, ignoring the catcalls of drunk men as she passes them, down another hall, towards the spa and pool area.

She approaches an employee door, pauses before glancing over her shoulder to check if anyone is watching her. I am, but I'm far enough back and off to the side that she doesn't spot me. And then she punches in a code she should not have and swipes what appears to be a universal card into the slot. The door unlocks for her, and she slips through it to the pool area, shutting the door quietly behind her.

What. The. Fuck?

How on earth did that just happen? How did security not catch that? I glance up at the ceiling, at the small black globes we have strategically placed, and realize we do not have one over that door. I have no idea where this girl got that badge or the code from. They are not given out to regular staff, let alone bar staff in one of our restaurants. A million questions racket through my brain as I take out my own badge and follow her out into the hot night.

The pool is still lit, even though it's night and the area is closed. It shuts down at eight this time of year, so the idea of this girl walking alone in a deserted part of the hotel sets me on edge. I hold the door, ensuring it closes without a sound, and those extra few seconds cost me everything, because I lost sight of her, and there are dozens of places out here that she could have gone.

Is she meeting someone? That Brent guy?

My thoughts flit back to my conversation with Cal. The notion that she could be involved in something illegal now doesn't seem so farfetched.

I catch a noise off to my right, like one of the loungers moving, scraping against the hardscape. She hisses something I can't make out, and my feet carry me in that direction before conscious thought can take over.

I spot her, over by the employee entrance of the spa, bathed in dark shadows, her movements cautious. Then what she does next causes my breath to lodge in my chest and my legs to grow weak. She's setting up a pallet on one of the lounge chairs, complete with blanket and pillow.

Oh my God. She's homeless.

This beautiful, sweet, angelic, perfect girl, who is terrified of the world, is homeless.

And sleeping outside in the pool area of my hotel.

What the hell has her running like this, using fake IDs and addresses and sleeping outside? *Goddammit, Mia!*

I want to storm over there. I want to grab her and haul her up to my apartment. I want to make sure she's safe, dammit.

My mind races, going over a million scenarios. Coming to a million conclusions. None of them are good. None of them are right. Men have forced her hand before. Men have told her what to do before. I won't be one of those men with her.

But I know one thing for sure, after tonight, this girl will not be homeless again.

Chapter Nine

Mia

I wake up to bright sunshine streaming on my face and the sound of people talking not even fifty yards away. I panic, not making any sudden movements or noise until those voices grow fainter as the people walk away from where I'm hiding.

How on earth did I sleep so late? It's well past dawn, and the pool area is coming to life, getting ready for the day.

I sit up slowly, peeking carefully through the bushes surrounding me, so grateful this is where I set up the lounger to sleep. No one is around, but I still hear people not too far off. I quickly roll off the lounger, hastily wrapping up the blanket and pillow and tuck them back in the notch. I decide to ditch the lounger where it is because there are too many people milling around to get away with moving it back.

Reaching down, I grab my backpack and gasp at what I find sitting directly on top of it.

An envelope that says, *Open Me*, in neat script. I glance around, half-expecting someone to be standing there watching me, but no one is here.

I don't open it yet.

I don't have time.

I shove it into my rucksack and get my ass into the spa bathroom as fast as I can without drawing attention to myself. There are two women in here, talking with each other as they put on their white robes, getting ready for whatever treatment they're about to have done.

They throw me a quick glance and a smile, but otherwise ignore me as they go back to their conversation. I move around the lockers, all the way back to the showers, and enter the far one I usually use. It's the most hidden and there's a small area set with towels, as well as a bench where you can leave any possessions. I strip down and shower at lightspeed before slipping into a pair of shorts and a tank top. I don't bother blowing out my hair since I don't have to work, so I just fold it into a quick braid, and I'm out the door, practically crying out my relief as I enter the main part of the hotel without anyone questioning me.

Suddenly, I feel claustrophobic in the massive building, like there are a million eyes on me. That envelope could be from Maddox, but somehow, I don't think it is. I think someone found me sleeping there last night.

They didn't wake me, and they didn't take any of my things. I know because I checked. I leave the resort briskly, my long legs carrying me forward, all the while unable to shake the sensation I'm being watched.

I make my way up Las Vegas Boulevard, before turning down a side street, and three blocks later, I'm at the laundromat I googled.

I've never washed my own clothes. Never once in my life. I had a maid for that, and she probably had someone to do it for her. But really, how difficult can it be? My work clothes are getting nasty, and so are the rest of my things.

I put everything I have into the washer before I realize I have to purchase soap separately. I get a packet out of the small vending machine, pour it in the way it directs on the label on the outside of the washer and start it. There is a coffee shop attached to this place, so I grab myself a small coffee and a muffin with more calories than I care to think about, and sit down, contemplating that envelope.

I can't help but look again, still unable to shake the feeling that someone is there. The hairs on the back of my neck have been standing at attention since I left the hotel, but every time I glanced over my shoulder, no one was there.

Did Niklas find me? Is this a warning?

I tell myself that if he did find me, I wouldn't be sitting here in the laundromat. I tell myself that if I am being followed, I'd know. It wouldn't just be a feeling. Niklas was nothing if not in your face. Nothing if not brutally direct.

I slide the envelope out of my pack and set it down on my lap, staring at the writing. I can't determine if it's male or female handwriting, and I figure that was intentional. The envelope is sealed, so I slide my finger into the open crevice on the side and tear away at the paper until it's open.

And then I start to shake uncontrollably.

My hand flies up to cover my mouth, smothering the sob desperately trying to climb out of my chest.

Inside is a hotel room key for The Turner Grand, which is my hotel, and a note.

I unfold the note, my hands tremulous. Sucking in a deep breath, I read the typed words.

Room 48-108 is yours for however many days, weeks, or months you need it. Please feel free to charge whatever you want to your room, there will be no charge to you. Whenever you're done with the room, just let the front desk know.

It's not signed, and for the life of me, I have no idea who would do this. Niklas's men certainly wouldn't. Or would they? Is this a way to corner me into a small, confined space where there are no cameras for security to see them? I don't know. But the idea of a free hotel room is too good to pass up. At the very least, I have to check it out.

Someone gave me a place to live. For free.

Did Maddox do this? Is this his way of sidestepping my refusal of his financial assistance?

Drawing my knees up to my chest, I bury my face into them and silently cry. I'm overwhelmed. I'm so grateful to this mystery person, but that gratitude quickly twists to fear. If it's not Maddox, what will this person expect when they make themselves known? Will they hold this over my head and demand things I have no desire or capability to give? Nothing is ever free in this world. Nothing.

How did this become my life?

Alone, homeless, working as a waitress and bartender, going by a fake name, and running from a man I'm terrified of.

The note said months. Aside from being insanely generous, I can't imagine living in a hotel room for months. It's far too conspicuous. In reality, I don't know how long I can stay in this hotel with these jobs. Either I need to switch to another one here or move on in the next few weeks. I can't get too comfortable. Can't ever let my guard down.

I finish washing and drying my clothes, pack everything back into my backpack, and then step outside in the heat. August in Las Vegas was probably not the best decision I've ever made. Most definitely not the worst, though, and I almost want to laugh at the irony of this. Do I ever make the right choice? No. I don't even have to think about that one.

I take the street that runs perpendicular to the Strip and weave a pattern that leads me closer to the hotel. My fingers dig into the pocket of my shorts, fingering the smooth rectangular room key.

My sneakers slap against the sidewalk as I hastily make my way. I'm too apprehensive, too curious to be cautious at this point. I hit the side entrance, bypassing the lobby, and going directly into the casino. And then I pause, searching around, but no one and nothing are out of the ordinary. Just gamblers.

I draw in a deep breath and walk straight through, past a few restaurants, to the elevators. 48-108. Locating the bank of elevators that will take me to my floor, I press my finger into the button until it lights up. My heart starts to pound so ferociously that I'm positive everyone around me can hear it. Blood rushes through my ears, and my vision sways as the heady cocktail of adrenaline and apprehension takes over.

A group of guys approaches, laughing and chatting away in their swim trunks and t-shirts when the elevator doors part. They wave me in first, and I immediately skirt to the back, tucking myself into the corner.

One of them turns over his shoulder, smiles at me and asks, "What floor, darlin'?" He's got a sweet southern accent, Georgia if I had to guess, and a nice smile. In another life, if I were a different girl, I'd give him a second look.

"Forty-eight, please."

He turns back around and presses the button for my floor. They're getting off on thirty-one, and it's just us in here, so I'll have a few floors to myself. It's a relief. But it's not. Their idle, inconsequential chatter is keeping me grounded. If it were silent in here, I'd be exploding off the walls.

They step out, and the cute guy looks back to me. "See you around, I hope."

I nod, give a forced half smile, and then the doors close. There is music playing in here that I just now notice, and my incessant bouncing seems to fall in sync with the beat.

The doors open twenty-eight seconds later, and here I am, on the forty-eighth floor. I step out, take a right, and reach a center area where with three separate halls feeding off it. I press my hands down on the cool marble top of the table in the center and do my best to steady my breathing. I know there are cameras in these halls, and I won't linger longer than necessary. Just long enough to catch my breath and slow my heart. It's not working.

Covertly, I unzip the outer pocket of my bag, locate my switchblade and encircle my hand around it.

A switchblade.

I can't stop the ironic scoff that bursts forth as I think about my only weapon. My father had guns all over the goddamn house and this is the only thing I have to protect myself with. Like I even have a chance if Niklas is waiting for me on the other side of that door.

Maddox was right about getting a gun.

Rounding the table, I pick up my pace and hike down the long hallway. And it is long. The room is all the way down at the end by the stairs. God, that gives me a real smile as I think about that. My fingers trace the placard that reads 48-108 and then the key in my hand. I open the blade as quietly as I can, peek up and down the hall to ensure that I am alone, take the deepest breath of my life, and then slip the key into the slot above the door handle.

I half-expect the light to flash red instead of green, or for the door to jerk open before Niklas drags me in. But neither of those things happens.

It makes an incredibly loud clicking sound as the locking mechanism disengages and then I turn the lever and open the door.

That's all I do.

I just stand here, holding the heavy door open and peering into the space, which from here appears like more than just a room. It's a suite, I think, and if I weren't so fucking petrified, I'd laugh.

I don't call out *hello* or *is anyone there*. That's the crap the dumb blonde in horror movies does. I may be naturally blonde and make terrible life choices, but I am not dumb.

Instead, I wait, and I listen, and when I'm positive I do not hear anything other than the hum of the air conditioning, I take a step in and allow the door to click shut as gently as it possibly can behind me.

Silence. And it *is* a suite, goddammit.

Off to my left is a small half-bath so I explore there first. No one. I open the closet by the door. Empty, save for hangers, two bathrobes, and slippers.

The living room is next. It's extensive and mercifully very open. Dark-gold and brick-red couches with alternate patterned chairs make up a seating area off to the left. To the right is a small kitchenette with two mini-fridges, a microwave and a sink. On the tiny dining table is a huge basket filled with assorted items I can't look at yet.

A door slams shut outside, and I jump ten feet in the air, poised with my knife held high as I stare back at my closed door.

Breathe. Right. That. I think I might vomit instead.

Spinning back around, I'm greeted with a bank of floor-to-ceiling windows facing the Strip and the mountains beyond. This room has to be at least five hundred a night, probably more. And the note said I could stay here for months.

What the fuck is going on? I figured I was going to get a bottom of the line room with a tiny bed and a view of the parking garage. Not a suite on practically the top floor with a million-dollar view.

I twirl around in a circle, but no one is here to greet me.

The bedroom. Christ, my heart. I'm desperate to grab hold of my chest, but I need to be alert. And knowing me, I'd end up stabbing myself. Ever so slowly, I creep along until I reach the bedroom. It slopes back, angling away from the main part of the suite, limiting visibility.

Crouching down, I pass the long desk that transitions into a dresser, and before I know it, I'm in a huge, king bedroom with the same gorgeous view. More Strip and more mountains. But no one is waiting to jump out and kill me. Or take me, which would be worse.

The bathroom is off to my left, and the door is open, showcasing a massive tub followed by an even bigger walk-in shower. Two sinks and more counter space than one woman needs.

I start to cry.

Big, ugly wracking sobs.

This is all just too much. That's when I notice the note on the bed.

I close my knife now that I'm satisfied no one is here lurking and go over, picking it up. It's typed as well, which frustrates me to no end.

"I hope you like your room—" Room? I snort. *"—It's yours. The basket in the kitchen is filled with assorted items I hope you will enjoy. Feel free to order room service. Go to the spa or salon. Anything you want you can charge to your room, no questions or strings attached. You are never to sleep outdoors again.*

I fall to my knees and weep out the massive tears that have been threatening since I stepped off the elevator. I have no idea what to make of this. No idea who my new benefactor is. Whoever they are, they obviously know I've been sleeping outside. Whoever they are, they're obviously rich. Whoever they are, they just became my hero, even if they'll likely turn into my nightmare.

All this opulence and counterfeit safety will no doubt come crashing down on me, but for the moment, it's mine to enjoy.

I run back out to the front door, and peek through the peephole. When I'm certain no one's there, I lock the door up tight and then drag a chair over from the living room and prop it against it, because that's what they do in the movies.

Next, I go for the basket filled with expensive cookies, designer chocolates, nuts, fruit, cheese and tons more. There is a bottle of very nice champagne tucked into an ice bucket with one flute next to it. One. Not two. Whoever did this for me is very deliberate. I also find another note.

I took a flier on the basket. I hope it's to your taste. The fridge on the left is stocked with food, but if it's not to your liking, just call down, and housekeeping will fill it with whatever you want. The fridge on the right is the minibar. Take whatever you'd like.

I don't have to be at work for six more hours. Grabbing a tin of peanuts, a block of cheese, an apple, and a bottle of water, I head for my new bathtub.

I'm going to soak in the thing until I figure out just what all this means while I try not to think about the unknown person who gave it to me.

Chapter Ten

Mia

I pull myself up and out of my oh-so-cozy bed, sleepwalking over to the view. My fingers press against the glass, and I smile. This feels like hope, and even though I'm foolish to let it, I can't stop it. In the five hours I've been in this room, no one came knocking. No one tried to break in. No one so much as called the phone.

I am alone.

For the first time in God only knows how long, I feel okay.

Not safe. Not fully anyway. But safe enough that I took a bath in the tub and a nap in the bed. Now I feel rejuvenated, and every time I think about my stranger—since Maddox vehemently denied everything when I called him—I want to cry happy tears. As much as I do not want to know who they are, I also wish I could thank them. Because calling this gift huge is an understatement. It's life-changing. It's mentally restorative. It's soul-saving. Amazing what a place to sleep can do.

I sigh wistfully, wishing I could spend the night in one of those robes, drinking that champagne and staring out at the Las Vegas night, but I can't. It's Sunday night, and the bar will be busy. The bar is busy every night.

Welcome to Las Vegas.

Setting my backpack up on the counter, I dig through until I find my uniform dress. I squeeze into it, lamenting the amount of bare flesh it shows, before I brush through my slightly snarled bedhead. I put on makeup, including that damn red lipstick, slip into my black wedges, because these are far better than the heels I wore that first night of work, and then I'm good to go.

Except my backpack. What do I do with that?

Anyone can access this room when I'm not in it, so I guess my decision is made. I pack everything into it, including some of the food from the basket, just in case I can never come back here, and then I'm out the door.

I hit the elevator in no time and then I take it all the way down, squeezed to the back behind the other people ready to take on the night.

Just before I enter the restaurant through the side entrance, someone calls out, "Mia." I spin around and find Brent on the opposite side of the large hallway, leaning against the façade that has a picture of a designer shoe store with the words Coming Soon plastered across it.

He knows my name. And he's waiting for me.

"Are you here for me?"

I stare him down, knowing he is, and wondering if he captures the double entendre.

He nods as he rights himself, sauntering over like he's got all the time in the world to stalk his prey.

Me.

I'm most definitely his prey as he enslaves me with his incisive stare. My heart kicks up into hyper-drive. My mouth bone-dry, my stomach in knots, and my skin prickles.

Is he the person who set me up in the room? Is this all a big ruse or way for him to demand sex or whatever he's after from me? Or does he work for Niklas? Jesus, how fucking stupid am I?

"I thought I'd try to catch you before your boyfriend interferes."

He reaches me, and in these shoes, I'm nearly six feet, a couple inches shorter than him.

"What is it that you want? I need to get in. They're expecting me," I add like this will make any sort of difference if he believes people would look for me.

"I think you know exactly what I want, Mia Jones." I swallow and shake my head, my eyes wide and fearful despite my best attempts at reining in my emotions. "You, Mia. I'm here for you. Why else would I come to this bar night after night? You're my reason for being here."

"I already told you," I whisper, my voice void of any strength or potency, "I don't—"

"And I already told you, I'm persistent. I always get what I'm after, Mia. *Always*. And right now, I'm after *you*."

Soul-crippling chills run up my spine. My breaths come out in short, unequal spurts. Fight or flight. I surreptitiously scan around, wondering if I could take him down and make a run for it. I doubt it. Something about this man, his size, his confidence, the way he's looking at me, says I'm not going anywhere until he lets me. Even if I scream.

"I make you nervous," he observes with a wicked grin. "Good. You should be nervous around men like me. I might be everything you think I am."

I swallow hard and step back.

He steps forward.

I shake my head.

He nods his.

"Are you?"

He shrugs and then shakes his head slowly, his eyes never wavering from mine. "Not in the way you think. One night, Mia. One date. Dinner. Talking. Just you and me."

There is so much more behind the last part of that. "How did you find me?"

"Call it fate, because that's how it feels to me. The important thing is that I *did* find you. And now that I have, I'm not letting you go."

I take another step back and, damn him, he takes another step forward. I can't think. My mind is a jumbled mess of too much adrenaline and limited innate survival skills. Because let's face it, if I had a proper set of those, I'd never be in this situation.

But despite the magnitude of his words that leave me quaking like the earthquake they mimic, his green eyes are sparkling, and his smile is warm and inviting. It makes me wonder if my fears are warranted. If this is simply the act of a charming man trying to seduce a woman. Sadly, I can't tell the difference anymore. There are a million things dancing behind those eyes, and I'm blind to all of them.

"My business in Las Vegas is nearly finished, so I'm on the clock. I know you said you don't date and the fact that I don't live here is a deal killer. But I travel here a lot for work. *A lot,*" he emphasizes. "So maybe if we tried dinner a few times, we could see how things went. Try me, Mia. You know you want to. We'll only talk. And eat, of course. Nothing more. It's not as sinister as you think it to be."

A date? He's got to be fucking kidding me. And the way he just transitioned from stalker to light and flirtatious is giving me whiplash. A derisive scoff passes my lips. I straighten my spine and fix him with my most assertive glare.

"You're good with the lines, Brent. I'll give you full credit on skill and effort. But I'm still not dating. And that's not going to change."

"I am good with a lot of things, and not everything I say to you is bullshit. But I get it. You're…unsure of my intentions."

That's putting it mildly. Then he takes a final step, and I find myself plastered into a wall. Pinned. There is a foot or two between us. But it doesn't feel that way. It feels like he's consuming me. Eating my fragmented soul piece by piece.

He opens his mouth to say more when we both catch movement out of the corner of our eyes.

Jake.

He's standing there like he was just about to go into the restaurant and spotted us.

Our eyes lock, my green ones to his brown ones, and for a moment there is nothing else. My heartbeat calms. My breathing returns to normal. It's the most nonsensical reaction based in absurdity, but it's still welcome. He smiles, those dimples sinking deep into his smooth cheeks. I smile back before I can help myself and that smile seems to alter something in him because he steps toward us.

"Sunshine," he greets me, completely ignoring Brent, who is openly scowling at Jake. "You coming in with me?"

The question is innocuous, but there is nothing innocuous about the way he asks it. Especially the way he emphasizes the word *me*.

"*Mia* and I are in the middle of something," Brent clips out, maneuvering his body so he's closer to me.

"Oh?" Jake replies, still grinning at me like he has a secret only he and I are privy to. "It looks to me like all you're doing is making her uncomfortable."

Brent's back stiffens, his posture becoming tall and wooden like this thought disgusts him. "I think you're jealous she pays me a hell of a lot more attention than she does you. Can't say I blame you, though." He chuckles, finding me again with something dark and deliberate in his eyes, as he talks to Jake. "There's a lot more going on between us than you know."

"I'm, uh…I'm going to head in now," is all I manage, using Jake's presence as my escape, and pushing past them both.

Taking in a much-needed breath, I walk as fast as I can without running. I need to think about that encounter with Brent. Analyze it fully when I have more time. Because I believe him. I think he is here for me. I think there is a lot more going on between us than I know.

What exactly? Well, that's the question, now isn't it?

I stash my bag in the back room, take some more deep breaths to prepare for what I know is waiting for me out there. By the time I reach the bar, say a quick hello to Diamond, who does nothing more than give me a curt nod, both men are in their usual spots—Brent sitting at the bar and Jake behind it. I pour Brent a drink of the same bourbon I gave him last night, before he can ask me for it.

"You never gave me an answer," he says when I place it in front of him. He reaches for my hand, but I don't give him access, and he gives up. "You don't have to give me one this minute, either. Think about what I said."

Sort of impossible not to.

"Dinner tomorrow night."

"How do you know I don't have to work tomorrow?"

He gives me that million-dollar smile. The one meant to be charming and reassuring. It's not. I've seen that smile before. I know it intimately.

"Because I asked your boss."

I'm hoping that's where he got my name from, too, but instinctively, I know it's not.

"I appreciate the attention. I'm beyond flattered—"

He puts his hand up, stopping me. "Not yet. Don't decide yet."

I give him a nod because I don't know what else to say or do. Nothing with him feels the way it should. But if he were working for Niklas, wouldn't he have already taken me? I'm honestly not sure.

I leave Brent there to sip his drink and fiddle around on his phone. I don't have time to waste. The bar is overflowing as the restaurant is filled to capacity after the weekend turnover.

Jake hasn't said much to me other than bar-related business since that scene out in the hall. It's a relief. He's another one I cannot figure out.

Yet, I think about him. More than I should. A lot more than I should.

And none of my thoughts are innocent.

Opening wine bottles might just be my bartending nemesis. It's difficult and requires leverage and short of sticking the bottle between my thighs to pull out the cork with the shoddy corkscrews they give us here, I've got nothing. And of course, two women order a very expensive bottle of white wine. I set the bottle down on the back counter, go through the routine of taking off the foil and twisting the corkscrew into the thick, meaty cork.

Then I pull. And I pull. And just as the cork is about to pop out, my elbow smashes into a row of glasses next to me, two of them tumbling to the floor and shattering. *Shit.*

I sink down, grabbing the small dustbin and brush hidden under the counter and begin to sweep up the shards of glass. I'm not myself tonight. Everything about today has turned my brain into a turbulent, chaotic, jumbled mess.

Once the glass is cleaned up, I empty the dustbin into the small trash can next to me. Just before I stand back up, I catch a large shard stuck in the rubber of the floor. Reaching out, I grasp it in my hand, give a good tug and yank it up, only to get jostled from behind as Diamond practically knees me in the back, pushing me over.

"Sorry," she calls out as she rushes down to her side, not even checking to see if I am actually okay.

Yeah, she's not sorry.

Sharp, shooting pain sears through my hand, and when I open my palm, that I had stupidly closed over the broken piece of glass I was holding, there is blood everywhere.

"Crap," I mutter, dropping the bloody piece of glass into the bin with the other pieces and taking in the wound that doesn't seem to want to stop bleeding. I grab a few bar napkins and press them into the wound.

"Jake?" He turns around, smiles, and comes over to me. "Can you finish off this bottle of wine and get it to those ladies over there, please?" I point with my good hand. "I cut myself and need to get cleaned up."

He takes my bleeding hand in his, ignoring the way I draw back from his touch, and uncurls my reluctant fist.

"Shit. This is a mess. You okay?" he asks as he examines the gash.

I nod, trying to extricate myself from his grip, but he's not relinquishing the firm hold he has on my hand.

"Kiera, can you finish off this bottle for those women over there and cover us for a few minutes?" he asks one of the bar-backs, even though it's not really her job to do so. "Mia cut her hand; I'm going to help her get cleaned up."

"Sure. No problem," Kiera answers.

"Come with me," Jake commands.

I shake my head. "I can do it myself, Jake. Really. It's not that bad."

"No arguing."

Jake grabs a first aid kit from a lower shelf and leads me through the bar, still holding my wounded hand, until we reach the bathrooms in the back. They're single bathrooms, and without hesitating, he opens the door to the men's room and guides me in.

The door shuts heavily behind us, and he locks it with an amplified *click.*

The sound of my exaggerated breathing and the blaring reality that I'm alone with him in a small, confined space, has me turning toward the faucet and away from him, to wash out my cut.

I turn the handle to cold and nearly jump out of my skin when the splash of water hits the porcelain. Lord have mercy, I need to get a grip. I feel his large, overpowering presence looming behind me, his thumbs brush up and down against my exposed arms and I start.

"Do you need help cleaning it out?"

"No."

He chuckles lightly, his warm breath skating across the shell of my ear. "Then why are you just standing here staring at the water like it's going to drown you?"

My eyes flicker up to the mirror, finding his in the reflection. He's so close. So tall and commanding. I feel his heart beating against my back. *Bump-bump, bump-bump, bump-bump.* It's a hypnotic rhythm mine seems to be matching, even when it's desperate to run five beats faster.

His molten chocolate eyes search mine, a concerned expression marring his handsome face before his lips quirk up into a lopsided grin. He reaches around me and takes my injured hand, his eyes fixed on mine as he places it under the cool water. It burns, and I wince, but I can't stop staring at him.

"Sorry," he whispers, letting the water do its thing before pulling my hand out and patting it dry with a cloth hand towel from the side of the sink. "Does it hurt?"

"A little."

He spins me around in a flash, pressing my back into the sink. I gasp and then whimper when he caresses my fingers with his.

"It's okay," he soothes, clearly thinking that sound was pain related. It wasn't. Not even close.

Drawing my hand up to his face, he examines the small cut on the top of my palm, just below my pointer finger, and then puckers his lips, blowing cool air onto the wound.

My body erupts in a shiver, and he steps closer into me, our bodies practically flush. My face flames, my chest rises and falls in rapid, succinct movements. The smell of his sweet breath mixed with his cologne is making me dizzy. It's also making me want to tear the clothes from his body and beg him to make me come right here in the men's bathroom at work.

"It's not bad," he whispers, urging me to look at him.

But I can't. I'm too nervous. Too wound up. This is excitement. This is anticipation. This is the type of rush I haven't experienced in a very long time. And that scares me as much as it thrills me.

"Look at me, Sunshine. Let me see those gorgeous eyes of yours."

I swallow down the thickness clogging my throat and look up.

Jake stares into me before shifting his focus to my lips. My tongue reflexively juts out to moisten them. Black pupils eclipse soft brown irises. He smirks, enjoying the effect he has on me.

"We need to get back."

"Not yet," he replies on a thick exhale. "I haven't bandaged your hand."

Right. My hand.

Dark, lust-laced eyes framed in black lashes, flitter to each one of my features like he's trying to memorize every dip, curve, and freckle on my face. My breath hitches at the intensity and my heart beats even faster, my cleavage heaving over the top of my dress.

"I think it should be good with some liquid bandage. The bleeding has mostly stopped."

"Whatever you think." *Because I have no idea what day it is right now, let alone how to bandage my hand.*

He reaches up and brushes some hair out of my face and that smile of his grows wider when he realizes I didn't flinch. Nothing shocks me more.

He leans in, his eyes locked on mine as he gauges my reaction to him. I can't determine what he's going to do.

Is he going to kiss me? Whisper something in my ear? Push the boundaries on how far he can go before I freak out? I don't know. But I'm thinking right now, I'd let him do whatever he wants with me.

Knock, knock.

"Just a minute," Jake calls out, and I close my eyes, blowing out a relieved breath. What the hell am I thinking? This has to stop.

And it does stop. Jake blinks, clears the wild desire from his eyes, and focuses on the task at hand—literally. He applies liquid bandage to my cut after making sure it's good and cleaned out. We exit the bathroom together, my head ducked down when we pass the man who was waiting to enter, because I do not want to see the expression he has. We come off as two lovers who just fucked in the bathroom of a restaurant. Sadly, I came pretty close to letting that happen.

Just before we reach the bar, he turns back to me, drawing my body close to his once more.

"You're okay?"

"I am. Thank you for helping me."

"Any time." His fingers glide across my cheek before he regretfully drops them back to his side. "Every time."

What the hell is going on?

I give him a tight nod and then I brush past him, going back to work, practically shaking myself at the clarity space provides me. How stupid am I to sink into a guy like that? To fall into a gorgeous face and eyes that say, 'you can trust me?' Those eyes say, 'you're safe with me.' They say, 'I'll give you incredible pleasure and no pain.'

And if nothing else, they serve as a reminder that I'm not safe with anyone.

Because I fell for charming once.

I fell for bullshit notions of safety and security. I fell for the man who promised me the world only to decimate it time and time again. I fell for it all—hook, line, and sinker—and this is where it got me.

Running.

Alone.

Terrified out of my very wits.

Like driving a car without any breaks. It doesn't stop no matter how much you will it to.

So yeah, it would be easy to give in to Jake. He might be everything those eyes promise him to be. But then what? I'm still the girl on the run using a fake name and sleeping in a borrowed hotel room.

Letting out a wistful sigh, I mix up a requested cocktail, ignoring the smirks and winks Brent continues to throw at me as he asks for his refills, patiently waiting for me to cave.

I won't. Because like I said, there is something about this guy that doesn't feel quite right.

Chapter Eleven

Mia

My eyes open to a sound. A sound I do not recognize, nor want to hear. A grating sound? No, maybe more of a tapping? Whatever it is, it's inside. My alarm has yet to go off, which means it isn't even seven yet, but I know something is wrong instantly.

He's here.

I throw myself out of bed, flipping on every light I can, before grabbing the metal rod I keep on the floor in my bedroom. Padding into the living room of the suite, I grip the cold metal so tightly, I can feel the blood draining from my knuckles. My heart thunders, adrenaline courses through me, and that all-consuming fear strangles me.

He's here, and I'm going to die.

"Don't worry. You're safe with me." I spin around at lightning speed to find not Niklas, but Jake. "Don't worry. You're safe with me," he repeats, smiling reassuringly down at me as if from a higher elevation. "I won't hurt you." His voice is soft, ethereal.

"I'm never safe." My words come out garbled. Like my mouth is filled with marbles. Like the sound did not come from my mouth, but from something next to me. Something on the floor? I look down to see my body, lifeless and bleeding. Niklas's blue eyes smile malevolently up at me as he hovers over my broken form.

I scream.

Springing up, I gasp, clawing at the sheets. Cold sweat soaks my entire body, making me convulse and shudder painfully. *It was a dream. It was just a dream. He's not here.*

My hands fly up to my face just as the sobs break free from the confines of my chest and out of my lips. I pull my knees up and lose it. Absolutely fucking lose it.

Rocking back and forth, I pick up my pillow and bury my face in it so that my neighbors don't hear me, and I wallow in the agony and terror that I still can't seem to shake.

I dream about Niklas most nights, but nothing this bad in over a week. The sad thing is, I don't even have a metal rod. I only have that stupid, insubstantial knife, and it's tucked away in my backpack. Useless. I should take Maddox's words to heart more.

Pepper spray. Maybe a gun. Probably both.

Sleep used to be something I always looked forward to. My nannies continuously joked about what an amazing sleeper I was, even as a new baby. Dreams were a world left mostly unexplored. A window into my subconscious and I couldn't wait for my next adventure.

But the quiet peace of those dreams altered drastically after Niklas nearly killed me. They became all about him. An endless stream of beatings I relive night after night. Part of me wonders if I'll ever feel safe again.

He doesn't know where I am. He's not here for me.

The truth is, I've been abused for most of my life. First from my father, then from Niklas. It's not even the abuse that has me so afraid. It's the idea of him killing me. Of the *way* he'll kill me when he's ready. When he's gotten everything he's ever wanted from me and I'm no longer of use.

He took me so close to that edge once, lost control completely, that while it was happening, I was sure I was never going to wake up again. I was positive he had killed me, and when I regained consciousness, it was a surprise.

A wake-up call.

Niklas was far more brutal than my father. My father was a believer in a good slap to keep his women in line. Maybe more with my mother than with me, because I rarely gave him anything to be displeased about. But Niklas? I still shudder at what that man has done to me.

It wasn't always like that. Didn't start out that way. But by the end, it was merciless.

Finally, after the crying subsides and I manage to steady myself, I climb out of bed and make my way into my bathroom. My reflection is pretty spot-on—I resemble the flat side of pavement after a truck drives over it. I splash ice cold water on a washcloth, pressing it to my red, swollen eyes. God, that feels good.

And when my face is somewhat back to normal, I throw my hair up into a high ponytail and don my running gear.

The Strip is a popular early morning running spot. Lots of stairs and plenty to keep your eyes occupied. Sprinklers are running over manicured shrubbery, men are power-washing last night's refuse off the pavers, and people are heading into work. Yet those lights. Christ, they never turn off.

I start out, taking a left and heading up toward the center of the strip, but within a block, I feel movement on my right. My head flies in that direction as I jump more to my left to counterbalance the intrusion.

But the moment I catch sight of Jake, dressed similarly to me, with that arrogant, master-of-the-universe grin, I narrow my eyes and slow my pace. He follows, matching me step for step. My hands prop on my hips, though I haven't been running long enough to need to catch my breath for longer than a second or two.

"What are you doing?"

"Running."

"Why are you following me?"

"For a smart girl, you're a bit slow on the uptake this morning."

"Pardon?"

"I'm not following you," he says defensively, an indignant edge to his voice. "I just happen to be out for a run and saw you. I thought it might be nice to run with someone. That's all. Christ, you're a difficult one."

"I am," I agree. "And I like to run by myself."

"Does that mean you don't want to run with me? Might get awkward since we're headed in the same direction. I could fall back and watch you run, but something tells me you won't appreciate the natural direction my eyes will take." He gives me that grin again. The one that hits me in the gut, filling it with a million tiny firecrackers, all going off simultaneously.

Even in his running gear, he looks like a runway model, and the way that shirt clings to the muscular contours of his chest, abs, and shoulders is diverting.

I should tell him no. I should tell him to fuck off and keep his alluring, chauvinistic self away from me.

But I don't.

I can't even explain why. Or at least I don't want to think too closely about it. That said, it will be fun to see if Mr. Pretty Boy can keep up.

"What's your routine like?" he asks as I stretch, grasping the top of my right foot and swinging it back until my heel meets the bottom of my ass. We're standing in front of a hotdog restaurant. The smell is not doing my stomach any favors.

"Why don't we do what you normally do, and I'll let you know if it's enough for me?"

He smiles the type of smile that shows me he's accepting my challenge with a cocky confidence.

Jake's amber eyes blaze. "Awesome, let's go."

He spins back around and immediately sets out at a good clip, assuming I won't be able to keep up with him. His arrogant ass doesn't know what he's in for.

We run up and down stairs and across walkways and through different hotels for at least forty-five minutes at a much faster pace than probably either of us typically does, but I'm not about to beg for mercy, and neither, it seems, is he.

Finally, we make our way back to The Turner Grand hotel we both work in, slowing down to a walk for the last half-mile or so.

"Wow," he pants, clasping his hands behind his head to draw more air into his lungs. "I don't think I've run that hard…well, ever actually. I'm soaked." He chuckles, taking off his shirt and wiping his forehead and neck with it.

If I wasn't having difficulty breathing before, I certainly am now. I trip over my own damn feet, righting myself before he can catch me. He smirks, knowing full well he's the reason for my sudden clumsiness. Mercifully, he doesn't comment.

But really, it's not my fault. His chest is sexy as all sin. He's toned and muscular without being overly built or bulky. He has a delicious six-pack and that lovely V at the bottom. Think Brad Pitt in *Fight Club*.

There's a tattoo on his right flank that, at first glance, is just a swirl of multicolored ink, but upon closer inspection is really an elaborate compass. The one on his chest, covering his left peck over his heart, is a pattern of numbers and twisting lines that come together to form…something. I don't know. It's mesmerizing. I've never seen anything like it.

Not that I have any experience with tattoos.

The ones on his shoulders and upper arms are all different. Mostly brightly colored and all intricately done.

Then I catch the scar.

I assume it's from a bullet, given the pattern, as it sears right through his left shoulder like a starburst.

Jake glances over, catching me in the act of checking him out. He smirks, throws me a wink, and says, "If you're going to stare at me that hard, you can touch. I don't mind. Or at least allow me to return the favor without slapping me."

I blush, my already red cheeks growing warmer. I'm too intimidated to ask about his ink. Or that scar. Sweet baby Jesus, that scar.

"I wasn't checking you out," I snap with an exaggerated huff, flipping away as quickly as possible, which only serves to make me appear guiltier. He playfully grins, and I feel his warm body draw closer for a beat before that heat disappears just as quickly. I don't have it in me to look at him, but I feel him all the same. I'm already too wound up, too…*excited?* just being this close to him.

I hesitate for a minute as we stroll in the relative silence of the early morning. The city is just starting to come alive, and I can already feel the heat of the summer sun baking the streets.

"May I ask you something?"

"Sure."

"Why did you want to run with me this morning?"

His head bobs away for the quickest of seconds before turning his focus back to me, an impish grin curling up the corner of his lips.

"Truth?" I nod, because I have zero room in my life for anything less. At least where others are concerned. "It felt like a good excuse to see you again."

"Jake—"

"Yeah, I know," is his only reply, and I leave it at that because I don't even know what I'd say to him. Especially after the bathroom incident a few days ago. Especially after enjoying his company this morning. That thought is almost capable of pulling an ironic smile from my lips. I'll deny that to my dying day.

We pause outside the hotel and, without prompting, turn to face each other. I have no idea where he lives or where he's going, but I do not want him to see me walk into this hotel.

"I was also worried about you," he adds, taking a step into me, crowding my personal space and bleeding sincerity into my neglected crevices with his magnetized stare. "You bolted on me the night I picked you up on the side of the road, and even though I've worked with you, fixed your fucking hand, I was still worried."

I swallow. Hard. He watches the roll of my throat as I do and I wish I didn't care. I wish it didn't matter to me that he's worried. That I didn't get hung up on the pathetic, destined-for-failure dream. That my whole body didn't come alive at the thought of this man.

"I told you, I'm fine."

He nods, rubbing a hand along his jaw. "I know. I can see that. Doesn't mean I don't care or worry. Do you want to run with me tomorrow?"

And this is the part where I should say no. Where I should say I can't run with him. In my three weeks of living here, I've never once seen him out running in the mornings. But I wonder if all that will change now.

How can I avoid this? Avoid him? Do I even want to?

"I can't tomorrow."

"What are you doing today? Wanna grab some breakfast?" he asks, moving in even closer to me to avoid a guy running past us. I take a step back, but I have nowhere to go. I'm against the stone fence separating me from the huge water feature. The lapping sound of water, spraying and splashing against rocks, fills the new silence I'm putting between us.

"Why are you so persistent with me?"

His knowing smile lights up his whole face, but he doesn't answer me.

I sigh, ducking my head and rolling it side to side, the muscles in my neck enjoying the stretch, before raising it again and staring straight ahead. Anywhere but at him. Looking at him makes it impossible to think clearly.

Christ, it makes it impossible to breathe.

I try to step around him, needing to get the hell out of here. Away from the musky, masculine, sweet scent of his skin and sweat. The heat of his body and the too-close stance he gets off on imposing on me.

He reaches out, grabbing my arm and bringing me to a stop. I yank away from his grasp, but before I do, he turns me to face him. His eyes are everywhere. Devouring me in a way I cannot ignore. In a way that has me craving his hands on my body and not just his eyes. And when those brown depths finally find mine again, the intensity in them makes it impossible to look anywhere else.

"I'm not playing a game with you, Sunshine. Yes, I'm attracted to you. I'd have to be dead not to be. And I know I can be an asshole sometimes and that I tend to send mixed signals. But the truth is, I want to get to know you. I want to see where this crazy connection will lead us." He pauses, and then cripples me with a devastatingly adorable lopsided grin. It makes his boyish dimples sink in, and for a moment, I forget the danger he poses. "Give me one day. One breakfast. Maybe a ride to somewhere. Followed by lots and lots of kissing. Dinner. A sunset possibly. And more kissing."

I shake my head, rolling my eyes because if I don't, I'll smile and he'll see just how much I want that. "Here's the thing about that, Jake," I start before I just as quickly stop. Why am I indulging him? There is no yes to Jake. Despite the way just one glance from him has my panties wet. "That's never going to happen. Ever."

He scrunches his eyebrows like he's hearing every word out of my mouth for the first time.

"So, it's not just me?" *Arrogant asshole.* He shrugs. Smirks. Winks. *Charming Bastard.* "Never say never." I shake my head at him, trying for absolute. He doesn't believe me. I can tell. "Can I ask you something, Sunshine?"

"Probably not, but you can try anyway." Why am I still standing here? Why am I still entertaining him? *Like you don't know*, the cynic inside me teases.

He snickers. "Okay then. I just want to know why you're not dating."

"Nope. Sorry, that's out-of-bounds."

"We have out-of-bounds questions?"

"Yup."

"But—"

"Basically, everything about me is out-of-bounds. I don't like to talk about myself, and I *definitely* don't like people asking questions. Thanks for the run. It was amusing watching you try and keep up."

And with that, I leave Jake behind. I shouldn't look back. I shouldn't care if he's watching me go. I shouldn't feel this…pull.

But I *do.*

I feel it and turn around and he *is* watching. He smiles when he catches me. Big. Bright. Beautiful.

"You like me, Sunshine," he calls out, not even caring about the people staring at him as they jog past. "I flip your world upside down the way you do mine. You're as crazy about me as I am about you."

I laugh before I can stop it, because he's practically yelling this, garnering more stares. But that smile. Jesus, it lights everything up. The Strip has nothing on him.

"I'm going to kiss you. Really fucking soon. And my hands will more than likely cop a feel."

I shake my head, biting into my lip to hide everything his words do to me. His grin only grows.

"You'll love it, I promise. I'll have you begging for more."

I stare him down, crossing my arms over my chest, trying for defiant, miserable to keep my blush contained.

"Never gonna happen, Jake."

"It will," he promises, his brown eyes so light. So perfect. So… everything I never knew was possible. "Since the first moment I laid eyes on you, I had a feeling I was gonna have to move heaven and earth to make you mine. And I will. Because there is something about you I can't shut off. It's just a matter of time for us, Sunshine. But time is exactly what I've got, and I'm not about to give up now. I'll win you over eventually."

Butterflies. Bright, sparkling butterflies. That's what I've got going on. They're fluttering everywhere inside me. Around me. I stare at him for another second, enjoying that adorable, I'm-safe-and-would-never-hurt-you boyishness. Before I remember that Jake is all man, capable of unspeakable things. Before I slap myself with a hard reality check.

Then I turn around and walk away. I don't look back this time. Because I believe him. He'll win me over. And then what will I do?

Chapter Twelve

Jake

If pussy-whipped had a definition in the dictionary, my goddamn face would be next to it. I'm a bartender. Again.

Typically, I only work in this restaurant once a week. And only as a waiter, I might add. This makes the third goddamn time bartending in ten days. And it's all because of her. Mia I-am-home-less-running-from-something-miserably-fucked-up-with-a-fake-ass-last-name Jones.

Yeah. Her.

Because I have no idea if she's sleeping in the suite I got her. The crafty little minx managed to evade me the last time I worked with her. I wasn't able to follow her. And stalking in daylight has its disadvantages.

Then Cal told me I was not allowed back for a few days. Prick actually restricted my access to her. I was going to tell him I own this whole place and can do what I want, but that would make me sound like the pretentious dick I strive not to be.

He also reminded me the girl told me—and not so kindly, I might add—to fuck off. She did tell me that, even if her sweet mouth would never utter such crude vocabulary. I might not have accepted it, but he was right. I needed distance. I needed to wash my brain clean of the girl who seems to have stained it.

It hasn't worked. Not even a little.

I did try to conclude she was using the suite since then, but short of pounding on her door or stalking her after she gets off work, that wasn't possible. And since I am still not known as the CEO, I can't exactly ask housekeeping. It's creepy. And definitely stalkerish.

I have, however, joined her for a run three other times. We have this unspoken competition going on. It's fantastic. I've never met a woman who can keep up with me, but not only does she do that, she pushes me harder. I feel like I'm back in the Army when I run with her. And hell, does that turn me on.

Then again, everything about her does.

We talk, but never about anything personal. She doesn't reveal anything about herself. She doesn't ask a lot of questions about me, either. But she does let me get close to her. She even laughs at my jokes occasionally. She's far from impervious to my flirting and has yet to switch up her running routine in an attempt to avoid me.

She likes me.

I know it.

It's there in the way she watches me when she believes she's unobserved. In the smiles she reserves solely for me, because they are most definitely different than the ones she gives anyone else.

When I came in tonight, wondering why I was chasing a girl for the first time in my life, she smiled at me, *again*, her cheeks warming to the loveliest shade of pink I've ever seen, and I knew the answer to my question.

This girl… Hell.

Sometimes she can be impossible to navigate, and then she does something like that. Making my world just a touch more vibrant with her sweet innocence and addictive vulnerability.

I'm the guy who can't get enough, and she's my drug of choice.

My warm and fuzzy moment didn't last long, though. Brent, who is evidently still in town, interrupted it.

Ten. Days.

No one stays in Las Vegas this long. No one.

He's still trying to gain access to my girl. Every time she spoke to that cocksucker, my fists clenched, and my jaw ticked.

And when she wasn't looking, he threw me smarmy smirks and knowing winks. I had to remind myself time and time again he wasn't worth getting arrested over, otherwise I would have kicked his ass. Yeah, I can be immature and juvenile when I want to be, but I rose above, and for that, I deserve brownie points.

That guy, Brent. Shit. He's good. I'll give him his player dues because he has been working her hard. He watched her all damn night.

Never took his eyes off her.

And whenever he spoke to her, that charm was spread on thicker than frosting and just as sweet. She sees through it. She has to.

Mia's shift ended when everyone else's did, and she slunk into the back room.

I linger, much the way I did the last night I worked here, but tonight, I am determined not to miss her. My intention is not to follow her for snooping purposes. I just want to make sure she gets back to her room safely.

All day, hell, for the last ten goddamn days, I've fought the urge to look her up. This is Las Vegas, and I have access to one of the best in-house security systems and teams in the world. A background check is nothing. It doesn't even take very long. A few hours at most for a basic one and that's all I need. Enough to know if she's a missing person. Enough to know some of her history. But I fought it. Have been fighting it.

Even though it's tempting as hell, I won't invade her privacy like that. I'm already overstepping with that suite. With the food I had placed in there and the expense account I set up. Probably the running, too, if I'm being honest. After all, I don't know her. Nothing real at least. She could be a fraud. She could be a con artist. A swindler. A thief. A criminal.

But she's not any of those things. I feel that deep in my blood. I have spent enough time with her now to know, but if I'm wrong about her, about that, then I deserve the repercussions, because she's sold me on her sad side. On the scared, homeless girl who just needs to feel safe. I'm not a hero. I'm not a saint, and I've done my share of things wrong in this world.

I lie to nearly everyone every day about who I am and what my purpose here is. And honestly, I'm okay with that con. I'm okay with that lie as it serves a greater purpose and that greater purpose is securing the futures of Turner Hotels and its staff.

But I can help this girl.

I can make her feel safe. I can give her a place to sleep and some food and anything else she requires to get through whatever it is she's trying to get through. I can run with her in the mornings so she's not alone. I can do that.

If she never gives me a second glance and we never become real friends or lovers or more, I'm okay with that too. Even if it's not what I want from her.

She's become part of my purpose. I don't even know how it happened, but I will not let Brent fuck with my purpose. I will not let that asshole use her the way I know he wants to.

I mean, hell, who stays in Las Vegas this long if they don't live here?

Mia exits the back room, and I follow.

"You're not staying for a drink with everyone else?" I ask as I reach her side. She doesn't so much as glance in my direction, her focus is locked on that exit door.

"No. I see you're not, either."

I grin, walking closely by her side. She lets me. She doesn't even try to adjust her position.

"You're the only reason I stayed this long."

She lets out a derisive snort. "Diamond said you don't date a lot. How come?"

I can't stop my laugh. "Why the hell are you asking me that?"

"I don't know," she laughs in return, shaking her head, pausing to peek up at me. "She said when you do date, you get bored quickly. Am I just another woman you want to get bored of, Jake? Once the thrill of chasing me is over, of course."

It's as if something shifts in her, her question goes from teasing and conversational to something resembling interest. It's that spark in her eyes. It's such a small thing, but when you spend a lot of time observing someone, you get to know them. Understand their facial expressions. Mia is telling me that my answer matters.

I shake my head slowly, because as I take her in, I don't think she's someone I could ever be bored with. It's been more than three weeks and my mind is nothing if not occupied with her.

And really, what the hell is Diamond talking about? I haven't dated any women in this bar. I've fucked none of them. In fact, if we're throwing down facts, I haven't fucked a woman since I came to this town. I've been way too preoccupied. Besides, the only women I meet work for me in one way or another. So, I've kept my dick tucked securely away like the smart man I sometimes am.

"I just don't get it, is all."

"Well, I don't get you, either."

"Touché. I'll stop prying."

"You can pry as long as I get to return the favor."

"What is it you want with me, Jake? I thought I already made my position clear. Yet you keep coming back for more and more."

"You like my more and more. You like me working with you. You like running with me and spending time with me. I know you do." She sighs, shifting her weight and pivoting away from me. She's not denying it. "I think your position on us needs amending."

"Amending," she half-laughs the word, crossing her arms over her chest and peering up at me in the dim lighting with those forest-green eyes that make me forget how to breathe. "What precisely needs amending?"

"For starters?" I ask, and she groans. "The friendship part. And definitely the breakfast part. We should go have a very early breakfast and then watch the sunrise."

She shakes her head, but she's trying really hard to hide her smile.

"It's late. I just want to go to bed."

"With me?" I point to my chest. That was a softball I couldn't resist. My lips quirk into my most charming smile so she knows I'm kidding. Well…

"No," she laughs. "That's not what I meant. I've seen you interact with the other staff, and I get it. Everyone likes you. You're fun and easygoing. You make me laugh and know more about me than I'm comfortable with. But I don't know you, Jake. Not really, anyway. And that's all I care about."

I don't skip a beat. "I'm single. Never been married. I'm right-handed. I graduated from high school, college and business school with honors. I like electronics and hate business. I was in the Army for two years and my father is recently deceased. I grew up in Baltimore, well, sort of, and I absolutely love baseball, particularly the Orioles. There. How's that?" I take a small measured step. Just enough to let her know I'm interested in whatever she's willing to give in return, without coming across as intimidating. "You're safe with me, Sunshine." She blinks, her eyes becoming glassy and wide as if startled by my declaration. "It's just breakfast and a sunrise. That's all."

A rush of air parts her lips, like she had been holding her breath that entire time and couldn't stand it a moment longer. She doesn't respond. A single tear breaches the ridge of her eye, slowly gliding down her soft cheek.

Reaching out, I brush it away. She lets me, with not even the slightest of flinches, and I have the greatest urge to kiss her. To close this insignificant distance and take her mouth with mine. To wrap her up in my arms and feel her warm softness against me. To lose myself in her sweetness. To let her know I mean everything I say to her.

She's always safe with me.

"I'm not safe with anyone," she says on the quietest of breaths. Her voice the barest of whispers that it takes me a couple of beats to comprehend what I think I heard. And when I know I've got it fully, when I accept she couldn't have said anything else, I'm rattled out of my lust-filled haze with a cold, hard slap. The power of her words drops an anchor straight through me, mooring me to the floor. Like a sailboat in stormy waters, my insides turbulent and ill at ease.

I stare at her, unable to formulate words. All I want to do is come up with something epic. Something that will blow her away and change her life and make her realize she *is* safe with me.

But there are no words for that sort of thing.

Nothing that can instill trust in a woman who's already had it shattered. *That* I'll have to show her.

"Come have breakfast with me, Mia. We can talk. I'll tell you anything you want to know about me. Anything at all."

Now it's her turn to be silent. She's tempted. I know she is. I affect her as much as she affects me. There is no hiding this sort of connection. It's intrinsic. Unable to be faked, ignored, or shutdown.

"It's late," is all she can manage as she twists back toward the door and hastily exits. I follow again because that seems to be what I do where she's concerned. I might just follow her anywhere, which is ironic considering I've never chased a woman in my life.

I won't lie and say I don't love the challenge. I do. Any man who says he doesn't is a liar.

But she's more than that. She's got this something else. This indescribable attribute that hits me in my core. That knocks me off balance and has me desperate for even just the smallest bit of her attention.

She pauses again when she notices me following her, spinning around to face me once again, exasperation punishing her beautiful features.

"You don't need to come with me. I can manage on my own."

"I know you can," I say, because that's what she's been doing up until this point. Managing.

"Then please don't walk with me."

"All right. I won't walk with you. Have a good night, Sunshine."

"You too, Jake."

She sinks her teeth into her full bottom lip, shifts her weight again like she wants to say more, but doesn't. She turns away from me, tossing her dark locks over her shoulder, and marches off. I watch as she gets to the end of the hall, and then I step out after her. I don't need to walk with her, but I sure as shit am going to follow her.

Stepping into the corridor, I move quickly, afraid of losing her before she reaches the elevators that lead to the guest rooms. I get halfway down the hall, but my attention is diverted the moment I step past a group of drunk bachelorettes.

Brent. What the motherfuck?

And when Mia notices him standing there, waiting on her, everything about her disposition changes. I can't hear him as he approaches her, but I know he's talking to her. The cocky bastard shifts his gaze to me for the briefest of seconds, like he knew what I was up to following her, and the challenge is clear as day. I told him to leave her alone that night in the hall when he cornered her. That was forever ago. But this guy is not getting the message.

He's not the one she's running from. I know this. She didn't even know Brent when he first started making his move. No. He's not the guy, but he is a threat to her all the same.

I move slowly, unsure what my next move should be.

She asked me not to walk with her, and if I intercede, again, well, I don't know how she'll react. But if he pushes her, even a little, hell, if he so much as touches her, I'll end him.

Thick waves of consternation surge from her, filling the space between them with a visible uneasiness.

Mia says something to him that has the prick smiling and shrugging. He leans in and hugs her. Actually fucking *hugs* her, her body squirming in his embrace, and my feet start moving before they stop just as quickly. She pushes him off, and he steps back, and then she steps back. She gives him a tight smile and a small half-wave. Brent doesn't offer much back. He just watches her walk off, same as I am.

The asshat turns to face me and just…stares at me. He does this for no longer than a few seconds, but it's long enough for me to read him loud and clear. He's telling me to back off. He's telling me she's his and he's a man on a mission to win. Finally, he smirks at me and saunters off like he doesn't have a care in the world, hitting one of the exits that branches off this long hallway.

I take off into a sprint, my eyes scanning everywhere for Mia. She's nowhere. *Goddammit!* I run in the direction of the elevators that go up to the guest rooms, but she's not there either.

No way she could have gotten this far. No way.

Spinning back around, I drag through the casino, my head whipping in every direction, looking at everyone, until I find her, standing against the wall on the edge of the casino floor, clutching her worn backpack, her chest rising and falling to an exaggerated rhythm. She's trembling, fighting to maintain her composure, though it's slipping quickly.

A rush of adrenaline bursts through my veins as sweet relief prickles my skin. I'm panting. Hell, I'm fucking hyperventilating. But I found her, and this bullshit is done. I'm her hero. I'm her fucking knight. And I'm the one who is going to make it all better.

Tears fill her eyes, falling down her cheeks one by one until they turn into rivers of anguish. She takes off, but it's without purpose or proper vision because she slams directly into me. "I've got you," I promise, wrapping my arms around her and holding her up against me.

"Jake?" She pauses, frozen in my arms for a half-second before she throws her arms around my neck, practically jumping up into me. "You're here," she cries, shaking with equal parts panic and relief. "You came back for me?"

"I was following you when I saw you running away from Brent," I admit. "I waited. I was giving you space. I wasn't going to walk with you." For some reason, this makes her cry harder. "What happened? What did he say to you?"

She just shakes her head in the crook of my neck. I guide her off to the side, into a small alcove, and then before I can even process my actions, I press my lips into the top of her head, inhaling the fragrance of her floral shampoo and holding her so close to me I wonder if she can breathe. I have no idea what I'm doing, but I also know nothing has ever felt so right before.

She loses all control. A heartbreaking sob passes her lips as she sinks into me, barely able to stand as whatever this is overpowers her. I whisper soothing words into her hair. Comfort her as best I can. She clings to me like I'm her talisman. Like I'm the dividing line between lost and found. Between salvation and destruction.

I'll straddle this line with her. She's got me. It's the craziest thing, but she does. She had me the moment I picked her up on the side of that deserted road. She had me the moment she looked up at me with those big green eyes of hers.

"Mia?" I speak softly into her hair that feels as smooth and glossy against my fingers as it looks. "What did he say?"

"Nothing," she wails. "He didn't say anything. It's me. It's all me. I'm a mess. You should have left me on the side of the road. I can't do this anymore."

I have no idea what she's talking about, but the hopelessness in her voice scares me. "Come on, baby. Let's get you upstairs."

"What?" She pulls back, wiping her eyes and the ring of mascara beneath them. My words startle her, snapping her out of her mini panic attack. She thinks I'm talking about her room, when really, I'm talking about mine. But at some point, I need to tell her. Not yet. It's too soon for that declaration. There are too many unknowns between us.

"Breakfast and the sunrise. I live here."

I've never brought a woman up there. In all the time I've been living here, I never wanted to. It felt like too much of a risk. There are too many questions, a million implications, that come with that step. Trust in another human can be a real motherfucker. It's not something I give away freely, but I want to bring her up there. I want to earn her trust as much I want her to earn mine.

"You live *here*?" Her cheeks are tear-stained and rosy. Her lips are crimson, her eyes bright and clear. God, she's so pretty.

"I do. Can I trust you?"

Her eyes volley back and forth between mine, a crease forming between her pinched eyebrows. "I don't believe in trust anymore."

Wow. That's probably the most heartbreaking thing anyone has ever said to me. How does something like that happen to someone like her?

I cup her cheeks and cover her mouth with mine. Because sometimes there are no words to fix broken, only actions.

She resists me, her posture wooden, but she doesn't pull away. My lips meld to hers, my tongue demanding access, and ever-so-slowly, her defiant mouth surrenders to mine.

Our lips and tongues move together, leisurely at first, like she's testing me out, making sure I won't take more than she's offering. I don't. I kiss her like she's the most precious thing my hands have ever held. My tongue brushes against hers as I gently press our bodies together, coaxing the most perfect whimper from the back of her throat that I greedily swallow down. She smells like tragedy and tastes like tears.

"I do," I whisper against her lips. "I believe in trust. Sometimes there is no other option. So, I'm going to trust you and take you up to my apartment. I'm going to make you breakfast, and then we're going to sit outside and watch the sunrise together."

I open my eyes and find hers right there, inches from mine, our lips still fastened together. Her eyes pierce into me, trying to see everything I hide from everyone else.

"Okay." She says it so softly that, even though our bodies are practically one, I still have to strain to hear her.

"Okay," I smile. I can't help it. That one okay feels like a yes. It's not. I know it's not. That okay is filled with a world of trepidation and a lifetime of broken promises. But right now, I'll take the small win. I won't even gloat about it.

My hand slides down her face, over her neck, down her arm until my fingers intertwine with hers. I press my lips to hers one last time, because I absolutely have to, and then I'm leading her out of this alcove, back into the fray that is a casino in Las Vegas on a Friday night at nearly four in the morning. It's bright, noisy and disorienting. It's filled with drunken chatter and voracious cheers of excitement.

But we find our way through, over to the private elevators that are reserved for VIPs, celebrities, and me. Once we step inside, I hit the button for my floor and punch in my private code.

"Who are you?" she asks hesitantly, almost like she doesn't want to know the answer, but needs to at the same time.

"I'm a lot of things." She peers up at me through her long, dark eyelashes. "I'm a waiter. Lately a bartender. I'm a bouncer in a club and pit boss in a casino."

"You're more than that. Aren't you?"

"I am," I say it with a smile that is meant to reassure her. That kiss, man. Hell.

I wait her out. I wait to see if she asks more questions, but she doesn't, and the only reason I can come up with is she doesn't want me to reciprocate.

The elevator doors slide open, and I step out, taking her with me. Her eyes wander around my place before they come up to mine, examining me. Figuring me out. And when she opens her mouth, I expect accusations.

But instead, I get, "What are you making me for breakfast? I'm starving."

Sunshine… Holy hell, Sunshine. This girl is quickly becoming a delicious addiction. One I don't know how to resist.

Chapter Thirteen

Mia

I met Niklas when I was a teenager. He blew in like a storm. Like a tornado, destroying everything in his path while covering up his destruction with perfect manners, a beautiful smile, and brains. I was sixteen, and he was twenty-six, but that didn't matter to me. Or him.

My father found Niklas, bred him to eventually take over his empire. As a result, Niklas became one of the sole fixtures in our home.

You see, I didn't have a lot of people in my life. Very few other than my maid and her son, but after he and I were discovered spending time together, he was no longer allowed to return. My parents had already pulled me out of school by that point, stating I would be better served with tutors. I protested vehemently, but my cries of discontent fell upon deaf ears. My mother did not want to be bothered tending to my homework or anything else that required parental supervision, and my father despised me being out in public.

The day I was photographed going into my school was the day my father pulled me out of school. After that, I didn't have interactions with people my own age. Practically none. Until Niklas came along. Not that he was my age.

My mother was never someone I could turn to. Not someone I was able to discuss with the concerns a young girl finds herself consumed by.

My maid educated me about sex. Enlightened me on periods and tampons and what boys are really after. But she was my maid, and I never felt comfortable asking her the questions that burned holes in my brain. The internet wasn't much better. Romance books? Well, those bastards gave me hope. A hope I didn't need and certainly should never have clung to. I saw light when there was nothing but darkness lingering just beneath the surface.

But that light… God, did I need it.

Niklas filled me with the illusion of that light. He gave me attention. He smiled at me and flirted with me. Something I had definitely never experienced in my sixteen years. He told me I was beautiful. He told me I was special and that he loved me. He told me I would one day be his, and then he'd take me away from my lonely life, giving me the world.

It was everything my young, naïve, self had fantasized of and more.

My father never seemed to care if I spent time with Niklas. My mother was too self-absorbed to notice anything I did, unless it was to criticize me.

Niklas caught my attention the first moment I saw him. I felt those blue eyes of his. They snaked a path straight into me and never let go. He gave me that first smile at my sweet-sixteen ball, which was comprised entirely of my parents' business associates and social friends. When Niklas moved across the crowded dance floor, heading directly for me, I practically vibrated out of my heels from excitement.

"Do you want to dance?" he asked, and I smiled so big, nodding my head like the young, eager teenager I was. He had an accent. One I wasn't familiar with, but it didn't take me long to discover it was German. I thought it was the sexiest thing I had ever heard in my life.

I had no idea Niklas was a predator.

A dangerous beast of a man who was capable of things I still can't begin to grasp. In my mind, I never figured a man who looked like that could be dangerous. That title always fell more in line with men like Jake. The quintessential tall, dark, and mysterious man. And those tattoos. To me, a man like him has dangerous written all over him.

Niklas looked like an angel. Fair and perfect.

Just goes to show you what bullshit appearances are.

Because here I am, in Jake's multi-million-dollar apartment on the very top floor of The Turner Grand hotel. My dark devil, who more accurately fits the mold of a dark knight. A savior instead of a punisher. Almost like Batman. A beautiful vigilante with a secret pain he tries to bury.

He kissed me with what was easily the most gentle and tender kiss I've ever experienced, and now he's cooking me breakfast while I hide in his bathroom, trying to rein in my overwhelming anxiety.

Where was this anxiety when I needed it all those years ago?

Nonexistent, that's where. I saw a pretty face and a gorgeous smile and those blue eyes and a way out, and I was done. Bought and sold in seconds. That's all it took for me to fall for him. The way Niklas held me when we danced? I would have done anything he asked of me.

He didn't try to kiss me that night. I was sixteen to his twenty-six, and there were eyes all around us. His hand never crossed those imaginary lines on my body. He never asked me for any of the things I was dying to give him. He just demanded my number, and when I all-too-happily gave it to him, he promised to call.

I was heartbroken. I mean, I'd always read in books and watched in angsty teen movies, boys say they're going to call and never do, right?

That was my first incorrect assumption about him. Because Niklas Vaughn was a man and not a boy and he did call me. That very night, in fact. I spent hours hiding in my bathroom talking to him. I fell in love with him that night in my very adolescent way.

But when my parents died two years later in a plane crash, everything between us changed.

I was eighteen, and he no longer had to hide me from the world.

He moved in, into my parents' house and my father's business and my bed, and took over everything. At first, it was a relief. I was a lost girl in a lost world, and I didn't know up from down or day from night. It was all…too much. Especially for a sheltered, neglected and partially broken girl who'd secretly hated her parents and the world they forced her to live in.

That relief did not last long.

But I didn't lose myself completely until that ring was on my finger.

I was not allowed to go to college or work. I was not allowed to have my own money; in fact, any cash I inherited, Niklas took over. I couldn't even argue with him. He made sure of that. I was not allowed to have my own computer, and he tracked my cell phone. I was not allowed to leave the house unless he was with me.

It was worse than when my parents were alive, because though my father would smack me around from time to time, and I was generally unloved and blatantly ignored, they were never as cruel as Niklas could be.

I was a prisoner. Physically, financially, and mentally.

I knew how deep in I was, and I had no clue how to climb my way out.

No one ever imagines they'll become that girl. The one trapped with an abusive man and terrified for her life on a daily basis. It's easy to judge her. To see what the outside world sees.

But the inside is something else entirely. The inside is a fear so raw and acute you spend every moment of every day in a heightened state of awareness. A constant state of second-guessing every decision, whether it's insignificant or not. The perpetual panic is all-consuming. Because one perceived misdeed and your life is literally on the line.

Those beatings. Just thinking back on them makes my body shudder. He was brutal, and I was powerless. The one time I attempted to leave him, he beat me within an inch of my life, and once I came to, he promised in no uncertain terms he would kill me if I tried it again.

Because he owned me.

I was his forever.

Till death do us part.

That leads me back to Jake. And that kiss. And that Brent guy. And fucking Vegas.

I'm not dead. Only my parents are. Which is why I should walk right out of this bathroom, get back on that elevator, and leave. Except, I can't make myself do that. Jake is the one who gave me that hotel room. I know it. There is no one else it could possibly be. Brent would have taken credit. But why would Jake do that? Especially for a woman like me. Sex? Possibly. I can't come up with much else.

But why not tell me it was him?

Why not throw down the hero card and see if that gets me to spread my legs?

He did it anonymously, and even though I know there is so much he's not telling me, I also know none of it is dark.

He is the opposite of Niklas in every way.

At least, I hope so. Because I see light when I look into his dark eyes. And this light is real. It's not a façade. I see the end of the tunnel I'm stuck in. Is that selfish? Without a doubt. Desperation lends itself to moral ambiguity. I should not bring this man into my ugly world.

And I won't. I will have breakfast with him. I will watch that sunrise. And then I will go back downstairs to my room and sleep off the emotional hangover Jake will no doubt leave me with. I wasn't lying when I said I no longer believe in trust. That's very true. But I want to believe Jake could be something good.

I splash some water on my face, wipe away the remnants of the mascara I cried off, and stare at myself in the mirror, tired of everything I see.

I left Niklas. And since then I've been trying to be strong. Brave. Self-possessed. Badass. But sometimes I feel like I don't know who I really am beneath the layers of polished politeness and perfect-girl routine. I need to find myself. Figure out who I want to be and how to get there. I'm trying. Maybe this breakfast is a step in that direction.

I exit the bathroom and follow the aroma of bacon all the way back to the top-of-the-line kitchen. I don't say anything as I approach him. I just stand here and watch as he moves with the ease and confidence of a man who knows what he's doing. I'll give Jake I-have-no-idea-what-his-last-name-is credit. He's certainly unexpected.

He spots me watching him and grins, walking around the large island and the counter until he's standing tall over me.

"Hey," he says, his voice low, his hand reaching out to touch my shoulder.

I turn away, and his hand drops back to his side. I cannot handle his touch. It leaves me defenseless. Like that night in the bathroom when he fixed my hand. I've fallen for kind touches before. For gentle hands and perfect words and longing looks. I've fallen for all of it. Like jumping off a cliff, that fall was fast and hard, and I landed in a sea of hurricane waters.

"You doing okay?"

"Smells good," I say instead, and he doesn't skip a beat.

"Glad to hear that." He winks at me. "Have a seat, Sunshine. It's almost ready."

Sunshine. That's what he calls me now. Is that what this is? Something light and bright and warm?

"I was in the Army for two years," he says to me as he continues to cook our breakfast with a smile like he didn't just knock the wind out of me. I instantly freeze, my ass halfway between the air and my seat.

He's talking to me.

"Yeah," he says, watching me closely with an indiscernible expression. "I was shot in the shoulder in Afghanistan and sent home. After that I went to MIT and then Wharton. I didn't know what else to do after I was discharged from the Army, so I went at my father's request. After I graduated, I dicked around New York City, bartending and waiting tables. It wasn't a bad way to spend time, and I was pretty damn happy doing it, but then my father died."

My ass hits that seat because if it doesn't, I'll fall over. He piles a bunch of scrambled eggs onto my plate along with some very crispy bacon and a piece of buttered toast. The bastard buttered my toast for me. And coffee. He gives me a big white mug of coffee, but when I spin the mug around to slip my fingers in the handle, I see it's not a blank mug. It says, "I do marathons (On Netflix)." A burst of laughter leaves my lips as I read this, and he winks at me again like he's easy and not dangerous at all.

Biting my bottom lip, I try to hide my smile, and once that's under control, I take a bite of the yellow fluffy eggs in front of me. He can cook. And he's so good-looking it's almost unfair. I love running with him in the mornings. And when he smiles at me with those twin dimples, my stomach turns into a quivering, jittery mass of excitement. Or melted butter as the metaphor fits.

This does not bode well for me and my plan to never look back.

"I loved MIT," he continues on despite my silence. "I was really good at school. And college was just…fun, you know?" *I wish I did.* "Even if I was a little older than the other kids there. Endless parties and crazy smart kids who all thought they were going to change the world. I never wanted it to end."

I hate that he's telling me these things. I can't stand that he's doing this. I don't want to know about Jake. I don't want to like him for more than what I already know. *Don't make me get attached to you, Jake.*

"For a while, I had illusions I was going to be a mechanical engineer but couldn't really find my way there. Wharton was to make my father happy when I couldn't come up with a real plan after graduation. He didn't like me waiting tables. He didn't like me riding motorcycles. He didn't like me doing anything I was doing. So, I went to business school and hated every goddamn second of it."

He takes a bite of his own eggs, standing across the counter from me while he eats, washing it down with a mug of coffee that says, "Accio Coffee" with a picture of a wand next to it. Who the hell has a Harry Potter mug? It makes me want to smile until my face hurts.

"Why are you telling me all this?"

He shrugs nonchalantly, but there is nothing casual about this moment or this conversation, and it's obvious he knows this. Everything he's doing with me right now is deliberate.

"Because I'm hoping if I tell you something real about myself, you'll grow to trust me. That you'll give me a little something back in return."

I shake my head.

"We'll go slow." He smirks, taking a sip of his coffee to hide his amusement, if that's what that look is. "I learned a lot at Wharton," he continues, after setting his mug back down on the stone counter with a clink. "But once I graduated, I went back to whatever the hell I was doing before. Then my father died."

I swallow hard, the food suddenly feels like it's choking me, and I have to guzzle down my coffee to dislodge it from my esophagus. My parents are dead, and I wish they had waited until I was twenty-five to die. That may sound wrong or fucked up, but it's true. I hated my parents. They were not good people, but their death only made things worse.

"And once he died," he continues, unaware of my internal struggle, "I realized my life would never be the same again. That everything I thought I could get away with, I couldn't. I was glad I paid attention in business school, because I needed it."

"You own this place, don't you?" I accuse, interrupting him. "The hotel? That's why you have all of those jobs and why you gave me my room."

He smiles, his dark eyes sparkling as he crunches down on a piece of bacon. "I have no idea what you're talking about, Sunshine. But you're fucking adorable."

"What's your last name?"

He laughs. "If I tell you my name, will you tell me your real one?"

All the blood drains from my face, and my fork slips from my fingers, clattering against my plate.

"I can't do that." I don't even bother to deny it. He knows. There was no question in his expression or tone.

"Sure, you can. You can tell me anything."

I shake my head, my hands trembling as I fold them into my lap so he can't see.

"Harris," he says and then sighs, setting his fork down and running a hand through his hair. His eyes meet mine, and there might be a dare in them. "Harris…Turner."

I nod. Turner. Turner Grand and Turner Palace and that other Turner on the Strip. Turner Hotels. They're a national name.

Jake Harris Turner gave me my hotel suite. He gave me that food, and he picked me up on the side of the road, and he held me in his arms downstairs while I was losing my mind, and he made me goddamn scrambled eggs.

He drinks coffee out of gimmicky mugs, and he told me his real name. He told me his real name when he absolutely did not have to and no one else, as far as I can tell, knows it. I've never heard anyone mention to me he's the owner of the hotels. An owner who works as a waiter and bartender as well as those other jobs he mentioned.

I trust him. Jesus Christ, I do. I trust this man, and my heart swells with that truth.

But Jake Harris Turner has a lot to lose.

I should never have come up here. I should never have let it get this far. If I were brave, I'd keep going. I'd pick up my things and leave. But I'm terrified of bus stations and trains. Airplanes are out, and I don't have enough money to buy a new car. I'm stuck here, waiting for Niklas to find me. If he hasn't already. Brent is a wild card.

What will happen to Jake when that happens, if I allow this—whatever this is—to continue?

He takes another bite of his food, watching me struggle before jutting his chin in the direction of my plate for me to do the same.

"Eat up," he urges. "The sun will be up in an hour or so, and I want to show you something before that happens."

I do eat. But only because I have no response to that. I know I need to go, but I find myself prolonging this breakfast, this time with him, for as long as I can. *I wish I didn't like you so much, Jake.*

When I'm done eating and drinking his fantastic coffee, he takes my hand and slides open an invisible door amongst the long panel of glass that makes up his wall. The early dawn air is cool but not cold, and my feet glide of their own volition over to the edge of the balcony. I didn't think Vegas had many balconies for obvious suicide reasons, but this place is all balcony. It just goes on and on. We're facing east right now, and I can see the very beginnings of the sun in the far distance.

Jake wraps his arms around me, folds me into his chest, and rests his chin on top of my shoulder, our cheeks practically pressed together. I can't help but flinch, to cringe from his touch and comfort. It's as unsettling as it is wonderful. He doesn't comment, and he doesn't let me go. He just holds me tighter until, eventually, my body relaxes into his. I'm safe with him, is what this embrace says. The offer is so tempting. But the price?

"This is my favorite time of day here," he whispers into the quiet darkness. We're high up from the Strip, so I can't hear any of the madness below. And the lights that adorn the Strip only seem to accent the impending dawn. "The sunset is spectacular, but it's the sunrise that sets the tone, don't you think?"

"Yes," I manage, utterly spent and emotionally overloaded.

Even though I'm scheduled to go see Maddox this morning, I have no idea how I'll manage that on no sleep. I should cancel and go tomorrow instead. I took his advice. I got myself a gun. An illegal one at that. Nevada doesn't have the strictest laws, but there are still laws. If I'd gone to a reputable dealer, I'd have had to give my information and produce a real license. Neither of those were an option.

I got myself a Ruger LC9s. It's small, concealable, lightweight, and pretty easy to shoot, according to the man who sold it to me. But he doesn't do lessons and he wouldn't let me come back to practice at his range. I have to go to a legit place. That's one thing, but signing up for lessons with a teacher is another. It can't be done.

"Do you know anything about guns?" I ask Jake, my heart beating just a bit faster as my words float out into the early dawn.

"Guns?" He turns me in his arms, staring at me like I just asked him if the sky is brown.

"Yes. Guns."

"Why are you asking me that?" His expression turns guarded, his posture more rigid.

I sigh. Maybe this was a bad idea. But I feel like I need help with this, and Maddox made it clear to me he wouldn't be the one to give it.

"Because I've always wanted to learn how to shoot one, so I figured…," I trail off, realizing just how unbelievable that sounds.

"Yes," he says quickly. "I know about guns."

I glance up, only to find him watching me with more concentration than he ever has before. "Would you teach me how to shoot?" I ask, going for broke.

"If you tell me why."

I should have known.

"You can tell me the truth. I won't tell anyone." His hand brushes my cheek, and I see it in his eyes. He means everything he says. No punches pulled, no lies, just brutal honesty. It cuts me to the quick. I don't remember the last time I saw that in a man.

"I'm not sure I can do that. I want to. I don't even know why, but I want to tell you things. But really, I'm just trying to protect you, Jake Harris Turner. Don't dig deeper into my world," I beg. Because if he pushes me, just a little, I'll cave. I'm so desperate for a connection. For something real.

"I'll teach you how to shoot," he promises in a hushed tone. "You don't have to tell me why. I'll help you."

Relief courses through my veins, warm and welcome like a drug. "Thank you."

He holds me tighter, kisses the side of my face, and then we watch the sun rise in all its glory. We marvel at the varying shades of pinks, purples, and gold. We cling to each other like this moment is as fleeting as it feels. And after that sun rises, I spin around in his arms and I kiss him.

I have to. It's a thank you. Because he managed the impossible. He made me feel safe. Even if it only lasted the fifteen minutes it took the sun to rise. His tongue invades my mouth, one hand sweeping down to the crest above my ass, the other knotted in my hair. A soft groan catches in the back of his throat as we kiss with abandon.

"Stay," he whispers against my lips just as I say, "I have to go." I blink up into those oh-so-dark depths.

"Do you have to?"

"Yes."

"Have dinner with me then?"

I shake my head. Because while this was a fantasy come true, reality always comes back with the light of day.

Chapter Fourteen

Mia

"Trying to outrun me?" I half-tease. Jake is kicking my butt up and down the Strip today. The sunrise changed things between us. No, correction, the sunrise changed everything. At least, it did in my mind. It's been three days since that sunrise, and we've run together every day since. He continues to push for more breakfasts and dinners and even lunches, and I continue to thwart those advances. I tell him it's better not to chase me.

I don't tell him the actual reason, but I think he knows. Not necessarily the details, but the rough outline. He's a smart man and can add pieces together easily enough.

I like him.

I'm drawn to him.

I feel safe with him, and worse yet, I'm starting to miss him when I'm not with him. It's all the kissing we've been doing, I think. He kisses like a rollercoaster. Fast, exciting, and with enough dips, spins, and swirls to make my head spin and have me screaming out for more.

He chuckles and slows his pace enough for me to catch him. Reaching out for my hand, he grasps it tightly before tugging me into his sweaty chest, kissing me as if to eliminate any shred of womanly doubt I was just having.

"I want to take you somewhere today."

I shake my head. I have no idea why I continue to draw this line in the sand with him, but I do.

"You said you wanted to learn how to shoot."

Oh. I wasn't expecting that. "Now?" I'm incredulous. I can't imagine there are shooting ranges open at this hour.

"Yeah. Now." He grins at me, and I love that he's just the right amount of taller. "I know the perfect place."

"I need a shower."

A wicked smile lights up his face.

"I didn't mean with you, dirty boy."

"I know, and it's a damn shame, because I'm dying to see you naked and wet in the shower."

"You're crass."

"Only for you. Now hurry. We're wasting time."

"You're the one standing here."

He nods as he watches me with barely contained lust. "Can't help it, I get hard as a fucking rock just looking at you."

I blush like I've never blushed in my life and turn my face away from him. *Jesus.* My breaths are sharp and ragged and not remotely related to our run. He tilts my face to his again and kisses me, pressing into me like he needs to prove his point. And yes, he's hard. Everywhere.

"I want to take you shooting."

"Okay. You can take me shooting. No more begging, though, Mr. Turner, it's pathetic."

He grins into me. "I want to kiss you more."

"I know."

"I want to do more than kiss you."

I grin against his lips, heat flooding me in ways I'm embarrassed to admit. "I know."

"This is Las Vegas. I doubt we'd even get in trouble if I fucked you right here in the middle of the Strip outside the hotel."

"Maybe not, but that doesn't mean I'm going to let you."

He growls like a caveman and then kisses me again, sweeping his tongue inside my mouth to taste me as he bends me back. Christ, this man can kiss.

"Let's go inside before I lose my mind any more than I already have."

He walks me into the hotel and over to the elevators, even though he still likes to pretend he has no clue about my hotel room. Whenever I bring it up, he tells me I'm crazy. I press the button, and when it opens, I step inside.

"I'll see you downstairs in half an hour."

"I take it back," he yells at me as the doors begin to close. He sticks his arm in between them, making them jolt back in surprise with a loud ding.

"What?" I ask completely baffled. Now he doesn't want to take me shooting?

"I can no longer be your friend or friendly or whatever crap you were saying."

"Why's that?" I'm trying so hard to hide my smile, my teeth sink into my bottom lip to cover it.

His eyes become heated as he takes me in, a cocky smirk pulling at the corner of his mouth. I can't get enough of playful Jake. Or naughty Jake. They're like my personal kryptonite.

"Well, for one, I'm picturing you naked in this elevator."

"I'm not." I roll my eyes.

He smiles the type of smile that has me clenching my thighs, desperate for some friction where I need it most. "I know. But I'm still envisioning you naked with your very long legs wrapped around me, my cock buried deep inside you." A rush of air passes my lips. "That's one of the marks of non-friendship. Picturing the other person naked while you fuck them till they come, and since I know you picture me, too, I think this friendship thing is done."

"You have a dirty mouth."

He grins. "You should see the way I fuck."

I shake my head, folding my hands behind me and gripping the rim of the elevator wall. If I don't, I'll launch myself at him so we can live out that fantasy this very moment. I swallow. Clear my throat.

"What are the other reasons? Because if we're no longer friends, you can stop stalking me on my runs, and you can get out of my elevator." I raise an eyebrow at him.

He's undeterred, positioning himself in the entrance of the elevator so the doors can't close. "I think I may need to date you instead."

I snort. "Nope." I reach forward to press the button for my floor again, pushing him out. He steps back, but God, the way he's looking at me...

"This is happening, Mia Jones. It's when and not if."

The doors close on him, and the moment he's out of sight, I let out a shaky breath. Because that right there, that fake name on his lips, is why I can't date him. It's why I should leave town and never see Jake Harris Turner again.

But I can't stop myself. I enter my room and get in the shower with the intention of allowing him to teach me to shoot. With the intention of letting him take me somewhere and kiss me again. Probably more, if I'm being honest with myself.

Every rule I make about him, I break.

Every. Single. One.

I give in to him with very little resistance. It's becoming easier and easier to blur the lines. To ignore reality and live in this world that still doesn't quite feel real. Like I'm living someone else's life. My parents would roll over in their graves if they knew I was working as a waitress and a bartender. They'd die all over again if they knew I ran away from Niklas and had slept outside for two weeks.

Thirty-two minutes later, I find Jake in the lobby, staring down at his phone. He's wearing a green t-shirt and jeans and sneakers. He looks like any other guy, except I assume the black duffel bag resting by his feet houses guns. Such a weird thought.

"Where are we going?"

He glances up from his phone at the sound of my voice, a smile etched on his perfect lips as he tucks his phone into his back pocket.

"I want to take you somewhere."

When a man says something like that to you, that he wants to take you to fire a gun at an undisclosed location, well, it should raise alarm flags, right? Especially when the man you're running from owned guns, knew how to shoot them, and once used the same phrase to draw you out into the woods, have violent sex with you, and then proceeds to beat you unconscious because you left the house to go shopping the day before and didn't tell him.

But Jake doesn't give me the I'm-going-to-try-and-kill-you vibe. He gives me a I-want-to-fuck-you-crazy—in a pleasurable, non-violent way—vibe. He said he wants to date me. And considering the tingle that thought produces inside me, I should tell him everything now. I should turn him down flat.

"Um—"

"Mia, please come with me," he requests softly, but his eyes are earnest and begging for trust. Mia. Shit. I really need to tell him. But now doesn't feel like the right time. It feels like the worst time in the world. Because once I do, I'll have to leave, and I don't want to.

And I do need to learn how to shoot my illegally purchased firearm, right?

"I guess I'm in."

"YOU OWN a gun and keep it in your apartment?" I ask Jake as he drives us away from the city into the blazing heat of the desert. I'm really just talking, stating the obvious, because he's taking me away from the city, and it's not even seven in the morning. I'm talking because if I don't, I might vomit all over his what-smells-to-be-new truck.

Jake glances over at me and shakes his head slightly, like he's reading my thoughts perfectly.

"Yes. I have a gun, and I keep it in my apartment. I was in the Army. I think I told you that at one point or another."

"No sarcasm right now, Jake. I'm hanging on by a thread."

He chuckles and takes my hand, giving it a reassuring squeeze.

"We'll talk more about me owning guns if you want. Probably not today, because I'm not really in the mood, but we will talk about it if you need us to."

"Too busy contemplating your plan to lure me away from the city and..." I widen my eyes at him. "Kill me?"

He laughs like what I just said is ridiculous. Maybe that should make me feel better, but it doesn't. Once upon a time, I was considered really smart. My tutors always told me I was and when I picked up four other languages like a native, I believed them. When I let Niklas move in, it was like he zapped out every single smart brain cell I ever possessed and replaced it with clay or mud or something thick and simple. Because that's what I had become. Thick and simple.

"We really need to work on this whole trust thing," he says dryly.

"I'm just edgy," I reply, glancing out the window.

"I can tell. And maybe when we go on our date, you'll explain why."

"Probably not."

"Hmmm...okay. What can I do to get you to trust me?"

"I do trust you, Jake. Well, sort of." I sigh. "I can't help it. It's just the way things are for me."

"All right, baby," he says on a breath. "But I'm not going anywhere. I want this with you. I want your full trust. I want your body and your mind and your everything." He squeezes my hand again as if to punctuate his perfect words.

"I wish you weren't so patient."

"I'm annoyingly patient—"

"And persistent."

He nods, his chestnut hair falling in his eyes, making him look boyish and innocent. "And persistent," he agrees. "That sort of goes with being patient. I guess what I'm saying is, I'll win you over eventually."

You already have.

"Why keep chasing me?" I ask before I can stop myself.

A smirk crawls up the corner of his mouth and it sits there as he mulls over my question. He's silent for the next few minutes until we pull into a field in the middle of nowhere. And I mean nowhere. There is absolutely nothing around us. Probably for miles. Jesus, what have I gotten myself into?

Calling this place a field is a bit of an overstatement. It's really dried out grass and cracked earth with the mountains in the distance. It's open land as far as the eye can see.

Jake puts his truck in park, shuts off the engine and turns, engaging me before I can get out. "It's not the chase or the thrill of the conquest," he says, his flinty brown eyes searing into mine. "You do keep telling me no, but you also tell me yes sometimes. Like this morning. And every time we run together. And the other morning when I made you breakfast, and we watched the sunrise. You definitely said yes to me then. And every time you let me kiss you and you kiss me back. But all that aside, it's quite simple really. I like you. I'm drawn to you in a way I haven't been drawn to a woman in a long time. Maybe ever. I spend time with you and once I'm back home alone, I want to do it all over again. I think about you. A lot more than I should. But it's there and I do, and I won't apologize for it. Especially when I know that you're right there with me."

"Jake, I—"

"I know. You've got a lot going on you won't talk about. I get it. But like I said, I'm not going anywhere."

He leans in and presses his lips to mine, cupping the back of my neck with his calloused fingers. Calloused fingers I'd love to have all over my body. He pulls my lower lip with his teeth and then gives me a wink.

He just proved his point completely, didn't he? He gets out of the truck, leaving me here with a dull, aching chest stuffed full of butterflies. Why didn't I tell him? It was the perfect moment, but coward that I am, I chickened out.

When I finally figure out how to breathe normally again, I hop out and find Jake standing in the center of…well, nothing really. Just a lot of brush and reddish-brown earth. The sun is just starting to rise higher in the sky, bringing with it an incorrigible heat.

"Come here," he commands, and I obey instantly. "Here," he

pulls a pair of safety glasses out of his duffel bag and hands them to me. "Put these on and show me your gun."

Wow, that's sexy. I don't know if it's his domineering presence or the absurd words coming out of his mouth that sound like something from a bad porno or an action film, but damn...

"Here," I say on a swallow, the sound practically choked in the back of my throat.

"This is a good gun for you. It's small and easy to use." I nod. "I'm not going to ask where you got it, because I really don't want to know. I also know you won't tell me why you're doing this, but if you go out and kill a bunch of people—or even one person—for any other reason than self-defense, and end up in jail, I'm going to be pissed as hell, and I won't bail you out."

"Noted."

"Okay." He looks down at me, any amusement gone from his expression; in its place is cold, sober deliberateness. "Do you know how to load it?"

I nod again.

"And I see you have the safety on so we're halfway there. Have you ever fired it?"

"No. I've never fired a gun before."

"Huh," he muses, his head bobbing up and down. "Then let's get started."

"Out here?"

He turns to me with a laugh. "Yes, out here. Don't worry, I own this land. I've used it for target practice before. You see that mound over there?" He points to his left, and I notice a large mound of dirt about fifty yards out. It even has a target on it.

"I'll never be able to shoot that far."

"Probably not." He takes my hand, the one not holding the gun that is, and leads me over until we're about twenty yards away. "Place your feet shoulder-width apart."

I do as he says.

"Good. Now hold the gun up like you're getting ready to fire."

I raise it up with one hand and aim at the target, but he takes my other hand and places it just so on the gun, raising my hands higher as he does.

"Take off the safety, aim it, and fire."

Holy crap. Suddenly, I'm hit with a rush of adrenaline. Nervous excitement routes a path straight through me. I'm scared out of my goddamn mind. Sucking in a deep, fortifying breath, I close my eyes, center myself, open them again, and press in on the trigger. The gun fires with a loud crack, and even though I jolt back a little, there isn't a whole lot of kick to it.

"That was good. Next time, keep your eyes open and on the target."

"Right. Sorry." I didn't even come close to hitting it. Nor did I realize I had closed my eyes. That's a bit embarrassing. I lift my arms the way he showed me, this time focusing on the center of the target, and fire again. I don't hit the target, but I do hit the mound.

"Better. Again."

I fire until I'm out of bullets and need to reload. I hit the edge of the target twice, but nowhere near the center of the bullseye.

"It takes practice," he reassures, taking my gun from me and reloading it. "You can't expect to come out here once, fire a gun, and be an expert."

"I know," I groan, but I'm still disappointed. I'm just starting to realize how innately competitive I am. "I wanted to at least hit the target."

"We'll keep practicing. But we're done for today."

I peer up at him, my eyebrows furrowed. "Then why did you reload my gun?"

Jake turns to me, placing my small weapon in my hand with the safety engaged. "Because you're learning how to shoot this thing for a reason. Don't you think it should be loaded?"

My stomach twists before it sinks into my feet. I stare down at the warm gun in my hand, hating everything it represents. Guns scare the shit out of me in general, but his words kill me. How do I rationalize this? I know I'm just trying to protect myself, but I can't believe it's gotten this far.

"Jake...," I start. I need to tell him. I suck in a rush of cool morning air and blow it out slowly. “Where did you learn how to shoot?” I go for instead and close my eyes, hating myself just a bit more for my cowardice. He fired a few rounds of my gun, hitting the center target each time. It was effortless for him. Second nature.

“The Army taught me. They did a damn good job of it, too.”

“Thank you,” I whisper, unable to meet his eyes. “For teaching me, I mean. I sincerely appreciate it.” I feel sick. I don’t know how much longer I can take this. Especially with what I know is coming for me.

Chapter Fifteen

Jake

Mia is a different woman after leaving the desert and the makeshift gun range behind. Quiet. Introspective. Rattled. I want to take her home with me. I want to take her up to my apartment and tuck her in my bed. But she needs her space, and I respect that.

I guide her across the lobby, regretting there is no way to access her floor from my elevator. Mine only stops at the forty-ninth floor, which is all villas. I should have given her a villa. That way, I'd have better access to her, but that made me feel…well, like a creeper, I guess. I don't know. I didn't do it, so now I have to take her to the fucking guest elevators every asshole uses.

She eyes me the entire way, waiting for me to say something I refuse to acknowledge. On the way home, she said it can't happen again. It felt like she was referring to more than the shooting.

"Why can't it happen again?" I ask before we reach the elevator. Because screw that. Being with her is too good not to happen again.

"You've done so much for me. And I'm grateful." She turns to me. "More than grateful. But I can't tell you more than I already have, okay?"

"You haven't told me anything."

She nods like I'm getting it.

"I'm not going to hurt you," I say slowly, carefully, like she's a caged animal I'm afraid of upsetting. "I promise you, I will never hurt you. Ever. I think you know that already, but I'll tell you a million more times until you believe it, if I have to. Because it's the truth. You. Are. Safe. With. Me. That means you can tell me anything. I'm in, Mia. I'm in. You've got me."

She blinks back her impending tears.

"Mia," I reach out my hand for her, and she reluctantly takes it, "Who's after you? Why are you so afraid?"

She doesn't respond, and I'm losing my last shred of composure.

"I don't know what to say. What to do. I know you ran away from home, because you pretty much said so that night I picked you up. You were afraid I was going to hit you." I glance over, checking her reaction to that last statement. "Right?" She's frozen, standing against the wall of the elevator, still holding my hand. "You had a panic attack that night after Brent spoke to you, and today we're firing guns."

"Please stop," she whispers.

"Just tell me what the fuck is going on!"

Her eyes widen, and I hate myself for yelling at her. Shit and fuck, that was so goddamn wrong. The elevator doors ping before they open, and even though it's so early, there are people milling about the casino floor.

"I ran for a reason," she breathes out softly, staring up at me like she's trying to convey a message I continue to miss.

"I know."

"From a dangerous man."

"I figured."

"Then don't go all caveman on me, demanding shit I can't give, okay?"

"Caveman?" I tease, because I hate seeing her pain. I point to my chest. "Me?"

"Maybe," she muses, relaxing some at my playful tone. "I guess you can count your lucky stars I think cavemen are sexy."

I give her a lopsided grin. Anything to let her know I didn't mean to yell. That I'm sorry if I startled her or scared her or anything else. I'm trying to prove she's safe with me and I'm doing a shitty job of it.

"Sexy, huh? You think I'm sexy?"

She shakes her head, biting her soft bottom lip as she tries to hide her smile. "I said I think cavemen are sexy. Not you specifically."

"Nah, you let me kiss you. You think I'm sexy."

Now she can't fight her grin. I reach out and cup her cheek, my eyes locked with hers. "You said shit."

She scrunches her eyebrows.

"You said shit. I think it's the first time I've heard you swear. You're this perfect, proper lady who uses these formal words with me like pardon instead of what. And now you said shit."

She shrugs a shoulder.

"We okay?" I ask.

"Yes. We're okay. It's everything else that isn't. You'd be smart to leave me alone."

"Probably. But I've never been good at doing the smart thing. Why start now?" I lean in and press my lips to hers before pulling back, my face inches away. "You're going to live in the hotel room I did not give you." *Kiss.* "We're going to call you Sunshine, because I know Mia is not your name." *Kiss.* "And you're going to see me again and again and again." *Kiss.* "And everything else we'll figure out as we go along." *Kiss.* "And when you trust me more than you do this minute, you're going to tell me absolutely everything there is to know about you."

"I can't afford that hotel room, Jake. And I don't like you paying for me."

"I have no idea what you're talking about."

She blows out an exasperated huff, but I think at this point, she's too tired to fight me.

I kiss her goodbye because there is no way I can't. She throws a smile over her shoulder and heads up in the elevator that will take her to her floor.

Here's the problem.

I'm crazy about this girl. And she has me teaching her to shoot a gun. And she just admitted she's running from a dangerous man. Lines are getting blurred. Right and wrong and smart and stupid all seem to be mixing into one. But I can't stop. I can't walk away from her. So now what do I do? Especially when everything I am, my whole world, is at risk.

Then I feel movement on my right. I turn to find Brent. Doesn't this guy ever sleep? He watched her go. Just as I did. I clench my fists so tight I can feel the blood draining from them.

"I thought I told you to leave her the fuck alone," I snap from beside him. If he's surprised by my outburst, he doesn't show it. He doesn't even flinch. He just keeps his focus on the elevator she just left in. "You were gone. You told her you were leaving, and you were gone. So what the fuck?"

"And I told you, you don't know shit." He spins around, pinning me with an arrogant smile and a menacing gaze that says I really don't know shit. "You think you can get her a hotel room, teach her to fire a gun, and keep her safe? You think you know what game you're playing or who you're fucking with?"

Ho. Lee. Shit.

"Who are you?" I ask and then that smile grows. The creepy asshole looks like the cat who just ate the canary.

"I bet you'd like to know. Especially since I know everything about you, Mr. *Turner.*" My heart starts to beat harder, punching out an angry rhythm against my ribs. "But try as you might, you won't know anything I don't want you to. And as for Fiona—" *Fiona?* "—I'll let you continue to play your hero games with her. I never relished the idea of her sleeping outside anyway." He takes a step forward, totally and completely unafraid of my extra height and weight. This tells me two things. One, he's probably packing heat, and two, he can absolutely handle himself in a fight. Well, that makes two of us. "But if you fuck with my objective, I will take you down. I do not give a flying fuck if you own this hotel. I will end you. Don't think I can't."

And then he walks away like he didn't just threaten me. Like he didn't just shake-up my entire world. I'm too stunned to respond. To charge him or have him thrown out. Because a guy like that does not make a threat he can't back up, and even though I can play it off like I'm the one in charge and invincible to the world, I'm not. These hotels are not. He could out me to the media this minute. He could ruin everything I've spent the last six months of my life trying to build.

Is she worth this? Worth the very real risk that evidently comes with her?

Yes, my subconscious answers before I can even finish my thoughts. It's not something I didn't assume about her before. I just never anticipated this. I presumed she was running from a guy who beat her. Not a man like Brent, who referred to her as an objective.

But first things first.

I count to ten so I can get my anger under control because right now I'm ready to plant my fist through concrete. Then I'm moving, quick and with purposeful strides. I hit the back door, the one no one notices off the casino floor because it's neatly tucked away behind a sign, and then I'm punching in my code and swiping my badge.

I get those three green lights and that beep and then I'm racing up the stairs, taking them two at a time. I punch in the next code and swipe my badge again and then I'm in the security tower.

We have a hundred screens taking up an entire wall. We have even more in the form of monitors, attached to computers or tablets. This is our control center where we can see any public space in this hotel in under a second, and all of it is voice-activated. We just have to say the command, and it's there. We have facial recognition, and along with that, any public information that is legally found on the internet can be ours within minutes.

We have other less legal, but not illegal, methods as well. All casinos do, don't fool yourself into thinking otherwise. Gambling is a cutthroat business responsible for hundreds of millions of dollars a year, mostly in cash. Think about that. Cheaters are everywhere. Everyone wants to beat the house and go home a winner.

"Cash—" Yeah, that's really this guy's name "—I need a face."

Cash turns away from the command board. This place is basically his home, and he rarely leaves. His discerning black eyes see absolutely everything, and this motherfucker is the definition of ruthless. He's also as loyal as they come and will keep his mouth shut about anything I ask him to do.

"Where?"

He's also a man of very few words.

"Outside the guest elevators with me. Five minutes ago."

He nods, doesn't ask any more questions as he picks up a tablet, punches in some numbers, and then his finger swipes around the screen until he gets me to where I want to be. Then he hands it to me. It's a playback of me standing there, talking to Brent.

I nod and hand it back to him. "That's the guy. I need everything you can get on him. Text it to me the second you have it."

"You got it."

His brevity almost makes me want to laugh. It might if I wasn't so fired up. What the hell is going on with this woman? Who is she? Do I dare look her up? I sigh inwardly as I pause at the exit, my eyes focused on the dozens of people working and the big monitors displaying feeds of people gambling and drinking and generally having a good time in my hotel. Do I look her up? If I thought curiosity was a nefarious bastard before, I know that for sure now.

I have no idea what this guy Brent is after with her. Does he want to hurt her? Kidnap her? Is he a hired gun? Police? No, I discount that last one immediately. Police don't dress the way he does, but he could be government. Ours? A foreign one? I have no idea how far or how deep this thing with her goes.

But I do know she's scared. That she's running from something or someone, and she'd rather work multiple jobs in a strange city and sleep outside than return to whatever life she had before. And if I had to place my bets, I'd go all in that she's a victim of regular abuse. Women don't flinch from men the way she does unless that's the case.

Do I look her up? Not yet, I decide. I'll start with Brent and see how far that gets me.

Then I have a very big decision to make.

Fiona. Shit.

I leave the security area and slowly move through the main floor.

I should go straight home, but suddenly I'm in no rush to be cooped up in my apartment with nothing but my thoughts. I could get on my bike and ride around town, but I don't want to leave her here alone until I know what's up with Brent.

That's probably not even the cocksucker's real name.

And just as I think that, I get a text. *Staying in this hotel, room 24-072, under the name Brenton Michaels. ID he showed the desk along with a copy of the credit card, attached. No other data available.*

What the hell? That doesn't even make sense. Everyone has some data to be found. Unless this guy is a professional. Or his name is as fake as Mia Jones's. But even then, his face should come up. Jesus Christ, he's a ghost.

I take a look at the photo ID. Los Angeles, California. I have no idea if this is legit or not, but if it's fake, it's flawless.

It's well after nine in the morning here, but I can't wait, so I find an empty seat in the Sports Book and make the call. It rings through to voicemail, and I hang up, but he's usually good about getting back to me. *Come on, Ryan. Call me back.*

If he does call me back, I should not be down here when he does. So, I get my sorry ass up and off the stool and make my way over to my elevator. The elevator doors open once again when I reach my place, and I'm immediately struck with images of Sunshine's sweet face staring up at me from across the counter as she ate the breakfast I cooked for her. Of the way she felt in my arms while we watched the sunrise.

I don't bother with lights. All the curtains are open, and both the lights of the Strip and the fireball of a sun give me plenty of illumination to see by.

I head for my bathroom and rinse my face, strip out of my clothes that smell like gunpowder, Sunshine, and desert. I throw on a pair of shorts and a clean tee and fall onto my bed. I'm exhausted. I haven't had a full night's sleep in months. But I'm too jazzed-up to try for a catnap now. My mind is racing. And just as I begin to settle down and my eyes finally close, my phone rings.

I have no idea what time it is, but I know it can't be that late. "Yeah?"

"It's ten-forty in the morning, Jake. I don't think I've ever spoken to you before midnight in all the years I've known you."

I smile into the sunlight invading my room. "I know. How's Seattle?"

"Well," Ryan drags out, "if you called regularly, you'd know."

"Asshole. It's not like you call me regularly, either."

"True," he laughs the word. "Seattle is great. Katie is fantastic, and if I have my way, my last name will be her last name by this time next year."

"Wow. That's…" I'm at a loss for words. My friend Ryan Grant wasn't always this commitment-minded.

"I believe the word you're searching for is awesome."

"Yeah," I say with a small chuckle. "That. I'm happy for you, man. You deserve it. I can't wait to meet her."

"Sure. Enough with the bullshit pretenses. What's going on? I'm going to assume this is work-related, but you should know, I play for the other side now. I'm all about fighting cybercrime, not contributing to it."

"And Luke?"

He chuckles into the phone again, the sound warm and welcome. "He's a gray area."

"Should I call him then?"

"I'm gonna be honest with you, Jake. That hurt. I've known you for what? Years, right? Since our very first day of freshman year when we discovered our other roommate, Tommy, was a douchebag. And you're going to call Luke, whom you've met like a handful of times? Dick move, dude."

"It's big, Ryan. Like I've suddenly found myself in the middle of some potentially big shit. I can't do this through the casino. It has to be done privately."

"Are we speaking on a secure line?"

Good question.

"I have no idea. This is not my world."

"Hmmm…it's not mine, either. At least not anymore." *Liar*. "So, here's what we're going to do. You're going to go to Walmart or some shit and buy something. After you do that, you can text me. I'll be in touch from there."

We hang up, and I rub my bleary eyes before I drag myself out of bed. I know what he's talking about. He wants me to get a burner phone. And now it seems I'm wading in deeper because a burner phone is not something I ever imagined I'd have to buy.

But that asshole Brent threatened me. Threatened to end me. He knows who I am, and he's after something from Mia. Fiona. Whatever the hell her name is. I may not know her secrets, but I do know her. I can't leave her alone and defenseless to the wolves. And this guy is definitely a wolf in sheep's clothing.

I haven't been able to stop thinking about her since the moment I set eyes on her, which I realize is only about a month ago. But so what. I see her nearly every day. We run together. We talk and joke and make-out like fucking teenagers.

I might just be falling for my mystery woman.

So, I'm going to get that burner phone. I'm going to text my old college roommate with everything I've got on this prick. And we'll see what comes up from there.

I never asked Ryan what he was into back in college. I knew. He was part of the underground hacking ring MIT had going on, and was in direct competition with Cal Tech. It's how he met Luke. Now they run a very successful information security company. But Ryan won that freaking hacking ring for a reason. He was the best.

Let's hope he still is.

Chapter Sixteen

Jake

I texted Ryan everything I have from my new burner phone four hours ago. And then I passed the fuck out. Part of me was tempted to text Mia, too. I have her number from her file, but I didn't want to freak her out and make her run. And then I felt guilty for that because maybe she should run. Maybe she'd be safer that way. Maybe I could help her do that.

Then again, if this asshole found her here, he can find her anywhere. Here, she has me. Here, she has a place to sleep and free food. Here, she has work. So, I won't scare her off. Not yet anyway.

When I wake up, I see I have a text on my new phone. Immediately, I call the number in the text. "This is Claire."

"Claire?" I ask with an unstoppable smile. "It's Jake."

"Jake," she laughs my name. "As in, Ryan's old roommate Jake?"

"Is there another?"

"One never knows, my friend. One never knows. I didn't get to be this sexy by not watching my ass." A laugh bursts out of my chest. Fucking Claire. "So, the boss man is tied up with some business crap, but he gave me a message for you."

And then she falls silent. "I'm waiting, Red."

"Jesus, give a girl a second to find it." She puffs out a breath.

"Okay, here it is. Ryan said this is a level one. As such, he's sending you a package with detailed instructions. It should be delivered…" She clicks some keys. "In like, oh, fifteen minutes. And this delivery service is never late, so make sure you answer your door when they ring."

"That's it?"

"That's it, honeypie. Well, except that since this is a level one, it's going to mean favors instead of money."

I roll my eyes at that. "Yup. I'm well aware. Tell him whatever he wants."

"Really?" she exclaims with genuine excitement. "Can I cash in on some of that action? Because I'd totally love to come and sit by the pool for a weekend. My skin has gone from porcelain to pasty."

I shake my head, unable to stop my smile. I love Claire. She's fun and just crazy enough to keep you interested. Ryan, Luke, and Claire are a team. A united front. I have that, too, but I'm hesitant to bring them in on this. At least not yet. Not until I can make some moves and shake some shit up.

"That's not part of the favor. That's a given. Whenever you want, Red. I gotta run. Talk soon. Give the big guy a squeeze for the help."

"Later, skater."

Claire disconnects the call, and I immediately hit the shower. The last thing I want is not to be ready for whatever the hell is heading my way. By the time I'm out and buttoning up my jeans, the buzzer from the elevator sounds. I run across the apartment, check the camera feed, and press the intercom button.

"Yes?"

"I have a delivery for Jake Harris."

"That's me. Come on up." I hit the button on my end, and it illuminates in the elevator, bringing this guy up to my floor. The elevator doors slide open, and he hands me a box, then hits the button for the lobby and the doors close behind him. That's it. No signature. No uniform. No other confirmation. Could this be any sketchier?

I take the package over to the dining room table, set the moderately weighted box down, and then open it up.

It's a MacBook Pro. An expensive one from the looks of it. A few wires and things that appear like they plug into the USB, including a goddamn portable firewall and a note. *If you're sure you want to proceed, turn on the computer and call the number.*

Jesus Christ. Just what the absolute fuck? *If I want to proceed*? Is Ryan messing with me or what? I know he's a paranoid bastard, but is all of this necessary? I feel like I'm being pranked. Like all of this is a joke or I'm a character in *The Matrix*. But it's not and I know that there is no going back once I make the call.

I stare at the computer and then I stare at the number on the slip of paper. No name. Just a number.

Scrubbing my hands up and down my face, I suck in a deep breath and let it out in the form of a growl. *It's just information. It's just a call.* But even as I think it, I know it's not true. This girl is scared of something very dark and sinister.

And this Brent guy is here on some sort of mission that has him making threats. Serious threats. I mean, he didn't exactly threaten to kick my ass. No. He threatened to *end* me.

So, this information is as much for Sunshine as it is for me. Right?

Right.

I dial the number first because I'm curious. I expect Ryan to pick up, but he doesn't. Luke does.

"It's about time, motherfucker," he says, chewing on something crunchy right into the microphone. God, that's annoying.

"What the hell, guy?"

"You tell me. You called Ryan in to research an asshole who we should not be researching."

"You found him?"

He lets out a derisive snort. "Of course, we did. Who do you think we are? Open the laptop, you pansy, and I'll walk you through this. Because nothing adds up, which tells me he's legit. Or he's on the stupid side and doesn't know about hacking unsecured networks, because he was talking with people on the dark web, linked into your network. But I don't think he's stupid, if you know what I mean. Accessing a computer like that is child's play. Like my goddamn baby niece could do that if she set her mind to it. And yeah, he was using a Tor browser to try and hide his activity, but it's not all that effective if you start on an unsecured network and leave your backdoor open."

"Awesome," I deadpan as I open up the laptop. "We do say it's unsecured when you log in."

"All the more reason this guy is either a fool, which he's not, or he *wanted* us to see this shit, which makes him even more dangerous. Anyway, check it out." He starts crunching into the phone again, and I set it down so I don't have to listen to it.

He wanted us to see this, Luke says. And he does. Because isn't that exactly what he said to me downstairs this morning? I'll only know what he wants me to?

What twisted game is this guy playing?

I plug in the firewall thing as well as the other stuff that's here, open it up, follow the instructions, and then a picture shows up on the screen. And a name that is not Brenton Michaels. I hit the speaker button on my phone.

"Gavin Moore?"

"Yeah," Luke says. "And that was the hard part, because his real name was the only thing on his computer that was well hidden. There wasn't much else on it, other than what he was doing on the dark web. As in, it's a clean unit, and nothing is ever that clean. This is not his regular computer."

I sigh, loud and hard, rubbing my hands over my face. A sick knot of dread twists in my stomach as my heart starts to pound.

"What was he doing on the dark web?"

"Feeling someone out mostly. He was emailing with some dude in German, using encryption software, talking about a missing girl." *A missing girl?* Jesus. I'm in way over my head now. "There was also mention of an exchange of money and a face-to-face meeting to collect the girl."

"What sort of money are we talking about?"

"No idea. It was not mentioned in the stream. What are you doing with this guy, Jake? This is not your area, man."

"He's been stalking a friend of mine," I admit as I plant my face into my hands and close my eyes. "I didn't like it, so I said something about it, and the bastard came back with more information on me than is publicly out there. And then he threatened me."

"Well," he says mid-chew, "there is a reason Ryan sent this to me. That's all I'm saying. If you need more help, I can do that."

I pause, staring sightlessly out the window toward the mountains in the distance. How deep do I want to go with this? I don't know Luke well enough to understand his level of crazy or what it really means to elicit his help.

"Not yet," I whisper. I want to talk to Maddox first.

"Okay. But be careful. This guy is not a pussycat. He will not be toyed with. If you change your mind…," his voice trails off, leaving his offer hanging in the air.

"I'll call for sure," I say, and I say it decisively. "I can't get out, but I'm not ready for the next level with this, either. It's this girl, you know? She's caught up in something, and I'm just trying to help her out."

Luke laughs. "It's always about a girl. Always. We are nothing without the better sex. My one piece of advice is that I would not roll with this guy for some piece of ass. Unless you're in love with her and she's the one and all that warm, fuzzy shit, get out now."

"Noted." But I'm not backing down. Not now. Not now that I have an idea what I'm—what she's—up against.

Am I in love with her?

Maybe.

It's a big fat fucking maybe, I realize. I might be some rich asshole who went to expensive schools and now runs a business pushing legal vices, but I'll be damned if I let this Gavin psycho get her. Hand her off in exchange for money. The man wanting her back will kill her.

Because she's not *missing*, she's *running*.

I'm setting myself and my company up for an unknown risk, all for a woman who won't even tell me who she really is. What her real name is. Stupid? You bet. But it's still not stopping me from doing this. From knowing that I'll protect her if I can.

I already know this is all going to blow up in my face. So, am I an idiot for going along with this, accepting that as a likely eventuality? Understanding I could lose her anyway?

No, I decide. I don't want that regret. I'd rather have this time with her than nothing at all.

Even if it gets the shit kicked out of me later.

"I can't say more to you, Jake. But what I can tell you is that I can help and I'm a friend. When you get to the point that you need both, let me know."

He ends the call, and all I can do is shake my head. This is big time. This is no screwing around.

Maddox. Do I want to involve my friend in this? He's former Army, like me, but he didn't check out after two years like I did. They turned him into a surveillance master. A guy at ease with walking on the shady side of life.

I pick up my real phone and call him. It rings through to voicemail and I don't dare leave a message or text him. I need to get my bearings, so I'll be able to think clearly. I stand up and walk over to the wall of windows. My eyes search along the horizon, but I come up empty. *What are you doing, Jake? Are you seriously ready to risk everything?*

What choice do I have now?

I need to get out of here. I need some heat and fresh air and wind on my face. And I need to do that with her. I don't think twice before I hit her number.

The phone rings and rings before voicemail picks up, informing me that it's not set up for this phone. Shit. My eyes scroll over to the computer sitting on my dining room table, filled with a world of waiting nightmares, and I text her.

Me: ***How do you feel about dinner and then a motorcycle ride through the desert to watch the sunset? This is Jake, by the way, in case you were confused on that one.***

I stare at the phone in my hand, touching the screen when it starts to go dark, willing her to text me back. *Text me back, Sunshine.* I do this for way too long, but then she does. That message bubble with the three dots springs up on my screen, and my smile is huge.

Mia: ***How did you get this number?***

Me: ***I'll tell you all about it over dinner.***

Mia: ***I can't.***

Me: ***You can. I'll meet you in the lobby by the west exit in twenty.***

She doesn't respond, so I take that as consent and get my shit together. I read over the crap one more time, wrap my mind around just what all of this means, remove the firewall, and shut down my new expensive toy. I lock it all away in my safe, and then I'm out the door, my leather jacket and an extra helmet in tow, even though it's hot as hell out there.

A ride and the sunset are just what's needed. I need to see her again. Talk with her. Get to know her. Then I'll decide what to do and say.

I like motorcycles. I wouldn't call myself a biker, but I like to ride. Tonight, with Sunshine behind me, is not the night to take out the racers. It's not the night to take out the really loud, vintage ones, either. Instead, I'll take out my Harley-Davidson Fat Boy S. It's pretty, comfortable with long footboards and a narrow seat. The ride is smooth and plenty fast enough for some excitement.

It's also sexy as a motherfucker.

I leave my apartment, hit the lobby, glancing around as I go, because now I'm beyond paranoid. What are you after, Gavin Moore? I mean, guys like that don't get where they are without a certain skill set. But I have things in my back pocket, too. Things he doesn't even know about. He may think he's got me pinned, but I'm far from down for the count.

Chapter Seventeen

Mia

It's amazing how quickly the body and mind forget. When I woke up a few weeks ago, I was homeless, sleeping on a lounge chair, and the thought of a man touching me in any way had me so filled with fear I wanted to vomit.

This morning, I woke up in a large, comfortable bed to thoughts of perfect kisses. And I don't like it. I don't like how quickly I've become complacent. How easily I fall back into a pattern that could lead to my death.

Don't get too comfortable, my inner voice berates me. My fingers glide across the picture of me and Niklas I brought with me as a reminder. My eyes close, and visions of that night come crashing down on me. My parents. The ball. Niklas. It was two months before my parents died, and this was the night he and I became… Niklas and Fiona. How I missed the warning signs, I do not know. Taking a deep breath in, I'm instantly transported to that night.

I've been looking forward to this night for the last four months since my father decided to throw me a ball for my eighteenth birthday. It's the first genuine thing he's done just for me. Even when I was sixteen and he threw me a ball, it was really to announce a takeover of another business. But tonight is only about me. It's also one of the only things my parents have agreed on in ages. That said, they did fight over my dress.

My father bought me a form-fitting, beaded, silver, strapless mermaid gown and my mother felt it was distasteful to reveal my curves. Said it made me look fat and that my cleavage was disgusting. The two of them went back and forth about it for over an hour until finally my mother retreated to her room because she had to take one of her pills to calm down. My father won that round, and he didn't even punish her, so I guess that's a step in the right direction.

The room is decorated in silver and white with black accents. It's beautiful and magical, and everything is sparkling. Twinkling lights, meant to match my dress, fine china, and crystal glasses.

For me. Tonight is just for me. As I enter the room on my father's arm, I can't stop the smile that lights up my face as I take it in.

"Thank you, Daddy. This is just like a dream."

"I'm glad, princess." He's never called me princess before. That brings my smile to a whole new level. My insides mirroring the warm glow of the room. "Now, remember yourself tonight. You're a Foss. You must behave like the lady you've been trained to be. I've arranged everything to my specifications. Do not *disappoint me, Fiona."*

I don't miss the threat in his voice and it takes everything in my power not to drop my gaze or cower away. The cold slap of his perpetual disappointment in me twists in my gut, superseding the warmth I had just moments ago. But everyone is watching us, so I maintain my poise and my smile, and say, "Of course, Daddy. I'll do my best to make you happy."

He nods. He knows I will. It's all I ever do. Try and fail at making him happy.

I hear my mother's sardonic scoff from the other side of my father. "She looks like a whore in that dress. There was no need to instruct her team to push up her breasts and do her hair and makeup that way."

"She looks like a young woman," my father growls out between clenched teeth, his jaw twitching as his anger over the topic refuels. "And if you utter one more word about it, I'll make you regret it."

My mother falls silent. She knows he never makes threats he's not willing to follow through on. I glance down. I don't think I look like a whore. I think I look beautiful, but my mother's words weigh on me, and I find I have to refrain from tugging self-consciously at my dress.

"Eyes up, Fiona. Never look down unless it's on another person."

My father leads me around the room, introducing me to everyone he wants me to meet. Other than the ball when I was sixteen, I haven't met anyone outside of my father's inner circle. Tonight, is different. Tonight, I meet everyone. Senators, congressmen, CEOs—even the governor of Texas is here.

Suddenly, I feel a strong hand on my upper arm, and when I turn around, I'm staring into a pair of familiar blue eyes. Blue eyes I haven't seen since Christmas. Blue eyes I've dreamt about since I was sixteen.

"Niklas," I say with a smile I can't contain, a flurry of butterflies filling my belly with nervous excitement. "I didn't know you were coming tonight."

Niklas grins knowingly at me, his eyes gliding down my dress in appreciation before they return to mine.

"I wouldn't miss your big birthday ball. You look beautiful, sweetheart." Niklas leans in and kisses my cheek.

My face heats as a flush creeps up my neck.

Winking at me, he steps around and addresses my father. "Mr. Foss," he interrupts with a confidence I envy. My father turns at the sound of his name and they exchange firm handshakes.

"Niklas, my boy. Good to see you. So glad you could make it to our little party."

"Thank you, sir. It's a special night for the Foss family, and I wouldn't miss it. I was wondering if I may take Fiona off your hands?"

My father doesn't appear surprised by the blunt question. His eyes skirt to me and then back to Niklas. And then he smiles. A real smile. One that says he likes that question. That idea. My heart soars.

"Of course, Niklas. I'm sure Fiona would love that. I've been hearing good things about your work on the White acquisition."

"Yes, sir. It's going precisely the way you designed it. I'm just grateful for the opportunity to put it all together. Should be a huge success for Foss Industries."

This pleases my father tremendously. I wonder what that feels like. I'd give anything to be on the receiving end of that look.

"Glad to hear it. And what are your aspirations beyond that?"

Niklas stares directly at me when he says, "Marriage. Family. Taking over the world."

He winks at me on that last one, drawing his gaze back to my father with a playful smirk that doesn't quite reach his eyes. My father laughs.

"And you're asking if you can take Fiona off my hands?"

Niklas nods, standing tall and proud as he stares directly into my father's steely gaze. "Absolutely, sir. She's an incredible young woman."

"I like you, Niklas. The world needs more smart-minded businessmen like yourself. Fiona is a lucky young lady for you to have taken an interest." My father removes my hand from his arm and extends it to Niklas. "Remember what we spoke about, Fiona."

"Yes, Daddy."

I bow my head to my father ever so slightly to acknowledge my understanding and will do as instructed. Niklas takes my hand with purpose, placing it in the crook of his arm. He guides us away from my father, toward the center of the dance floor. I can feel the eyes of every person in this room on us. Niklas is older than me by ten years, but he doesn't treat me like a baby. He makes me feel like a woman. Like something beautiful and special. Like I matter.

"Do you want to dance with me, Fiona?"

I peer up at him through my lashes, my face heating under his steady gaze. He always makes me blush. He doesn't even have to speak. "Yes, thank you."

"You know, you don't have to be so formal with me. We've been so very close for two years now. To the day, in fact."

I nod because I'm positive my father is watching us, and no one has a clue just how close Niklas and I have been in these two years. Niklas takes me in his arms, one hand on my lower back, his other holding mine as he leads me around the dance floor like we own the room.

"You know what this means, don't you?"

I shake my head, smiling, unable to rein in my elation as I dance with him. Niklas is a fantastic dancer. His movements are fluid and flawless. No doubt he's had the same level of instruction I've had.

"It means you're mine, Fiona Foss. It means I've staked my claim and now no other man in the room can have you. No one else can ever *have you."*

I blink at him. "How do you figure that?"

"Because your father gave me your hand, knowing my intention with you. And I have the honor of the first dance."

"Oh." I look away, embarrassed. The thought of belonging to Niklas fills me with a warmth I have no name for.

"Does that please you?"

"Please me?" I laugh, trying to hide just how much. "You make me sound

like a piece of meat. Besides, you're twenty-eight and work for my father. I don't see how one dance matters all that much."

He shakes me roughly, forcing my full attention back to him. His eyes harden, dismayed, I think, though his fake smile never falters. I frown. Maybe I should have kept my mouth shut. What if he tells my father about my insolence? I don't want to upset Niklas. He's nice to me. One of the only people I'm allowed near. I love him. He doesn't criticize me. He doesn't slap me. He doesn't make me feel like I'm nothing. He tells me he loves me, and I honestly can't remember the last time anyone else said those words to me.

"I work for your father," he sneers the words, and for a moment, I'm surprised, "so I can be near you. So I can learn his company. I have no choice if I want what's due to me. It should be mine already, but he's making me work for it. But you, Fiona, you won't make me work for it."

I don't know what to say to him. I don't quite grasp his meaning, so I stay silent, doing my best to enjoy this dance that feels like it turned on me.

"Do you remember the summer after you turned sixteen?"

"Yes," I whisper softly.

"Do you remember when I kissed you that first time?"

I nod, my face growing warmer by the minute.

"You were so sweet and young and innocent. I've spent this whole time kissing you, touching you, knowing I couldn't do more with you. Knowing I was going to have to wait and be patient before you would become mine completely."

"You're embarrassing me, Niklas. Is that what you're after?"

"No, Fiona Foss," he hums my name like it evokes something within him. Something deep and dark and forbidden. "I'm after you. *You're mine now. You've been mine since that first kiss when you were sixteen, and I was twenty-six. It's why I claimed you. You're a woman tonight, Fiona. No longer a child. I'm tired of waiting for what's been mine in secret for years. I'm going to put a ring on your finger, and we'll be everything. Foss and Vaughn."*

"And you think I'm just going to agree to that? To marrying you? What if I don't like you?" I smile so he knows I'm not serious. I like Niklas more than I've ever liked anyone. And if I marry him, he'll take me away from my parents' house. Away from my father's hand and my mother's words. Away from this prison of isolation, and out into the world. I'll make friends. Hell, I could even go to college. I could have a life. One I've been sorely missing for eighteen years.

He chuckles, pulling me into his chest a little tighter, the dancing and his promises making me dizzy. "I know you like me. You like me every time I see you. And you let me kiss you every time I see you, including last Christmas." He leans into my ear, his hot breath tickling the sensitive skin, eliciting chills. "Do you want to do more than kiss me, Fiona?"

My breath hitches.

"You're still a virgin."

I turn away from him. He's making that warmth inside the pit of my stomach spread everywhere. He growls in my ear. "I love that you waited for me, sweetheart. You're mine, and tonight, I'm going to make it happen. Tonight is the beginning for us. I've wanted you for so long." His tongue licks the shell of my ear, and I whimper. "Do you understand me? Do you understand what I'm saying?"

"Yes," I say breathlessly. "I understand you, Niklas. I'm yours."

I've never wanted to be anything more.

"Gutes Mädchen," he purrs in German, his fingers trailing up and down my back, tickling the exposed skin before dropping back to my waist. I can't describe the delight that consumes me when he praises me. When he calls me 'good girl.' I've pleased him. He doesn't want to punish me. He wants to make me his. To take care of me.

Niklas wants to marry me.

That means he loves me.

I've never been this happy in my whole life.

When I think back on myself that night, I hate what I see.

Small.

Meek.

Naïve.

Lost.

Blind.

Rarely do I have positive thoughts about Niklas or my parents. Typically, I relive my father's raised hand or my mother's vicious words. And Niklas? There are no words for what that man has done to me over the years.

Rubbing my hands up and down my face, I glance toward the window. The sun is still high in the sky, and I've been hiding in my hotel room all day. Since Jake and his kisses and the guns. Guns. I can still smell them on my hands. Am I actually capable of shooting another human being? Of shooting Niklas?

He was my first kiss. My first everything. But I never felt a tenth for him what I feel when Jake kisses or touches me.

I never lost myself in Niklas the way I lose myself in Jake whenever he simply glances in my direction.

After the night of my eighteenth birthday, Niklas made it clear he considered me his. I construed that to mean his girlfriend. And for the two months prior to my parents' deaths, that's how it felt.

We spent a lot of time together. He began coming over regularly for dinners with my family. My father promoted him to a senior executive role—his second-in-command—the day before he died. Three days after the funeral, after the will was read, Niklas took over both Foss Industries and my entire world. I wasn't given a choice in the matter.

I wouldn't call Niklas sweet, and he certainly was never gentle, but his attention and affections felt vital. Especially in the absence of any other. Like breaching the surface when you've been underwater too long. I needed him after my parents died. Or so he told me. I was lost with no life skills to speak of and he came in and took over everything. Took all my fears and worries away. And so, I entered into a new reign of intimidation. Of being controlled.

I overlooked so many warning signs. So many patterns and behaviors that should have tipped me off to his true character. Truth is, I was terrified of losing him. Terrified that if I made a fuss about all those things I foolishly ignored, he'd break his promise of giving me the world. Irony at its best.

I had nothing for myself. No money. No friends. No love.

All I had was Niklas's empty promise.

The moment my parents died, he put a ring on my finger. It wasn't flowery. It wasn't romantic. There were no professions of love or him getting down on one knee. No. It was just a step in his master plan, and I fell for it. Desperation made me gullible and stupid. Or maybe single-minded is a better way to look at it. I was out of my depth, and Niklas fed me every single line I needed to hear. He was all I had, all I knew, and I clung to him.

I told myself he loved me. I told myself I loved him.

Looking back now, I don't know if I did or didn't. I have no frame of reference when it comes to the definition of love. I've never seen it. Felt it. But I've sure as hell envisioned it. Longed for it. Deluded myself over it.

Am I doing that again with Jake?

It doesn't feel like that. It feels real with him. Maybe that's what scares me most.

My tears. I can't stop them. They bleed me dry and leave me empty. I run into the bathroom, throw open the glass enclosure of the shower and start the water to full blast hot. Steam quickly billows out, and I focus on that sound. On the sound of water slapping against the marble. On slowing my breathing.

Never again, I tell myself. *I'm safe here*, I promise myself.

Glancing around the large bathroom, I wonder if this feeling will ever go away.

Stripping down quickly, I step inside the shower and turn my face up to the stream. I'm okay. I got away. It took me four weeks after that last beating before I was healed enough, but I did it. I stole the gardener's car, and I fled.

And in the four weeks I've been here, he hasn't found me. Three more years. That's all I need. I can run and hide for three more years. I can do this.

Chapter Eighteen

Mia

After one of the longest showers of my life, I step out, wrap a towel around my body, and blow out my hair. It's too long, but I'm not about to spend any of my hard-earned money on a haircut. That's something I might have to do myself.

My phone is sitting on the nightstand next to my bed. I never use it except for internet research and when I pick it up, almost reflexively, to search my name, I find a text from Jake, asking me to go for dinner and then a ride to watch the sunset.

Sunrise and now sunset.

I really should leave town. I should pack up my meager belongings and go. My plan was to go to San Francisco, somehow find a way to procure a fake passport, and then go to Australia. That's about as far from Germany, or Texas, as you can get.

So why am I still staring at that text?

For the same reason I'm putting on jeans instead of shorts. Because weeks of running, hiding, and lying are wearing me down. So much so, that a few hours with Jake this morning has my mind going in places it absolutely should not be. Like I said, it's amazing how quickly the mind and body forget.

I don't flinch when Jake touches me anymore, and that took

alarmingly little time. I want him to touch me. I want his kisses and his coffee. I want him running with me every morning. I want his sunrises, and now I want his sunsets.

"Don't do it, Fiona," I say to myself. I haven't dared to call myself Fiona in a very long time. Not since I left.

Niklas always called me Fiona. So did my parents. The only person who ever called me Fi was my maid, and only ever when my parents couldn't hear. I lift the picture of me with Niklas once again and stare at it. Stare at him first and then me.

Jake won't hit me. How is it I know that with absolute certainty?

Maybe because he's so very different than Niklas ever was. Niklas was never gentle. Niklas never held me when I cried or made me breakfast or did anything for me. Our world was entirely wrapped around him. I went from one prison to the next so seamlessly that I didn't even see the ruse until I was in over my head.

Jake Harris Turner, you should stay away from me.

Yet, here I go. Leaving my backpack inside the hotel room. Walking away from everything I own and willingly going out into the balmy evening with Jake. A man who might have as many secrets as I do. He wants me to know him. He wants me to trust him. I sigh at that thought.

That doesn't stop me from pressing the button for the elevator. It doesn't stop me from smiling politely at the other people who join me as we descend to the first floor, and it definitely doesn't stop me as I meander my way through the casino, past the burger joint and alcoholic slushy place over to the west entrance. Or, in this case, exit.

My heart rate finds another octave as I spot Jake, dressed in a black t-shirt that hugs those muscles and tattoos like it can't get close enough, and dark low-slung jeans. He's got two helmets by his feet and a leather jacket swept over his shoulder.

"I want you to wear the leather," he says as I approach him. "You're far too pretty to have your skin marred with road rash."

"That happens frequently with you?"

He grins at me, his eyes playful as they feast on me. "Never. And tonight will not be a first."

"Motorcycles are dangerous." I guess I'm just full of irony tonight.

"Only if you don't know how to ride them. I do."

"You're very tall," I say, tilting my head and staring up at him. His brown eyes are so warm and deep, I feel I could easily get lost in them and never be found again. "That's really saying something because I'm five-nine and you tower over me. And you're strong. You're all muscles and bad-boy tattoos and dark hair, and you've got scruff lining your jaw."

His lips twitch as he tries to suppress his amused smile. He steps forward, towering over me even more than he was moments ago, further proving my point.

"Do you typically enjoy stating the obvious, or are you going somewhere specific with your blunt observations?"

"This is going to sound ridiculous, but I have to ask anyway, and I need you not to question my question."

"Um. All right," he says through a laugh.

"You said you weren't going to hurt me."

His gaze turns steely as his posture shifts from relaxed to unyielding in a flash. "Is that your question?" His voice is like a knife. Cold. Hard. Sharp. But I don't think it's for me. I think it's for the question I asked him.

"Yes."

"*Never.*" He stares directly into my eyes, that one single word bleeding from him with raw sincerity. He doesn't touch me, but I know he wants to. I feel his restraint, see it in the twitch of his hands and arms, and I think I might love him for that. For understanding what I need even if it fights with what he wants.

Jake is a good man. And he'll never hurt me.

I see it. I believe it. And I nod. "Okay. Where are we headed?"

"Dinner."

"Then where?"

"East."

"You're aware the sun sets in the west?"

"I am," he grins crookedly, "but the place I want to take you is east of here."

"Okay."

"Yeah?"

I wish he weren't so incredulous. It makes me second-guess my decision. "Yeah. What the heck."

"*Heck*?" That smirk turns into a full-on smile, complete with dimples and then he reaches out a hand for me. "Shit, you're so cute. I never stood a chance at resisting you." His arm snakes around my waist, and he tugs me into his large, warm body. My hands fly up to his chest to steady myself. "Look at me," he commands.

I obey automatically, but there is nothing punishing in his tone, and I relax into him. Dipping his head, he kisses me, holding me so close. One. Two. Three kisses, before he draws back, running his nose against mine.

"You won't regret trusting me," he breathes against me before releasing me completely.

I already do, I think. But I take his proffered arm and allow him to lead me outside. It's hot out. Like close to, if not already, a hundred degrees hot. Whoever said dry heat made the temperature more bearable was a fucking asshole. It's *hot*. There is no getting around it.

"It'll feel better on the bike," he says as we reach what appears to be a private area of the garage, and then I notice a line of cars and motorcycles. Some classic. Some new. All expensive. He guides me to a black motorcycle with chrome in just the right places. I'd be lying if I said this thing didn't make me wet. This bike is the epitome of sex on wheels. He could approach any woman on this thing and they'd happily hop on the back without any hesitation. The man riding it certainly doesn't hurt that.

I let out a small giggle at that, when something occurs to me. "Is this a date?"

"A date?" he parrots, unable to contain his grin as he quirks an eyebrow at me. "This is most definitely a date."

"Wow," I muse glancing up at the cement ceiling of the garage, thinking about that. "I've never been asked out on a date before. I feel like I should have put effort into this. Put on more makeup and done my hair differently." A date. It sort of makes me giddy.

"You've never been asked out on a date?" He's incredulous.

"Not like a real one, no. My love life was more of a setup than traditional."

He stares at me with the most befuddled expression I think I've ever seen on anyone's face before. "Right. Um." He swallows audibly, shakes himself out of his daze, and says, "Well, I think you look beautiful the way you are now. Come on," he urges. "I don't want to miss the sunset."

His colorful tattoos slip under the hem of his short sleeves that cling as desperately as ever to his large, very powerful muscles. He slides over and onto the bike effortlessly, and then reaches out a hand for me.

I hesitate. How could I not? But once his dark eyes meet mine, I know there is no going back. My hand slips into his and then I'm behind him, my arms wrapping snugly around his middle, my chest to his back.

He smells like sandalwood body wash and man and sexiness and Jake.

This moment is everything I expected it to be.

Exhilarating.

Dangerous.

Terrifying.

Electric.

Life-changing.

That last one especially, because like I said, there is no going back. More importantly, I don't want to go back. And I'm not even talking about my former life.

"Put on your helmet," he directs. "We're not going far for dinner, but the ride into the desert is a good one."

I release him to do as he commands and once I'm wrapped in leather and hard plastic that makes me feel more secure than I probably should on this deathtrap, he starts the bike, revs the engine, which is loud and so powerful my body vibrates from the top of my head down to my toes, and then we're off. I squeeze his middle and squeal out before I can hold it back.

He laughs, covering my hand that's holding his waist, patting it. "I've got you, Sunshine."

"Hands on the bike, Jake," I yell out, and he laughs harder like I'm being ridiculous.

We flow through the garage until we're outside, the Strip heavy with traffic. And every time we stop, for one reason or another, one of his hands finds one of mine, squeezing or gently caressing or just holding.

I don't think my heart has ever beat like this. His touch feels like everything I've never experienced before. Like the softest sand you can't help but dig your toes into just as the ocean rushes up to greet you. Like the most decadent dessert that both melts in your mouth and makes your taste buds scream for more. Like a cool breeze on a hot day or the sun's warming rays on top of a snow-covered mountain top.

I can't seem to get enough of it.

It takes us forever to get out of this traffic and off the Strip, but oddly enough, I don't mind. I enjoy the time, unabashedly people watching, hidden securely under the face visor and pressed against a man who should not make me feel as safe as he does. Women are dressed for a night of fun. Men are watching them with obvious lust. People are drinking. Having fun. Smiling and laughing. Walking and talking and staring at every oddity they encounter.

I mean, let's face it, women in bejeweled bikinis with feathers on their backs are not a rarity here. This city is a spectacle. But it gets in your blood and under your skin, and suddenly you find yourself staying in the last place you ever thought you'd be.

Once we get off the Strip, the streets open up, the wind on our faces, whipping against our bodies. I hold on tight, terrified to let go, yet so intoxicated I can't seem to stop smiling.

We hit a flat stretch of nothing, and I hear him yell, "Are you ready?"

"Ready for what?" I scream back, but if he responds, it's lost in the wind and the roar of the powerful engine because in the next second, we're flying, racing so fast. I scream again, only this time it's all nonsense. And if I thought I was holding on tight before, then I was so very wrong. We only do this for a few minutes before we're pulling into what can only be called a dive bar.

Jake parks his bike, cuts the engine, and then helps me off before doing the same, removing his helmet in the process. I take mine off, shaking out the wind and helmet hair.

"Don't judge, okay?"

I stare at the dirt-colored building that does not look like it's in the best repair and then back to him.

"I'm not."

"You are, and I don't blame you. It looks like a shithole, but they make the most incredible Spanish tapas here, and I swear, the inside is very different from the outside."

"Tapas?" I snort out a laugh, because this place does not look like they do tapas.

"Trust me."

That word again. Trust. It might be my least favorite word in the whole of Webster's dictionary. "Sure. Who am I to question anything on my first official date?"

He throws me a funny look before taking my hand and leading me inside. And he's right. The inside is completely different than the outside. It's…romantic and funky. The walls are blood-red velvet with various pictures of scenic Spain everywhere. The lighting is dim, but not dark, glowing from crystal chandeliers and sconces, red roses on the tables next to flickering votive candles. Multicolored beaded curtains separate the entrance from the dining area and every table is small, quaint, and private.

"This is perfect."

Which is why I do my best to push down the voice in my head that reminds me it can't last.

Chapter Nineteen

Carolina seats us at a booth in the corner. It's not all that crowded here. A half a dozen tables filled, and if you're not a local or don't know about this place specifically, you'd drive right past it without a second glance.

We're surrounded by those nineteen-seventies type crystal beaded curtains. Surprisingly, it creates a more intimate atmosphere than being a cheesy cliché.

Sunshine leans down and presses her nose into the rose adorning the table, holding her dark hair back so it doesn't catch fire in the small flame of the candle that's next to it. Her eyes close, and when she breathes out, she smiles. I can't help but watch her.

I told myself earlier in my apartment, and then again on the ride over here, that I didn't care. That her secrets don't matter to me. That I was protecting her from whatever messed-up shit had her running. But I still find myself sitting down on the crushed-velvet bench seat across from her, debating my next steps. This woman has me tied up in knots.

I'm potentially risking so much for a woman who won't even tell me her name.

And for what? A pretty face? A connection? That doesn't exactly make her the love of my life. I sigh at that. Luke said not to continue with this unless I was in love. That the risk is too great.

Love.

Is that what this feeling is? I have a connection with her unlike any I've ever experienced before. I felt it that first night in my truck, and I felt it in the bar when she first looked up into my eyes with her startled expression, and I've felt it every moment with her since.

I can't brush her off. Can't put her aside. Can't get enough of her. The idea of another man touching her makes me psychotic with jealousy. *I* want to touch her. Pleasure her. Make her smile and feel nothing but happiness for the rest of her life.

Shit.

And when she leaves in a few days or weeks or months, it will be like she never existed in this town. That's how I'll force her to be for me, too. After a few days, maybe a week or two at most, it will be like she never existed. But even as I try and convince myself of this, I know it's a lie.

She's not someone you forget. She's someone who gets under your skin and stays there. An itch that can never be scratched. The one you think back on when you're eighty and regret you didn't do everything differently with. That you didn't put a ring on her finger and make her yours for life. That's Mia.

A bitterness settles over me. *Mia*. She's not Mia. She's someone I don't even know, and my natural desire and inclination to protect her is obscuring my decision making. I won't be blindsided again.

Her eyes flit around the restaurant, taking in everything they can. My eyes don't leave her.

"Who are you, Mia?" Her head snaps in my direction, eyes wide and lips parted as she sucks in a rush of air. "I know I said it didn't matter, but it does. It fucking matters because you fucking matter and I can't do this. My eyes are always open. I see everything. But I didn't see that goddamn sniper, and I didn't see my father's heart attack and now I can't see anything beyond you. I don't even know your name."

"I'm just a girl who needed a new life." Her eyes close slowly before they reopen, and she pins them on me as she steeples her fingers, laying them against the wood grain of the table. "I get I'm asking a lot of you. None of this is lost on me. And if you want me to go, leave that hotel room and your hotel and this date, I will. I probably should anyway. Things are getting…complicated. I like you too much, and I think you like me, but I'm not someone you should like, Jake."

"I'm willing to take the risk," I tell her, knowing just how much I mean it. "And you're right, I do like you. Like you cannot even imagine. I don't need details. I don't. I just need…something." I close my eyes and drop my head back against the seat. I hate that I'm begging her. It's weak. And pathetic. And evidently ineffectual. "Christ, I don't even know what I'm saying. I don't know how to navigate my way through anymore. I just want you to trust me. I feel like if you tell me something real, it doesn't even have to be a big something, then I won't go crazy the way I've been going."

I feel her hand on my face, running along my cheek, my eyes open and I drop my chin to face her as she leans across the table to touch me. *She's touching me.* It's the first time she's initiated contact with me and the significance of it is not lost on me.

"My eyes are right on you, baby. I see you. And I feel like I'm climbing all these walls and chasing you up mountains when I'm not even sure you want me to catch you. I don't even know what I believe anymore. Just please, say something. Anything. This is never going to go our way if you can't trust me with the truth."

Sitting back, she stares at me. One. Two. Three seconds.

"My name is Fiona Ramsey-Foss."

Foss. Fiona Foss. Fiona Ramsey-Foss.

I know that name. Why do I know that name? I search my brain, threading small pieces together that eventually form into something substantial. "You're Foss Industries?"

Tears well up in her eyes. "My father was Foss Industries," she whispers achingly soft. She's an heiress. Why does an heiress run off in a shit car, get herself stranded, sleep outside, and then work in a bar in Vegas? "My parents are dead, and I want nothing to do with the life they left me with."

I don't know how to make sense of those words. "What does

that mean? You don't like the life of money and privilege they planned for you?" I realize the second those words tumble from my mouth, I shouldn't have said them. They're hypocritical, first of all. But they're also wrong. There is so much more to her story than that. Someone has been hurting her, and I have no place to judge her. "Shit. I'm sorry. I didn't mean that. I know that's not the situation."

But I'm angry at her because the only reason I know *her* name specifically, other than her last name, is the fact that I saw her picture online about four years ago and she was as memorable back then as she is now.

"You're married," I continue, the contempt in my voice unmistakable. "You're married to Niklas Vaughn. Your last name is Vaughn. Not Foss. It was plastered all over the news when you got married. I can't believe I didn't put this together sooner. So, you're running from your husband, and now you've wrapped me up in your drama."

"You don't know anything about me," she snaps, those tears running down her cheeks, and even though I'm pissed, I can't stand that I made her cry. "You read the bullshit they wrote about me in the paper or on the internet and think you've got me all figured out. Well, fuck you. I didn't ask for your help. You offered it. But maybe it's better this way." She moves to get out of the booth, but I can't have that, so I grab her arm, pulling her back down. She yanks herself free of me like my touch is acid on her skin. "Don't touch me," she hisses.

"I'm not going to hurt you."

"I trusted you," she accuses. "You asked me to trust you and I did. I told you my name and you threw it back in my face."

"You're right, I did that. I did exactly that and I'm sorry. I'm so unbelievably sorry. But I need to know…"

Her arms cross over her chest as she stares defiantly out into the restaurant. She's not running. Not yet, but it's right there. I can feel it.

"What else do you feel you're entitled to know?"

"Are you running from your husband?"

"Yes."

"Fiona?" She doesn't respond. "Look at me, please." She does, but it takes her a very long, stubborn minute. I give her that because well, I fucked this all up. "I'm sorry," I say again once I have her full attention. "I shouldn't have reacted like that. I don't give a shit your father was Foss Industries. I really don't. But I do care about the fact you're running from Niklas Vaughn. And I *really* care about the fact that you're married to the prick."

Now that I know who she is, it's going to be impossible to think of her as Mia. But I have to. I despise the fact she's Fiona Foss-Vaughn. This thing just went way beyond complicated. Niklas is the CEO of Foss Industries. And she's married to him. He also has a reputation for being a ruthless asshole. And Gavin Moore must work for him. That's who he was messaging with in German on the dark web.

Jesus Christ, this is the craziest thing I've ever been involved in, and I fought in Afghanistan, run hotels and casinos, and am friends with Maddox Sinclair.

Her lips twitch, and I find mine doing the same. Why? I have no freaking clue. "You care that I'm married, huh?"

"Yes," I tell her, no longer able to contain my grin. "I do. It's bothering the shit out of me, actually."

"Would it make you feel better if I told you he never really asked? He just put that ring on my finger and told me I belonged to him. It was all very *Princess Bride*."

"Very romantic. Sounds like a great guy."

She giggles, and I swear I've never heard a more beautiful sound. "Well, he sort of was once, which is why I didn't see it coming. But that's a story for another time. I don't consider him my husband, and I don't consider myself married. I left him and my ring behind along with my name. If it were up to me, I'd be divorced by now."

"Noted," I say, still smiling like the idiot I am, because we do this well. This fight and tease and makeup stuff. It's like we can't stay mad at each other. Even for a few minutes. "And your father's company?"

"That..." she looks away. "I can't talk about that with you. You know my family name, and you know about Niklas, but that's as far as I want to go right now."

I sigh. I hate that answer, but I respect it all the same. She's just looking out for me. At least, I hope that's her reason. She did say she trusted me, so I guess that's what I'm going with.

"Can I still take you out on this date?"

"Seriously? You expect me to sit here on a date with you? This is the worst start to a date in the history of dating."

"Probably, but you said you've never been asked out, so you really have nothing to compare it to. For all you know, all first dates start off with tears and demands."

She laughs, and I stand up, because I can't take this another second. I round the booth and squeeze myself in next to her, taking her arms and placing them around my neck.

"You have a lot of ground to make up for," she says against me.

"I know," I tell her as I kiss the spot under her ear. "I'm really sorry I screwed this all up. But I'd still like to treat you to dinner, because the food here is too good to pass up, and then I want to watch the sunset and spend the evening with you."

"But not the night?"

I draw back, catching her eye. "That an option?" I raise an eyebrow at her. Fuck all if my dick doesn't react like it is. Like it's a goddamn invitation.

"Isn't it considered slutty to have sex on a first date?"

"Not in my book, but I'm a guy, and generally, we're into slutty. That said, slutty is not a word that could ever come to mind when I think of you. Ever. And to be fair, I made you breakfast that morning. I don't count the shooting or the running, so this is sort of like a second date. You definitely have sex on the second date."

"No," she says, shaking her head. "I read in a book once that a girl should never give it up before the third date."

"I'm gonna be honest with you here." I cup her cheek, kissing her full, soft lips because they're right there and I want to, and I don't give a fuck if she is technically married. That asshole hit her. As far as I'm concerned, that voids out that forced piece of paper.

"That's a dumbass rule. In fact, I don't think it's something that should be mapped out."

"No?" she asks, her voice soft, her breaths coming out just a bit faster. Her pupils are dilated and her cheeks are flushed. God, this girl. She takes my breath away. She's the reward. The peak at the top of the mountain. The oasis in the desert. The hidden cavern behind the waterfall. The one worth fighting for.

"Definitely not." I kiss her again, sweeping my tongue in and tasting her sweetness. "I think spontaneity is the way to go."

"I've never been spontaneous. Not a day in my life."

"You should try it." I smile against her lips, before I glide across her jaw, hovering over her ear. "Makes life more fun." She shudders, and that shit drives me wild. If I don't pull back this instant, I'm going to tug her onto my lap in the middle of this restaurant for all to see. "Let me buy you dinner. Date number two. Proper date number one."

She licks her lips as she opens her eyes. "Okay."

"There will come a time with no more tears. And love and trust will not break your heart, or have you running. They'll give you strength instead of fear. They'll make you whole."

She shakes her head at me like she doesn't know what else to do. "God, Jake Turner, you might just be the best thing ever." Funny, I feel exactly the same way about her. But even as I think that, stare into her pretty green eyes and fall just a bit harder, I wonder just how dark this is going to get for us.

Chapter Twenty

Fiona

When Jake reacted to my name like it was poison on his tongue, making sneering comments about how my life of privilege was too much for me, I should have smacked him across the face and left. Because I shouldn't be here with him. I shouldn't be doing any of this. He's right. I'm technically married. Even if I don't think of myself that way.

I tried to divorce Niklas. It just didn't go so well. In fact, it nearly cost me my life.

Does it count as a marriage if the guy only married the girl for financial gain and power? If it was bred under false pretenses? If the husband physically, verbally, and psychologically abused the wife? I tend not to think so.

But being with Jake is different.

And I like it. No, scratch that, I love it. I love him holding my hand and being jealous of Niklas. I love the attention he gives me. The way he looks at me. No one in my life has ever made me feel like this. Ever made me feel like I was worth anything to them other than a negotiation tool. A commodity to be traded and used.

So, even though I shouldn't be doing this, and I know it, and Jake most definitely knows it, I can't make myself stop.

Dinner. I wasn't lying when I said I'd never been out on a real date. I was with Niklas, legitimately, for four years. Four. Freaking. Years. Four years in a relationship without one real date that didn't consist of a business dinner. Never once did he ever take me out for dinner just because. Or hold my hand because he enjoyed the way it felt. Hell, the man never kissed me unless he was planning on fucking me.

Jake kisses me like he has no other choice but to kiss me. Like my kisses are the key to his sanity.

Before I was eighteen, Niklas and I were a secret. A secret I coveted. A secret that got me through my father's maltreatment and my mother's criticisms. Niklas was the epitome of charming.

But once my parents died and he married me…well…everything changed. Looking back, I realize the day he became CEO of Foss Industries was the day he stopped being the perfect husband and turned into the monster of my worst nightmares.

But here's the thing. Niklas may be the CEO, making ridiculous money, but he comes from nothing. From less than nothing. His mother died when he was a newborn, and his father died when he was ten. His aunt brought him to the States shortly after that, and they lived in a studio apartment in the shit end of the Bronx. Money became an obsession for him. There was no such thing as enough.

Niklas does not consider himself a salary man. Not when he's surrounded by the billionaires of the world. That's where I come in, because not only do I have Ramsey money from my mother's side, but I have Foss Industries and Foss money.

Now comes the kicker. My parents' will dictated I had to be twenty-five to inherit fully.

Twenty-five. I'm twenty-two now, and since I'm married to Niklas, he's my next of kin. He'll be the one to inherit if I'm dead. It's how I know Niklas will come after me. It's how I know he won't stop until he finds me and lures me back. Because between Ramsey and Foss, well, I'm worth a lot. Enough to put Niklas at the top of any circle or power list he could ever want to be on.

But if I die before I'm twenty-five…good luck to him because that money ends up in probate, I guess. It's why filing for divorce makes me a dead woman walking. He'd rather take his chances with a dead wife and probate than let me divorce him.

I never knew if his determination with owning me was a product of financial ambition or some obscure twisted affection. And if I'm honest, I still don't.

Jake orders all kinds of food. I let him. I even smile when he does it in Spanish, even though I speak the language fluently. I like this date. He's trying to impress me, and it feels genuine. He doesn't care who I am. About my parentage or lineage. He talks to me like he's interested. He asks me questions and leans forward every time I answer like he doesn't want to miss a word that comes out of my mouth. He smiles and laughs and touches me whenever he can manage it.

As happy as I am in this moment, I'm also incredibly heartbroken.

It can't last, can it? Not when Niklas Vaughn is searching for me.

Then there's Brent.

I lied when I told Jake that he didn't say anything to me. He did. He said a lot of things. One of them was that I shouldn't discount him so quickly. That I was doing myself a great disservice by doing that.

Honestly, I wouldn't have thought much of his statement if it weren't for the way he said *disservice*. Like I was actually risking something by saying no to him. Like he knew exactly who I was and was giving me the chance to save myself through him.

And when he hugged me, he whispered in my ear that now that he'd found me, he wasn't going to let me go. That's what brought me to tears. Because it didn't feel like a threat.

It was a promise.

Jake and I don't drink any wine with our dinner. We sip on sodas and water and then after Jake pays the bill, we get back on that bike of his, riding east at a million miles per hour until we begin to trail through mountains and other small towns, until finally, we reach the Valley of Fire.

It's fairly empty here, probably because it's summer in the

desert, but Jake seems to know his way as he rides us into the park. There's an observation area off to the right, but he bypasses it and continues on the road.

"Where are we going?" I yell. It's the first time I've bothered to talk since we challenged the land speed record for motorcycles. He doesn't hear me. Or he feigns deaf because he doesn't respond.

He just drives east a little longer and then stops on the side of the road. "Here," he says, taking off his dust-covered helmet and helping me off the bike. I need to walk, so I'm grateful for the break. "This is us." He removes my helmet for me, and after I shake out my long hair, he takes my hand.

I stare in awe at the fiery red rocks and sandstone formations with brilliant contrasting colors of white, lavender, and purple. And when the setting sun hits them just right… Wow. There are no words for that type of glow. For that level of brilliance. The sun is a wonder. I now understand how this place got its name, because if I thought those rocks were red before, they are blazing fire now.

I can't pull my eyes off them until I feel Jake's fingers under my chin. He turns my face to his and then his lips are on mine once again. It's a quick kiss, but no less passionate than any before it.

"You make it hard to breathe," he says against my lips. "The sun has nothing on you."

I want to laugh at that line. Poke fun at its cheesiness. But my barb is strangled silent in my throat as I catch his expression. Hell, he means it. And my heart is in so much trouble. I don't know what to do with this. I'm a mass of conflicted anxiety. My brain is saying run. Hide. Get away. And my heart? God, it's saying so many things. It's like it's finally woken up after hibernating for years and now it's so voraciously hungry it can't be denied.

He takes my hand, and we climb some of the crazy rock formations. It's incredible, one of the most magical places I've ever been. And when I'm sweaty and tired, we watch the sun set, the way it lowers in a ball of orange fire as the mountains engulf it, swallowing it down until there's nothing left but the smallest remnants of its warmth and light.

My body is tucked into Jake's, much the way it was when we watched the sun rise, and once it's securely behind the mountains, the light takes on a different form—softer, gentler, more intimate.

He guides me over to a small patch of earth. "I have a blanket," he says. "We're really not supposed to be here after dark, but I won't tell if you don't."

"That depends on what we're doing out here."

"Having a picnic." I stare at him, and he gives me a cheeky grin like he's reading my mind. "I can be romantic. Don't let the motorcycle and tattoos make you believe otherwise."

I never will again. He lays out a blanket in a flat spot on a large boulder with a perfect western view. He helps me to sit and then does the same, holding me close as we lie against the warm stone.

"Can we forego the picnic?" I ask hesitantly, not wanting to ruin the special moment he planned for us. "You just stuffed me beyond capacity."

"We didn't have dessert, but if you prefer to do that back in civilization, I'll understand."

"Civilization? Like your balcony?"

He rolls over to face me, propping his head up with his hand and grinning so big I can see his white teeth in the paltry remnants of daylight.

"Yeah. Like there. I'll happily feed you dessert there if you want."

"I don't know," I say as my eyes take in all the spectacular nature around me. The stars are just starting to come out, and already that show is something else. "I sort of like it here."

"Yeah?"

"Yeah."

"How's this then? We lie here until it's good and dark, which won't be much longer, and then we go back to my place. I cooked you breakfast, but I'm kick-ass at pouring chocolate sauce over ice cream."

"Is that right?"

"Without a doubt."

"And what if I like caramel?

"Shit," he laughs, hugging my body against his and locking those eyes on mine. "I don't have any of that." He grins impishly, and my stomach dips. "But give me a chance, and I'll give you whatever you desire."

Oh, I just bet he will…

Chapter Twenty-One

Jake

I don't want to take her back to my place. I mean, I do. I'm dying to get her alone in my apartment again. But I also don't. I want to take her up in a helicopter, so she can experience the Strip and the mountains from the air. I want to take her to a private dining room in a five-star restaurant. I want to take her to a premier show and have us sit front and center.

And if she were just any other girl I was trying to impress, I'd do all of those things.

But she's not just any other girl. It's why I'm glad I took her to Cuchi Cocina. It's why I love that I took her to the Valley of Fire. She's dined in the best restaurants. She's flown in private planes and helicopters. She's been to the best shows in the world, I'm sure of it.

But this is her first real date with a man. And I don't think anyone has ever held her while they simply watched the sunset. And I don't think anyone has ever put her on the back of a motorcycle. I bet no one has ever made her a damn ice cream sundae before because it's too prosaic for the likes of Fiona Foss. *Vaughn*, I correct myself. Shit. That one sucks.

But fuck all that other crap. These are the best kind of dates. The very best of moments, and I'm spending them with her.

My father might have been in the same class as hers, financially speaking at least, but that's not how I was raised. My mother was an elementary school teacher, and yes, my father did pay child support growing up, but I lived in a small two-bedroom house. I went to public school in a Baltimore suburb and shot hoops at the town courts.

I didn't grow up the way she did. My mother made sure of that. She wanted me to be a normal kid, and now, more than ever, I'm grateful to her for that.

I never turned into a Niklas Vaughn. I don't know his background, but an obsession with money never dictated my life the way I bet it does his. I may have money now, but I know how to walk, how to live, on the real side of town. It's where I'm most comfortable if I'm being honest. It's why I still ride motorcycles and only wear expensive suits when I have to. Give me a pair of jeans and a t-shirt and I'm a happy man. Give me ice cream out of the carton with chocolate sauce instead of a soufflé or expensive pastry any day.

I think Fiona is like this, too. I think she wants simple. Easy. I can be that with her. I'm just not sure she'll let me.

But right now, with this woman, I'll take whatever I can get.

We don't linger much longer. It's dark as hell, and I have no idea what sort of wildlife lurks out here. I get on the bike and help Fiona do the same, and then we take off, heading back west toward the bright lights of Las Vegas.

Tonight might have been one of the best nights of my life, and hopefully, it's not over yet.

That doesn't stop my mind from going back to Gavin Moore. What am I going to do about him? I'm at a disadvantage, I realize. Because he's got a purpose and I'm not exactly sure what it is. I mean, I can guess, right? I assume he's after Fiona. I assume he's working for her husband. But is he here to take her back to him? To kill her? And when does he plan to do this? Is he bringing her husband here to Vegas, or is he kidnapping her?

I hate unknowns.

But that's what everything with her feels like. An unknown.

I have work tomorrow. I'm a pit boss for a few hours, and I'm wondering if it's worth trying to find Maddox to tell him what's going on. What I'm involved with.

I stop at a grocery store and Fiona and I run in for ice cream and caramel sauce. She's a Phish food girl, evidently, though it took her the better part of ten minutes to pick out a flavor she liked. I don't think she's ever had Ben and Jerry's before. I'm a New York Super Fudge Chunk guy. Not a dealbreaker, though. I can live with Phish food. I still bought both, because I want her to try mine.

We make it back to the garage at the hotel, and I park the bike in its usual spot. I help her off, and I take her hand and the bag of ice cream, and we walk, hand in hand, back into the hotel, through the casino and over to my elevator.

"I have work tomorrow morning," she says, her voice quiet. I wonder if she's as exhausted as I am. I feel as though I haven't slept in years.

"At Rhe Bistro?" She nods. "I have work tomorrow, too." She glances up at me. "I'm a pit boss for a few hours."

"Then maybe I should go so we can get some sleep?"

I shake my head. "No. This date is not finished until we've had dessert."

The elevator doors part for us, and I tell her to go out on the balcony while I make the sundaes. She doesn't argue, but she is more subdued than she was when we were watching the sunset.

Her mind is working. Her wheels are spinning, and I know she won't tell me why, no matter how hard I press. Time. It's running out on me. At least, that's how it feels. Like I'll blink, and she'll be gone.

Everything feels like it's moving in fast-forward. Or maybe it's just the contrast to how slowly my life was moving before. Before Fiona, my life was predictable. I'm not even saying that as a bad thing. It was just…life. I went through the motions, but emotionally, I was disconnected from it all.

And now? Now, everything seems to be coming at me all at once. All because I pulled over to help a stranded car on the side of the road.

I walk outside, the warm night air brushing across my face as I find her all the way down on the far side by the pool.

"This is nice," she says, reaching in to touch the glowing blue water. "And warm. It's like a bath."

"Unfortunately, it gets like that in the summer. The sun heats it all day."

"Vegas feels hotter than Dallas, and Dallas gets plenty hot."

"Then this should help cool you down." I hand her the bowl of ice cream and then I take her hand and lead her over to a lounge chair. We sit, staring out at the lights of the Strip while we eat in companionable silence. I don't have anything to fill it with right now, and I think she's there with me. We've breached the gap instead of falling into the abyss. I know her. I know her story, for the most part. I know who she is, and she knows who I am, and we're still here, in this together.

"I have to leave town," she whispers, and my heart sinks. Maybe I was wrong about that last thought. "The longer I stay, the more vulnerable I am. The more vulnerable *you* are."

I think on that for a moment. Let it settle. When I realize I don't give a shit, at least about me, I say, "I don't want you to leave."

She sighs, and it sounds like longing. It sounds like heartbreak. "I don't want to leave, either."

"I can keep you safe, Sunshine. I can. You just have to trust me." She shakes her head, her chin trembling and her green eyes growing glassy with her unshed tears. "Stay with me. Don't go." I cup her face in my hands, forcing her to see me.

"Jake," she whispers, but I cut off her protest with my mouth.

I kiss her. Hell, I kiss her like I've never kissed a woman before. Because this is the kiss. The one that changes everything between us.

I slide my tongue against hers, invading her mouth, tasting what can only be described as pure heaven. I command every inch of her as my fingers thread through her hair and down her body, cupping her ass. I lift her, moving her over the arms of the loungers until she's straddling me.

"Please," she begs, and that word, coming from her sweet

mouth, does something to me. It makes me fucking insane. It makes me hers.

One hand tangles in her hair, holding the back of her head, the other is on her waist, but I feel myself trembling against her. *I'm trembling*. The sensation is so completely foreign, then I realize she is also trembling, because this is so much more than kissing and touching.

"Please what, baby? Tell me. I'll give you anything you want."

She draws back and searches my eyes before she rolls her hips slowly into my rock-hard cock. My eyes close momentarily as pleasure surges through me.

"You, Jake. I want you."

I grab the back of her head and slam her down, our lips crashing together. It's messy and hot, all teeth and lips and tongues. I want to consume her. I want to claim every inch of her body. Her mind. Her heart. She's mine.

And I protect what's mine.

"Fiona," I breathe against her.

She shakes her head. "Mia."

"No." I pull back, meeting her eyes, holding her face in my hands. "When we're alone, like this, you're Fiona. Or Sunshine. Or maybe Fi, because that's kind of cute and somehow fits you."

She blinks at me. "I'm not sure I want to be Fiona Foss anymore. I certainly don't want to be Fiona Vaughn. I like being Mia Jones. I like being your Sunshine."

"Fiona Ramsey-Foss—" *Because I will not call her Vaughn* "—is the most beautiful woman I've ever seen. The most incredible woman I've ever met. She's so fucking strong. So much stronger than she realizes or gives herself credit for. You should always want to be her. Always."

A tear rolls down her cheek, and I reach up to swipe it away. This is not about tears. This is about her, and she needs to understand that I mean absolutely every word I'm saying.

"You mesmerize me, Fiona. You've woken me up and brought me back to life. There is no going back now."

"I'm a mess," she half-sobs.

But I'm smiling. Because this is one of those moments. One of the goods ones. One that should not be overlooked or brought down by crying.

"Good. Because I am, too."

She smiles back at me, and I swear, she's never looked more stunning. My breath actually catches in my chest, and my heart stutters out an extra beat.

"Then I think you should kiss me. I think you should kiss the hell out of me, actually, until I can no longer speak or think. And then I think I'm gonna need you to make love to me, Jake Turner."

Christ. "I can do all of those things."

"Thank God," she laughs, wiping at her remaining tears, before lowering her face back to mine. I kiss the hell out of her, because she asked me to. I kiss her until she's not talking, and hopefully, her brain has shut off for the night. Our tongues tangle and dance, passion and heat flowing between us, swirling around us before it rises up and dissipates into the Las Vegas night.

My hands slide up the back of her shirt, feeling the silkiness of her skin. I've been dying to touch her. Dying to watch her as I make her come with my body. My cock is so hard, I can hardly stand it.

But she asked me to make love to her.

Not fuck her.

And there is a difference. I might have never experienced that particular distinction before, but I sure as hell am now. Any asshole with half a brain can fuck. Only a man who knows the worth of the woman he's with can make love. She's placed so much trust in me tonight, and I refuse to break that.

Because one thing is certain.

She's not leaving. No goddamn way.

I kiss her harder, her body wrapped up in mine. Pulling her shirt over her head, my mouth glides down the smooth column of her neck, nipping and sucking as I go, taking my time to worship her. My hand cups one of her perfect breasts, squeezing gently, but hard enough so she moans, throwing her head back as I rub my thumb across her puckered nipple, straining through the lace of her bra.

"Jake, yes."

I growl before I can stop myself. "Say it again."

"Jake," she pants my name, rocking her hips into me. "Jake, yes."

Jesus motherfucking Christ. "God, I love it when you say my name like that."

"If you want me, Jake, don't let go. I'm so unsteady. So out of my depth. I don't want to fall."

I stare into her eyes. It's dark out here, but it's also not. It's moody. Hazy. But I see her. I see her, and she's asking me not to let her go. To hold her and make sure she doesn't fall.

"I promise, I won't let you go." She blinks at me, the desperation in my voice, in her expression is making me high. "But I want you to fall, Fiona. I want you to fall hard. I want you to fall so hard there is no turning back."

She doesn't respond. And for a moment, she looks torn. Stricken. Terrified. But if there is no going back for me, there sure as hell is no going back for her.

I'm in this. She's in this. And we're leaping together.

I roll our bodies over, her on her back and me covering her. She shivers, her skin touching the cool fabric of the lounger. Her hands grasp the hem of my shirt, tugging it up. I reach behind my neck and grab the collar, yanking it over my head and tossing it aside. Her eyes rake me in, covering every inch of my chest, arms and abs. Tentatively, she reaches out, wanting to touch me, yet afraid to. She undoes the buttons of my well-worn jeans, her fingers trembling as she goes.

It might be my total undoing.

How can one woman be this sexy? How can I be this turned on by one simple gesture?

"Lie back. Eyes on me," I command, my jeans left undone, sitting low on my hips. I strip her down completely, leaving her bare beneath me. "So fucking beautiful," I whisper as I take her in, because damn, she's a sight. Large—but not too large—breasts with perfect pink nipples. Slender, taut stomach that slopes into the curve of her hips and her bare pussy and then down into her legs. And damn, those legs. I've had far too many fantasies about those legs.

I lower myself down, my body sinking into her softness, basking in her warmth. My eyes close quickly, before reopening, needing to see her, watch her.

My fingers caress a trail down her body, my eyes following the path. I pinch her nipple, roll it between my thumb and finger. She whimpers, wiggles just enough so I know she likes it.

Lower. Lower. Until I'm pressing two fingers into her wet pussy and finding her swollen clit with my thumb, rubbing it in slow circles. A moan escapes the back of her throat as her body bows, arching and pushing down on my fingers.

Hell, that's hot. She's writhing beneath me. She can't stop moving. I've never felt this sort of sensation before. This incredible build. This insatiable need. I'll never get enough of her. Ever.

She's it for me, and she doesn't even know it yet.

"Do you trust me?"

"Yes," she pants, and the speed of her answer makes my heart soar and my cock grow harder.

I give her a wicked grin, the coarse stubble on my jaw following the same pattern down her body as my fingers. I part her thighs, stare at her pretty, glistening pussy, and drop my face.

"Ah! Oh my God, Jake." Her fingers fly down, gripping and yanking my hair, like she's unsure if she wants to pull me closer or push me away.

My mouth explores her. Tastes her. Licks her. Sucks her clit in and laps up her sweetness until she's fucking my face with abandon and screaming so loud I'm sure all of Vegas can hear. Her pussy clamps down on my fingers as she comes, her face an exquisite picture of pleasure.

I crawl up her body, kissing and licking as I go. I can't seem to stop. I can't get enough. A satisfied grin etches on my face, and she's most definitely echoing it times a million.

"What was that?"

I laugh, nuzzling my nose against her cheek. "The first of many."

"I've never had an orgasm before." She blushes furiously, her face turning away from me ever so slightly with her embarrassment. "I mean, not from someone else."

I groan out something unintelligible, and then my mouth is on her, kissing and nipping and exploring, my tongue swirling with hers.

"Taste yourself on me, Sunshine. Taste your first real orgasm." She moans, and my blood roars in my veins. "I'm really glad you find cavemen sexy, because you telling me I'm your first, makes me want to beat my chest like one. You have no idea what that does to me. I'm going to give you everything that other asshole couldn't. I'm going to ruin you, Fiona, for any other man."

My hands cup her breast, my lips skimming and licking the swell.

"I need you inside of me, Jake. Please."

I let out a shaky breath, my hooded eyes feasting on her. "I thought you were beautiful before," I whisper, suddenly overwhelmed in a way I never expected to be. "But God, you're so much more than that. I don't think words have been invented to describe women like you. Stunning and perfect just don't seem adequate." My mouth covers her nipple, licking and sucking. It drives her wild. She's crazed, scraping her nails down my back, leaving marks I wish I could see.

Before she can say or do anything else, I'm pulling down my jeans and wrapping myself in a condom I snagged out of my wallet. Her hands go to my shoulders and glide down my chest like she can't touch me enough. Like she needs to learn every surface of my skin. I'm right there with her. But the second I cover her with my body and sink deep inside her, she no longer cares about any of that.

"Are you ready for me, Fiona?" I ask, freezing my body in her incredible heat. God, she feels so good. "Tell me, baby. Tell me you want me as much as I want you. I'm nuts about you. I'll never get enough, and this is only the beginning."

She nods, blinking her eyes up at me. "This is so…" She pushes out a breath. "I'm so… Take me. I'm yours."

That's all I will ever want to hear.

I pump into her, pressing her down into the lounge chair that creaks in protest with every move we make. I kiss her, touching her wherever and whenever I can. We both moan, loud and long, because this is so insanely good. Mind-blowing. I had no idea it could be like this.

We move together like our bodies were made for each other. She meets me thrust for thrust, sweat lining my brow and gliding down my back. Her mouth comes up, kissing me, taking me deeper into her body as she wraps those legs around my waist.

I'm fucking her. I'm making love to her. I'm everything in between with her.

I feel my climax building, but I hold off, not daring to go near the precipice until she falls first. And just as I think that, she begins to tremble, shaking uncontrollably, her pussy squeezing like a vise grip on my cock so hard I see stars. Her nails claw at my shoulders, somersaulting me over the edge until I can't help but let go, her name an expletive on my lips.

Panting heavily, I lean in on her, but I'm too tired and weak to move.

"Am I crushing you?"

She shakes her head, her nose rubbing against mine.

I draw back once I'm able to see straight. I won't lie, it takes me a while to get there. Standing upright, I dispose of the condom and am back on the lounger with her in an instant.

"Come here," I say softly, bending down and picking her up into my arms. I cradle her against my chest and drop back into the chaise, holding her close, my nose pressed into her hair. "That was incredible," I whisper against her. "Are you okay?"

She nods, meeting my eyes, her unstoppable smile telling me everything her words can't. Our eyes lock, heat swelling from within me, and then I roll her on top of me, desperate to watch her ride me.

I'm hard again already. This girl. Fuck.

She sinks down on me, fucking me. Taking what she wants. What she needs.

And when we're done, when we're both sweaty and smiling and

completely out of breath, I kiss her, wrapping her body up in mine. I've made love to her twice, but I can't stop kissing her. I've never been intimate with a woman before. I've fucked plenty, but I've never been *intimate*. There is a difference. I realize that now, here, with Fiona.

But I need the rest of her story. There are things present that are bigger than both of us and I have to know what I'm in for.

Because I am in for it. I could care less that she's a billionaire's daughter. I could care less that she's technically married to another man, though she swears to me she's left him and that life far behind.

I've fallen in love with her.

That should scare me. But it doesn't.

The only thing about Fiona that scares me is losing her.

And as our kisses grow from urgent and passionate to sweet and languid, she sinks into me further. I pull back and just look at her, my eyes gluing to her heavy ones. She's wrecked. I smile softly at the woman in my arms, press my lips to the tip of her nose, then her forehead, then her lips.

I bundle her up in my arms to keep her warm against the desert night, and she lets out a contented sigh. We fall asleep together on the balcony like this. In this interlude we find ourselves trapped in. It's perfect.

So why do I have the sinking feeling everything is falling apart instead of coming together?

Chapter Twenty-Two

Jake

"It was a sniper," I tell Fiona as my fingers caress the soft skin of her collarbone and chest. Everything about tonight feels surreal. I don't even necessarily know why, it just feels like something out of a dream. Like I died and went to heaven, and when I got there, God said, here you go. You can have this woman because you've been a good person.

But the irony of that is I can't have her. Not really anyway. This will all come tumbling down on both of us. It's just a matter of when.

We passed out on the balcony, but when I woke up at two in the morning, freezing my balls off with her snaked around me like a vine, I picked her up and brought her into my bed. We didn't fall back to sleep, though. We've been up talking since, even though neither of us has had much sleep lately. I don't care, and neither does she.

"A sniper?" she parrots softly, her fingers tracing the raised scar on my shoulder.

"Yeah," I say, looking deeply into her green eyes that are now more the color of a forest in the paltry light of my room. "Not the worst wound to get, I guess."

"And this?" she asks, playing with the lines of the tattoo on my left peck above my heart.

"Believe it or not, my father was an incredible artist. I've had this image since I was a boy. My father gave it to me on a card for my eighth birthday. He was always drawing. After I enlisted in the Army, I drove to this well-known tattoo parlor in Baltimore, because that's where I was living at the time, handed the artist this picture and told him to ink me up."

"Is this his name?"

I shake my head, my eyes glazing over as I remember the day I had that done. I'd been home from Afghanistan—well, the hospital in Germany—for a week when I attended the funerals of two of the soldiers who died the day I was shot. All I could see were their dead eyes.

They eclipsed everything. They haunted me. I couldn't shake it.

I wanted to die with them for a while. One left behind a pregnant girlfriend and the other had a wife and a son.

Me? I had no one. I mean, I had my parents, both separately, but it wasn't the same. Watching those families weep over their fallen soldiers? Shit. Guilt is a possessive bitch. She clings onto you when you need her least, and holds on as she rides you to a hell of self-loathing and self-destruction.

"No. I did this after," is all I say because I don't know how to talk about that. It's been nine years, and I still haven't accepted it.

She nods, leaning in and kissing their names. I shudder, a lump forming in the back of my throat. We're quiet for a few moments. Contemplative. Both lost in our worlds.

"Tell me about your last girlfriend."

A rumbling chuckle bolts past my lips as I scrub a hand over my face. "You want to hear about my last girlfriend?"

"Yep. I do."

"Why?"

"I'll tell you after you tell me."

I chuckle again, running my fingertips up and down the bony prominences of her spine. "Her name was Kerith. She was smart and pretty and kind and more of a loner than I was. I dated her at Wharton for about a year."

"What happened?"

I shrug. "We graduated. She got an offer from a large accounting firm in Miami and I didn't give a shit enough about business to apply for anything. She was ambitious, and I wasn't. She left, and I didn't try to stop her or go with her."

"Huh," she says.

"What?"

"That was a while ago, right? I mean, you didn't just graduate."

"No. That was a few years back now."

"No girlfriends since?"

I cringe to myself. "No," I admit. "I didn't particularly want one. I dated, some girls longer than others, but I wasn't big into commitment."

"Hmm…"

"I was just lost, Sunshine, and didn't want to bring a woman into my mixed-up world. Or head, for that matter. But once my father died, everything changed. I became focused. Driven. I'm good at this job, and I like it."

She tilts her face to find mine in the darkness as if challenging me.

"Fuck that, I love it. I really do. It's just…fun, you know?" She smiles, but it's half-hearted. I cup the side of her face. "Don't let my past experience with women make you wary of me now. I'll be yours if that's what you need from me."

"Mine?" she giggles. "You barely know me, Jake Turner."

I shake my head. "I know you Fiona Sunshine Foss. I know you," I repeat, because I do. My consciousness recognizes hers. Two lost souls that somehow found each other. "I know you blush easily. You bite your lip to hide your smile. You're right-handed but can do pretty much anything lefty, too." I cup her jaw, caressing her cheek with my thumb. "You're smart and a fast learner. You genuinely like bartending but hate waitressing. You're in phenomenal shape and can outrun me if you wanted to. You're a shitty shot but have a competitive nature you don't feel comfortable showing. You're from

Texas and when you get agitated or scared, your accent comes out thicker. Pink is your favorite color, because you wear it whenever you're not in your uniform. You like chocolate ice cream with caramel sauce." I kiss her softly, rub my nose against hers. "You feel lost and alone, even when you're surrounded by people." She lets out a shaky breath at that last one, like she's been holding it the entire time I was talking. "I know you, Sunshine, because you're my girl."

"Your girl." She shakes her head. "That seems so…barbaric. And yet so very perfect."

I kiss her. I kiss her swollen lips and claim them as mine. I claim her. She *is* my girl, and I'm keeping her. Even if that makes me sound like a two-year-old. No going back. No hiding away. I'll take on her prick of a husband and disembowel him like the pig he is.

"He's going to come for me," she states as if reading my mind, unable to even meet my eyes. She's staring down at the tattoo on my chest, still tracing the lines with her finger. "Niklas was never grounded. Never rooted in place. Gravity flows through him, making him believe he owns it like he does everything else. Like he can manipulate it to his every whim and walk on water if he so desires. He grew up poor and found us with a plan. Money. Niklas never wanted me. It took me far too long to figure that one out. He wanted the Ramsey-Foss fortune. He saw me, and he saw his ability to take over Foss. He swept me off my feet with flowery words and attention I was starved for. But there was never any truth to his lies. Then my parents made a fatal mistake. At least for me. Their will dictates I don't inherit the main part of the estate until I'm twenty-five. It's more than just money, though. I hold sixty-two percent of Foss Industries. I could run him off the map, but not until that point. Until then, he's the CEO. He's the one in charge. In three years, everything changes." She blows out a steady breath like just getting all that out was painful, before she finishes it up with, "He's going to find me and take me back."

"How come you never went to the police?" I realize it might be a stupid question, but I have to ask.

A bubble of laughter flies out of her mouth. "It wasn't an option for me. First, it would have looked bad on Foss Industries, and I wasn't raised to air our dirty laundry out for all to see. That may sound like a bullshit excuse, but it's not like anything would have been dealt with privately. The press would have been all over me, and in case you missed it, female victims are forever seen as the culprit. It also wouldn't have done anything. Foss Industries, with Niklas as the CEO, donates over a million dollars a year to various police charities. He's been pulled over at least a dozen times for speeding and never once been issued a ticket."

She falls silent, and I tilt her chin up until she finds me. "And?" Because I know there is more.

She stares at me, deflating as oxygen passes her lips. "And the one time they came, the one time I called them, they saw the bruises on my face and body, and didn't even arrest him. They gave me medical attention in our home and then left, telling me they couldn't do anything unless I filed a restraining order, which I believe is a lie. I asked them what that entailed, and they explained if I had one, and he came within the boundaries of that order, they could hold him or temporarily arrest him. That's it. If we were married and living together, all bets were off. Niklas proceeded to beat me unconscious after they left, warning me if I ever called them again, he'd kill me."

Christ. What the police did is not even legal. "We'll just have to tell him he can't have you back," I promise, holding her face in my hands, making sure she believes me because I will never lie to her. I will never let her down, and I always keep my promises. Always

Fiona leans in and kisses my lips softly. "I want to be just like you when I grow up."

I laugh, rolling her so she's on top of me again, her glorious soft tits pressing into my chest. Her warm body flush with mine. My cock stirs to life. It's late, or early, depending on how you look at it. I haven't had a decent night's sleep since she blew into town, but I don't want to go to sleep. I want to stay awake and talk to her and make love to her and tell her things I've never told anyone before.

Fuck it. You don't get too many of these moments with someone, and I will not squander it.

"What else do you want to be when you grow up?"

She looks down at me, her face hovering inches above mine. She's smiling. I like this Fiona best, I realize. Happy. Vibrant. Playful.

"When I grow up, I want to be a professional swimmer," she says this so seriously I can't help but grin. "And I want to help women and children who come from abusive homes. Be a social worker who specializes in that. And I want to destroy men like my father and Niklas who believe because they have money, nothing and no one can touch them. And I want to be happy. Right now, I smile, but really, I'm just crying through it."

I reach up and press my lips to hers. "What else?" I whisper against her.

"I want to be a good mother and wife one day. I want to hold my child's hand when I walk them to school. I want to be on the PTA and make homemade brownies for bake sales. I want to grow a garden and cook delicious food with the things I grow. I want to be good at something. I want to matter to someone."

"You matter to me," I interrupt her without filtering myself. "And the rest of that, well, I don't see why you can't do all that. Except for being a professional swimmer. That might be off the table."

She shakes her head. "I'm a really good swimmer."

I laugh, kissing her nose. Her cheeks. Her eyelids as they flutter closed. "I guess you can be anything you want to be when you grow up."

"Maybe," she muses. "But all anyone sees when they look at me is money. It's like having cancer or being a movie star. That's all I'm known for, and it's all they think about when they speak to me. I'm not just Fiona; I'm Fiona Ramsey-Foss, the billionaire's daughter. Or worse, Fiona Foss-Vaughn. The heiress. The woman on the arm of Niklas Vaughn. And I'm not asking for sympathy. I realize many people would kill to have the resources I have, but there is nothing glamorous about my life. It's mostly pain and heartbreak."

"Then it's a good thing you ran away."

"Guess so," she smiles.

"Just so you know, I don't see money when I look at you. I wouldn't care if you were the Mia Jones I met weeks ago on the side of the road and didn't have a penny to your name. I'd still like you."

Her smile shines bright in this dark room. Fi rubs her nose against mine. Releases a deep contented sigh. "I like you, too. And I'm really glad you didn't rape and kill me that first night. You're a lot hotter than Leatherface."

I pinch her side, making her squeal and squirm. I kiss her hard because I can. Because she's mine. For now, at least. Time, right? It's out to get us all.

"I'm afraid of falling for you," she admits, her cheeks growing warm, but her steady gaze does not waver.

"It might be too late for me."

She shakes her head against me like I'm not getting it. "It's dangerous for you, Jake. For Turner Hotels. Niklas will stop at nothing to bring me back. If he ever knew I was here with you…" She shakes her head again, her eyes as grave as I've ever seen them.

"So, he owns everything now?"

"*Runs* everything. He doesn't own anything. It's all in a trust, waiting for me to take over. And he's restricted as hell now, thanks to my parents' will. I haven't signed a will making him my beneficiary. But he's been pushing for it recently."

"Jesus, Fi."

"Yeah. He might try and kill me."

The words sound like they're meant to be taken in jest. But her tone is goddamn serious. I can't begin to imagine uttering words like that. Believing your husband is capable of killing you. Of wanting you dead. How does a person reconcile that? I honestly have no idea. And how is she lying here with me, smiling and sweet and so fucking good? God, this woman. She astounds me with her strength.

Sitting up, I cup her face in my hands. "You're here now. And you're safe."

"He'll ruin your life," she states, almost like she's thinking aloud. But then her words turn to a warning. "When he finds me here with you, he'll make sure he takes away everything you have."

"Are you trying to warn me off?"

"I probably should be."

Dipping my head, I kiss her. I kiss her like I've never kissed her before. Because this is the one that counts the most. "You're worth the risk. And I can more than handle myself."

"That's what all the heroes say before it all falls apart."

Chapter Twenty-Three

Fiona

"Where are you headed dressed like a bible salesman?"

Jake's wearing a suit, and not the nice suit I saw him wearing that morning I bumped into him. This one has a black jacket that looks like it's moaning in protest as it desperately clings to his muscled arms, shoulders, and back, black pants, white shirt, and a red tie. He looks like he's going to a Christmas party or a funeral.

He chuckles, reaching for his coffee and taking a sip. The mug he's drinking from this morning reads, "You're all fucking idiots until I've finished this." It made me laugh so hard when I saw it, I actually sprayed my coffee out across his counter. Not my finest moment. My mug has a picture of Yoda and it reads, "Coffee I need or kill you I will." I mean, who has mugs like this? I realized something very important this morning. Jake, this gorgeous, sexy, tattooed, mysterious man, is a closet nerd.

I think it might be the hottest thing ever.

"Work. Not at the restaurant. I'm a pit boss at The Turner Palace down the Strip."

"Oh," I say, sinking back into my seat. His eyes bounce down to my lips like he's reliving our kisses from very early this morning in his bed, and I feel the color begin to rise in my cheeks.

"I'm a pit boss, a bouncer, and a waiter, remember?"

"Yes," I say, trying to hide my smile behind a forkful of eggs. "I remember. I just didn't realize pit bosses dressed like that."

Jake woke me up obscenely early this morning because he wanted to make me breakfast again. I have to get going. I have to be at The Bistro at seven-thirty. It's almost six-fifteen now, and I need to shower and change into my miserable uniform. But I don't want to leave. I like it here. He's making it impossible for me to run and never look back. Everything this man does pulls me in deeper.

He leans against the counter, propping his elbows up on the cool, marble counter and pins me with a gaze that instantly has me swarming with butterflies.

"Will I get to see you again later?"

I hesitate. I really should say no. I not only had sex with him, but I stayed the night, sleeping in his arms.

"Let me rephrase. I want to see you later. I have a crazy day tomorrow with one meeting after another, and then you're working in the bar by the time I finish. So please, Sunshine, spend the evening and night with me again."

"Okay," I say softly because there is no way I can say no. That took alarmingly little persuasion. I'm in way over my head with Jake. With his kisses. With his passion. With his promises of safety. How am I supposed to say no to something that feels so good?

His phone rings from the other room, and he throws me a wink. "Be right back."

Jake runs across the apartment to grab his phone, and I decide to be helpful and do the dishes. Something I've never done before. I turn on the water at the sink, pick up a sponge, add some soap, and get started on the pan.

"Hey there," a deep male voice rumbles behind me, a firm finger tapping me on the left shoulder. I startle, dropping the pan into the sink with a loud clang.

Spinning around, I slam into a beast of a man. He's a solid nine inches taller than me and easily two-hundred-and-fifty pounds of muscle. It's not Jake, and I scream out the loudest, shrillest sound I can manage. I can't even look up at his face. That's how terrified I am right now. He lifts the thick meat-hooks he calls hands, coming directly at me like he's going to shut me up.

Before he can grasp my shoulders, or my neck more likely, I raise my knee as hard as I can, connecting with his balls. The behemoth lets out a loud howl of pain, grasping his groin and staggering back away from me. I kick him in the side with my foot and he drops to the ground, his head narrowly missing the marble of the island. He falls hard, curling up into a fetal position as he continues to groan.

But as he was falling, I realized my mistake. Maddox. Holy shit, I just attacked Maddox. What the hell is he doing here?

"What the fuck is this?" Jake yells, running into the kitchen and over to me. His hands cup my face as he searches me for any signs of harm.

I'm too rattled to speak, so instead I point to Maddox, who is still on the ground.

"Your crazy girlfriend just kneed me in the junk," Maddox growls, his voice thick with pain.

Jake glances down to the floor and lets out a surprised half-laugh before he turns back to me. "You kneed him in the balls?"

I shrug and then bite my lip to hide my smile.

"And kicked me in the flank, dude. Don't forget the fucking flank shot she got me with."

"You kneed Maddox Sinclair in the balls and dropped him to the ground?" Jake's incredulous, and I can't stop the bubble of laughter as it rises.

"It's not funny. I should be proud of you for getting the drop on me like that, but this freaking hurts," Maddox whines like a small child as he cups his family jewels once again.

I roll my eyes. "You're being dramatic," I tell him, before my tone turns sympathetic. "I'm sorry. I didn't realize who you were. You startled me, and I reacted."

"Yeah," Maddox groans, rolling onto his back, blowing out a couple of deep breaths in rapid succession. "A mistake I'll never make again."

Jake bursts out laughing. "Jesus Christ. No one has ever gotten the drop on him. Ever. You're amazing. I think I might need to marry you."

"Glad I could help bring you two closer together."

"Sorry," I apologize again, feeling just a bit bad. And if I'm being honest, secretly awesome. I just kicked his ass. I put this giant, muscled man on the floor, and in all the weeks we've been training, I haven't managed that. Not once. I'm smiling. I know I shouldn't be, but it's sort of unavoidable.

Maddox manages to right himself, using the island to help hoist himself up.

"Are you okay?" I ask concerned.

"I'll live. I just wish you hadn't taken out my future children in the process. Usually, a woman has to sleep with me before she castrates me." Maddox smiles and when he does, all of his hard features soften.

I giggle a little at that. I might still be a bit giddy. "Just doing my part for womankind."

Maddox's eyes widen, and Jake laughs, wrapping his arms around my shoulders and kissing my face.

"Besides," I quirk an eyebrow at him, crossing my arms over my chest, "who sneaks up on an easily excitable, unsuspecting female? Really, this could all be construed as your fault."

"My fault?" Maddox points to his chest. "You're a real spitfire this morning."

I shrug.

"At least all those hours of training have paid off."

"*What*?" Jake's eyes bounce back and forth between us. "How do you know about that?" Maddox freezes, and so do I. "You two know each other? How?" And then a light of realization flashes in his eyes and suddenly, it's like all the pieces come together for him. He pivots to Maddox, his gaze steely as he points a stern finger at him. "You. You're the one who gave her the universal keycard. You're the one who got her the jobs at Valaria's and The Bistro. You're the one who's been training her." Jake turns to me. "Did you know about my friendship with him all this time?"

He's hurt, and maybe a bit suspicious, and I can understand

both, but I shake my head. "I had no idea you two knew each other until a few seconds ago. Maddox never mentioned you were friends, and I only said your name once in passing."

"So...," Jake trails off, unsure of his next question though he's clearly all questions.

"We'll talk about it later," Maddox says to him in a tone with an expression I can't quite read. I think it's the sort of unspoken thing best friends do. I mean, that's all I can come up with, even if I've never experienced it firsthand.

"I think that's my cue to leave."

"I'll walk you down." Jake takes my hand. "I need to talk to you," he says to Maddox, the playfulness of the moment is swallowed up by a dose of harsh reality encased in a meaningful tone.

"That's why I'm here."

Jake nods, leading me to the elevator. He kisses me the entire ride down, one hand on my lower back, the other in my hair. He walks me, hand in hand, to the other elevators and then proceeds to get in with me to ride up to my floor.

I don't question him. He's walking me home, I realize. He's showing me that last night wasn't just sex. Is it possible to fall harder for someone already? I meant what I said. I'm terrified of this thing between us. I just wish it didn't feel too perfect to stop.

We kiss goodbye at my door, his lips brushing across mine. And when I release my breath on a sigh, he does it again.

"So goddamn sweet," he whispers against me, and I shudder. "I'll see you later, Sunshine. Have a good shift."

He releases me, throws me a wink, and then walks off, back down the hall to the elevator, leaving me standing here wondering how to keep him out when he's already in.

I enter my room, secure no one is here, and then I shower off a night of desert winds and hot sex. I shouldn't be smiling as much as I am. I shouldn't be as excited to see him again later as I am. And I should not be addicted to this...feeling. God, this feeling. I don't think I've ever felt this wonderful in my life.

I change into my whore outfit, and then I get to work. I am not a great waitress. I forget orders, and I spill more than I should, and sometimes I'm slow when I need to be fast. But I'm learning, and thus far, people are nice enough about the things I get wrong.

My shift goes quickly, mostly because it's non-stop brunch-goers, desperate to get their huge breakfasts after a night of too little sleep and too much partying. Once two o'clock hits and the restaurant winds down—it closes at two-thirty until dinner time—I press my body into the cool subway tile wall of the back room and close my eyes for a beat. I'm tired. I haven't had nearly enough sleep since I set foot in this town.

For a girl with no formal education who has never worked a day in her life, I feel like I'm getting by okay. The skill set I was taught would have been better served for a lady in society—ballroom dancing lessons, proper manners, and table etiquette. I'm fluent in four languages besides English. But I've never cooked a meal in my life. I've never washed a dish—until this morning—and last night was the first time I'd ever been in a real grocery store.

And I'm ashamed of this.

It's disgraceful, not to mention embarrassing as hell. If it weren't for Maddox, I doubt I would have gotten either of the jobs I have. And yeah, I did lie a little bit on the applications. I didn't exactly have a choice. No one would ever hire a person like me otherwise. Fiona Foss knows how to exist in her world, but Mia Jones seems to be just a bit fucked in hers.

"Mia," Julien, my boss and the owner of this restaurant, startles me out of my quiet moment. I open my eyes and pivot my head to him. He's a nice man. Older. French. He likes to swear under his breath in French because he doesn't think anyone understands him, but I do. "You finished?"

I nod.

"Get your things, but there is one customer sitting, sipping his coffee. You can go after he leaves."

I glance over at the round clock on the wall. Two-twenty-five. He has got to be kidding me. I don't say anything, though. No complaints leave my mouth as I straighten my spine, offer Julien a weak smile, and then head out into the dining room that is completely empty save for one person. Well, one man, who has his back to me as I approach.

I set down my backpack by the hostess stand, two seats away from him. I open my mouth to speak, to ask him if he'd like more coffee, but my voice lodges in the back of my throat as I finally catch sight of the man waiting on me. Brent. His green eyes find mine, and he smiles playfully, taking in the ridiculous costume that never fails to humiliate me.

"Good morning, beautiful. Miss me?"

"What are you doing here?" My voice comes out as a breathy whisper, and I hate that. I hate how easily I come unglued around this man. He raises an unnaturally high level of fear in me in comparison to our easy back-and-forth. But something is not right with him. It's never felt right.

"Relax." He holds a hand up, that smile slipping a notch like he knows just how close to the edge I am. "I'm not the bad guy in your story. I might have come on a little too strong before, but women generally tend to like me."

"I don't doubt it." I raise an eyebrow, crossing my arms over my chest, feigning composure. He needs to get the freaking point already.

His eyes sparkle with mischief and maybe a touch of astonishment. I blush instantly, realizing the way that sounded.

"Yeah? I knew you found me attractive."

I shrug. "You can be charming when you want to be." He leans forward, and I hold up my hand to stop him from getting closer.

He nods with a shrug that says, I had to try. "I can't believe your boyfriend lets you work in that." He whistles through his teeth.

"What I wear and where I work is no one's business but mine."

"Well then…" He grins, and I blanch before I can stop it. "Trouble in paradise?"

"What do you want, Brent? Why are you back?" I remember him telling me he comes here a lot for business. But all his card said was his name, personal contractor, and a phone number. That was it.

"I never left."

I suck in a rush of air and step back, bumping into the table behind me. "Why haven't you left? You told me you were leaving."

"I couldn't leave this town without you," he says simply, his voice completely sober.

I don't know why I wasn't expecting that answer, given the person and his relentless pursuit laced with veiled threats, but I didn't.

"But my question is, why do you look like you're skipping town?"

I furrow my eyebrows, trying to play dumb, knowing I'm not even close to pulling it off. "I'm not skipping town," I sorta lie. I'm still undecided.

Brent's attention slowly, deliberately, drifts to my backpack sitting on the floor.

"Does he know?"

My eyes narrow, and my posture turns wooden. "Jake is none of your business."

He grins. "No, beautiful, he's not. But you are, and I don't like you putting yourself at risk."

My eyes widen and my mouth pops open. I want to ask him why I'm his business, but I don't. Instead, I go with something safer.

"How do you figure I'm doing that?"

He picks up his coffee mug and takes a sip, his eyes never wavering from mine. I swear there's an amused grin there. "Well," he starts, setting his mug back down and licking his lips.

He's gearing up, I realize. Setting the stage and building suspense. I fucking hate suspense. It never ends well for the blonde in the story. Though, I guess I'm technically not a blonde anymore.

"You walk around carrying a bag that's bigger than you are. That bag is never far from your person, which tells me you're not exactly a permanent resident anywhere, and I'd wager being separated from it for any length of time makes you uneasy. Am I right?"

"Who *are* you?" I know Brent is not who he claims to be. His observation skills are more astute than the average flirtatious asshole. He's been in this town for weeks and every single night I've worked at the bar—except for last week when I thought he was gone

—he's been there. He's not some businessman here for work. He's here for me. He has to be. Nothing else adds up or makes sense.

But from what angle?

FBI? Hired mercenary? I have a guess, and that's what terrifies me most about him.

"I'm a friend," he says warmly. Earnestly. "Someone you can trust. Someone who will look out for you if you let them."

I shake my head, emitting a torrent of frustrated air, losing my patience quickly. "Who says I'm looking for that?"

Brent's features soften further as he reaches out a hand for me. I pull mine back, but he leaves his hand there, so close to me that I'm finding it difficult to think clearly as an all-too-familiar panic ensues. I wish he didn't look like this. I wish he wasn't gorgeous and charming, while challenging every survival instinct I've ever acquired.

"You're afraid of me touching you," he states, and my eyes climb up to his. "I saw it that first night when Jake touched you, and you flinched. I think you're over that small problem now, though."

"What the hell are you doing here?"

"Aren't you really asking if I came here for you? Because if you are, the answer is yes."

"I—" I stutter, looking around the restaurant. No one is here. It's completely empty, and now that I focus on it, there are no sounds coming from the prep area or the kitchen. My head whips in the other direction, and the doors are closed.

My heart begins to race, thrumming through my ears. I can't think as everything begins to dip and sway. My stomach rolls and I feel like I'm going to be sick.

He's here for me. I knew it all along, and yet, I fought my instincts. I fought my better judgment, and now he's either going to kill me or take me back to Niklas. Probably the latter, because I am worthless dead.

He's talking, watching me closely, but I can't hear anything he's saying. It's just noise that echoes through my skull like the blades of a helicopter going around and around.

"Sit down, Fiona."

Fiona. He called me Fiona. His voice finally breaks through my panic, and I take a step back again, stumbling just before my knees give out on me and I fall toward the ground.

"Hey now," he barks, flying out of his chair just in time to catch me.

I fight him. My senses finally kick in and I attack with everything I have. I slap his face, scratching his arms while kicking and screaming as loud as I can. His hand covers my mouth, and he picks me up, dragging me to the back of the seating area away from the glass doors of the restaurant where any curious onlookers might see.

"Stop fighting," he growls when I bite the hand covering my mouth, but his grip on me does not relent. I thrash, doing everything in my power to get away, but he's big and strong, and I am so very small and outmatched.

Sobs wrack my body, shaking me down to my very core.

"I'm not going to hurt you," he barks. "I'm not. I swear to you. But you have to calm down because I need to talk to you and I need you coherent for that. Can you do that? Can you calm the motherfuck down, or am I going to have to sedate you and try this again later?"

Sedate me? My stomach rolls, and my body retches, dry heaving against his hand. He twists me around, shaking my shoulders and locking eyes with me from inches away.

"I. Am. Not. Going. To. Hurt. You." He enunciates each word with so much force my sobs turn into tears, and then I collapse against him, my head pressing into his chest as I let go. I should have left last night. Last week. The one before that. Why did I stay so long?

"If you're not here to hurt me, then you're here to take me back to him."

He lets out a loud sigh. Like he's tired. Like this is all just too much for him, and he wants it to be over.

"That's what I'm hired to do, yes."

I shake my head against him, pulling back and slapping his face as hard as I can, savoring the sting in my palm and fingers. His cheek reddens, but he doesn't flinch, and he doesn't retaliate.

"I'd rather die," I spit, my soul bleeding out. "I mean it." I pull back and meet his eyes, letting him see my tears and my anguish and my determination. "That last time Niklas beat me, when he nearly killed me, and I woke up alone on my bedroom floor in a pool of my own blood and vomit with broken ribs and an unrecognizable face, I promised myself he would never do that to me again. That I would get away from him, but if I couldn't, then I'd die. I'd take my life and my money and Foss with me. I'd leave him to fight probate against a note and pictures to prove his abuse." His features harden, and I can't determine what that look is supposed to mean.

"Sit down with me, Fiona. Let's talk."

I do sit down, but only because I can no longer stand. I need to formulate a plan, and I need to hear exactly what he has to say before I know what has to be done. What my options are.

"How did you find me?" I ask before he can launch into whatever he's about to tell me. I can't make the same mistake again.

He grins, and that expression just makes me so much angrier than I think I've ever been. It's like he's mocking me. Like I'm this stupid little girl who doesn't know how to escape without being found by the bad guys. I don't, but who needs that reminder in the form of a smug smirk when the proof of that is sitting across from me.

"Your car."

I blow out a breath and lean back in my seat.

"You had it towed to a shop owned by a man I've done business with in the past, and when I was putting out feelers for your whereabouts, hoping to get some leads, he got in touch."

I nod. I don't know how to navigate that one. I forgot all about the car. Jake mentioned he had it towed, but by that point, I had already abandoned it and when Jake told me what he had done with it, Brent was already in front of me. I guess tow-truck guys can be on the shady side of life, so vetting them out to see which mercenary they've worked with and which they haven't isn't exactly an option. I highly doubt Jake had any clue what he was bringing down on me when he had it towed to that guy's shop.

Mercenary. That's what Brent is. I may not be worldly, but I do know a hired killer when I see one. I just wish I had put it together before now. He didn't dress the part then the way he is now, and he had that business card and all that charm going for him.

He's good, I realize. Knows how to work his mark.

"I take it Niklas knows I'm here in Las Vegas. Is he here already, or are you supposed to take me back to Texas?"

Brent—I bet a million dollars that's not his real name—leans back in his seat, much the way I'm doing, and folds his arms across his chest. He's in all black. Black t-shirt and black jeans and black boots. If he weren't so good-looking, large, and powerful, you'd miss him. You'd look past him as just another man. But he's not, and his handsome features might just be his biggest weakness.

"Niklas does not know you're here. I never told him I found you."

I stare at him, blinking a couple of times because it feels like I'm missing something here.

"I found you, Fiona. It only took a couple of weeks, but I did find you. And when I found you, I watched you. I watched you for two days before I ever approached you in the bar. What I saw when I watched you is why I haven't told Niklas I've found you. I told him I was close. That I had some leads, but that you're moving on from place to place quickly and efficiently."

"Why would you do that?" I ask, my bewildered tone so very light.

"Because it didn't take a genius to see you were much more than a rich girl who ran out on her husband. Niklas told me you were spoiled. That you were entitled. That you wanted more power and possessions, and he was trying to rein you in. That you didn't like the life he was giving you and this was your way of protesting. It was quite possibly the biggest bullshit story I have ever heard, which was why I took the case in the first place. Niklas is not your standard guy. I know this better than most. And this is not my typical job. I don't do missing people."

"No. You just make them go missing," I hiss out and then shut my mouth. I have no idea why I just said that, but he doesn't look angered by my harsh accusation.

He grins and nods his head slowly, watching my reaction to his non-verbal confirmation of his profession.

I blow out a breath, running my finger along the edge of the butcher-block table.

"Rich girls who run off and throw tantrums don't sleep outside. They don't avoid eye contact, and they don't jump anytime someone, particularly men, come near them. They also don't work two jobs, dressed in basically nothing, to earn pocket money."

I snort out indignantly. "So, you figured out my bastard husband beat me. Good for you. Now what?"

A chuckle rumbles up the back of his throat. Rubbing a hand across his lightly stubbled jaw, he leans against the table, closing the distance between us by half.

"I'm not the only one he hired to find you, beautiful."

I gasp, my eyes reflexively searching around the restaurant like someone else is going to pop out at any moment.

"They're not here. I made waves in a few different places to make it appear like you could be there. But it's only a matter of time, Fiona. I found you and they will, too."

I shake my head, my eyes narrowing and my eyebrows pinching together. "Why would you do that?"

"Because I may be a lot of things, but I do not tolerate violence against women. Ever. Not under any circumstances."

"But—"

"I'm a killer?"

I nod as he finishes my statement, swallowing down the lump in my throat. He laughs, reaching out to run his fingers across my cheek. I let him. I might be too confused and terrified to stop him.

"I'm not what you think. If you make it to my list, chances are, you've done something very bad to put yourself there. I rid the world of the bad, but not necessarily in the name of good. Don't confuse the two. Don't confuse this. I have my reasons and my reasons are all that matter."

"Is that supposed to make me feel better?"

"No, Fiona. Because the world is better off without the people I rid it of. But you? You are not one of those people. Even though I was simply hired to find you and bring you back to Niklas, I knew what I would be taking you back to and I won't let that happen."

Tears well up in the backs of my eyes and I swallow, pushing down my useless emotion. "So, you're going to…help me?" I shake my head. "I don't understand."

Brent gives me that million-dollar grin. The one he's given me every time I've seen him in the bar. "Like I said, we need to talk."

Chapter Twenty-Four

Jake

I smile the entire walk down the Strip. I could get in my truck and drive it, but with the traffic here it actually takes longer than walking. Besides, with my jacket slung over my shoulder and the sleeves of my shirt rolled up, it's not unpleasant. You get used to the heat. I mean, no one gets used to a hundred and ten in the shade. That shit gives you a glimpse of what hell must feel like.

But eighty-five, I can do. The heat we had going on yesterday is gone, and now we're back to reasonable. My eyes spot The Turner Palace up ahead, and I take it in for a moment. It's not gimmicky like some of the other hotels on the Strip. My father was more into simplistic beauty, and he certainly accomplished that with this one. It's got an old-world vibe to it, made mostly out of glass and white sandstone.

I hit the side ramp, walk past the illuminated requisite Vegas water feature and then coast through the main lobby. It's Sunday morning, and there's already a very nice line at check-in. I watch it a minute, and when I see it moves steadily along, I continue on my path. This is the largest casino of any of our resorts. It's clean, relatively well lit—for a casino—and nicely ventilated, which means you can barely detect cigarette or cigar smoke.

I make my way through the throngs of slot machines that are flashing lights, buzzing and clanking loudly over to the high-limit tables. That's usually where I camp out first, because, believe it or not, those tables are more crowded during the day. At night, the whales are with their wives or mistresses. They take them to dinner and shows. But during the day, they like to play, and that's why I'm here.

I say my hellos to a few of the dealers as I reach my position in the center of the ring of tables. In this area, we have three blackjack tables, two craps tables, one roulette wheel, and one Pai Gow table. Typically, each dealer rotates every sixty minutes with a 'breaker' who fills in during dealer break times. It's a well-run machine, and each of the dealers in this section has been with our hotel for at least five years. That was my father's requirement for high-limit tables.

These dealers must be flawless, personable, well-groomed and trustworthy. My father might have been a lot of things, but the man knew his business. He practically built up this hotel with his bare hands. It was our flagship that he turned into three on the Strip and then into a national chain.

Some of the other executives have been wanting to go global. Branch out to Europe, Asia, and try our hand at a resort in the Caribbean. It's a goal certainly, but I want to see how the changes we've enacted in our resorts affect our business before we discuss international markets.

My gaze focuses on the players at the blackjack tables. They're a rowdy group of guys, at the end of their party weekend. They're laughing and drinking—even though it's only a little after ten in the morning—and giving each other shit like they've known each other forever. They also look too young to have the type of money they're throwing around, considering it's a five-hundred-dollars-a-hand table. But they could be like Fiona. Rich kids born to rich parents.

Fiona.

Just her name makes me smile. I can't get her out of my head.

I love that she kicked Maddox's ass this morning. I might not have even been kidding about the whole marrying her thing. She's perfect for me.

In the back of my mind, I know I'm in trouble. Not just over the girl. But over everything she could possibly represent for me. I would love to play the role of the bad-boy bartender who rides a motorcycle and has zero fucks to give. But I'm not that guy anymore.

Fiona Ramsey-Foss-*Vaughn* is dangerous. Her husband, Niklas Vaughn, is dangerous, and I'm playing the only hand I have with her.

Protector. Lover. All around savior.

I sent Maddox on an errand this morning. The fact that he knows Fiona, knows some of her story, is an asset. An ace in the hole. Because Maddox is not someone you fuck with. And he's protective of Fiona. There was no arm-twisting. No special favors I had to promise. I told him the situation, and he said he was in. That was it. All it took.

But he has far less at stake than I do.

I may want this woman in a way I've never wanted one before, but that does not make me stupid. It will not make me careless. I think back on my conversation with Luke, and I know I need to be offensive with this. I need to be smart. Pervasive. If I want to save my woman *and* my empire, I have no other choice.

I watch the guys a little longer than I should, a little longer than is required, before I move to the next table. My eyes scour the casino floor, and every time I do this, I hate the piece of me that loves it here. I push addiction. I make money off the vice. Alcohol. Drugs. Sex. Gambling. I don't discriminate.

And then there's Fiona.

Pure. Sweet. Innocent.

None of those adjectives match the world I'm engrossed in. But I can't give her up. She's a part of my blood. The beautiful storm on the horizon you can't take your eyes off of, even when you know it's going to blow your fucking house down. That's her. Unassuming beauty. Brazen destruction.

I push my temptress aside and focus on my work. Close to the end of my shift, five hours later, I'm watching over the roulette wheel when I feel a slap on my shoulder and the large presence of too many muscles on my right.

"Sup, man?" Maddox asks, eyeing the tables the same way I am. "I'm surprised to still see you here. I figured you'd be done by now."

"No rest for the weary or the wicked, my friend. What's your excuse?" I question, moving over to the Pai Gow table.

Maddox is my head of security. And not just in one of the casinos or hotels. He's it. We served together until the sniper hit me in the shoulder. He completed two tours, eight years in total, and when that was up, I talked him into coming on board with me. He's intimidating as hell. The guy looks like an NFL defensive end. Think J.J. Watt big—and quietly brilliant. Tactical in all of his endeavors.

So, the fact that Sunshine took him down like tipping over a domino is fucking hot. I won't even lie about that.

"I just finished checking up on the things you asked me to when I heard you're still down here dicking around. I have some of what you were looking for."

"And?"

He gives me a look that says I'm an asshole for even asking that here. "And between your Seattle boys and me, we were able to come up with some shit. Some shit that's meant for a *later* discussion," he emphasizes, staring at me intently while I try to focus on the goddamn gaming tables. "When are you off?"

"Half hour."

"She worth all this?"

I hate that question. I get it, but I still don't like it. I clear my throat and straighten. "What do you think?" I clip out. "You know her. You've been lying your ass off and training her this whole time."

"Of course, I have. You would have done the same. Why do you think I sent her to you?"

"*What*?"

"Don't *what* me, guy. She needed someone to take care of her more than I could. It's why I have her working at Valaria's. It's why I asked Cal to have you train her that first night."

"You set me up with her?" My eyebrows knit together. *Methodical bastard.*

"Don't look so surprised."

I sigh. I should feel hoodwinked, but I don't. I'm grateful he went to such extremes. Both for her and for me. "We have to be smart about this..." He nudges my shoulder, urging me to continue when I don't elaborate. "Why are you smiling at me like an asshole?"

He laughs. "Because I've never seen you look like this over a girl."

"Fuck off. Are we having a girlfriend moment here? Are we sharing our innermost thoughts and feelings, sweetheart? You know what this really is."

Maddox rolls his eyes at me, not fooled for a second. "Yeah, you're a lovesick bastard who has gotten in way over his head."

"Yep. One in the same."

"Then I hope it's the real deal, brother, because we're about to walk the line," he says with a sadistic smile. He likes the game. Always has.

His threat is not for me. Not really. But it is a threat. Something is headed our way. Or it's already here. I know it. I feel it pumping through my blood like newly injected heroin. Only instead of getting me high and numbing me up, it's grounding me, focusing my thoughts and making me hyperaware.

It's also making me anxious to see Fiona again. I hate that we both had to work today. It's no longer safe for her. Not with that asshole Brent sniffing around again.

"What's he doing here?"

"Not the place, brother, but he's a professional."

I sigh. I already knew that, but hearing it confirmed only frustrates me more. "I might be totally fucked. I can't get—" I pause mid-sentence, my phone vibrating in my pocket. "Fiona."

"Why is she calling? I thought you told her to go to her place after her shift was done and wait for you." Maddox checks his watch. "That was well over an hour ago. It's almost four." Maddox leans in to stare down at my screen like he can't believe it, either.

"No idea," I mumble. I slide my finger across the screen and say, "Sunshine?" Maddox is waving me out of here. There are no phone calls allowed by the tables. "Everything okay?" I point at the ground, and he nods, understanding that I'm asking him to do my job while I take this call. I walk past the partition rope and over toward the bathrooms because it's quieter there than it is on the floor.

"I'm sorry to call, Jake. I didn't know what else to do." My heartbeat picks up a notch at her tone. She sounds shaken to her core. "I can't do this anymore. I…care about you. So much. Please believe that. It's why I have to go…," she trails off.

"Fi?" I rub my hand back and forth across my forehead. "You're not going anywhere. You can't just run off."

Nothing is making sense, and then Maddox is there next to me, his phone pressed to his ear, a sick expression on his face. "We need to go," he mouths to me. I shake my head, but it's not a no. It's a what-the-fuck-is-going-on shake.

"I have to, Jake," Fiona continues. "It's for your safety. For everyone's safety. Please try to understand."

No way. Just no fucking way am I letting this girl go.

"I'm on my way," I say without a moment's hesitation. "Meet me by our entrance, Fi. You stay there, and you wait for me to find you. Don't leave, baby. Wait for me, and we'll work this out together. You're safe with me," I remind her.

She blows out a relieved breath and then disconnects the call. She didn't agree to meet me, but I know my girl. She'll be there. She doesn't want to leave, she told me so last night. Something's changed. Something's wrong.

"No. I want first and only access to video. I don't care. I want to see it, and I want to see it the second I get there," Maddox shouts, his eyes locked on mine. "What the hell do you mean the guy is waiting on us?"

"That Cash?"

He nods. "Just hold him there, Cash. Do not let him leave." Maddox disconnects the call and then turns to me. "Our friend found his way up into our security booth. He's there now, waiting on you and me." Maddox stares me down at that. We both know what it means. He lets out a sigh and runs his hand through his hair. "You told Fiona to wait for you?"

I nod, and Maddox shakes his head like he's pissed at the entire planet.

"I need you in the security booth, Jake. He wants both of us, and I want to make sure he knows what's up, but you need to find Fiona first."

"Agreed. Let's go."

"What about your shift?"

Right. Shit. I grasp onto the ends of my hair and tug. Fiona needs me. She's freaked out about who the hell knows what and is now getting ready to run. A freaking hired gun is now staking himself out in my security tower. And I'm a goddamn pit boss. Jesus Christ.

"I got it. I'll grab someone we trust from a quiet section. Don't worry. Go take care of your girl and then find me. This shit has to be taken care of. And, Jake?" I pause at the sound of my name. "You know it's coming down, right? You know this is just the start?"

I give him a tight, determined nod. "Storm's coming."

"Let it rain."

And so it begins.

"I gotta get to Fiona first. I'll call you the second I'm done. Get to that Gavin guy," I call as I start to walk away from him. "I have a really bad feeling about this. A really bad feeling."

Maddox throws me a wave that says he's got it. Me? I just run out of the casino, and all the way up the Strip. I don't stop until I've reached The Turner Grand, and I'm dripping sweat and panting for my life. Fiona. I just sprinted over a mile in eighty-five-degree heat for a girl who wants to run from me the first second she gets.

Awesome. I think I've officially hit a new level of moron.

And really, what the motherfuck? How could she do that? How can she possibly think of running after our night together? After we talked and worked so much out?

I make my way through the lobby that is uncomfortably quiet and subdued, past the casino, and across to the west entrance. And when I get there, I spot Sunshine, her back to me, her eyes fixed on the pane of glass that comes in the form of the door beyond.

For a moment, I can't make myself close the distance. I know what it means if I do. It means I might have to say goodbye to her. It means I probably *should* say goodbye to her. She's married. Even if she doesn't consider herself to be. Even if the prick beat her whenever he got the chance.

Even if he doesn't deserve her and I do.

Sucking in a deep breath, I slowly approach her.

I hear Sunshine sniffling a little, and even though she hasn't turned around to face me, from the sudden shift in her position, I'm pretty positive she knows I'm behind her. She's wiping furiously at her cheeks as she tries to regain her composure.

"Don't try and talk me out of leaving. I…" She looks up at the ceiling, blowing out a heavy, despair-saturated breath. "I need to leave." She swallows, clears her throat, and turns to meet my eyes. "It's not safe here for me or for you. There are too many forces at play, and I can't control or stop any of them."

"You were just going to run? Just like that?"

She's so beautiful. Red-rimmed eyes and rosy cheeks and messy dark hair and long legs. I need her to stay. She can't go.

Fiona glowers, shaking her head. "It's not how I want this, Jake. You know that. You're…you've. Christ." She blows out another breath, this one soft, and wipes at another tear that's fallen. "I don't even know. You're important to me, okay? You're more than that. A lot more and I'm scared. Everything is coming down on me, on us, and I need to leave. I'd never forgive myself if something happened to you."

The problem with this moment is that I get it. I get her wanting to go. Her feeling like she needs to. She might even be right. I honestly don't know yet. But I do know I'm not just going to let her run off with nothing but her backpack and nowhere to go. That is not happening.

"Come here," I whisper, taking her hand, and pulling her into me.

She doesn't resist and that has me smiling despite the gravity of this moment and this day. I inhale her scent and close my eyes, needing this with her. My heart is still racing, and I have no idea if it's from the run up the Strip or the threat of losing the woman in my arms. I'm thinking it's the latter, because the idea of her leaving unravels me.

"Let me figure out what's going on, okay?" I draw back, cupping her face and staring intently into her eyes. "Come upstairs with me. Stay in my place. It's safe up there. *You'll* be safe up there. Let me find out what happened, and then we can decide *together* once we have all the facts."

She searches my face before refocusing on my eyes, bouncing back and forth between them, her green to my brown. "Okay. I'll stay in your place for an hour, but then I'm leaving," she says this like it's a warning. "I thought I could be normal with you. I *want* to be normal with you. More than anything. But I'm not normal. And maybe I should be more grateful than I am. Maybe I should just be happy that I'm alive. But I'm not. I'm fucking resentful. I'm fucking angry. And I'm swearing, Jake, which isn't something I typically do, and that pisses me off too."

I can't help but smile at that. She may be having an existential crisis at the moment, but she's goddamn adorable. "Come on," I say, reaching out and taking her hand. She glances down at our fingers as I intertwine them and sighs. Her eyes reluctantly make the journey up to mine.

"You can't talk me out of going," she warns. "I need to. I don't want to, but I need to. It has to be done."

I lean in and kiss her sweet mouth. "Maybe," I whisper against her, "but I'm gonna try like hell to change your mind."

"I know you will. And part of me loves you for that. So, okay, let's go upstairs and talk. I have a lot to tell you. A lot you need to know."

I kiss her crazy. I can't help it. That one *okay* feels like *please*. It's not. I know it's not. That okay is a mess of a half-baked promise.

I press my lips to hers one last time, and then I'm leading her away from the exit and back toward the elevators. Back into the fray of the casino. It's bright, noisy, and disorienting, and Fiona sinks further into my side as we go. Just before we reach the elevator, my phone rings.

Maddox. Shit. That Gavin guy.

"Hey," I say, my eyes on Fiona who can't seem to pull hers from the floor. We reach my elevator, and I press the button. "What's going on?"

"I need you in the control room. I need you here ten minutes ago."

A healthy cocktail of adrenaline and dread courses through my veins. "Okay," I draw out, trying to regain my equilibrium and think. "Let me take her upstairs, and I'll meet you there in a few."

"No," he says in a tone I don't know how to argue with. "You can't do that. Because fuck it all, I need you here, Jake. This very second. This guy's got a gun in here, dude. A freaking gun. And he knows shit he shouldn't know. Put her on the elevator and get your ass here. Now."

Maddox disconnects the call. He doesn't even wait for my answer. When I look down at Fiona, she's watching me with an indiscernible expression. I realize she probably just overheard everything Maddox said. And I realize there is something behind her eyes I don't understand. Something deliberate. Something hidden. Something that is so unlike the Fiona I know.

"Do you know about this?"

She nods her head. That's it. A fucking nod.

"Is that why you're trying to run again?"

Another nod, but this time, her eyes shift. I feel like someone just shut off all the lights in a store full of glass, and my eyes haven't adjusted to the darkness yet. I can't see anything that is going on around me, but I know what's there, and one wrong move will bring everything crashing down on me. Whatever this is, it's about to take me out at the knees and I'm three steps behind.

"I know a lot more than I should. He's coming for me, Jake, and filing for divorce is not going stop him. Divorce is not an option for him. He'll kill me long before I get there."

I wrap her up in my arms, and I kiss her. My tongue slides into her mouth, tasting her before I force myself back. I cup her face as I stare into her green eyes.

"I know my world starts and stops with you. Your face is the first thing I see in the morning before I've even opened my eyes and the last thing I see before I fall asleep. And not because you're beautiful, but because you're all I want to see. All I'll ever want. I love you, Fiona." I brush my thumb along the crest of her cheek. "So goddamn much that the thought of you leaving, of me not seeing you again, rips a hole through me that could never hope to close. I know you think you're broken. I know you think you're damaged beyond repair and that being with you is dangerous. But I don't see any of that when I look at you. When I look at you, I see your resilience, your strength, your kind heart, and your amazing smile that lights me up. That sets me on fire." I rub my nose against hers. "You set me on fire, Fiona. Stay. Don't run," I plead. "Be with me. I swear, I'll always keep you safe. But more importantly, I'll make you *feel* safe."

Fiona lets out a whimpered sob, tears running down her face as she stares up at me. Her lips pull up into an all-encompassing, beaming smile. "I already told you, I'm yours."

I smile, brushing my nose against hers again, my eyes closing.

Then she whispers, "I'll stay, Jake. For you. For us. I'll readjust the plan. I don't think I can leave you. Come find me when you finish up." She places a soft kiss on my lips. "I love you, too, by the way. So much. I will love you till my heart stops beating."

Till her heart stops beating. I can only hope that wasn't a threat of things to come.

I press my lips to hers again, lifting her in the air and not giving a damn that we're in a busy hotel. *My* busy hotel.

"I have to go, but I'll be back. You know my code, so just go up and wait for me."

"I will. Be safe."

"You too." But as I say that, I wonder if we'll be able to keep that promise.

Chapter Twenty-Five

Fiona

I press the button for the elevator, staring at Jake as he walks away. Shoulders raised, head held high, steps bursting with confident determination. The perfect package. The perfect man.

And he loves me. Jake loves me. This day, I swear. It almost makes me want to laugh. *Almost.*

The doors slide open, and I step backward into the elevator car, my focus fixed on the casino floor beyond. On Jake, who is no longer visible.

I punch in the code for Jake's apartment, the elevator doors slowly closing, locking me in the car and shooting me up fifty stories. My stomach dips at the rapid ascent, my thoughts scattered, and my mind chaotic. Gavin has a plan, but I can't leave now. I told Jake I'd stay. That I was his, and I meant it.

I need to tell him.

The elevator dings, announcing my arrival, and the doors open once again. I step out, pivot to face his spacious, sunny living room, and close my eyes when a hand covers mine, yanking it behind my back and pinning it against my spine at the breaking point. Another hand firmly covers my mouth.

I try to scream, but any sound that manages to pass my vocal cords is completely muffled by the pressure of his hand. I know this hand. I know the smooth texture of the fingers. I know its size and the spicy scent of its skin. I hate these hands more than anything in the whole world.

"Fiona, sweetheart, I'm so happy to see you." His voice is light, casual, like he doesn't have a care in the world. Like I haven't been hiding from him for more than a month.

I swallow down the bile that's rising up my throat, threatening to choke me. I swallow down my fear and try my best to steady my heart rate. I know what I can't do and that's panic.

If I panic, I die.

My eyes close, and air passes slowly through my nostrils. I can do this. I reach my free hand up and take his hand away from my mouth. He doesn't fight me on this, yet.

Niklas Vaughn, the devil in my nightmares, is in Jake's apartment.

I was never supposed to see you again.

"I didn't mean to startle you." He takes the hand he has in his firm grasp and spins me around to face him.

I blink at him, stunned stupid. And my heart? Well, I didn't know a heart could beat like this without a person dying on the spot. My skin crackles with anticipation. My system overloaded with adrenaline.

Slow down.

Breathe.

Don't panic.

"I have to admit," he continues with that smooth voice of his wrapped in a faint German accent. "This is not how I expected to find you. And using the name Mia Jones? Really? It's almost like you're trying to evade your husband." He chuckles at this. Like it's all just a big, fat joke. Ha. Ha. I don't laugh, but mostly because I think I've forgotten how to breathe or think or speak. "I still can't fathom how you made it this far in the gardener's car. Especially when we have so many at our disposal."

"I didn't have a lot of time to plan before I left," I respond without thinking my answer through, my voice stronger than I would have imagined. It hardly registers the fact I'm about to pass out on Jake's beautiful hardwoods. "How did you find me?"

He chuckles, the sound like warm butterscotch. But it's mirthless. Sardonic. Like he's the lion, and I'm the tiny field mouse he's playing with.

"Did you really believe I wouldn't have people out to find you? That I would let you get away?"

I shake my head. I didn't. I knew this moment was coming. I didn't need Brent—whose real name is Gavin—to confirm that for me this morning. I saw him coming after me the moment I left. I saw it the way people see the oncoming car seconds before it crashes into them, helpless to do anything to stop it.

"I don't like your new name, I have to say. Though, of course, I always loved your name as Fiona Foss-Vaughn."

"How did you find me?" I demand again, needing to know. It wasn't from Gavin, unless he set me up.

His eyes darken, and I realize my mistake instantly. He pushes me back toward the living room without allowing me to turn around and get my bearings. He just pushes me hard and fast, his hand still clamped around mine, my feet stumbling back blindly as I go. Niklas shoves me down onto a chair, and I brace for impact, stunned when he doesn't follow that move up with a punch to the face.

He is tall, muscular, and rigid. Fists clenched, jaw tight, left eye twitching, though his gaze is nothing if not controlled. He's ready.

Poised.

He raises his hand, and instinctively, I shut my eyes in anticipation of the blow that never comes. Heavy hot air gusts out of his mouth instead, and I open my eyes to find him running his hand through his fair hair and pinching the bridge of his nose as if trying to stave off a headache.

"How did I find you?" he barks, his darkened eyes wildly scanning the apartment around us. Jake's apartment. My lover's apartment. "My schönes mädchen, the truth of the matter is, if you want something done properly, do it yourself. It took a while, but it wasn't impossible, *Fiona*," he emphasizes my name like a reminder. Like a warning. "The people I hired were…ineffective at locating you. One believed you were in Los Angeles, but I knew better. You've always hated L.A."

I nod. "Yes. You know me so well."

He smiles, and I return it. I smile big and bright. Why, you may ask? To keep Niklas calm. He likes me sweet. Docile. Totally subservient. But most importantly, he likes me when I stroke his massive ego while openly adoring him. The calmer he is, not only am I safer, but the more inclined he is to lower his guard. It makes *him* vulnerable, not *me*.

Niklas bends down, effortlessly scooping me up into his arms and cradling me against his chest. I freeze, my body wooden, my natural reaction to his touch, but I don't fight him.

"Sit with me, my love."

Niklas kisses my forehead, setting me down in the middle of the long, comfortable, leather sofa. Then he sits on the far end. I stare at him, and he pats his thigh for me to come to him. I know this game. This is where I come to heel. And like the good little trained puppy I am, I immediately oblige, crawling on all fours for him until I'm settled into his side. Hating myself for giving him what he's after.

"Good girl," he purrs, only now I don't feel the same rush of pleasure those words used to give me. Instead, they make me sick. He buries his nose in my hair and inhales deeply, sending icicles up my spine and down my arms. "Much better." He kisses the side of my head. "I've missed you so much."

I close my eyes and let out a shaky breath. I cannot remember a time he was this tender with me. When he called me his love or said he missed me. Instead of softening me to him, it fills me with fury, fueling my hate.

Fucking bastard with his mind games.

"I know why you left." I don't respond. "I deserved it." That catches my attention, and I shift on the sofa to face him. The devil with the face of an angel. Blond hair. Piercing blue eyes. His hair is the same light blond as when I left, but it's longer now. It curls on the ends close to the collar of his shirt and hangs over his forehead. His eyes are still the same piercing blue. Clean, angled jaw and perfect white teeth when he smiles. I hate those eyes. I hate his mouth, maybe more than his eyes.

He looks the same, but different, and I can't quite place the change.

I'd love to say I don't feel anything for him. That my hate far outweighs any other emotion.

But I'd be lying.

We had good moments, light moments, before we fragmented. For years, he was the only person to ever show me affection or pay any attention to me. The first person to ever make me feel like I was worth more than my parents' bank accounts.

Even if it was all lies.

"I hurt you."

"Yes," I say, managing to force my words past my lips despite our proximity and the way they're trembling. "You did. A lot. Years and years of hurting me, Niklas." I don't know if it's being in Jake's apartment that's making me brave, but these are words I've never uttered to him before. Not in this way. Not this directly.

"I lost control over myself, Fiona, and you suffered from that. I love you. You're my world. I was your first kiss. I took your virginity. I am your *only* lover," he stresses the word, maybe seeing if I'll disagree with him on that. I'm not as stupid as he thinks I am, so I keep my mouth shut. "Perhaps next time you'll speak to me before fleeing? It appears this could have all been cleared up with a simple conversation."

He wipes my tears and kisses my cheeks, and I feel like I'm dying. Like my soul can't possibly recover. He's going to take me back. He's going to force me to go back with him. There was a plan, and now that's destroyed, all because he showed up.

"I'm waiting for my apology, Fiona. And I expect it to be good. *Satisfying.*"

Shit. He presses my hand against the fabric of his pants, directly over his hardening cock, and I don't know what to do. My heart thrums so frantically I feel the pulse in my toes as I search the recesses of my mind for a way out of this. If I say no, he might force me. He's done that before. But I'm definitely not about to say yes to him, either.

Think, Fiona. Goddammit, think!

"I'm not ready for that yet," I blurt out, knowing it's weak and ineffective. "I need time to process everything you've said to me."

"There is nothing to process. You'll believe what I tell you because it's the truth. You'll suck my cock because you're my wife, and you've angered me by leaving. Because you made me travel thousands of miles to come get you. Because I'm sitting in another man's apartment."

If Jake comes home, Niklas will hurt or kill him. I can't let that happen. I honestly have no idea what this man is capable of at this point. "Let's go home," I say softly, swallowing down the physical revulsion those words bring me.

"We will." I let out a breath and move to stand, but Niklas doesn't let me move. He doesn't let me breathe. He holds me so close and so tight my ribs compress in on my lungs. His other hand jerks my jaw up, forcing my eyes on his. "I want your mouth on my cock while we wait for your lover to come home."

"Niklas—"

"Tell me I'm wrong, Fiona. Lie to my face and tell me this man, this Jake Harris Turner, has not been inside your body."

Blood rushes through my ears like a train at top speed. Loud and thunderous. My vision blurs, and I can't decipher if it's from panic, lack of oxygen, or my tears. *Smack.* My head whips to the left. The entire right side of my face burning with white-hot heat.

I hear Maddox's words echo in my head. *Don't panic. Listen. React.*

I'm done here. Done with him.

Time to go.

I suck in a restricted breath and push Niklas back, crawling out from under his bruising grip and dropping onto the floor. The elevator. I need to get to the elevator. But he'll stop me before I can even press the button, let alone get inside and flee. My gun. Holy Christ, my gun is in my backpack by the elevator, but it's buried in the main pouch because I'm a stupid, stupid woman.

I crab-walk backward, stuck between the couch and the coffee table. If I stand up this close to him, he'll grab me and pull me down. Most likely backward.

Niklas watches me for a moment, shock and amusement dancing in his eyes. But that doesn't last long. It takes him less than a second to realize my intention.

"What are you doing, bitch?" I see his names for me haven't changed in the month I've been gone.

It's time. God give me strength; it's time.

"I'm not going anywhere with you, Niklas."

His eyes widen as he stands up, tall and imposingly fearsome.

The elevator. My backpack. The gun. They're all I'm thinking about. But my focus is entirely on Niklas.

I spring to my feet when I reach the end of the coffee table and turn to run like I've never run before. I hear his footsteps come up behind me. His hands wrap around my neck, yanking me back before I even clear the chair he initially set me in. But inwardly, I smile, because it is exactly what I knew he would do. He yells something I don't pay attention to as he starts to squeeze.

Not today, Niklas. Today, I will take you down. Not the other way around.

I bend my knees into a partial squat, step to my left, plant my dominant foot, and elbow him in the stomach with all my strength. His grip on the back of my neck falters as he leans forward, clutching his stomach. Before he can pull himself together, I spin around, face him directly, and thrust my foot in his stomach.

He barks out something loud and unintelligible, the hand that had been pressed against his abdomen crunches beneath the impact of my foot. I replant my feet and deliver two front punches to his face, back-to-back.

He staggers, practically tumbling backward over the glass coffee table. He recovers faster than I anticipate, certainly faster than I had hoped. He lunges for my retreating form, catching me, pushing me, knocking me down to the ground. My cheek smacks against the hardwood floor, as does my knee. I'm momentarily dazed, unable to regain my bearings until he flips me onto my back.

My body zings with anticipation, my old wounds aching in

protest. His fist connects with my jaw, pain exploding from within. The familiar taste of metallic copper fills my mouth.

Blood pools so quickly from where my teeth mashed into the soft inner tissue of my cheek, I let it drool out onto the floor, just as he slams his foot into my stomach, the way I did his.

"I'm not going to kill you, Fiona. I'm going to torture you. I'm going to make you my prisoner. You're mine," he taunts, laughing evilly as he wipes blood from his mouth and spits on the floor. "There is no running from me."

This is the moment.

I'm in pain, I'm bleeding, I'm down on the ground, and I'm a little dazed from hitting my head.

I breathe. In. Out. In. Out.

I hear him. He's coming for me.

I open my eyes as his fist rapidly descends for my face. I roll over before I can even blink, and he punches the unforgiving floor instead of my face. He howls out in agony, clutching his fist with his other hand.

Scrambling up as fast as I can, I kick him in the side so he falls awkwardly onto the coffee table, and then I run for the elevator to hit the button. I know it's not the smartest thing I can do. I know it's going to take forever for the doors to open and then close. But I don't have a choice at this point.

I can't beat him. I can only slow him down.

I make it just to where the button is, but I'm pulled back before I can press it. My phone rings from the confines of my backpack that is lying a solid five feet from me. I know it's Jake, and that makes me even more desperate.

Niklas has my neck again, and he's squeezing so hard, I'm choking for air. He screams in my face, but all I can do is whimper. He hits me, and I smack back on the floor, my vision gray and crackly.

He straddles my waist, hovering over me with a stare so malevolent I know there is no going back for him now. My hearing is wobbly, but I don't miss it when he says he's going to kill me.

I'm too broken, too hurt to fight him off. He strangles me harder and my reflexes kick in along with any remnants of adrenaline still flowing through me. I'm clawing and kicking and gasping. I find no purchase, nothing to make it stop, and no air to fill my burning lungs.

This is it. I'm going to die. I can't stop him. Multicolored stars splash in front of my eyes, life slipping away along with my last breath.

My phone rings again, but it's too late for that.

My world stops. My heart, my breath, my mind, all stop.

Chapter Twenty-Six

Jake

"How the fuck did he get in this room?" I bark at Maddox as I give Gavin Moore, the asshole who threatened me and has been after Fiona, my most menacing death glare. I point at him, turning my attention over to Maddox. Maddox isn't giving me anything to work with. And really, this doesn't seem like the moment to hold your poker face. This seems like the moment to show your level of crazy and hope it's more than the other asshole's.

"I found him here," Maddox deadpans, and I think my eyes might have just bugged out of my head.

"What do you mean, you *found* him here?"

Maddox opens his mouth to answer, but Gavin cuts him off with, "What he means is when he arrived in the security tower or whatever you call this place, I was sitting here waiting for you. Or him. Or both, I guess." He shrugs like it's all just so blasé, and he's bored with explanations and details. "Where is Fiona?"

"None of your fucking business," I seethe. "He's carrying a weapon?"

Gavin rolls his eyes, crossing his large arms over his broad chest. He's in all black and has the air of a professional killer. It's a look on him I haven't seen up until this point, but after everything Luke and Maddox told me about him, I know that's exactly what he is.

"Of course, I'm carrying a weapon. At least, I was until your man-muscle over there confiscated it." He juts his thumb at Maddox, rewarding me a wolfish grin. "I let him have it, but it was only to demonstrate my goodwill and all that friendly shit. But really, we're getting off target." He snickers. "Pun intended."

Gavin doesn't look around to see if anyone else can hear us. We're in a soundproof room in the back. He must be aware of this, like he seems to know everything else. He angles forward in his chair, digging his elbows into his thighs and throwing me an expression I've only seen in the military. The face before you're about to interrogate someone and are willing to get the information you need by any means necessary.

"Where. Is. Fiona?"

"Somewhere safe. That's all you need to know."

"Good. Because I have reason to believe her psychopath husband, Niklas Vaughn, is either on his way to Las Vegas or is already here."

That stops my heart. One. Two. Three. It takes three seconds before it starts beating again.

"Does Fiona know this?" Maddox asks, and right now, I'm sort of pissed at him. Because he's just leaning back against the long table, with one ankle crossed over the other and his hands in the pockets of his jeans. He looks far too casual for this type of conversation.

"No. And for the record, this was not part of the plan. Fiona and I set everything up earlier this afternoon, and now it's all fucked up. She was to meet me after changing out of her work clothes. That was supposed to be at 16:15. But she didn't show, and this asshole could be here any second. She and I need to figure out a plan B, which means I need to speak to her. It also means you and your man-muscle here, unfortunately, need to be in on it."

"What do you mean you set up a plan with Fiona?"

Gavin sighs like I'm trying the last of his patience with all my questions. I'm about two seconds from putting my fist through his smug jaw.

"Again, that's really not important. Yes, Fiona and I spoke earlier this afternoon. Yes, we came up with a plan, even if I sort of hung back on the full extent of mine. It's not about me and her. I care about her, I want to help her, but not in the way you do. This is about fucking over Niklas Vaughn. This is about revenge."

I take in a deep breath and pace around in a circle, my hands on my hips, thinking through everything he's saying. I believe him. I hate that I believe him, but I do.

"That's why you contacted him on our open network? So, I'd find you and see what you were up to?"

Gavin nods his head like I'm finally starting to get it. "Yes. I knew you were an overprotective bastard and would do everything in your power to keep her safe if you thought me a threat. You did, and I'm grateful. I don't want anything to happen to her."

"Tell me about this revenge plan. Why Niklas Vaughn? It can't be about Fiona?" Maddox questions.

Gavin stands up so suddenly, both Maddox and I spring into action. Maddox with a fucking gun drawn. Jesus, no wonder his hand was in his pocket.

"Slow your cocks there, boys. I think better when I'm moving. If I wanted either of you dead, you would be, and you wouldn't have seen it coming. I may be former military, same as you, but my psych profile sent me in an entirely different direction."

Maddox sets his gun on the table, right next to Gavin's. Maddox likes his firearms small, compact, and powerful. Gavin's is an FN Five-SeveN. Those guns are meant to kill. They have special Kevlar-penetrating ammunition. So yeah, things just got real in our small room.

"Talk," I bark.

Gavin stoically walks over to the glass wall that separates us from the rest of the security area and places his fingertips on the pane. "I've known Niklas since I was eighteen, and he was twenty-two. He interned for my father's company in Denver while he finished up his senior year in college." He sighs, running a hand through his hair.

"My family has money. Not Foss money. Nowhere close, but enough money to draw attraction." He lets out an incredulous scoff and a headshake. "My father instantly liked him. Niklas is a charmer if ever there was one. And when he took a liking to my older sister, no one batted an eye."

He spins to face us, pressing his back into the glass and pinning Maddox and me with his discerning gaze.

"I left shortly after he showed up. I went into the Army, and I traveled around, learning my trade. But when I came home, needing to dry out after a particularly difficult job, my sister was different. She was always sweet and innocent and full of life. But when I came home, she was quiet, reserved…jumpy," he adds, turning his head to catch my eye. I get what Gavin is saying. She was like Fiona was with me when I first met her. "She never admitted anything, and hell, did I push. She said Niklas loved her. She said he would never hurt her. When I saw them together, well, I couldn't tell to be honest. Gabriella insisted she was just going through some depression but would be okay. I believed her like the idiot I was and left shortly after for another job. Four months later, she was dead. Hung herself, is what the coroner said, but I hacked his shit and read the report. Strangled seemed a closer description considering there were some defensive wounds. I was pretty sure Niklas paid the prick off to call it a suicide, but I couldn't be positive. The evidence just wasn't conclusive, and I was angry, looking for anything to cling to. Anyone to blame other than Gabby."

"Then what?" Maddox prompts, waving his hand in the air to keep this moving when Gavin falls silent.

"Niklas vanished," Gavin drawls. "Left Denver immediately after the funeral. A few months later, he popped up in Dallas, working for Foss. I watched him, but everything seemed on the up and up. The moment Fiona turned eighteen and her parents died, they announced their marriage. Gabby was a grown woman when Vaughn moved in on her, but Fiona was only sixteen when Niklas blew into Texas." His eyes grow hard, the unforgiving determination of a killer etched in his features. "When Fiona ran, the stupid asshole called me to find her, thinking I was an idiot who didn't know what he was really doing to her and would help him. So yeah, I want my revenge, because after seeing how Fiona is, how afraid she is of male attention and physical contact, I know without a doubt he killed my sister. That it wasn't suicide. If I can keep Fiona safe in the process," he shrugs, meeting my eyes once again, "all the better."

"You're going to kill Vaughn," I say simply. It's not a question, but Gavin surprisingly shakes his head, a look of pure determination in his eyes.

"Then what are you after?" Maddox asks, standing up just a bit straighter, his hands on the table, resting comfortably next to his weapon.

"Death is too good for him," Gavin declares. "If I wanted him dead, I'd have killed him ages ago. I'm a patient man. I've been biding my time. I want him in ass-raping prison for the rest of his life. Or at least long enough for it to completely destroy him. Then I'll kill him."

"Does Fiona know this?" I ask.

"Some of it. The prison part," Gavin exclaims, pushing off the glass and moving until he's directly in front of me, nose to nose. "She would have never agreed to the rest. Girls like her don't know street justice, but guys like us do. I informed Fiona that I have information on Niklas, which I do. I told her it's illegal, which it is. I promised her he could go to prison, which he will since I'm a vengeful fucker. Guys who look like Niklas and have his sense of entitlement don't do well in prison. I'm counting on that. If things don't go my way for whatever reason, I'll end him."

Gavin smirks, staring off out the glass wall and into the security tower. Maddox and I exchange glances. I don't know what to make of this guy. He's ruthless and honest and protects women. I like him, however odd that is. Maybe it's our like-minded goals. Who cares, really?

Gavin shifts his weight, turning back around to face both Maddox and myself. "She thinks I'm going to Dallas with her to help put him away in some white-collar prison for the next fifteen years. There will be nothing white-collar about his prison, because I will ensure he ends up in the place of my choosing."

"But you think he's here now." That's Maddox, and he's standing up straight, tucking his gun into the back waistband of his jeans. Once it's secured the way he likes, he picks up Gavin's gun and hands it to him. Gavin nods his appreciation but doesn't do anything to conceal his weapon the way Maddox did. He just holds the thing like it's an appendage he feels naked without.

"Yes," Gavin answers. "Shortly after Fiona and I parted ways, I got a message from Niklas telling me he found her in Vegas. It's why I'd like to get Fiona—"

"I'm calling her now," I interrupt. The phone rings and rings and rings. She doesn't answer, and now my heart is really starting to go, sweat slicking the back of my neck. *Where are you, Sunshine?* I try her again and get the same result.

Sick, hot, nauseating dread fills my gut. Like pouring cement into a bathtub and trying to run the water. If he already has her, I am going to rip him apart. Fuck Gavin. He's not getting his revenge. This asshole is mine, and if he hurts one pretty hair on her beautiful head, I am not just going to kill him. I am going to torture him and enjoy every second of it. Fiona called me her caveman, and she was right.

That girl is my universe, and you don't fuck with a man's universe.

"She's not answering. Something is wrong," I tell them.

Maddox's eyes blaze at me, and for a moment, we have a private conversation that only people who really know each other, understand each other, can have. *I'm going to get more guns*, is what his look says. Mine says, *I'm going to use them.*

I try her one last time with the same results.

I want to chuck my phone across the room. I want to slam my fists into the glass walls. I might, in fact, be losing my mind. I can't believe I let her go up to my place without me. I can't believe I let her go up without checking it out beforehand.

Stupid. So motherfucking stupid.

"I have to find her," I snap at someone, anyone. "I have to find her now. He's got her. I know it."

"Where is she?" Gavin asks.

"My place."

"Let's move," Gavin barks out. "But if you kill that dickhole without me there to pull the trigger, you and I are going to have some serious issues. I want him in prison, but I'll settle on death if I have to."

"You think I care?" I breathe fire and pulse venom.

"You will."

"I'm coming with you," Maddox asserts, his voice perfectly calm. His massive hand grips my shoulder, and it's his non-verbal cue to get my shit on straight.

Because this is about to go down, and I cannot lose my temper. Not yet. Not before I know exactly what's going on with Fiona and if she's okay.

I don't wait for anyone else. I just leave the soundproof room and march my way through the security tower. I make my way down the long, narrow staircase, taking the steps two at a time, until I hit the casino floor. It's busy in here tonight. A lot of happy cheers from the craps tables.

None of it registers.

None of it matters.

I sprint across the casino, my misguided confidence driving me forward. Driving me to her. If she's even with Niklas. I have no idea where this thought comes from, but in my gut, I know she's with him. I know he has her. Maddox catches up quickly, having the advantage of a few extra inches on me and long-ass legs. He doesn't speak. He doesn't have to.

We reach the elevator, and I take a moment to catch my breath.

"One of us should get off on the forty-ninth floor and take the stairs up the last floor, entering your place through the back," Maddox recommends softly so only the two of us can hear.

I nod. I can't quite speak. I'm getting myself ready for whatever I'm about to face, including my own death. It's not the first time I've faced it. Not by a long shot.

I'm not hesitating, though. I'll go freely, and I'll go willingly, because I'd die for Fiona. If I'd die for my country and my fellow soldiers, you bet your ass I'd die for the woman I love. It's really that simple.

But it won't be that easy to kill me. I've been shot before, and out of the three of us who were there that day, I'm the only one who survived. There is no trade here, and there is no tit for tat. It's going to be a dogfight.

Fiona would have picked up. She would have called back if she had missed the call.

This isn't right.

The elevator dings, and the three of us enter quietly. Maddox hits the button for the forty-ninth floor, followed by mine. The doors close, and we take off, my heart hammering against my ribs, sweat dripping down the back of my neck.

The elevator stops, and Maddox steps out without prompting. I catch him running full speed down the hall.

"Niklas might not be there," Gavin says. I count to twenty, giving Maddox enough time to get himself somewhere useful, and then I move my finger away from the door-open button and press the one to make them close.

"Do you really think that's the case?" I ask.

"No," Gavin answers bluntly. "I think he has her. And they might already be gone. There's a good chance they might not be in your apartment."

"Are you a good hunter?"

"The best," Gavin replies.

"Good. Because I'm thinking if he took her, hurt her, then prison is too good for him."

Gavin smirks, eyes me hard, and then we both fall silent as the elevator starts to slow.

Chapter Twenty-Seven

Jake

Gavin and I exchange glances, both of us staring at the open elevator door. No sound. It's absolutely silent in there. It could be because Fiona is standing, waiting for me to walk out. It could also be because she's not here.

"Stubborn fucking woman, she was supposed to come with me," Gavin hisses, under his breath.

I hold up three fingers, and he nods. Then I count them down until I get to one, and we step out together. It's hot in here. Or maybe that's just me because I'm sweating as I've never sweat before and I served in the goddamn desert.

Click.

The cock of a gun behind us freezes us both.

"That better be a friendly, Jake Turner, or I swear I won't hesitate to kill the motherfucker, splattering your nice apartment with blood."

"You really are a sociopath, aren't you?" Maddox laughs from behind us. I sigh out my relief, sagging for a flicker of a second before jumping back into high-alert mode.

"I prefer morally indifferent," Gavin offers wryly. We spin

around to face Maddox, who does not look happy. "Where is our lady?"

Our lady? *My* lady. Fiona is mine. And I do not like the fact that I'm standing here in my foyer in my quiet ass apartment with nothing but these two assholes beside me.

"I haven't seen her yet." Maddox holds a finger up to his lips, indicating they could still be here. "She's not in the utility room, laundry room, kitchen, living room, or here, obviously. But...," then he trails off with an upthrust of his chin. I spin around automatically and so does Gavin and now we're staring at my messed-up living room.

Before I can think or stop myself, I amble toward the disarray, glaring down at the blood on my floor. *The blood on my floor.*

What did Gavin just say about splattering my nice apartment with blood? Someone beat him to it. My jaw clenches so tight I'm shocked I'm not chipping my teeth. My coffee table is shoved back. The chair on its side. *So much blood.*

Where are you, Sunshine?

I don't think I've ever been this terrified in my life. I can't lose her.

I sprint toward my bedroom, flying through the closed door. Why is the door closed? My bed is made, and I'm positive I did not make it this morning after Fiona left it. No way she would have come in here, made my bed, closed the door, and then fought Niklas? Or one of his hired goons. Jesus, that almost feels worse than Niklas. Maybe because I like to imagine on some level, the sick bastard cares about her enough not to kill her.

"He made the bed," I say aloud, not even caring if they hear me.

"Who? Niklas?" Gavin asks, his tone incredulous. Clearly implying that making a bed is beneath him, but I think it's a message. It's his way of saying he knows what I've been doing with Fiona. His way of saying he was here and he has her, and now, it's like she doesn't exist for me. My bed is made. All traces of our night together are lost.

Or maybe I'm reading too much into this. Who the hell knows?

"Where is she?" I ask, my stomach twisting into a sick knot.

"Cash said there is no video of them leaving here, dude," Maddox says, his voice suddenly whisper-quiet.

Our eyes lock. "They're still here? How?"

"Not freaking possible," Maddox rejects. "I checked everywhere."

"Do you have video on the freight elevator?" Gavin asks, glancing at Maddox first and then me with a tilt of his head.

My eyes widen.

Gavin nods.

And then the three of us bolt across the apartment. Maddox took the stairs up. But the freight elevator is all the way in the back, down its own hallway. Goddammit. How could I have been so freaking stupid to overlook the freight elevator?

"There is more blood," Gavin yells as we approach the hallway. "He definitely came back here."

"Shit," I bellow. "We're too late." I turn and run back to the main elevator. "You two take the freight. Maybe he didn't get too far ahead of us. Maddox, call Cash. Have him get any video feed that's even remotely close to there."

I hit my regular elevator, slamming my fist into the call button. I don't wait to find out how Gavin and Maddox do with the freight. They're both equally capable.

The doors immediately open for me, and I rush in, punching the button for the lobby. But it's slow. So goddamn slow and I need to move fast. I'm bouncing off the walls in here like a caged lion waiting to strike.

The side of my fist meets the fabric wall just as the doors open. My feet carry me forward without thought. My eyes scanning everywhere, left and right and straight ahead.

I don't see Fiona or Niklas. They're not here. My phone pings a text and I pull it out of my back pocket to see four words.

Event Wing, West Side.

Shit. That's clear on the other side of the damn casino. Sucking in a deep breath, I take off again. Dodging patrons and bumping into drunks. I can't move fast enough.

I'm going to lose.

I'm not going to reach her in time, and if he makes it out that exit, well, he has all of Vegas and beyond at his disposal. He'll be a ghost.

And she'll be gone.

The corridor for the event wing is long and wide and has a million doors that lead to a million conference rooms and ballrooms. He could be hiding out with her in one of these rooms. It's a rare day we don't have at least one function or conference going on, but it appears today is one of those days. The hall is completely devoid of people, which is eerie in and of itself, considering I'm in one of the most popular hotels on the Las Vegas Strip.

My lungs burn and sweat drips down the side of my face and neck.

I'm about to call Maddox, or even Cash, when I hear it. The slamming of a door. It could be any door, but instinctively, I know it's an outside door. They just sound different when they close. Maybe it's the fact they're glass-paned instead of solid wood. Or maybe it's the fact I know he's trying to escape without drawing a lot of attention. I don't know. But that's where I go.

The remnants of the Las Vegas sun catch my eye through the line of glass doors leading outside. There isn't much out this way, just a circle drive for cars and limos to pull up, and a long driveway that is lined thickly with shrubs before it hits a random side street.

The asshole is good. I'll give him that much.

I take a half-second to pull some much-needed air into my lungs, mentally thanking Sunshine for making me run so hard these past few weeks, and then race ahead. Tugging the door open, I squint against the intrusive sun, covering my brow with my hand, and then I spot them.

At least, I think it's them.

A tall man in a black jacket and jeans is speed-walking away, a smaller figure I cannot make out all that well at this angle being dragged along beside him.

She's alive. She's on her feet.

Hopefully, that means her injuries aren't so bad.

I fly forward. "Niklas!" I bellow, and just as he turns around, I'm there, launching myself at him. He lets go of Fiona, who begins to drop back toward the ground. I don't mean for her to fall, and as we're all going down, I reach out for her, attempting to draw her body onto mine so I can break her fall. But it's impossible, and the three of us hit the ground hard.

Niklas grunts but recovers faster than I do. I'm more concerned about Fiona, who is an absolute mess. Niklas jumps on me, but he's nearly as bad off as Fiona is, and all I see is red. All I see is what this motherfucker did to her.

I can't let that stand. There are few things lower than hurting a woman, and now I'm starting to understand Gavin wanting Niklas to end up in ass-raping, hard-knocks prison.

Hell might be a day at the spa compared to that.

We'll have to see which place he reaches first.

Niklas lands a punch square to my jaw, but it hardly registers, the pain a quick zap of electricity.

I roll us, using the full force of my weight and strength to get us there. Niklas is a big guy. A strong guy. Even as banged up as he is, he's still putting up one hell of a fight. He punches up, landing a blow straight across my jaw, the metallic taste of blood pooling in my mouth. I hit him back, savoring the crack of his jaw against my closed fist. We trade punches back and forth, scraping at each other, both desperate for the upper hand.

His knee fires from behind, hitting me square in the back. Inadvertently, I lurch forward, and he uses my momentum to roll me, plastering my back to the asphalt. Before I can catch my breath, his elbow slams into my throat.

I choke, gasping for air, giving him a moment's reprieve from my assault. Hoisting himself up and onto his feet, he runs toward the street, dodging my outstretched hand as I try to trip him up. A feral growl glides past my lips, and I'm on my feet. But Fiona...

"Baby?" Crouching down beside her, I gently run my fingers along her bruised cheek. Her left eye is swollen. Her lips split and bleeding. Her face covered in purple welts and long gashes. Her breaths are labored, pained.

I've never tasted murderous intent before. I've felt it directed at me. I've held it in my hands as it bled to death in the desert heat.

But never once, in all the times I pulled the trigger and took a life, did I feel this…wrath. This explosion of hatred. My muscles twitch, aching to perform the deed my head and heart are commanding.

But Fiona.

I can't leave her like this.

"How bad does it hurt?"

Fiona blinks, like she's coming back from somewhere else, and then her pale eyes meet mine. They lock, holding onto me, and I realize just how much I love her. Because she smiles, trying for brave when everything she's feeling is pain and fear.

Out of the corner of my eye, I catch movement. Maddox is here. Finally.

Lowering himself to one knee, his eyes meet mine. They say, *move, asshole.* They say, *get the prick and make him pay.* "I've got her," Maddox promises. "Go. And give him a good one for me." He lifts a limp and injured Fiona up and off the ground, cradling her into his chest like she's made of glass and could shatter at any moment. She whimpers, saying something I can't hear in a low, sweet voice.

I stand, watching him walk over to the entry of the building, holding her soundly in his arms.

"How is she?" I yell, turning back to the now-empty street, searching left and right for Niklas.

He wouldn't have gone far. Fiona is still here. Fiona is still alive, and his pride, greed, and misplaced confidence make him arrogant. Make him stupid.

"I'm okay, Jake," Sunshine tries to reassure, but she doesn't sound okay. She sounds banged-up and beaten-down, but she's coherent, and she's speaking, and I'll take what I can get.

A rush of air hits my lungs, and I feel like it's the first breath I've taken since I left the security room. It gives me a rush, a surge of adrenaline that forces me forward without the benefit of sight.

"Jake," Fiona calls urgently after me, begging me with her tone not to go after him.

My head swivels around and I catch her eye as she's held tenderly in Maddox's oversized arms. "I'm so mad at you, Sunshine. You better not die on me, or I swear to God, I'll chase you into the afterlife."

She gives me a half-smirk, her face pale, her skin clammy. My girl is in so much pain. "I love you, too."

Niklas growls from beyond my sightline, yelling something in German I don't care to try and figure out. *Ha! I knew you wouldn't go far.*

"I've got her," Maddox calls as Fiona argues with him, not wanting to go. Wanting to stay out here with us. I don't care where he's taking her. I know Maddox will protect her. That he'll take her where she needs to go and watch her with his life. That's just the sort of guy Maddox is. It's why he's my brother.

Gavin comes out of nowhere, like the stealth fog of death, a gun in his hand, his body poised. Our eyes meet, and silently, we move along the road, angling our bodies against the tall shrubs. I don't hear anything. I can see even less.

But I know he's here, more than likely, armed and waiting for just the right moment to spring.

Chapter Twenty-Eight

Jake

There are certain moments in your life that are defining. And I don't mean milestones like graduation or marriage. I'm talking about moments when you have a situation in front of you and a choice to make that will change the course of your life. It should come with a pause. A tingle up your spine. Some warning light that says, hey, this is it. This is your moment, so don't fuck it up and make the wrong choice.

But it rarely does. It's why people end up with regrets.

As I stand here, stalking the shrubs lining the road at the back of my hotel, I have no regrets when it comes to Fiona. But I'm also coming to grips with the knowledge that she might have been my moment.

It wasn't when I was shot in the desert by that sniper. It wasn't when my father passed away, and I was left with an empire to run at the age of twenty-nine. It was when I pulled over on the side of the road in the middle of nowhere and found a woman sitting in her car with terror in her eyes.

That one rash decision to pull over and help a stranded motorist changed my entire life.

The way she looked up at my hooded face, unable to see me,

though I could see her. The way just the sight of her had my breath stopping in my chest. The way my heart inexplicably jumped when she first spoke to me.

Fiona has forever changed the fabric of my life. Marked it with indelible ink. Branded it with her sass, smile, and sunshine. *My* sunshine.

And Niklas Vaughn will never be able to hurt her again.

I don't care how he goes down, whether it's through death or prison. But he is going down. Today is the day. This is the moment. And I'm ready for whatever is coming.

Gavin is directly across from me, on the opposite side of the street, hugging the hedge, his gun held up chest-high, ready. Mine is, too, and if you've ever been shot or know what the fear of a bullet is like, then you know the true nature and impact of the weapon. It's not something I take lightly. Not something I revel in possessing, and definitely not something I delight in using.

I get the impression Gavin can't say the same.

The hard line of concentration around his eyes, combined with the confident upturn of his lips, tells me he's been here before. In a position very similar to this. But really, I think the personal nature of this hunt is what's driving him with surgeon-like precision and hotheaded glee.

The sound of bushes rustling catches our attention. It's on my side about ten feet ahead, and without a word or a sound, Gavin crosses the street to stand beside me. Except, instead of being behind me, he's in front. I can't decide if this is a position I want him in, but my opinion was not asked for, and I'm certainly not afforded an argument as he rolls his head to me with a glare.

"He's mine," he mouths.

I nod, but inside I'm not sure if that's a promise I'll be able to keep.

"Where are you, you coward?" Gavin yells, the sound so startling, so unexpected, I practically trip over myself and squeeze the ready trigger in my hand. I have no idea why Gavin is intentionally giving up our position. He does not strike me as the type of guy who does anything without intent. He's painfully patient. His pursuit of

Sunshine proves that. The way he mapped this whole thing out proves that.

So what the hell is he trying to do?

"You tried to kill, Fiona. You're a depraved, sick fuck, and I personally will take tremendous pleasure in hearing all about the ass-rapings you will receive in prison after all your money, power, and possessions are stripped."

No sound. He's not luring Niklas out of the bushes, which is the only possible reason I can come up with for his intentionally baiting the lion we're blind to.

Gavin laughs, loud and maniacal, like he's lost touch with reality.

"Did you love her, Niklas? Did you care when you ruined her? When you beat the life from her eyes? When you strangled the breath from her body?" I pull on his arm, begging him to shut up, but there is no stopping Gavin. He's a bleeding, heartbroken force of nature. "Did you know about Fiona and her money before you killed Gabriella, or did that come after?"

Goddammit. I don't know what to do. I don't like this game of hide-and-seek. I don't like being out here, so exposed when Niklas is so very well hidden.

"I guess the call of young, money-filled pussy was too much for you to resist."

Now my fists clench. And I want to punch Gavin for saying that about Fiona. But…German. I'm hearing muttering in German. Then a shot fires in our direction, whizzing dangerously close to my head. So close I feel the breeze of it as it barrels past me.

Instinctively, I drop to the ground, hitting the pavement and the curb hard, just as Niklas releases another shot. This one skims Gavin's arm, leaving a nasty flesh wound and a long trail of blood in its wake.

Gavin doesn't even flinch. That's how lost he is in this right now. Concrete explodes not even three feet from us, splintering and raining tiny clay-colored pellets mixed with green leaves from the bushes on us.

"That was pathetic," Gavin taunts. "You're quick on the draw there, Nik. You like that in the sack, too, big guy?"

Jesus Christ. Gavin has got to be kidding me. Because Niklas Vaughn has us exactly where he wants us. We're sitting ducks out here like this, and if we're not careful, next time he won't miss.

I tug on the back of Gavin's pants, urging him to get down. He doesn't. Instead, he rolls his head over his shoulder and winks at me. The bastard actually winks at me.

And I have to tip my hat to him, because now in addition to German ranting, I catch movement in the bushes. *Crazy, brilliant bastard.* Gavin holds a finger up to his lips, urging my already-silent lips to stay so. He refocuses on the bushes, points his gun in the direction of the voice, adjusts it two clicks to the left and fires.

One. Two. Three shots. *Pop. Pop. Pop.*

Niklas catapults out of the bushes, clutching desperately to Fiona's gun, and I blow out a relieved breath that he didn't have it drawn before when we were scrapping on the ground. Gavin raises his hand just as Niklas does the same, but this time, I fire first.

A warning shot.

A graze across his shoulder.

Niklas jolts back, his bruised and beleaguered body overreacting. He fires haphazardly, wildly, missing us by a mile. He recovers quickly, aiming at Gavin, who jumps to his side and rolls on the ground.

"I don't want to kill you, Niklas," Gavin roars. "So how about you drop the pretty lady gun and we talk?"

Niklas turns to face Gavin head-on, staring him down with his bloodshot eyes, one so swollen, it's nearly shut. He is bleeding from practically everywhere on his face. His gun is still held chest-high, but it's a struggle, his hands shaking with the effort.

"No one can have Fiona but me," is all he says, but he makes a point to catch my eye. A warning. A do-not-try-and-fuck-with-my-possession warning.

"Is that why you made my bed? To try and send me that message?" I laugh. "That's funny, man, because not even two hours ago, Fiona was telling me how she's mine."

Niklas raises his gun at me, and I do the same, a solid twenty-five feet between us.

"I wouldn't do that just yet, Nik. Jake here is a damn good shot. Can you say the same from this distance with those injuries?"

Niklas glances in Gavin's direction, but his gun never lowers.

"While I have your attention, tell me how you killed Gabriella."

Niklas's eyes widen for a fraction of a second before he restores his stoic mask. But it was there. In that half-second, his features were lined with shock. Not at the accusation, but at the fact Gavin knows the truth about what happened to his sister. The aim on his gun falters.

"Did you mean to kill her? Did you enjoy it?"

Niklas stares Gavin down for a long, hard moment, the tension mounting, building to a deadly crescendo, a finality that can only end one way. Niklas aims his gun at me again, and before I can press the trigger, I hear, click. *Click?* Out of bullets or a misfire? Gavin laughs, squeezing the trigger.

The loud pop of gunfire rings through the air. Niklas's left leg jerks awkwardly beneath him and he cries out in pain, blood pouring past his fingers as he tries to staunch the wound on his knee.

Gavin's words are manic now, his tone shrill. "Tell me!" Gavin demands again, his voice like jagged glass. "Tell me about Gabriella, and I might let you live to become someone's bitch in prison."

Niklas points his gun at Gavin with a shaky hand, grinning painfully like he's won, and we've lost. He fires in rapid succession, spraying bullets at both of us. This time, I don't hesitate. I've had enough of this back-and-forth shit.

I fire, hitting the hand holding the gun. Niklas howls, capturing his now mangled hand as the gun drops to the ground with a clank. Gavin and I race over in a flash. I kick the gun away, and it skids about ten feet until it hits the opposite curb. Gavin rears back and plants his foot into Niklas's ribs.

Niklas coughs, sputters, spits blood on the ground. "I didn't intend to kill her. Just leave her. I wanted Fiona." His voice is thick with pain and garbled from his injuries. He locks eyes with Gavin, and then smiles, cruel and unapologetic. "But I won't lie and say I wasn't happy the bitch was dead." Gavin fires his gun, the bullet striking Niklas directly in the forehead, between the eyes, and that's it.

Niklas Vaughn is dead.

Stepping back, I spin around, my hands running through my hair, before I scrub them up and down my face, blowing out a breath. I tuck my gun into the back of my jeans.

"You okay?" I ask.

"No," Gavin replies, standing over Niklas's body, staring down at his lifeless form with so much disappointment in his eyes. "I wish I had shot him in the stomach and watched as he slowly bled to death in agonizing pain. That was too easy. Too quick. I wanted him to know what true fear feels like."

I shake my head. I have no response for that. Gavin spits on Niklas's body, and I realize that's why he didn't want him dead. Why he wanted him in prison. There is no satisfaction in death.

I walk away, back toward the entrance of the hotel where I left Fiona and Maddox. Fiona. I quicken my steps before I break out into a sprint when I catch sight of her on the ground by the door.

"She collapsed before we made it to the door," Maddox yells to me as I approach. He's sitting with her, kneeling on the ground. "She begged to stay, and I didn't exactly want to move her. I don't know the extent of her internal injuries."

I reach them and drop to my knees. *The extent of her internal injuries.*

My body covers hers in a protective hold, my face inches from hers as I cup her cheeks in my hands. "I've got you, Sunshine. Breathe, baby. You're not breathing." She's not. At least not enough. And if I thought my heart was pounding before during the freaking gunfight, if I thought I knew what panic-induced adrenaline coursing through my system felt like, I was wrong. "Breathe, Fi. Goddammit, baby. Breathe."

"She's in shock. She heard the shots and started to lose it. I've been trying to calm her down," Maddox says, but his voice sounds like it's so far away, garbled and tinny. I can't focus on anything other than her. Her green eyes are open and she's staring back at me, but I don't know if she's there. If she's able to hear me. "Ambulance is en route. Gavin, if he's done, you need to leave, bro. Cavalry is five minutes out. Leave me with your gun. I've already made the call to get this taken care of."

The call. Shit. I know what that means for Maddox. I know who he called and what he just did. Only I can't think about that right now. About the repercussions.

"Fiona, look at me," I beg. "Focus on me. Please, baby, you're scaring me. I love you. Breathe."

A surge of air forces itself into her lungs, and she gasps out, crying like I've never seen anyone cry before. "Niklas is dead?" I nod, and she closes her eyes, shaking her head back and forth. "Are you sure, Jake? Are you absolutely sure?"

"Yes. He's dead, Fi. I promise." I run my fingers along her cheek and through her hair.

A rattled sob escapes her lips. "I feel…relief. So much relief. He'll never hurt me again. He'll never hurt anyone else again." Her eyes open and lock with mine.

I lean down and gently kiss her lips. "Never," I whisper and then smile against her. "No one will ever hurt you again. You kicked his ass pretty good."

She grins, but then it slips. "I didn't win. I didn't beat him."

I rub my nose against hers. My competitive girl. "You fought him, Fi. You didn't back down. The rest doesn't matter. It's done. It's you and me now, Sunshine. Us. You're safe. I swear to God, Fiona Ramsey-Foss, I will always keep you safe."

"You better," Gavin interrupts my tender moment, and I angle my head to find him. He's smiling down at Fiona, looking as bad as I feel, but a serene glaze lights up his eyes. "Or I'll come back for you, Jake." He winks at me. "I'll be in touch, beautiful." He kneels down and kisses her face. "Both you and my sister are free now."

And then he's gone. Running off as the sirens grow increasingly loud.

Chapter Twenty-Nine

Fiona

The sky is one of those pale-green, ominous-looking things. And the air is oh so calm. Not even a stray breeze to be had. If this were Texas, I'd be thinking tornados, though we don't typically get those this late in the season.

In Las Vegas, however, it means a nasty storm is on the horizon. And generally, those are not my favorite. But right now, I'm sort of welcoming the ensuing chaos. A flash of lightning illuminates the sky only to be followed by a crash of thunder moments later, and then the pounding of rain as it hits the glass of the windshield.

I spent two nights in the hospital. Broken ribs and a serious concussion. Bastard nicked my lung when he broke one of those ribs, too.

The police showed up just after Maddox and Jake put their hands all over Gavin's gun. The guys told the police their version of events, and I suppose, it wasn't difficult to believe. There was nothing on video other than Niklas trying to drag me out of the hotel and Jake running after us. But once we hit the long drive that leads out of the event area, the footage ends, because there are no cameras there. Good thing for Gavin.

I don't remember a lot of what happened after Jake arrived

outside. A lot of yelling and gunshots. And pain. God, the pain was intense. So much worse than the last time Niklas nearly beat me to death.

The police questioned me for long, relentless hours. My face was all over the television as the press got one detail wrong after another. It was ugly and overwhelming. All I wanted was to be left alone to think. To process.

I left immediately after I was discharged from the hospital. That was two weeks ago. *Two*. Honestly, it feels more like a lifetime. At the very least, months. Jake told me he was coming with me, but I insisted going back to Texas was something I needed to do alone. I left him with promises of coming back after facing my demons.

Jake accepted it about as well as a person accepts a terminal diagnosis. He fought me hard. Fought *for* me, and I love that about him. Jake is a fighter, but instead of using his fists, he uses his brain and his heart. Finally, after a lot of persuasion, I left alone.

But something unforeseen occurred when I got to Texas. When I stepped foot inside the big, empty mansion. When I saw family pictures and wedding pictures and closets filled with clothes that will never be worn again by their owner. I went somewhere dark. Somewhere beautiful. I breathed in possibilities. A life renewed.

And I cut off all ties with the outside world. For the first time in my life, I had freedom. Real freedom. It was a lot to absorb, to come to grips with.

My family was dead, my husband was dead, and I was free.

"He's gonna be madder than a cut snake," Maddox drawls with a shit-eating grin as we drive toward the hotel, past the event area. The event area that changed all our lives.

Maddox presses the button on his steering wheel and Jake's sexy baritone booms through the speakers of the Bluetooth. My heart picks up pace at the sound of it.

"I'm going. You can't talk me out of it this time."

"You can't fly tonight," Maddox deadpans, trying to contain his grin. "You know, storms and whatnot. It can be dangerous." He turns to me with a dopey grin and a shrug that says, *I have no idea what I'm saying.*

I hold in my laughter.

"I need to get to her, Maddox. It's been weeks, and she's barely returned my calls or texts. I'm dying here."

Guilt sweeps over me, making my gut sink like lead. Maddox reaches over and quickly places his hand over my folded ones in my lap. He gives me a reassuring squeeze before releasing me and returning his hand to the wheel.

"Marry her," Maddox suggests, that stupid grin growing so wide I can see his pearly whites in the dim lighting of the car. *Asshole.* "I don't give a shit that you've only known her a couple of months. I'm not even saying you need to do that immediately. But you'd be a fool to do anything else."

I smile to myself at that, shaking my head. Jake chuckles into the phone, the sound giving me chills, and the man isn't even in front of me. Lord, I have it bad.

"What's wrong, Maddox? Jealous?"

"Yeah, motherfucker. I am." Then he clucks his tongue, running a hand through his hair and throwing me a sideways glance. "She can throw one hell of a punch." Another wink in my direction and I reach across and punch him in his huge, muscular shoulder. I think it hurts my hand more than it hurts his arm. "Go get your shit, get your girl, and bring her back here where she belongs. And tell her I was right about the rescue. She'll know what I mean."

"I will. Has he contacted you yet?"

Maddox shifts uncomfortably, throwing me a sideways glance. Whatever they're talking about, Maddox doesn't want me to know about it. "Not yet. He will when he's ready. Of that I have no doubt."

"And what will that mean for you?" Jake pushes and then sighs. "I wish you hadn't done it. I'm grateful but now you're stuck. Conti doesn't mess around."

Conti? What the hell are they talking about?

"I'll handle it," Maddox promises with a sharp tone. "You focus on getting your girl back. Before she decides to pick me instead."

"You're a jerk," I say the moment the call is disconnected, and Maddox breaks out into a peal of laughter.

"Oh come on," he says through his amusement. "That shit was funny as hell, and you know it. He's all the way down the Strip at a meeting, but he's gonna go home to grab a bag before he tries to fly out and get you. Good thing we're gonna beat him home."

I nod. "Good thing. What was Jake asking you about? Who's Conti?"

Maddox shakes his head, his gaze severe. "Don't mention that name again. And don't ask Jake about it either. You weren't supposed to hear that."

"Maddox—"

"I mean it. It's for me to worry about. Not you. Never you. I don't want Jake involved in it either. Understand?"

I swallow thickly and nod.

Jake announced himself as the new CEO of Turner Hotels. It had to be done, even if it was a little earlier than he'd planned. He needed to make a statement about the shooting and Niklas, and if he didn't do that as the CEO, well, it would have looked bad. Not just for him, but for the company. It also would have leaked sooner or later. A secret like that can only be held so long.

Questions circulated around my relationship with Jake. He never commented publicly about it, and I certainly never said anything to anyone, not that I spoke to the media. I was technically a married woman. Even if I stopped feeling like one years ago. I think a dog's chew toy is a more accurate description of what I was.

Lucky for us, this is Las Vegas. And Vegas does not have a long memory. In fact, this city prides itself on its ability to roll with the punches. To not get hung up in the regular daily crap of the world.

Maddox drops me off with a hug and promises of dinner tomorrow night. I like Maddox. He's the equivalent of having a grizzly bear for a brother. I enter the hotel and meander my way through the madness until I reach Jake's elevator. He changed everything after Niklas got in. His code is different, and he had a keycard insert installed. He added cameras in the elevator, as well as in the foyer that leads into his apartment—both feed directly to the security tower.

Maddox explained everything when he handed me his keycard.

Setting my stuff down by the entryway closet, away from the elevator, I forgo turning on the lights in favor of the wall of glass. It's beautiful here at night. Especially when the room is dark.

This room.

God, I can barely think about the last time I was in it. But I don't focus on that now. The wall of glass is calling me.

The storm is not in town, it's out in the mountains, though we're getting the tail of it with the rain. Sliding open the door, I step out onto the balcony and am instantly soaked.

Lightning flashes through the sky, the following bolt of thunder startling me in the best possible way, a jolt of excitement coursing through me. This is likely stupid. But I cannot seem to care. It's the most alive I've felt in so long. Turning my face up to the sky, I close my eyes and let the rain drench me. Wash me clean of my past.

"What the fuck are you doing out here?" Jake yells, and I startle once again; the effect on my body the same as it was with the lightning and thunder.

Spinning around to face him, my eyes are wide, lips parted. He rakes down my body like he can't believe I'm here. Like he cannot believe I'm standing on his balcony in the middle of a rainstorm.

Not an inch of me isn't saturated with rain water. My long hair is plastered to my face and body, my dress, which is white, is clinging desperately to my skin.

My eyes drop, following his line of sight. My nipples are hard, straining through the now-sheer fabric of my dress, and bra, my white panties are also visible as is the outline of my pussy beneath. Every inch of my skin is on display. I should feel embarrassed, but I don't.

Maybe it's the fire in his eyes. The way he licks his lips. The bulge in his pants.

In four swift strides, Jake crosses the balcony, capturing me in his arms, and pressing me into him with an unforgiving grip. My ribs still hurt. It's only been a few weeks and my body is still feeling the effects of that day. Sore ribs. Headaches. But in this moment, I don't care. Jake. He's all I see.

"What are you doing standing out on my balcony in the middle of a lightning storm?" he bites out harshly.

"It was beautiful," I pant, my voice breathless. "I wanted to watch it while I was waiting for you."

"From fifty stories up?" His tone incredulous. "This place is like a lightning rod. You could have been killed."

I pull back from his embrace and smile softly. "The storm is in the mountains." I point a long finger out into the sky just as another bolt does in fact hit in the mountains. "See. It's not close. We're just getting the rain."

"Since when are storms known for their predictability?" He sighs, running a hand through his now soaked hair. "Sort of like you, Sunshine. You're a goddamn storm of unpredictability. How did you get here?"

"Maddox came and got me. I called him."

"Maddox?" he grounds out. Yeah, Maddox was right about that whole madder-than-a-cut-snake thing. "You called *Maddox* and not me?"

I shrug, smiling up at him, staring into his beautiful obsidian eyes. God, this man. He makes my heart beat like nothing else. Rain hammers around us, loud and unforgivingly violent.

"I did. I wanted to surprise you, and you would have gone all caveman on me if I called you first."

He shakes his head, anger and disappointment raging through him.

My hand comes up, cupping his face, forcing him to see me. To hear me. "I needed time, Jake. I needed time to figure everything out for myself. I've never had that. I've never been alone. I've never felt in charge of my own life. There's always been this…void."

"What void?"

I blow out a torrent of air, staring sightlessly off into the distance. "I always felt like I had a hole in my soul. Like where I should be filled with things, meaningful things, I was empty. I never had any love or attention from my parents. I never had friends or school or hobbies. I was told what to do and how to do it, and I did it, because if I raised even the smallest amount of resistance, I paid for it. It's why I clung to Niklas so desperately. He promised me a way out and he ended up being something so much worse than what I had with my parents. I didn't realize just how much I need *this*." I wiggle a finger back and forth between us. "How empty I've been for so long. How alone and lost and unconnected."

"And did you fill that void in your time alone?" he asks softly, but his expression tells me he's not sure what he wants my answer to be.

"No, Jake." I wrap myself around him, pressing my face against his drowned shirt. "*You* filled my soul. You filled it until I was overflowing. I just didn't know what it was until I took a step back. I want to be complete in myself. And I think I'll get there. But I don't think I can do that without you." My head draws back, my chin resting against his shoulder as I peer up into his eyes. "I'm sorry I didn't call you much, and I'm sorry I've been out of touch. I hate thinking that I hurt you. I swear it wasn't intentional, and the distance was not about you. It was about me and maybe that's selfish after all we went through, all you did for me. Probably is and for that I apologize. Sometimes, we just need to hit the pause button and let the rest of the world spin on without us. But I'm here now and I want this. With *you*. I love you, and if it's okay, I'd like to stay."

His hands cup my cheeks, and his lips descend upon mine. He kisses me like he wants to devour me. Like he can't get close enough. Like he'll never get enough. My lips glide against his, cold and wet from the rain. When my tongue meets his, heat explodes inside me, zapping me with electricity and turning everything on. His fingers rake through my hair, tugging hard enough to make me whimper against him.

"I missed you," he breathes against my mouth. "I fucking missed you. My world was so goddamn empty when you were gone. I don't *want* you to stay. I *need* you to. You own me, Sunshine. You will always own me, and I'll face anything that comes our way if it means you're mine on the other side."

My heart rate picks up as anticipation slams into me, causing my breath to hitch, my stomach to coil, and my skin to tingle. I can't even play it cool. I'm pure lust. Pure need. Judging by the inferno in his gaze, he's right there with me. He lifts me effortlessly into his arms, my legs wrapping around his waist, but instead of kissing me the way I expect him to, he just holds me close, watching me intently.

"Do you trust me?"

I expel a heavy breath, blinking at him. I think about that. Really and truly let his question marinate until it settles in my bones with absolute truth. I nod, slowly, deliberately.

"With my life," I tell him.

"Thank God," he whispers, and then his mouth raises to mine, his teeth clamping down on my bottom lip, sucking it into his mouth before he does the same with my top lip.

A crooked grin curls up the corner of his lips when I moan. Jake deepens the kiss, desperate to capture the sound and taste of it. I shiver, and with another bolt of lightning and crash of thunder, we come back to our surroundings.

"Let's get you inside. It's dangerous as hell out here, you crazy thing."

I giggle into him, clutching his neck even tighter. He carries me through his apartment, my body shivering, sinking deeper into him as we're blasted with the air conditioning. He holds me tight against his warm, hard length, our bodies leaving a trail of water as we go. We bypass Jake's bed and head straight for the shower.

Setting me down on the marble counter, Jake opens the glass shower door and starts up the water to hot. He turns on the steam, too, because this feels like that type of moment. He catches me watching him and stares at me with so much affection, my chest clenches and my stomach flutters.

This day changed on me. I wasn't entirely sure how Jake would respond to me after my two-week absence. His soft expression quickly morphs into something else entirely as he takes me in. My white dress is plastered to my body like a second skin. The silky fabric turned sheer. My long brown hair clings to every place it touches.

"God, just looking at you." He shakes his head in disbelief. "You make it so hard to breathe."

My head dips a little, my pale cheeks coloring. "How can such a simple sentence light me up like this? Set me on fire? Or maybe it's just you, Jake." His eyes stay locked on mine as he snakes an arm behind my back to unzip the second-skin dress. The fabric kisses down my curves, falling to the floor with a wet slap. "Do you think I should go back to blonde?"

Jake grins, taking me in. Stepping forward, he pulls his sodden shirt over his head before removing his jeans. He approaches me, slowly, methodically. When he's standing before me, he whispers, "Take off your bra and panties." I suck in a shaky breath but do as he requests. "Your hair is beautiful. I don't care which color it is. I noticed you when you were blonde and fell in love with you when it was brown. If it were reversed, it wouldn't have changed the outcome." And then he reaches for my hand, leading me into the shower that could easily fit two more people comfortably. But right now, it's just us. And it's perfect.

Simultaneous groans fill the air as the warm water hits our frozen skin, but before I can say or do anything else, he yanks my body into his arms and kisses me. Jake's mouth hungrily consumes mine, his hands exploring every dip and curve of my body.

"I love you," he whispers against my lips.

"I love you," I whimper against him, my hands becoming as frantic as my voice.

"Tell me you're mine, Fi. Tell me you're not leaving me again."

"Never," I moan as he finds my clit with the pad of his thumb, his fingers pumping in and out of me. "Oh God, yes, Jake."

"Does that feel good?" I can only nod. "So fucking beautiful," he says reverently. "Your skin is turning the most perfect shade of rose." He continues to tease me, torture me until he's on his knees in front of me, looking up. "The most beautiful woman I've ever seen," he whispers, almost to himself. That's how light his voice is.

Jake leans in and takes my peaked nipple into his mouth, squeezing my other breast with his large hand. I cry out, back bowing as my hands fly down to tug on his hair, forcing his head to stay exactly where I need it to.

He chuckles against me, eliciting a wave of chills across my overheated skin. My legs are already quivering. "You're so close, aren't you?"

I nod, my eyes at half-mast.

"I know you. I know you inside and out."

My body hums into him as his mouth glides down the taut expanse of my stomach until he reaches my pussy.

"I'm going to fuck you with my mouth, and after this pretty pussy comes on my tongue, I'm going to spend the rest of the night buried inside you."

"Now," I moan. "I need you inside me now."

"Not yet." Jake kisses my mound and then moves lower, raising my left leg up and tucking my knee over his shoulder for better access. He runs his nose up and down. Licks me once before pulling back and driving me insane with his teasing buildup. "I can't get enough of the way you taste. Of the way your body writhes and clamps down around my fingers and tongue." He inserts two fingers inside me, and I can hardly breathe. "So hot and wet. Just for me. Only for me."

I moan so loud my voice cracks with the effort, my head falls back, pressing against the marble of the shower.

"God, everything about you makes me hard."

"Please, Jake," I beg, unable to stand it another minute. I'm too wound up, too tightly coiled.

"So fucking mine," he breathes into me, blowing on my clit one last time before he sucks it into his mouth, his fingers pumping in and out at a faster pace. I shatter, screaming his name over and over again until I'm sagging against the wall of the shower, boneless and spent, but not nearly done. Jake stands up, holding me against him. "Here or bed?" he asks softly, running his fingers down my hair.

"Both."

He nods in agreement, lifting me up into his arms and entering me in one smooth motion. He groans, closing his eyes for the briefest of moments, savoring the way this connection feels, because it's too intense not to.

I watch him, then close mine.

"Open your eyes," he commands before I can fully sink into this all-encompassing sensation. "This is not the moment to keep them closed. Watch me as I watch you. Love me as I love you."

Jake begins to move, our bodies connecting over and over again in a perfect rhythm. He's giving me everything. Fucking me with abandon. It's mind-blowing. It's intoxicating. It's everything I never knew I was missing.

And when we come, my eyes are still on his. I know we don't have it all figured out. I know we still have obstacles ahead. I know it won't always be this perfect.

It's life.

And life is ugly and brutal when it's not beautiful and serene. It can be hard as hell and money doesn't change that. Money doesn't make that bite sting any less. At least not when it really comes down to it.

My life has been broken, shattered repeatedly.

But I'm ready to put it all back together. To fix all my broken, ugly parts. And Jake will be with me, holding my hand the entire way.

Epilogue

Three years later

JAKE

Fiona is a mess today. An absolute wreck of a woman. For any other person, turning twenty-five would feel different. It would almost feel pretty cool, knowing you're now officially in your mid-twenties. Old enough to know better. Young enough to still do what you want.

But not for her.

She's been on the phone all day with lawyers, dealing with her inheritance. An inheritance she doesn't want much to do with. She sold off the majority of the shares of Foss first thing, giving up ownership. Then there's the Foss money. And the Ramsey money. I don't know the exact amount, but I know it's big.

Big enough that she's been pacing around her office in our new house for the last two hours, rubbing that spot on her back that bothers her so much, and worrying her lip with her teeth.

We bought this house about two months ago. A casino is not a place to raise a family. It's not the place where a child should grow up. And considering my Sunshine is thirty-eight weeks pregnant, almost to the day, we moved out of my rooftop apartment. It wasn't right for us anyway. Never exactly felt like home.

But this place does. Especially the back of the house that has an entire outdoor living area. It flows effortlessly from the inside and has a fireplace, outdoor kitchen, outdoor living room with a crazy television setup Maddox likes possibly more than I do, and a pool. A big fucking pool with a waterfall and Jacuzzi and a shaded area, because Fiona says all that sun is not good for children's skin.

Whatever. I still have way too much to learn about this baby stuff.

The best part of this house is the view. We can watch the sunset over the mountains every night, and if I don't go to get her now, we'll miss it. The sun sets early this time of year, and even though it's not exactly warm out, I'm hoping she'll go for a swim with me. Maybe even let me make love to her under the waterfall.

I make my way through the house, past the remaining boxes we have yet to get to, until I'm hovering on the threshold of her office. She's still pacing back and forth between the window and her desk, but instead of that spot on her back, now she's rubbing her belly.

She's so pretty it hurts.

I notice she moved her textbooks into one corner, some open, some closed. I wish she had called me to do that for her. I don't like her lifting anything.

Almost immediately after coming back to Vegas, Fiona started taking classes at the University of Nevada in Las Vegas. Evidently, she wasn't kidding around when she said she wanted to be a social worker who helps abused women and children. It's become her passion. Her focus. She has another year or so on her bachelor's degree and then, knowing my crazy, tenacious girl, she'll start in on her master's.

I have a feeling this inheritance of hers will help set up some sort of facility.

As for us, I married her six months after she came back. Honestly, I couldn't get her there fast enough. I was done chasing, and she was done running. We didn't do it in Vegas, it felt like too much of a cliché. Instead, I took her back to Baltimore, where my mom still lives, and we had a quiet ceremony there. Just close friends and immediate family. It's only gotten better from there.

Even after everything that went down with Maddox and Anthony Conti. Maddox made the call that day. The call to have Niklas Vaughn and the mess we made taken care of. And in doing so, that put Maddox directly in the path of Vegas' most notorious mob boss.

"Sunshine," I bark just loud enough to get her attention. She spins around on her heels, now rubbing that sore spot on her back again. I tap my watch, and she nods.

"I have to go, Charlie. Just please do what I ask and stop giving me guff about it. You're my lawyer, and this is what I want to do." Fiona ends the call and sets her cell phone down. "I'm opening up a shelter."

I nod. *I knew it*, I mentally fist pump into the air.

"It's going to have a lot of crap in it I can't even begin to think about."

"Come on, baby. Let's go have a swim and a fuck."

She lets out a snort. "Always so romantic."

"That's me, remember?"

She rolls her eyes, crossing the room until she's in my arms, her large, round, beautiful belly with our child growing in it, pressing against me.

"Yeah, I remember. I shouldn't let the tattoos and motorcycles fool me."

I kiss her sweet soft lips and whisper, "You got it. Happy birthday, Sunshine Turner."

She laughs into me. "That's what I'm calling the place. Sunshine."

"Yeah, I don't know. We might need to work on that one."

She shrugs a shoulder and takes my hand, letting me lead her away from her stress. We get to the edge of the pool, and I start to strip her down. I'm hard. I've been hard all day just thinking about this. Actually, I'm hard any time I think about her.

"Mine," I whisper into her as her maternity dress billows onto the hardscape. She shivers because, as I said, it's not warm out. Or maybe it's me making her shiver. Regardless of the reason, the pool is heated just enough for the water to feel amazing.

"Yours," she whispers back to me. "Now, get naked."

"Whatever my wife wants, my wife gets."

I give her an impish grin, but before my pants hit the ground and definitely before we enter the water and I enter her, she lets out a loud, "Ohhhh." She looks down. I look down. There is a very large pool of liquid at her feet. She looks up. I look up. Our eyes lock. "Shit," she says, and I laugh. Fiona Foss-Turner does not swear. Hardly ever. But she's learning to do so more. I'm helping her with that. Swearing keeps people sane.

"Well, I guess we'll have to put this fun moment of water kink on hold then."

She nods, gnawing on her lip nervously.

"Are you hurting?"

She shakes her head.

"Have you suddenly lost your ability to speak?"

She nods this time, and I wrap my arms around my nervous girl.

"We're going to be fine, Fi. Let's put your clothes back on, I'll get your suitcase, grab you a towel or something to stick between your legs so you don't get…fluids in the car, and then we'll go to the hospital."

"Okay," she whispers. "I'm scared. And excited. And I might just be freaking out, because now it is starting to hurt a little."

I cup her face in my hands, and I look directly into her eyes. "We've got this together."

Eighteen hours later, the doctor places a tiny, slimy, baby boy with a cream hat on his bald head, wrapped in a white blanket with pink and white and blue stripes on it, onto Fiona's chest. Fiona is exhausted but smiling and crying a lot of happy tears.

"What should we name him?" she asks softly, reverently. Names. Oddly enough, we never really discussed those. We don't do a lot of future talk. It's been more about living in the present for us.

It's taken a while for Fiona to adjust to life. To live it without fear. Not an easy task when that's all you've ever known. But my brave girl puts on her brave face and tackles the world on a daily basis. It's one of the many things I love about her. So yeah, names. Shit. I probably should have put some genuine thought into that.

Not that it matters. He's perfect. His mouth is already latched onto Fiona's nipple, because my little champ is mad smart and knows where the good stuff is and how to get it. Fi's head is cast down, watching him in wonderment as he feeds from her body. I'm watching both of them, because this is the moment, I realize. The moment where everything comes together and it's all just so…perfect.

I am my beloved, and my beloved is mine. Those are the words we spoke at our wedding. It's a Hebrew saying originally, and I can't think of a better way to express this swell inside of me.

I kiss Fiona's forehead, and I kiss my nameless son's forehead. He smells sweet. Like baby powder and sugar and something that feels so strongly of home, my chest constricts, and I have to swallow down the sudden urge to cry.

He's a little red and puffy, especially around the eyes, but I assume that won't last. His eyes are a blue-gray color, and that won't last, either. I'm hoping he gets Sunshine's green. He'll be tall, I think. And strong like his daddy. Yeah, this kid is going to kick some serious ass. Probably score some, too. I snicker at that. Who knew having a kid would be this fucking amazing?

"Toby," Sunshine says, and I immediately shake my head.

"Guys named Toby don't ride motorcycles. Guys named Toby get the shit kicked out of them by guys who ride motorcycles."

I hear one of the nurses chuckle off to the side, and it reminds me that we're not alone in our little bubble of tiny Baby Turner.

"What if I don't want him to ride motorcycles? They're dangerous."

I roll my eyes at that, knowing she can't see me, but she tilts her head up at the last second and catches me.

"No motorcycles," she says in a stern, motherly intonation that is beyond sexy.

"We'll talk about that when he's older, but Toby is on the veto list."

"All right, big daddy, you come up with one."

I lean down and whisper into her ear, "I'm going to make you call me that at some point." She giggles and pushes me away. "Zac? That's tough, right?"

"Zachery?"

"Too formal. Zac Turner. Short. Strong. Badass. What do you think?"

"I like it. What about a middle name?"

I think on this for a moment. "Henderson," I finally come up with. Her brows furrow in confusion. "I picked you up on the side of the road outside Henderson. It was the moment that changed my life. Where everything started falling into place. It was the moment that gave me you, and now him."

"Henderson," she repeats, this time with something close to awe in her voice. "Welcome to the world Zac Henderson Turner. Who knew running away and getting stranded on the road to Vegas would get us here?"

*** The End

Thank you for reading Touching Sin! Get more of Fiona and Jake in Maddox's story and meet the feisty heroine who puts this sexy alpha through his paces? Grab your copy of CATCHING SIN today!

Subscribe to my newsletter for a FREE copy of one of my books as well as the latest updates on new releases, promotions, giveaways, etc.

Also by J. Saman

Wild Minds Duet:

Love to Hate Her

Hate to Love Him

Crazy to Love You

Love to Tempt You

The Edge Series:

The Edge of Temptation

The Edge of Forever

The Edge of Reason

Start Again Series:

Start Again

Start Over

Start With Me

Las Vegas Sin Series:

Touching Sin

Catching Sin

Darkest Sin

Standalones:

Just One Kiss

Love Rewritten

Beautiful Potential

Reckless Love

Forward - FREE

End Of Book Note

Alright people. It's that time again. That time where I'm super depressed that the book is done and I write a ton of (non-edited) babble. Except, this time, I have a lot to say. Like a lot. So if you're totally done with me, you can move on to the chapter excerpt part.

THANK YOU! As always, you readers are what rock my world and I love and appreciate you endlessly!!

If you know me, then you know, I don't usually do suspense. Is this book suspense? No idea, but we'll go with it. I write weird twists. I write characters who are REAL. I write flaws and reality and ugly that turns into beautiful. But this book is so different. I feel like I keep saying that with every new release, but it's only because I get bored like an ADHD rabbit. I know I should have gone with boy meets girl, boy loves girl, boy loses girl after he fucks up and then boy gets her back. But I didn't want that for Fiona. I wanted her to always be sure in the love Jake was giving her. So I left trope lines behind. Don't hate me. I'll come back to you, I promise. I love my tropes too.

Before I get started, I'm going to apologize for lack of female friends. I missed them and I kept thinking…hmmm… where can I add one. Oh right, I can't. Because Mia/Fiona would not have opened up to one. It just didn't work and I'm sorry for that, because I feel like she could have used a girl to get real with. I have plenty of that coming in the next books.

Now that I got that over with…this book. Let's start at the beginning. It's a compilation of 3 (yes, I fucking said 3) books! Fully written books at that. Sigh. It started before I wrote Forward (my first book which I released in 2016!). In fact, one of the dudes in the first story was named Levi. Anyhoo, I wrote that original story in two different forms. And I could never get it to come together. One was a love triangle (it wasn't great). One was where the MH was an FBI agent and it just came down to him lying to our lady a lot and I hated that. So I ditched it no matter how many times I tried to fix it. Did I mention we're talking like 80k words each time? Yeah, that sucked.

Third time, I started writing a story where this girl ran away from her abusive finance and found herself in the damn Rocky Mountains with the best man in the world. Like I seriously fell in love with him. This is where Maddox spawned from and in case you missed it, I love him too. But this story… it didn't work either. Actually, I'm taking a lot of that book and putting it into the 3rd in the next series I'm working on.

Moving on. I went on a girls' weekend to Vegas. The idea grew and then after a conference in the same city a few months later, I spent the entire flight home writing the first two chapters. And once I got rolling, I never looked back.

Ryan, Claire and Luke. Ha, did you think I forgot about them? Never. I miss them like they're my long lost family and I've been seriously considering writing a story about their kids who I wrote into the epilogue of Start With Me. There is so much potential there. We'll see. But I missed them so hey, they're there. And they just…fit into this. If you haven't read me before, those characters are part of my Start Again series.

Here's the part where I address Fiona technically being married. Some of you might hate me for the 'cheating'. And all I have to say is, the fucking asshole beat her! He beat her until he nearly killed her! So I think that voids the piece of paper. Voids the legality of it. Because that's not marriage. That's not love and Jake loved her. So, I have zero regrets about it. If you hate me because of the technical cheating aspect of this, then so be it and I respect that and I won't hold it against you. In truth, I don't normally do that sort of thing.

I'm writing this way before the book is released and because of that, I have no idea how much money I raised for charity from pre-orders. But if you did buy it as that, thank you! There are woman and children out there who need help. Who need hope and fucking Mia/Fiona was one of them. Money was not her solution, though she technically had oodles of it. Freedom was. A new life was. And if we can help women out there get some of that, then I want to do my part. Have I mentioned I have 3 girls who I hope grow up in a better world than I did? Not that mine was bad, but you get where I'm going with this if you're a parent/mom.

Next up: I'm releasing a book in early December that is going to be part of a box set which comes out in January. It's going to be wide (meaning other retailers than Amazon) This box set is going to be super cheap. 99c for over 20 authors. That means I'm going to release the box set book at 99c and keep it there and when the box set comes out and I have to pull it from resale. I'll post the second in the series around that time.

I needed a new team so we're starting there, but I'm thinking Maddox and Gavin need a story and the Seattle crew isn't fully asleep yet.

Okay, last thing, a special shout-out to my transatlantic love, Claire and her family. I named the baby at the end for her husband because I love them so. And to my nursing girls. You crazy ladies gave me this weird brainchild by forcing me into a weekend of fun Vegas style.

Now I'm done rambling. Thank you! Thank you for sticking with me. Thank you for reading my book(s). Thank you for supporting me. You have no idea. I have other books if you find you like me and want to read more and haven't. Also, keep reading for an excerpt from the first chapter of my next book, The Edge of Temptation.

XO ~ J. Saman

Oh, please leave a review! I'm an indie and need all the help I can get.

Love to Hate Her

Viola

The air is hazy, thick with the cloying scent of weed as I meander my way through the throngs of people laughing, smoking, and generally having a great time. I don't belong here. At least that's how it feels. Especially since I have a sneaking suspicion what I'm about to discover.

"Hey, Vi," Henry, the bassist for the band, calls out to me with shock etched across his face as he grabs my arm and tugs me in for a bear hug. His tone is an infuriating concoction of surprise, delight, and panic. "What brings you out here?"

I'm tempted to laugh at that question, though it's far from funny. As such, it forces a frown instead of a smile. It really should be obvious. But maybe it's not anymore, and that only solidifies my resolve that I'm doing the right thing tonight.

Even if it sucks.

"I'm looking for Gus," I reply smoothly without even a hint of emotion, and his grin drops a notch.

Knowing that my boyfriend of four years is cheating on me should resemble something along the lines of being repeatedly stabbed in the back. Or heart. It should feel like death is imminent as the truth skewers my faith in men, my sense of self-worth, and my overall confidence into tiny bite-sized pieces of flesh. I should be a sniveling, slobbering mess of heartbreak. I should be nuclear-level pissed while simultaneously seeking and plotting a dramatic scene and meaningless revenge.

That's how it always goes for girls like me versus guys like Gus. And maybe I am just a touch of all those things. But right now, I just want to get this over with and go home.

"He's umm…," Henry's voice trails off as he makes a show of scanning the room as if he's genuinely trying to locate Gus amongst the revelry. My bet? He knows exactly where Gus is and is attempting to buy him and his current lady of the minute some time.

"It's cool," I say, plastering on a bright smile that I do not feel. "I'll find him."

Because when you've been friends with someone your entire life, in a relationship with them for the last four years, you don't expect them to betray you. You expect loyalty and honesty and respect. *You expect fucking respect, Gus!* Gus cheating and lying about it is none of those things.

"I can find him!" Henry jumps in quickly. "I'd probably have a better shot of locating him in here than you will. Ya know, cuz I'm taller so I can see around the crowds better. Do you want a drink or something? Why don't you go make yourself a drink while I look for him?"

I shake my head and step back when he moves to grasp my shoulder.

Henry pivots to face me fully, a half-empty bottle of Cuervo in his hand, his eyes red-rimmed and glassy. He crumples, his shoulders sagging forward.

"It's not what you think, Vi. It's not. It's just…" He waves his free hand around the room as if this should explain everything. Sex, drugs, and rock 'n' roll. This room is the horror show definition of that cliché.

I don't begrudge Gus or his bandmates success. I'm sublimely thrilled for them that their first album is taking off the way it is. It's been their dream–*our dream*–for as long as I've known them, and that's forever.

Which is why I should have ended it when Gus left for L.A., and I left for college.

I knew the temptations that were headed his way. I knew women would be throwing themselves at him and that I was going to be thousands of miles away living a different life.

Does it excuse Gus's actions? Hell no. Have I cheated on Gus once while in college? Absolutely not, and it isn't like I haven't had my own opportunities to do so.

But do I understand how this happened? Yeah. I do. I just held on too long.

"It was coming anyway," I tell Henry. "But it's nice to know he won't be lonely."

Yeah. That's sarcasm. And I can't help it, so I might as well allow the bitterness to make an entrance and take over the sadness that's been sitting in my stomach like a bad burger you can't digest. Especially as Gus has been adamantly denying his trysts, and Henry pretty much just confirmed them.

Henry's like a fish out of water, and I lean in and give him a hug. I always liked Henry.

"He's going to be so broken up about this, Vi. He loves you like crazy. Talks about you all the time."

I pull back, tilting my head and shrugging a shoulder. "That doesn't matter so much, though, does it? I'm at school, and he's out here with…" Now it's my turn to gaze about the room, my hand panning out to the side, reiterating my point. "Good luck with everything, Henry. I wish you all the success in the world. You guys deserve every good thing that's headed your way."

Henry scowls like I just ran over his dog as he shakes his head no at me. "You can't end it with him. You're a part of this. We wouldn't be here without you. We wouldn't be anything without you. You're like…," he scrunches up his nose as he thinks, "our fifth member. Our cheerleader."

"Maybe once," I concede, swallowing down the pain-laced

nostalgia his words dredge up. The backs of my eyes burn, but I refuse to let any more tears fall over this. I cried myself out on the flight here, and now I'm done. "You guys don't need me anymore. You have plenty of other cheerleaders."

He opens his mouth to argue more before just as quickly closing it.

"Stay safe, okay? And be smart," I add.

"You too, babe. I'm gonna miss you."

This is the moment it hits me.

I'm not just saying goodbye to my relationship with Gus, but to my friendships with these guys. To late-night band practices and weekends spent down by the lake just hanging out. I'm saying goodbye to my entire childhood, knowing that we're all headed in different directions, and there is no middle ground with this. My throat constricts as I try to swallow, my insides twisting into knots.

Bolstering myself back up, I hold my head high.

I need to find Gus, and then I need to get out of here.

Wild Minds, the band that Gus is the second guitarist and backup singer for, opened for Cyber's Law tonight. *The* Cyber's Law. One of the hottest bands in the world. They're also on the same label that just signed Wild Minds. This show is a big deal. This contract an even bigger one.

This is their start.

They had given themselves two years to make it big. They needed less than one.

Heading toward the back of the room, I skirt around half-naked women dancing and people blowing lines of coke. It's dark in here. Most of the overhead lights are out, but the few that are on mix with the film of smoke, casting enough of a glow to see by way of shadows.

I bang into a table, apologizing to someone whose beer I spill when I catch movement out of the corner of my eye. Jasper, Gus's fraternal twin brother and the lead singer of the band, is tucked into an alcove, a redhead plastered against him as she sucks on his neck.

Where Gus is handsome, charming, and completely endearing, Jasper is the opposite.

He is sinfully gorgeous, no doubt about that, but he's distant, broody, artistic, and eternally happy to pass the limelight to an overeager Gus. Jasper was actually my first crush. Even my first kiss when we were fourteen. But that's where it ended. Since that day, and without explanation, I've hardly existed to him.

Sensing someone's watching, he pulls away from the girl on his neck, and our eyes meet in the miasma. His penetrating stare holds me annoyingly captive for a moment before he does a slow perusal of me. Unlike Henry, Jasper is not surprised to see me. In fact, his expression hardly registers any emotion at all. But the fire burning in his eyes tells a different story, and for reasons beyond my comprehension, I cannot tear myself away.

He tilts his head, a smirk curling up the corner of his lips, and I realize I've been standing here, staring at him with voyeuristic-quality engrossment for far too long.

But I don't know how to break this spell.

The smoldering blaze in his eyes is likely related to what the girl who was attached to his neck was doing to him. Yet somehow, it doesn't feel like that.

No, his focus is entirely on me.

And he's making sure I know it.

A rush of heat swirls across my skin, crawling up my face. I shake my head ever so slightly, stumbling back a step.

Noticing my inner turmoil, Jasper rights his body, forcing the girl away. She says something to him that he doesn't acknowledge or respond to. He runs a hand through his messy reddish-brown hair as he shifts, ready to come and speak to me when my field of vision is obscured.

Gus. I'd know him in my sleep.

My gaze drops, catching and sticking on his unzipped fly.

"You're here," he exclaims reverently, the thrill in his voice at seeing me unmistakable. I peek up and latch onto the fresh hickey on his neck. A hickey? Seriously? I didn't even know people still gave those. When I find his lazy gray eyes, I want to cry. Especially with the purple welt giving me the finger.

"I'm here."

He wraps me up in his arms, and I smell the woman who gave him that hickey. Her perfume possessively clings to his shirt, and I draw back, crinkling my nose in disgust.

"What's wrong, babe?" His thumb strokes my cheek. "Long flight?"

I step back, out of his grasp.

"Your fly is unzipped, and you have a hickey on your neck."

He blanches, his eyes dropping down to his groin while immediately zipping his family jewels back up. "I just took a leak."

I nod, but mostly because I'm not sure how much fight I have left in me. It *was* a long flight. And a long eight months before that. But still, it's one thing to know your boyfriend is cheating on you; it's another to see it in the flesh, literally.

"And the hickey?"

"Not what it looks like, Vi. I swear."

I reach up and cup his dark-blond stubbled jawline. My chest clenches. "Don't lie, Gus. It just ruins everything. I don't want to hate you, and I think if you lie to me now, I might."

He shakes his head violently against my hand, his expression pleading. "You're here, Vi. You're finally here. Nothing else matters."

"But it does. It all matters. The distance. The way our lives are diverging. I love you, Gus, but it's not like it used to be with us. None of it is." I swallow, my throat so tight it's hard to push the words out. "Let's end this now before it turns into bitterness and resentment."

"I could never resent you."

I inwardly sigh. He really doesn't get it. "But your penis might. You're fucking any woman who looks at you. Where does that leave me?"

"You seriously flew out here to end it?" He's incredulous. And hurt. And I hate a hurt Gus. Even if we're not the stuff of happily ever afters, I do love this man. I'm just not so sure how in love with him I am anymore. He broke my heart. He broke my trust. And absence hasn't made my heart grow fonder. It's made it grow harder.

But I still don't want him hurting. He's my…*friend*?

Shit and hell, he's my friend.

And God, I'm going to miss him.

So I hug him. I wrap my arms around his neck because I need to. I ignore the scent of that faceless girl because I need to feel him close to me, even if for the last time. That lump is back in my throat, and my eyes are once again burning with those tears I refuse to let fall. Gus squeezes me, gripping me as if his life depends on it, and it's breaking me apart.

"Would you rather I ended it on the phone?" His face meets my neck, and my eyes fling open wide, only to find Jasper watching us from over Gus's shoulder. A curious observer, and my insides hurt all over again. His expression is a mask of apathy lined loosely with disdain. The way it's always been with me. All that earlier heat a thing of the past. I don't care either way.

"I don't want you to do it at all," Gus's voice is thick with regret as he holds me. "I love you, Vi. I love you so goddamn much. I just…"

"I know. I really do." I squeeze him back, feeling like I'm losing the only good part of my childhood in saying goodbye. "We're just in different spaces now, with different lives, and that's the way it's supposed to be."

He shakes his head against me, holding me so close and so tight, it's hard to breathe. He smells like that girl. But he smells like him underneath, and I cling to that last part because the scent of some unknown meaningless girl hurts too much. It rips me apart, knowing he did that to me.

To us.

I close my eyes for a moment and push that away. It's useless at this point, and I don't want to leave here more upset than I already am.

"Don't end it," he pleads, cupping my face and holding me the way he always has. "I can't lose you."

I lean up on my tiptoes and kiss his cheek. Tall bastard. "And I can't come in third. I handled second well enough, but not third."

"Third?"

"Music first. Other women second. Me third. I need to end this Gus, or I'll hate you, and I'll hate myself."

"No," he forces out, but it's half-hearted. We're nineteen, and just too young. There isn't enough of the right type of love between us to fight harder for something we both know will never work. He doesn't want to be the bad guy. The cheating guy who pushes his long-time sweetheart-best-friend away. "You're breaking my heart." A tear leaks from my eye as I battle to stifle my sob. "I'm in love with you, and you're ending it." I blink back more tears, watching as he accepts what's happening. "I'm going to regret this," he states matter-of-factly. "Letting you go is going to be the regret of my life. Years from now, I'm going to hate myself for not making you stay."

But you're not fighting for me now.

"And that's why I have to go." I lean in and kiss him goodbye and then run like hell.

I make it outside, the heavy door slamming behind me. Warm, stale air brushes across my tacky skin, doing nothing to comfort or bring me clarity. I'm a mess of a woman as useless tears cling to my lashes.

"You're leaving already?" Jasper's voice catches me off guard, and I start. Why did he bother following me? "You just got here."

"Yes," I reply, twisting around to face the green eyes that have been fucking with my head since I caught them ten minutes ago. "You can't be surprised."

"He loves you. He's just lost in this life, ya know?" I shake my head at him. Jasper takes a long step in my direction, wanting to get closer and yet hesitant to. "So that's it? You just walk away from him?"

"Am I supposed to ignore the fact that he's been cheating on me?"

"No. I suppose not. And I can't make excuses for it either."

"What do you want, Jasper? You can't honestly tell me you're disappointed to be rid of me."

"I see we're at the zero-fucks-left-to-give portion of the evening."

I shrug. That just about sums it up.

His eyes, filled with anger, indecision, and frustration, bounce all around, the street, the lights of the neighboring storefronts, the crowd still dispersing from the show, everywhere but at me. I can't stand this any longer, so I turn away and start to walk out into the Los Angeles night, away from the arena where Wild Minds–the band and the boys I've loved my whole life–just performed.

"It's yours," Jasper calls out, and I'm so confused by his hasty words that I freeze, turning back to him. His expression is completely exposed. Utterly vulnerable. And he's staring straight at me. Directly into my eyes in a way he hasn't dared since we were fourteen. My heart picks up a few extra beats, my breath held firmly in my chest. God, this man is so intense, I feel him in my fingernails.

"What is?" I finally ask when he doesn't follow that up.

"The album," he answers slowly, reluctantly, like it pains him to confess this, his darkest secret. "Every song on it is yours. All of them, I wrote about you."

I stand here, lost in space as I grasp just what he's saying. What it means, as random lyrics from random songs on their album flitter through my head. Song after song filled with the most achingly beautiful poetry.

"Jasper?" I whisper, my hand over my chest because I'm positive my heart never beat like this before.

But he is already at the door, having confessed his sins without waiting for absolution.

"Why did you tell me?" I yell after him, praying he'll stop. Needing him to explain this to me. *Why did you tell me, Jasper? Why did you pick this moment to ruin me?*

His hand rests on the frame of the now open door, his head bowed, his back to me. "Because I didn't think I'd ever get another chance, knowing I'll probably never see you again." He blows out a harsh breath. "But it doesn't change anything, Vi. Absolutely nothing. So you can move on without us and pretend like I never said a word."

And then the door slams shut behind him.

Jesus.

It takes me forever to move. To force myself to try and do just that. To try and forget his words and ignore the havoc they just created.

Knowing it's futile. Knowing those words will reside in me forever.

Want to find out what happens next in this forbidden rock star romance? Get your copy of Love to Hate Her today!

Made in the USA
Monee, IL
15 December 2023